Swords and Crowns and Rings

Published with the assistance of the Literature Board of the Australia Council

Contents

The doctor left husband and wife alone. He stood looking down at Mrs Hailstone as she sat with the shawled baby in her arms before the kitchen stove. 'No mistake, eh?' he said, and sighed.

'No, sir,' said Mrs Hailstone. 'Little pudden limbs, and see his hands!' She spread out the minute, fan-shaped hand.

The doctor ran his hand over the silky skin of the baby's face. He felt the bulging frontal and parietal eminences.

'Poor little devil, it's a damned shame. And he's a healthy child, too. God knows how Hanna will take it; he's a morose lump of a man.'

The doctor waited several days before telling him and his wife that their son was a dwarf. Mrs Hanna, who had been listless since the birth, said nothing but, 'I thought something was wrong. He doesn't look right, somehow.'

But Walter Hanna, his face suddenly plum red, stood straight up and belted his wife across the face. 'You did it, you sow. It's your fault, smoking like a chimney all the time you were carrying him. I told you, I told you every day.'

The doctor was a hot-tempered man. He spun the grocer about, shouting, 'I ought to flatten you, Hanna! It's no more her fault than it is yours. These things are handed down. It's hereditary. The child could have been crippled or imbecile. How would you like that, man? As it is there's not a thing the matter with him except that he'll never be as tall as others.'

'I wish to God he'd been born dead,' cried the father.

The remark, even more than the blow, seemed to put life back into Mrs Hanna. As a girl, she had been wild and humorous, full of go, a woman with crimson cheeks and crowded teeth that seemed to have a life of their own. Into her strong-boned face there now poured the old red. Fierce as a new-whelped bitch, she glared at her husband.

'That's my girl,' thought the doctor.

'You mongrel, Walter,' she said. 'This is our son, no matter what's amiss with him. Never you breathe again that you wish him dead, or I'll put poison in your tea, I swear to God I will.'

The father threw a hand over his eyes and stumbled from the room, sobbing.

4

'Pay no attention,' advised the doctor. 'It'll upset your milk. Besides, he'll come round in time.'

But Walter Hanna never did. From then on he hated life; he could have gouged its eyes out. The infant was six months old before his father could bear to look at him. Always a secretive man, Walter Hanna became glum and silent. Trade fell off at the shop. People who had taken their custom to Hanna's since Walter's father's time were depressed by his surliness and went to the Chinese General Store instead. The sympathy the birth of the child had engendered for him amd his wife faded.

'We've all got troubles,' people said. 'Why does he make so much of it? Peggy Hanna's come to terms with it, but Walter's taken it real personal.'

Walter Hanna's inward sufferings were terrible. After the birth of Jackie he had an endlessly busy conviction that he had done something wrong. He thought the child's deformation a judgment. But why?

It seemed to him that his life had been blameless, indeed, exemplary. Just over ten years he had been engaged to Peggy Hough, while she'd looked after that tyrannical old cow of a mother, bedridden with asthma, able to bring on an attack whenever Peggy broached the subject of marriage. He'd been faithful, respectful. He'd never laid a hand on her in a place that Father Link would not approve. He was, in fact, undersexed almost to the point of impotence, and had found distasteful the warm-blooded Peggy's passionate disposition as disclosed in the marriage bed.

Could that be the reason for the mishap with the child? It wasn't natural for a woman to be the way Peggy was, was it?

He spent more and more time in the front room with the clocks. His uncle the watchmaker had left four or five to him – the carriage clock with the wooden works, the grandmother with the ship painted on the face, the grandfather with the green enamel weights. As he had grown older he had added more to his collection. They were his only true friends, reliable, unemotional, firm and single in their intention of life. Ever since his twelfth birthday he had wound them according to schedule, checked and oiled them regularly, kept them clean.

The hour struck like an orchestra; but the front room was scarcely used and the noise never bothered Mrs Hanna. It was to her a remote angelic chorus of tinkles, bongs, and portions of tunes.

She cared for no one and nothing but the infant. After the first shock and grief of the child's disability, she made up her mind that no matter what sort of a mess God Almighty had made of her son there was no reason why she shouldn't try to improve on things. In this the doctor was her strong ally.

'I'll tell you this, Peg,' he said; 'it rests with you and Hanna to work it either that the child feels himself a monster, fit for nothing but jeers and cruelties, or he accepts the way he is and gives the world as good as he gets. He's got to feel himself special. Can you put your mind to it, Peggy?'

Mrs Hanna's eyes sparkled. 'Show me how,' she said. 'But you can count my old fella out. It's not in him to help when he sets his jaw against it.'

The doctor opened the glass-fronted cupboard behind his desk.

'I've taken it upon myself to send away for some books on dwarfism,' he said, 'some medical – and they're for my own education – and some for you and Jackie, to show you both that there have been plenty of dwarfs that have led natural happy lives, married full-sized people and produced full-sized children. And there were some that became famous: there was a French statesman who was a dwarf, would you believe it?'

'It isn't the riches that bother me,' said Mrs Hanna, 'but the happiness.' She gave a little whoop of excitement. 'Do you think I can do it, doctor?'

'No woman could do it better,' he said soberly. 'See here, Peg.'

He opened the top book and showed her the picture of a little man, Alypius of Alexandria, under two feet high, described as an excellent philosopher and mathematician, hardly anything more than spirit and soul.

The doctor looked at the mother. 'Do you see what I mean, lass?'

'I do see, I do. I must make his soul grow, to make up for the other. God help me, is it in me to do it?'

'If the child takes after you,' thought the doctor, 'the task won't be so hard.' But he said nothing, putting the books in her arms, and pushing her smiling from the room.

Mrs Hanna ran home, forgetting her husband's silence and depression, thrusting the books excitedly before him. 'There've been others that have done well, why not our Jackie? The doctor says we can turn him out tough enough to face anything!'

Wordlessly the father turned the pages, bitterly eyeing the paintings of pale-eyed, potato-nosed Flemish dwarfs; arrogant, richly clad diminutive women who belonged to queens and duchesses; Italian feasts, all lanterns and shadows and flushed revellers, gathered about a jolly little monster who sprang from an ornamented pie. With a cry of outrage he slammed shut the book.

'We've got no choice, Walter, don't you see?' said Mrs Hanna with pity. Almost for the first time she sympathised with his shame and suffering. 'I've been heedless,' she said, 'heedless and hard. But it hasn't been easy for me, either, you know. Last month when Mrs Moy over the road had her little girl, like a doll, perfect like a doll, I was so jealous I could have chewed rope. But it wasn't to be. We got Jackie the way he is and we have to help him all we can.'

Without a word her husband left the room, and the books were not discussed again between Mr and Mrs Hanna. Sometimes the mother hoped that he listened while she read to the enthralled Jackie tales of clever and heroic dwarfs, dwarfs that were the finest goldsmiths and jewellers in the world.

'He understands every word I say, I do believe,' Mrs Hanna told the doctor. The doctor rolled over the two-year-old child, already muscular and extremely active, prodding him till he shrieked with laughter.

'Of course he does,' he said. 'If brain weight is important, and many scientists think it is, Jackie's is about one-nineteenth of his body weight. Mine is only one-thirty-second; yet it's served me well enough.'

Sometimes, too, the mother slapped Jackie as she recited the list of his blessings, his good eyesight, his strength, his home, his ability to be like those other heroic little people in the books. She slapped him to make him remember and wept stormily because she had to. The doctor shook his head over this but admitted she had to work with the child according to her own nature.

Walter Hanna died when Jackie was five, never having really recovered from the birth of his only child. He came down with bronchitis, and went off with double pneumonia, very angry, fighting for breath, his last words to his wife being: 'Wind clocks. Schedule on mantelpiece.'

In his later years, when forgotten memories of childhood began to return to him, Jackie often recalled his father, clear as day, sitting on a stump with a rabbit rifle across his knees, hoarsely crying, 'Why?' Jackie remembered, too, that he was a man with a rupture, and wore a clumsy truss that bulked out his trousers and often gave off a smell like a hot-water bottle. He sometimes had mentioned that his feet hurt, and he had had flat, thin hair that smelled rather sweetly of sweat and pomade. The older Jackie ached for that man, the questions unasked, the sorrows and disappointments never understood or lamented by his only son.

Mrs Hanna had loved her husband with a pitying, exasperated love. Her grief after his death was genuine and unbearable. She threw herself into it as though into the path of an oncoming train, hoping it would destroy her quickly. She carried on with the run-down shop, trying to scrape a living out of it, and out of sympathy many of the old customers came back. She spoke freely to them of her bereavement, explaining her guilt and remorse over the estrangement that had existed since Jackie's birth, her inability to get the child's father to see things her way and help her to make Jackie as normal and carefree a child as possible.

But that was not the whole story. Part of her grief was because her youth had gone into the grave with him, years and years, pell-mell, packed into the coffin, into the grave, under the sod, with nothing to show that it had ever existed at all.

After all the customers had gone and she had locked up the shop, the false consolation of their compassion faded and sorrow submerged her once more. Puffing cigarettes until her throat burned, she walked distraughtly about the unlighted cave of a place that smelled of mouldy oats and pollard, half-scrubbed floors, and damp, greening potatoes. The street lights shone subaqueously through the ginger-beer bottles in the window. Shadow-shows went on outside the window, people meeting, kissing, quarrelling; and she watched them enviously.

The neighbour, Mrs Early, had fed Jackie and put him to bed. 'He's been a devil again,' she said, admiringly. 'Out in the tree like a possum. Wouldn't come in for half an hour, and not a stitch on his little rumtum but a singlet.'

The bereaved woman pulled down the blankets from the tittering, heaving heap that was her son. His sparkling eyes, the most beautiful she had ever seen in a human face, looked back at her. They were grey as the dawn, with black velvet bands around the iris, and the lashes were like a foal's.

'The Nun's going to build me a treehouse tomorrow,' he said.

The mother, looking into those eyes, saw nothing of her sad husband or herself. Perhaps he was like her father, who had died young.

'He says I'm a luck child,' said Jackie.

'So you are,' cried Mrs Hanna, gathering him to her breast. The child's face struggled up to her shoulder and he said excitedly to the neighbour: 'And I'm going to put my wee iron stove in it, and cook grapes and snails and me and Cushie Moy'll eat them.'

Mrs Hanna was aware that the Nun had every intention of courting her when the year was up. A man she had scarcely known in her husband's lifetime except over the counter, she had nevertheless heard and absorbed his history. He was gardener and handyman at the convent, and in Kingsland it was thought uniquely amusing that his name should be Jerry MacNunn.

The Nun was a large man of sixteen stone. Because of a wound inflicted during the Boer War, he limped and was often in pain. He was down and out when he came to Kingsland in the depressed years after the war. He first went to the parson who gave him a shilling and his hopes for a clean and temperate life. He saw the Seventh Day Adventists, but they were vegetarians and gave him a bag of carrots.

The Nun sat on the railway station trying to eat raw carrots and cursing his leg and his luck. He was not a Catholic, but in desperation thought he'd go to the priest. It wasn't Father Link then, but the old tough from Clare, McTigue, face speckled like a bantam hen, knuckles broken and splathered from scrapping in his youth. He was saying his Office in the windy presbytery garden when the Nun put on the bite for a doss-down in his tool-shed.

'Never,' said he between two psalms. 'The last time I was fool enough to let a couple of whining miseries from up-country sleep there, they got off with me hedge clippers and a grand chisel. What's the matter with you, a great lump of a man like you, that you've no job or a place of your own?'

'I've got this crook leg,' began the Nun, already incensed at the other's brutal manner. 'I was at Mafeking . . .'

'And so was every other bloody loafer,' snorted Father McTigue. 'Go and sleep under the bridge where all the vagrants go.'

And he walked off into the dusk intoning. The Nun pondered a moment or two on whether to go after him and pull his biretta down over his lugs, then went vengefully away to sneak through a window into the nearby convent kitchen to help himself to some Christian charity. Fearlessly he bogged into half a leg of mutton and a loaf of bread, and was away on what was left of the steamed pudding when the lay sister returned from the refectory and discovered him. She went flying off like some wingless black bird, squawking.

In came the Mother Superior, tall, commanding, kindly.

'What are you doing here, young man?' she inquired. The Nun stared challengingly, meanwhile shovelling in the last of the steamed pudding. The Mother Superior cut him bread and butter, made tea. Wordlessly, she poured it out, and fetched him the sugar. At the end of the meal, the desperate man rose.

'Where's the axe and the woodheap?' he said.

That was how he started, or, as the town wits said, got into the habit. It was said Father McTigue gave the Mother Superior, Sister Bonaventure, a tongue-lashing, but she stood firm. The convent needed a handyman for the gardening and the firing, to fit new washers and clean out the cesspit. Mr MacNunn could board at the home of any one of a number of respectable hard-up widows.

As time went on, the Nun and Father McTigue became friendly in a guarded way, and even had sparring matches: the Nun, because of his game leg, standing on a handkerchief like Young Griffo the old featherweight champion, and dodging with the whippy speed of a snake every blow the priest aimed at him. Once or twice Father McTigue landed a stinger, and the Nun was not slow in returning the compliment, so that Father McTigue said Mass for a week or two with a lop-sided jaw or a nose like God's wrath.

Still, all in all, they got on well, and when Father McTigue went to his reward the Nun was one of the pallbearers, and got drunk afterwards and belted up two fellows in the pub who'd said the wrong thing.

The Nun wasn't a religious man. He thought the whole caper was a racket. Yet, when he heard of the hasty carrying-off of Walter Hanna, he said, 'Praise be to God', having caught the expression from the Sisters. Then, in an inexplicable state of excitement, he prematurely chopped off the heads of the three young ducks he'd been fattening for the nuns' Easter Sunday dinner, thinking all the time of the comfortable woman Mrs Hanna, her hearty wailing laugh that had been so often cut off short as she suddenly recollected whose wife she was. A woman to laugh a lot and cry a lot: the Nun had a spookily dislocated vision of her putting her frizzy dark head on his shoulder and dropping tears all over his neck. He felt half-melted at the thought.

But Mrs Hanna was still in a sense living with her husband. The sorrows and disappointments of her life with him were still sharp within her; the memory of his inertia and apathy still aroused sadness but not sympathy or forgiveness. He permeated the house like the slowly fading smell of his pipe.

Throughout this dreary twilight of her bereavement the Nun sometimes made an almost mysterious appearance, mending the fence, pruning the fruit-trees and, as he had promised, building a treehouse in the fig-tree outside Jackie's window. The little boy moved all his treasures there. He could scuttle out of his window and along a branch in an instant. As well as playhouse, it was his refuge from threatened punishment.

For by the time he went to school Jackie Hanna was a perfect devil. Mrs Hanna's years of work to make the child believe that he was as good as anyone else and better than most had succeeded eminently. He was as outgoing and mad-headed as a young dog, and because of his great strength and agility always leader of his peers. At six the bulging of his forehead was more noticeable, his belly protruded a little, a certain massivity began to show in his short legs. But his hair was like black feathers, his eyes astonishingly beautiful when he lifted them to the world that moved above him.

Children his own age accepted him for what he was. Older ones, embarrassed by his difference from themselves, sometimes teased and mocked him, particularly his rolling dwarf's walk. He was quick to retaliate, seizing his tormentor around the body, digging his head into the belly, oblivious of blows and punches, and steadily squeezing. After the teachers had rescued three or four wheezing, hysterical children from his grip there was no more teasing.

Jackie had a fatherly kindness towards his chief playmate, Cushie Moy from the big house across the road. Her real name was Dorothy, but when she was three months old her father, in a rare moment of humour, had looked at the fat infant and said, 'She's just like a little cushion!' So she had become Cushie, a name that suited her physically – for she had remained chubby, a little golden-haired Britannia – as it did spiritually, for she was easily bullied, and had an obsessive desire to be loved.

She idolised her handsome father, a man in a sincere dark suit, an important man, and chief accountant at the Bank. Her mother had been a Miss Jackaman, from the newspaper-owning family in Sydney; and the town of Kingsland was well aware that all the money was on her side. From the wilful girl who had married beneath her she had developed into a snobbish, isolated woman. Her voice was cultivated and mild, but she was not mild. Inside she was raging, and the hapless Cushie, born perceptive, knew it.

Mrs Moy thought it fitting and rather charming that her child should become a little playmate to Jackie Hanna. There was something there of a baby princess playing with the court jester. Her social sensitivity to the situation was proven when she first idly asked Cushie what games she and Jackie played under the pepper-tree or in the treehouse.

Cushie, shrinking, for almost everything she did was inexplicably wrong, said that they played fairy stories. Cushie was the princess, and was rescued from various perils by the brave dwarf. Sometimes, she added, diffidently, she worked a spell and Jackie was turned into a prince at the end, and then he too wore a crown and lived happily ever after.

'Jackie says I'm a real princess because of my hair,' she mumbled, wary of a scolding on the evils of vanity. But her mother, smoothing a fawn eyebrow and sighing, was abstracted, remembering her own golden hair, its opulence, and the balls to which she had taken it, the crowning splendour of beautiful and talked-about Belle Jackaman. She looked suddenly at Cushie with a cat-glitter, seeing not the child but the child's father, the cause of her exile from riches and admiration.

A year after Walter Hanna's death, the last of his clocks ran down. Contrary to his dying instructions, Mrs Hanna had never wound them. She had a superstitious dread of doing so, though each Sunday evening she had gone to the front room to sit awhile, as he had done. The clocks died one by one. The light feminine ticks, the dull clatter of the clock with the wooden works, the resonant bongs and whirrs, all ceased until there was silence in the front room except for the chime of the 400-day clock, coffin-shaped, with a mirror in its base that reflected Mrs Hanna's face as a convex orange in the corner of a distorted room.

'Ah, shut up,' she said. 'Or I'll give you such a crack in the kisser!' She had her hand raised, edge first, as her irascible mother had raised hers to clout her in her childhood, when suddenly the thing died. It was uncanny.

Though she knew the clock was due to run down, the circumstance of its stopping filled her with dread. It seemed like an omen. She was so nervous from the fright she had had that day that she itched all over. She took a pin from her hair and scratched her head gently, and after a while she began to breathe easier.

'Ah, God,' said Mrs Hanna. A thought came to her. Perhaps the clock's sudden demise was indeed an omen. Perhaps it was a sign sent to tell her that poor Walter was out of purgatory and on his way to paradise. The idea fired Mrs Hanna and she had an imaginative vision of Walter, his back to her, climbing a long winding road up a hill. There he went, slowly – no, stepping lightly, towards the great rays that fanned from the hilltop as they did in the Sunlight Soap advertisement in the shop.

'Good-bye, Walter,' she whispered. There seemed nothing else to say, so she added, 'I'm sorry about everything.'

Enlivened by this experience, she left the front room and returned to the kitchen which needed a scrub. Wielding the brush vigorously on the drab, brittle linoleum, she puffed at a cigarette, dropping the ashes in the water and over her bosom, and in between times whistling, her heart becoming lighter every moment. Jackie was home, he was safe. He had brought Cushie home, and had stood up to Mr Moy, an important man at the Bank, without being bashful or afraid.

'There's a jumped-up snot, if you like,' she mused. A faint trepidation stirred within her as she thought of that other snot, Mrs Moy, who was jumped-up even higher, and what she would probably say on the morrow. But she didn't care really, for Jackie had more than proved by his escapade that he had become what she had set out to make him, an ordinary tough, mad, worrisome kid.

'But he could do without the swearing,' she confessed, making herself a cup of tea and grinning reminiscently as she did so.

Jackie and Cushie Moy had long anticipated their expedition to the hills. When they were four years of age Jackie had informed the little girl of his belief that dwarfs lived in the hills, a whole race of people like himself. He showed her pictures in his books – the black elves working at their goldsmiths' forges, outwitting the giants, helping Thor, crafting a wig of living gold for goddess Sif, after wicked Loki had snatched her bald.

Cushie and Jackie knew of no hills but Paddy's Range, the breakwind and fence about their town, gnarled, hostile hills that in the summer hung their wooded salients with smudges of bushfire smoke, and in the winter gushed rainwater, the streams splitting the greenish-blond slopes like white veins. They looked like hills where dwarfs lived. Also the children knew that Paddy's

Range was old goldmining land. The ground up there was so torn, so pig-rooted and blighted, that it was now useless for anything but lean sheep pasture, and that only in a good season.

Rarely was Cushie allowed to come to play for the whole day. On this occasion it was because her baby sister Olwyn had been ill in the night, and Mrs Moy thought she should take her to a children's doctor in Ghinni Junction, the next town down the line. Mrs Moy had not liked asking the favour, so Mrs Hanna had great pleasure in granting it. It did her good to see the posh young woman shivering a little in the chill of the unswept shop, one white lady's hand fluttering to the pearl pin that shone in the lace jabot, or nervously testing the placing of the foot-long hatpin that held a winged hat upon her ringleted pompadour.

'Sure I will, Mrs Moy!' she said heartily. 'The two of them will be safe as houses in the backyard.'

'I'm very obliged, Mrs Hanna,' returned the lady, adding with an admirable diffidence, 'I'll be pleased to er . . . recompense you for your trouble.'

Mrs Hanna, pushed neatly into her place, turned dark red but retorted with meretricious exuberance, 'Never think of it. It's a poor world if one mother of children can't help another!'

Mrs Moy, thus riposted, showed no sign of it, but continued, gently smiling: 'Mr Moy will call for Dorothy shortly after five, and you must tell him if she hasn't behaved well.'

She flashed the tense child a look that made Mrs Hanna promise herself she'd give Cushie a jellybean the moment her mother had gone.

'She's always good,' she protested. 'Me and Jackie love her, don't we, dotie lamb? So go on now, Mrs Moy, be off with you and that poor baby, and mind you bring good luck home with you.'

It was wonderful how the very sight of fashionable, superior Mrs Moy brought out in Peggy Hanna the coarsest Irish desire to tease.

'Now then,' she said to Cushie, 'Jackie's not up yet, as it's Saturday, so you run away upstairs and tell him to come down and we'll all have a dog's breakfast.'

This meant eating out of tins anything handy, bully beef, sardines, apricots. It was mucky and delicious, and one of the little girl's great joys. Clutching the jellybeans, red for her and black for Jackie, she scampered off, already in a daze of happiness and peace.

'The whole day,' she said.

'We'll go and find the dwarfs then,' said Jackie. 'See what a fine day it is on purpose!'

Jackie was always right, and Cushie believed every word he said.

They set off after breakfast. Jackie had not thought to tell his mother where they were going. With no intention of deceit, he had gone into the shop and asked her for provisions for an expedition, easy to carry, for they were going a thousand miles. She gave him walnuts, raisins, two chocolate bars, and a bottle of ginger beer, saying, 'You'll not be needing lunch, seeing as you're having a picnic. And Jackie, make certain Cushie wears her sunbonnet every minute, for you know how her mother is about freckles.'

The children drank the ginger beer first, for it was easier to carry that way, and set forth. The town was small, and soon they passed the ramshackle shanties on the outskirts. Several people saw them, a quaint pair, the chubby golden-haired girl in the starched red sunhat and the hearty, stout Jackie, rolling along beside her with a seaman's gait.

They stopped beside the train tracks to watch a train go by and, satisfied, crossed the railway bridge and followed the dirt road towards the hills. It was a fine winter's day, but it followed long rain. Puddles lay everywhere, flitting with discs of light.

'They're dragon scales,' said Jackie.

When the road came to an end, sheep tracks led up the slopes. The sheep had chosen easy grades, and the children climbed quickly. Soon they saw in the sunlight the muddy river showing its intermittent gleam, a serpent of brass.

'I thought we'd see the sea,' said Cushie.

But the hills were a wall about Kingsland, some far, some near, showing gloomy gullies and abrupt stony fells where the stunted scrub clung like grey and bronze lambswool.

The children had not known their town was so small. It was an islet in the wide valley, a taut thread of railway track connecting it with another, smokier island to the south, Ghinni Junction.

Extensive, livid green patches of undrained bog still marked this marshy vale, and as the cloud shadows slid across the landscape they saw a myriad lakelets darkening and shining in a slow blink.

Cushie was not a talker. She stumped along behind Jackie, ever higher and higher, eyes on the track. Supple wet brown leaves stuck to her buttoned boots.

'Is it far now?'

'No, not far.'

'Where do your people live then?'

'In the stories it's in the mines in the hills because the dwarfs dig gold and make swords and crowns and rings.'

'Could you make a crown?'

'I expect so,' he said confidently.

The country was folded and crumpled and scarred from the old workings, the gravel dumps meagrely covered with grass and thorny vines. But the bush had returned to the gullies, tall stringy-barks with trunks black from January fires, mountain casuarinas and swamp grass. Rapid sharp whistles, very shrill, sounded from this cover and the alarm signal was followed by an undulant rag of blinding green that streaked low out of the gully, stretching, condensing, swinging into a tight orbit, scintillant with tiny eyes, breaking up into a chain that billowed over the rise and vanished into the deeper vale beyond.

'Wild budgies,' said Jackie. 'Frightened.'

She saw the eagle far above, apparently standing on the tip of one wing. Burning in sunlight, the blue turning the ends of all his feathers to dazzling fuzz, he gave one skelloch of rage or deprivation, and rowed away as slow as a king.

Bringing her gaze back to earth, Cushie said, 'There's smoke over there.'

The ruined stone building had crumpled in upon itself; it was like an outcrop with a crooked stovepipe at one end.

A little smoke and a thin dirty smell of damp burning wood came from this chimney. Yet it seemed impossible that anything living existed in the derelict corrie, where ancient fragments of machinery mouldered in the wet grass, and rusting metal rods stuck up out of the earth like bristles.

'Is that where they live, your people?' whispered Cushie. Jackie surveyed the hut doubtfully. Presently there emerged from a hole in its drystone wall an aged Chinese. He seemed rather afraid of them, but gave each of them a dried peach, hard as leather, wherein small worms writhed feebly.

A wire stretched behind the hut. On this rattled the stiffened hides of rabbits. The old Chinese looked anxiously at the children, showed a few dark-brown teeth, and retreated through the hole.

'He's not them,' said Jackie.

Down the steep gully they saw a creek, noisy and shallow, beggarly willows around it. The children slithered and scrambled down the wounded slopes, where the hide had been ripped off almost a century before. Cushie felt sad and afraid. Her pinafore was yellow and white with clay, her boot clumped with it.

'Mummy will be angry with me,' she said. At the dismaying thought she began to snivel. But Jackie did not hear. He had reached the creek where it was deepest, dammed between two little rapids.

'There's fish!' he said. Cushie forgot to cry and slid down towards him. She peered through the clear water, where little fish flinched from place to place, and a brown butterfly drowned within reach of her hand. She scooped it up, but it was soaked and dead. The sun came out again and the children saw small spotted trout suspending themselves in the shallows as the eagle had done in the air, dragging one fin, balanced against the current. They were creatures of stone colours, yellow, cream, and chocolate.

Cushie's sunhat fell into the creek, and the fish vanished. This new catastrophe vividly brought back the image of her mother; she saw her standing there with the strap, and a terrifying look of disapproval and dislike.

'I want to go home!' she wept and at the thought of what waited for her at home she sobbed all the more. Jackie fished up the red sunhat and wrung it out.

'No, you don't,' he argued. 'We haven't found any dwarfs yet and we haven't had lunch.'

Talking persuasively, spreading out the hat on a bush to dry, finding a flat stony patch to be their table, and two tottering mossy green slabs of wood to lean against for chairs, he coaxed the little girl out of her terrors. He cracked the walnuts and gave her the meats, counted the raisins and put her share on a leaf.

'Is it magic food?' she asked hopefully.

'It *looks* magic,' said Jackie, unwilling to lie. For in truth he was tired, his short legs ached, his wet shoes had rubbed his heels sorely. Though they had called down many black holes in the ground, many cobwebbed burrows in the cuttings, and got back echoes, the echoes were not answers but mindless jabberings.

The orderly, industrious dwarfs of the stories could not live here.

'Perhaps they live in other hills,' he confessed. Glumly they ate their repast, sitting on the two old miners' tombs but knowing nothing of them or the wild golden history of the blighted watercourse.

Cushie said, 'Listen!'

Above the sound of the wind palavering in the gullies he heard the clanking of a chain, scraping and thumping. The children scrambled to the track again, and followed the sound until they found it.

A terrifying half-creature humped in dusty garments of patterned umber, its lower half showing gleams of bright metal. Near by was a bloody rag of fur. In this the creature, as if ravenous even in its terror, swiped its beak so that fur fibres puffed in the air.

'It's the eagle, caught in a rabbit trap,' said Jackie. A dreadful excitement filled him, a thrumming was in his ears. To see it close, the frowning insane eyes, the great wings unfolded, thrashing, hooking at the air, sweeping a wide circle in the dust! The bloodstained beak gaped; no sound came out; it slashed at the metal teeth that gripped its leg, at the leg itself. The teeth peeled down the leg a tiny fraction; blood dribbled on the ground.

'Help it, help it!' screeched Jackie. Cushie joined in. They danced like lunatics, delirious with excitement and horror, screaming and bawling, until suddenly the old Chinaman rushed onto the scene, chattering and laughing and carrying a muddy sack and an axe. He threw the sack over the eagle's head, and chopped off its imprisoned leg. It must have been in mistake, for the man yelped with anger or vexation as the bird tottered a few yards, dragging one wing, scooping helplessly with the other, blood splashing the dust.

Once it got off the ground for a few feet, cannoned into low boughs, and fell. Yet it was determined to live, flapping lop-sidedly into the deeper shadow of the trees, the man after it, slashing and shouting.

Cushie lost her head altogether and ran away down the track, shrieking dementedly. Yet her cries did not drown the noises behind, which reminded Jackie of a thrilling, disgusting day long ago when his father had tried to chop the head off the Christmas hen and only wounded it, so that it ran for ages about the yard, shrieking and bubbling and bleeding until it fell dead with its yellow feet up.

They passed the old rabbiter's hut, and skimmed, slipping and sliding and often falling over, down the track. Cushie's white stockings had torn knees; her own knees were skinned. Jackie's shirt was ripped. In a shared hysteria they lay for a while in the shelter of a broken monolith of concrete and squalled and thrashed their limbs.

After that they went exhaustedly down the hillside, taking the wrong sheep track and having to climb through a barbed-wire fence and skirt an old clay-pit half-filled with stinking water where bobbled a bloated monster that turned out to be a thrown-away mattress. Every way they went was shown eventually to be the long way round. Yet they were not lost, for the town was always in sight, lying beneath in a growing lake of winter shadow. The sun still shone on the hilltops and uplands, where wet rock faces fired up like western windows.

'Why is it day up there and not here?' asked Cushie.

'I don't know,' said Jackie, 'but I'll know when I'm seven.'

Now the children were silent; every step Cushie took downwards into the imperceptible gloom of Kingsland made her more afraid of what was to come.

Jackie feared that it was more than five o'clock and Mr Moy would be standing in the shop looking at his gold watch and being mad. His own mother was ofen mad. She flew straight up into the air like a stepped-on chook, and when she came down again all unpleasantness was over. But Jackie was aware that Cushie's parents were different. She was often strapped, and did not seem to know for what reason. She was sent to bed in a dark room, too, and tended to associate the dark with punishment and disgrace.

The children were seen afar off, and met by the police sergeant in a motor-car. Jackie had never been in a car, and was thrilled and exhilarated. But the closer she got to the Hanna shop, the more afraid Cushie became, until at last she was speechless and pale as beeswax.

Mr Moy had, perhaps justly, blamed Mrs Hanna for the whole thing. She had discovered the children's absence when she had dashed back into the kitchen to fix herself a bite to eat between customers. Even then the silly woman had not been alarmed, though the two had never wandered away before. She thought they had gone down the street to visit a friend.

'Without asking permission?' cried Mr Moy, taken away from his desk, forced to leave the Bank, an unheard of thing, the moment it closed its doors at midday. The face of the manager when the flushed, aproned shopkeeper flapped in, shouting to all that the accountant's daughter had been lost for two hours or more! The woman was idiotic as well as common.

'They're only six,' cried the common woman, outraged. 'They don't always remember to ask if they can do this or that! Lord, Mr Moy, can't you remember yourself at that age, silly as a chicken?'

His celluloid chops flushing, Mr Moy ignored the question.

'Mrs Moy will be home on the six o'clock train,' he stated, 'and what I shall say to her I cannot imagine.'

'No use asking me,' snapped Peggy Hanna; 'and I'll be obliged if you remember that my Jackie is gone missing as well.' She noticed the man's hand trembling as he snapped open his watch once more and added forgivingly, 'But there, don't worry your head; the youngsters are right as rain. My Jackie is as sensible as a cat when it comes to safety.'

The police sergeant had said the same thing, and as it happened he was right. Still, it was after five when the car pulled up outside with the two dirty, muddy, bloodstained scapegraces in it, too scared to get out. Then Jackie rolled forth, sparkling-eyed, and gratefully Mrs Hanna aimed such a skelp at his ear that he was almost knocked sideways with the wind of it.

'The devilment of you, taking off and not telling me!'

Then she put him aside and took Cushie in her arms, saying, 'Don't cry now, lovey, you're home safe.'

'I lost my sunhat,' blubbered Cushie, 'and Mummy will be angry with me.'

'Of course she won't,' said Mrs Hanna soothingly; but looking at the father's face she saw that she was telling lies. So did Jackie.

'It was all my fault,' he said. 'I thought of going. It wasn't Cushie. And she was very good and never howled very much even when she fell down the bloody hill.'

'I *beg* your pardon!' said Mr Moy cuttingly.

'Granted,' said innocent Jackie, and he had the temerity to seize a piece of the sincere dark trouser-leg in his filthy fist and beseech: 'Don't give Cushie a belting. She didn't know we weren't allowed to go.'

But of course Cushie was whacked by her mother all the way up the stairs into her room, where she was brusquely undressed with many a severe comment on the state of her clothes, and dumped into bed. Cowed, the child was silent as the mother turned at the door.

Mrs Moy herself was drained and cold with fatigue. The long worrying day, the journeys with the train-sick, cranky Olwyn, the frightening warnings of the doctor, had exhausted her. Half her anger with Cushie was because the child had added one more burden to the day. She hated chastising her daughter. It seemed to her that was the duty of a nanny, not a mother. And Cushie's extravagant reaction to blows that scarcely ever reached her legs shocked her.

'You silly little thing!' she said. 'You're not really hurt. Stop making such a fuss! Daddy will think you're a coward.'

Cushie could not tell her that the blows meant nothing, but the disapproval everything. Woebegone, she kept her eyes shut.

'Now, don't sulk,' said Mrs Moy. 'I'm going downstairs to get you some supper.'

As she closed the door she had an impulse to go back into the room, take the child in her arms, rock her till she was calm, tell her she wasn't a bad, wicked girl any more, but loved and precious, her own chick, her dotie kitten. Where had these inexplicable words come from? These kitchen endearments that no lady would use? Mrs Moy, with a nostalgic dart of pain, remembered that her mother had said them to her, after she had pushed one of her sisters down the stairs and been severely punished.

When she brought up a tray of supper for the penitent, she found Cushie asleep.

Jackie, on the other hand, splashing and sliding around in a hip-bath before the kitchen stove, snorting the soap out of his nose and drawing faces with lather on the front of his mother's apron, spent an exciting hour telling her at breakneck pace about the fish, the Chinaman, the eagle on high in the sky, and the awful manner of its imprisonment and mutilation. Mrs Hanna accepted the eagle's fate in a prosaic countrywoman's way.

'What do you expect?' she said, dabbing his cuts and grazes with a solution of Condy's crystals. 'I bet the rotten thing had been robbing the traps and ruining the rabbits' skins. Them wedge-tails are only pests. They even eat the new lambs, I've heard.'

But Jackie was looking with amazement at the dark brown patches staining his skin. 'If I painted my nose with that stuff would I have a black nose?'

Before she could answer, he had grabbed the cottonwool and painted his nose.

'Serves you right,' said his mother.

She gave him his supper and put him to bed, and in a moment he was asleep, dreamless, flushed, his blackened nose burrowed into the blanket. It was then that she felt worn out, overcome by the anxieties of the day, remembering that it was the anniversary of her husband's death, and she was alone. A fearful apathy and weariness of life almost submerged her. She looked about the untidy kitchen, the dirty dishes, the puddled floor.

This was the evening the last clock stopped.

On Monday morning Mrs Moy swept into the shop to express her alarm and displeasure at the children's adventure. But Mrs Hanna, still caught up in a joy both calm and inexplicable, refused to be nettled and agreed that Jackie had been both foolish and naughty to take Cushie off on his quest.

'It's them fairytales,' she explained. 'But he knows better now. I hope you'll still let the little one come and play, for they're as good as gold together and never a squabble out of them.'

Mrs Moy flushed faintly. 'There was a question of bad language,' she said. 'My husband was horrified . . . a child of six!'

'There's no telling where the children pick it up, is there?' lied Mrs Hanna rapidly.

'We wouldn't like Dorothy to learn any common expressions,' said Mrs Moy. 'You understand?'

'I do, I do!' said Mrs Hanna. 'I'll not let young Jackie get away with it, I promise you. Oh, he'll get a tongue-lashing, if not worse, now that you've brought it back to me mind.'

Jackie got up tired and cantankerous, obscurely displeased about the failure of his quest, violently hating his deep-dyed nose, and knowing that he'd never dare take it down the road to play with the boys.

So when his mother treacherously attacked him about his use of a bad word to Mr Moy, he retorted as vigorously.

'But it *was* a bloody hill, it was a *bloody* steep hill.'

'You're not to say *bloody*!'

'You say it, you bloody well know you do!'

'If I don't half-kill you for that, you young devil!' said Mrs Hanna, 'You just wait till I get to you!'

But, being sensible, Jackie was away around the brown-sugar barrel and the kerosene drums and half-way towards the door before his mother could count four. Bad luck for Jackie that the door opened then to let in the Nun, come with the Sisters' weekly grocery order. He grabbed Jackie by the coat collar and held him, the little boy flailing and spitting, and doing his best to get the Nun around the hips and squeeze the tripes out of him.

'You need help, missus,' observed the Nun.

Jackie let rip with an oath, and the Nun gave him a cuff across the ear that felt like a blow from a handful of candles. The boy

examined Jackie every six months for signs of the orthopaedic and optical deterioration that his books told him sometimes went with dwarfism. But the boy was radiantly healthy, like a tree or a young bear. The grotesqueness of his shape, becoming more noticeable as he grew, did nothing to mar this image of joyful vitality.

'You've done a great job, Peggy,' said the doctor, 'and you, too, Nun.'

The War had begun, and young men disappeared from Kingsland in small flurries of beer, tears, and band music. News of battles flickered like harmless lightning over the town. Jackie, growing up, in and out of mischief, had a pantomime idea of 'The Front', a remote country coloured like jelly babies, populated erratically by camels, Arabs sitting around the wells of Beersheba, Huns in spiked helmets, and our brave boys. The only one of these with whom he had been at all familiar was Cushie Moy's youthful uncle who died of wounds at Gallipoli.

The uncle had, in fact, been a dingy, barking adolescent who stumbled through life as a junior bank clerk under the critical eye of his elder brother, Cushie Moy's father. Their temperaments were in constant opposition, their leisure times filled with uneasy silence or venomous bickering.

Mrs Moy, who had brought her indifference towards the young man to a high level of unkindness, was able to squeeze out a tear every time she spoke of his gallant death, and Mr Moy thought this most becoming of her. But the passionate Cushie, thus brought for the first time into contact with death in her family circle, and rendered stone-cold by terror, endured the mourning atmosphere for a week, and then broke – with a spectacular fit of bawling and vomiting during the memorial service. For this she was slapped and put to bed. She was seven and never forgot her Uncle Graham's demise.

She had hardly recovered from this event before the town hall bells tolled for young Baillie Nicolson, football star and champion runner, Kingsland's hero and only son of John Nicolson, the town bagpiper and the Nun's closest friend. When the news came it was a Saturday so wet and blowy that even the football had been cancelled. Mrs MacNunn had plunged off against the gale towards the school, where the parish ladies held a sewing circle every third

Saturday. She had gone before the news of Baillie Nicolson's death was posted up outside the post office so she was not there to support her husband.

It hit him as though Baillie had been his own brother, not for Baillie's own sake, but for the piper's. Old melancholies he had forgotten since he came to Kingsland, childhood wounds and bereavements and horrors, rose up from some place in his soul and nearly swamped him. He lay flat on his bed staring at the ceiling.

The thick cobwebby light of winter afternoon buried him. There was nothing, he thought, but himself alive in the grave of the world. The dead despondency that had so often characterised his mood before his marriage came to him again as he thought of his friend Nicolson.

Some, like his own father, had kids and they punched and kicked them. But those kids were still alive. Nicolson had cherished his only son like a bloody great diamond and now that diamond was lost. Nicolson was a man in solitary now, that hard hawk of a man.

'I got to go and say something to the old piper,' he thought, 'and I don't know what to say.'

Jackie watched the fire die down into a grey ruff of ash, streaked with gasping ruby. He had overheard the man who came briefly to the backdoor, and he knew that Baillie Nicolson was killed. He waited for a long time for his stepfather to come out of the bedroom, while the house became colder and darker.

Jackie listened to the lift of the wind, the sudden seething as it found trees to scruff. He tried to distract himself with it as it tried the windows and proved a rattle, whistled through the keyhole as with pursed lips, shouldered the house and the shop, knocking the creaks out of the timber, hoying down the chimney and dusting the hob with ashes, skiffing under the house and across the floor so that one end of the mat reared up at it like a cobra and dropped again.

He was sad and lonely, feeling less than eight years old.

The Nun, sunk in lethargy, heard a new sound above the reeding of the wind, a scrabble at the door. A little sun of light leapt up against the hollow greyness of the hall.

'What you light the gas for, Jack?'

Jackie pushed himself farther into the bedroom. 'To keep me company. What are you doing, Dad? You sick?'

The Nun said, 'A man's a cur. I oughta be down at the Princess saying something to the old piper.'

'He's not down at the pub, Dad,' said the boy, eager to help.

'Sure he is. Bellowing boozed. Where else would he be after hearing what he heard today?'

'I seen him go past, Dad,' said Jackie, 'A long time ago. On the steamroller.'

The Nun sat up like a shot. 'Heading which way?'

Jackie pointed. 'There were lots of people running along behind.' He caught his stepfather's arm, 'I can go with you, can't I, Dad?'

The Nun was hastening into his oilskin. 'You rug up then, and leave the light on for your mother.'

He limped out, leaving the backdoor swinging. The two of them bored through the gale.

Jackie tugged the edge of the oilskin. 'I hear something funny,' he shouted. The stravaiging wind brought extraordinary sounds down the main street, a fearful stridulation, pierced intermittently by a grinding crash. Looking through the swimming air towards the park, the Nun could see little but a group of people trickling about some central point, breaking up, coalescing, flying apart. The steamroller's calliope uttered an exultant shriek.

'Holy God!' said Jerry. 'What's he up to?'

John Nicolson had learnt his trade at a Clydeside engineering works, and twenty years before he had begun work in Kingsland as borough engineer. But his long drinking-bouts had driven him farther and farther down the ladder until now, loyally retained by a council comprised mostly of his old friends, he worked spasmodically driving the steamroller.

Drenched and hatless, he sat the grotesque vehicle like a mahout, rain spilling into his untied boots and out again. It streamed down his skull so that his thin ginger hair was invisible; his face was purple with drink and cold. To the little boy, staring up at this towering, silent figure, it seemed that the eyes were as red as blood, like a dragon's eyes.

'Chris'sake, what's he up to?' shouted the Nun.

'He's run amuck,' answered someone, thrilled to death. 'He's gone and demolished the cottage where him and the boy lived, and now he's got it in for the Gallipoli memorial. Man's a nut case.'

'Ooo-ahh!' gasped a child's voice in Jackie's ear. 'He's smashing up the new monument!' it said, now becoming the voice of Cushie Moy, who stood beside him in a crimson coat, holding the hand of her furred mother.

'Come away at once!' said Mrs Moy sharply. 'The man's mental, he's dangerous!'

But Cushie, mad to see this astonishing spectacle, whined and yelped, pulling against her mother's gloved grasp, and straining all the time to see the reef of white marble rubble, and the obelisk, cracked as though lightning had struck it, standing lop-sidedly on its concrete platform.

A man near by sobbed angrily. 'No respect for the dead . . . our poor boys . . . Baillie wasn't the only one . . . my young brother died in France, didn't he? . . . wants to get his own back, he says . . . why doesn't he go and flatten Dr Zimmermann's surgery then . . . dirty Heinie . . . why don't he?'

'Hypocrites! Damned bloody hypocrites!' howled Nicolson suddenly, and the steamroller squealed into movement.

'Is he,' demanded Mrs Moy in a stricken voice, 'talking about *our side?*'

As the steamroller trundled dinosaur-like towards the monument, the sobbing man scrambled up over the rear, and snatched John Nicolson around the neck, clawing and shouting. With one sweep of his iron arm, Nicolson tossed him backwards into the crowd. The front roller collided violently with the shattered marble, grinding over the fragments and jerking back and forth across the wreckage. The noise was so great that no one could hear the stream of imprecation or blasphemy spouting from the driver's mouth.

Alarmed and embarrassed by this rare drama, Mrs Moy seized Cushie by the back of the coat and switched her away, willynilly taking Jackie as well, for Cushie had hooked herself to Jackie's arm.

'Can't you get some sense into him, Jerry?' bawled someone.

Clumsily swinging his game leg, the Nun dragged himself up on the juddering vehicle.

'Put an end to it, you old galoot,' he begged. 'Come on, chum, turn it up and we'll have a grog and talk it over.'

Piper Nicolson heard. He turned his red eyes on the Nun. 'I lost my lad, did you hear, Jerry?' he said. 'My grand lad.'

He shoved the lever, and the monster moved forward with catatonic slowness, nuzzling the face of the monument with an abrasive shriek. With a groan the obelisk came out of the ground like an uprooted tree. Majestically the steamroller tilted forward and buried its bow in the hole.

The children's desire to see this wonder was overwhelming. They dragged away from Mrs Moy and rushed towards it. Cushie goggled at the wreck in horror and delight.

'They'll never, never get it out,' she said.

'We can have that for a war memorial instead,' said Jackie, and they screamed with laughter.

The sound drew the attention of Piper Nicolson, sitting amidst restraining hands, dazed and glowering.

'Would you look at it,' he bawled, 'running around on its bit legs, alive and kicking, and my boy Baillie dead and rotten. My lad that was a cricketer and a runner, and saved the day in the Shield match for the shire last year. Dead and rotten, and that deformed wee turd of a creature still above ground. What justice is that?'

A hush fell over the crowd, though mostly they were farm workmen, not sensitive or used to stepping delicately around other folks' feelings.

Cushie felt the silence, and remembered her shock and panic at her uncle's death.

Jackie, who had not understood the drunkard's words, still looked up into the wet, corned-beef face with fascinated expectation of more excitement.

It was Jerry MacNunn who said calmly. 'I've never yet belted a man silly with the drink, nor one who's had the news you've had this day. But me and you are finished, John.'

The piper began to blubber. Cushie and Jackie, appalled at adult emotion, turned their eyes away.

The Nun drew Jackie away. 'Come home, boy, your Mum'll be wondering where we've got to.'

Jackie looked round for Cushie, but her mother was hurrying her down to the park gates. The rain began again and blotted out the crimson coat.

'What was the matter with Mr Nicolson, Dad?'

'His boy Baillie is dead and his heart's broke.'

'If I went to the war and I was shot, would your heart be broke?'

'Yeah,' said the Nun. 'Now shut up.'

The next school day, Cushie Moy, full of indignation and sympathy, blurted out to Jackie what her mother had told her the drunken piper had meant. He was certain that Cushie's mother must have made a mistake, and hastened to his mother and stepfather for reassurance. As soon as he saw his mother's angry eyes he knew that Mrs Moy had translated accurately.

He asked, trembling, 'Was that what he meant, Dad?'

His mother made a movement towards him, but the Nun checked her abruptly.

'Yes, that was what he meant. But you got to remember he was talking out of a bottle.'

The boy, bewildered, baffled, said, 'Did he mean that I don't deserve to be alive because I'm not as big as Baillie Nicolson? What's deformed mean, Mum? Cushie Moy didn't know.'

'Cushie Moy ought to keep her little gob shut!' said his mother fiercely. 'And that goes for her Lady Muck of a mother, too. Talking to a child about such a thing!'

'Am I deformed?' muttered the boy. 'Is it awful?'

Mrs MacNunn made a cat-like sound, and the Nun shot her the hardest look she had ever had from him.

'I'd like a cup of tea,' he commanded, 'and so would the old Jack, after a long cold day at school.'

'Why did you send Mum away?' asked Jackie. 'Isn't she to know what's wrong with me?'

'I sent her away because I'm going to say some nice things about her and I don't want her with a big swollen head,' explained the Nun. 'Because then it wouldn't fit that funny new blue hat, would it?'

'No,' said Jackie with a glimmer of a smile. He felt that if his stepfather could make jokes things weren't so bad.

'Piper Nicolson said a bad thing to you,' admitted the Nun. 'A lying thing, too, and one he'd cut his tongue out rather than say when he was sober.'

'Why'd he say it then?'

'You remember Father Link's big cattle dog when she was run over, and he was trying to help her, and she chewed his arm and wouldn't let go? It was like that with the old piper. He was hurt bad because of Baillie, so he pushed over his cottage and then he pushed over the War Memorial – and then he said a cruel thing to you.'

'What did he mean though, about me being alive when I shouldn't?'

The Nun had been thinking through the night. He had had more thoughts about life than he had ever had before. Now he gave the child his conclusions.

'How old are you, Jackie? Eight years old, is that right? Then it's eight years since your Mum gave you your life. She didn't take it away from anyone to give it to you. She didn't take it from Baillie Nicolson. She didn't ask you to pay for it. She gave it to you to keep until you don't want it no more.'

'Sister Peter says . . .'

'Never mind what Sister Peter says. What's that egg-bound old chook know? I'm giving you the drum. Mum gave your life to you. Nothing anyone says, nothing Piper Nicolson or anyone else says, alters that. It's your life and you've got to get every last ounce out of it and enjoy it like hell. But at the same time you've got to be as decent a bloke as you can. See?'

The child nodded doubtfully. The Nun felt helplessly that he hadn't got through, but he had no more philosophy to give.

Jackie did not again refer to the incident. But before he went to sleep that night he felt that his stomach was full of stones. A tiny crack in life had opened, showing him equivocal things he had not even guessed existed. He had become aware of the adult world and wary of those in it.

Of course he had always known they were there, abstracted giants lurching about on the periphery of the real world. But now a massive shift in perception had taken place in his brain. He understood that those ambiguous beings, who were both servants and masters of the children, observed and judged him. There was no guarantee that they would do either aright.

Still, *he* knew what he was. Their judgment, though it might hurt, as Piper Nicolson's had hurt, could not alter that. Nevertheless, Jackie was changed. The ruthless confidence of his infancy had been eroded.

Through some deep instinct he avoided Cushie Moy. At school he saw her watching him wistfully and anxiously, turning away quickly when she thought herself observed. For a long time he missed her, in his turn spying on her from the treehouse, a lonely little girl skipping on the path in her big garden, or playing solitarily at houses amongst the dripping trees.

The piper got twelve months in prison for wilful destruction of private and public property. The magistrate, apparently personally injured by the profane and inexplicable attack on a public monument, observed that he might have imposed a sterner sentence but that he had taken into account the unsettling nature of the news received by the accused that day. He added that it was not the British way to react to bad news in such a manner, or where would we all be? Recommending the prisoner to bite the bullet like a man, he called for the next case.

Thus everyone came out of the death of Baillie Nicolson a little different.

Shortly after her eighth birthday, Cushie Moy was sent away to boarding-school. When the final arrangements were made for Cushie to attend the Mount Rosa Academy for Young Gentlewomen, Mrs Moy was smitten with the strangest pang. Emotions she had forgotten flooded her heart. Her hand quivered as she laid it upon the tumbled hair of her daughter, helpless with terror and tears.

'Cushie . . . Dorothy . . .'

At the sound of her christened name, which she would be forced to adopt as an alias in the alien surroundings of the Academy, Cushie hiccuped with anguish. She was a messy weeper, grunting, snorting, and in no time at all grimy with the tumult of her woe.

Half of her mother's will inclined towards shaking her severely; the other half, melting under the force of her confused feelings, impelled her to take the child into her arms. Cushie, who was never embraced because 'ladies do not behave like kitchenmaids', was overcome by the sweet odour of her mother's person, clung like a limpet, and wept patches of sticky wetness into Mrs Moy's silk blouse. Suddenly, like a sideslip in time, Mrs Moy recalled doing the same thing to her mother, when Papa had volcanically forbidden his headstrong youngest daughter any more clandestine meetings with the gloriously handsome young man in his accounting department. Mrs Moy could, for a moment, actually feel the whalebone in her mother's long corset, sense once again on her cheek the slippery texture of the taffeta bodice.

'I adore him, Mama. I'll die if Papa won't consent. I *will* marry him, Mama!' she said imperiously.

And so she had, eloping on her twenty-first birthday, and ruining her life. But, ah, she remembered the turbulence of that passion!

Becoming for a little while that twenty-year-old Belle Jackaman, Mrs Moy touched Cushie's hair tenderly, saying, 'You must be educated and taught to be a lady. Your grandfather is a wealthy man, and some day you too may be required to take your place in society, so you must become accustomed to the company of young ladies of your own class.'

'I want to stay home,' snuffled Cushie. 'I like it here!'

'If by here you mean this village, this repository of clods and peasants,' said her mother, 'you are well out of it; and before you're six months older you'll thank me for sending you away.'

Cushie realised that the compassionate stranger had vanished.

'You'll forget what I look like,' whispered Cushie, defeated. 'You'll love Olwyn better than me.'

Mrs Moy looked at her freezingly. 'Your vulgar jealousy of your sister only proves how much you need the discipline of Mount Rosa,' she said.

So Cushie vanished from Kingsland. Jackie never forgot her. Every holiday he looked for her. Sometimes she returned home, other times Mrs Moy and Olwyn went off by train and spent the holidays with Cushie in some distant city.

On the day the Piper was due to leave the lock-up, the Nun took time off from the shop and went down in the train to fetch him and bring him home.

'You forget quick,' said his wife with rare bitterness.

'True,' said the Nun.

He scarcely recognised John Nicolson. In a year he had become old and fat, softness all over, dissolving pork, the radish flush gone from a face now rubbery and grey. They went to a shoddy hotel for the night, and for a long time the Piper looked at himself in the glass.

'Months since I laid eyes on my dial,' he said.

'I got the pipes safely put away,' ventured the Nun. But his friend did not answer, staring at his reflection.

'Would you like a drink, John?'

Troubled, Jerry said nothing while the older man drank himself into a stupor.

John Nicolson did not return to work. Living on a small Imperial Army pension, he went from one scrubby boarding-house to another, ending up amongst the Aborigines and tramps in the tumbledown shacks at the edge of town. But Jerry went to see him regularly, and sometimes Jackie accompanied him, for Jerry was under the impression that the boy had forgotten all about the day that the Piper knocked down the Gallipoli memorial.

But Jackie had not forgotten. An obscure pain touched him each time he saw old man Nicolson. It was neither fear nor hate, only recognition. The old man was a signpost, impersonal but important. He had indicated an unsuspected division of roads.

But, loving the Nun as he did, Jackie would have died rather than allow his stepfather to guess that he remembered anything at all about that rainy day long before.

Twice in the year they were ten Jackie found out that Cushie was home for the holidays, and lay in wait for her. The first time they both were petrified with shyness, not looking at each other, but seeing with some inner eye every tiny marvel of change.

Cushie was still plump and dimpled, though she was beginning to shoot up. She was already much taller than Jackie. Her golden hair was dressed in thick short plaits with curled ends, her skin sleek and blushing.

But she dropped her glance in the same old way, and he saw her mouth quiver.

'Come and play,' said Jackie.

'Mama won't let me,' she said. 'I have to play with Olwyn.'

'You ask her,' he pressed.

But he did not see her again. The second time they were not so much strangers, and spoke a little of unimportant things, the air electric between them. Each represented to the other an enigmatic compound of imagination, romance, otherworldliness. Jackie asked no questions about Mount Rosa, Cushie made no inquiries about their old school companions. They were content to be with each other and feel the air tense with unknown expectation.

'I'll write you a letter,' he said.

'No. They might read it.'

'I'll put it in our secret hiding-place,' he said.

The secret hiding-place was an unused beehive amongst the shrubbery near Cushie's gate. Cushie thought about nothing else all day, filled with a thrilling alarm and delight. Her excitement was such that she forgot the demure expressions and attitudes learnt with such boredom and misery at Mount Rosa, and began sarcastically bickering with the bronchitic Olwyn, who hardly knew her at all and was querulously disinclined to know her better. The stamping tantrum and coughing fit that followed caused Cushie to be sent upstairs to her room.

But this time Cushie, though she was a girl of ungenteel appetite, did not mind going without dinner.

It was winter, and Mr Moy liked to dine early on such cold dark days. Cushie listened from the top of the stairs, waiting till he was well away on the table conversation. His smooth face would be engraved with a smile, but there would be no smile underneath, for he found almost everyone and everything unsettling. He treasured up each little slight and act of ill-will until he had a boxful of spiders, ready to jump out and bite him every time he opened the box.

Cushie did not know this. She attributed his constant complaints about the Bank, the War, the Government, the world, life itself, to an obscure burden he bore. It was called business worries and, according to the girls at Mount Rosa, was commonly suffered by fathers. She longed to help him, for she still loved him achingly.

Her attitude towards her mother had changed. The experience of being torn from her and hurled into Mount Rosa's abyss of homesickness and bullying had hardened the girl a little. The wound was still there somewhere, but it was covered with scar tissue. Her father had not sent her away: It was her mother who had her banished to boarding-school. A daughter of Bede Moy would never have been classified as a gentlewoman unless she were also a daughter of Belle Jackaman, of one of the oldest established and most respected families in the country.

Now Cushie crept down the stairs and out into the garden. It was a foggy evening, with blue spectral glimmers everywhere. Kingsland was still lit by gas, and its familiar smell, the very essence of home to Cushie, hung dankly about the trees. She groped gingerly in the ivy-covered beehive, hoping that Jackie had already visited it. A tight-folded wad of paper met her hand. She undid three buttons on her bodice and slipped it into the constricted front of her chemise. Though she was fevered to be back safely in her room, a hard-earned caution made her do up the buttons and tidy her hair before she crept back into the kitchen hall.

Olwyn was helping her mother carry the sweets course into the dining-room. Live-in servants were unheard of in Kingsland. Mrs Moy managed with a gardener, a handyman, and a daily woman who cooked the evening meal before she departed for her own home.

Olwyn's face, pinched and monkeyish, crinkled into a spiteful smile.

'Cushie's supposed to be in her room and she's been outside!' she said.

'I was just putting Tib outside,' said Cushie. She tossed her head at Olwyn. 'She was in your room, not mine! I heard her mewing.' She escaped past the pair of them, hearing with some triumph her mother scolding Olwyn. 'How many times have I told you not to let that cat into your room? You know the fur makes you cough.'

Cushie was not able to lock her bedroom door, so she hastened into the lavatory. There she unrolled the many careful pleats of Jackie's note.

'I love you,' it read. 'I really do.'

A wild unchildlike exultation filled her. Rapt and justified, she stayed in the arctic cubicle until Olwyn came whining to the door. Then she carefully tied the note in her handkerchief and pinned it inside her knickers, which was the only inviolable place she could think of. She felt that she had come out of a twilight that had been her world since she was born. She was loved, for the first time. She knew that her father did not love her, that inexplicably she disappointed him. Her mother loved her, she supposed, but only as a mother loved a child, not because she was uniquely herself. But now a person loved her for herself.

Pushing past the hopping Olwyn, she glided away to her room like a swan. She was always to remember this evening as one of purest joy. For a long time she sat at the open window, staring and melting into the shifting fog until her dress was sodden with damp, and she shuddered, aware of the asperity of the wind lifting the fog and ruffling the river noisily on the gravel bars.

Hurriedly she stripped off her clothes and got into bed. She wanted to stay awake the whole glad night, but in five minutes she was dead to the world.

The next morning she awoke ill, and spent the last few days of the holidays in bed with a congestive cold. Her mother looked after her assiduously, but could not refrain from reproaching her with bringing a cold into the house.

'Daddy and I take so much care that we don't bring germs into the place, because of Olwyn's chest. But there you go, leaving the window flung wide on a foggy night, thoughtless as a bird!'

Cushie bore these reproaches humbly. Desperate lest Jackie took her non-appearance to mean that she had been shocked or amused at his letter, she waited on successive evenings at the window until she saw him in the shadows beside the fence. In the dusk he crept closer until he was below her window.

'Were you angry?'

'No. It was lovely.'

'Why haven't you come outside?'

'I'm in bed with a bad cold.'

Jackie slid away into the shadows. She did not see him again, but it did not matter.

The long War seemed to these children of Kingsland to have lasted for ever. Yet it had made little difference to them. Food was plentiful, the shops were full of goods, school and sports went on without a break, and if a young man's face was missed here and there in the crowd few people noticed. Families endeavoured to present a dignified front to the world; it was not good form to lament sons and brothers sacrificed for King and Country; they must smile bravely and be proud. Out of the young country's population of scarcely six millions, sixty thousand of her fittest and ablest young men were dead, and three times as many mutilated, blinded, disabled.

'Bloody, bloody war!' grumbled the Nun.

'You can talk,' said his wife. 'You were ready enough to go in 1900.'

'Yeah,' said the Nun, 'seventeen years old and with a head full of soup.'

Privately he was ashamed that he'd ever taken rifle in hand against the brave and tricky Boers defending their homesteads.

'A dirty scuffle that was,' he said. He shook out the newspaper, a pennyworth of sports, reports, auctions, advertisements for patent medicines and the local picture show, Tattersall's sweep results, steamship news.

Mrs MacNunn fanned herself. It was November and the temperature was eighty degrees. Her gauze combinations were sticking to her body, and the elbows that stuck out of her summer-sleeved striped fuji dress were moist and pink. She pegged up her damp hair on top of her head and said, 'I'll get my hair bobbed, I swear I will.'

'No, you won't,' grunted Jerry. 'Smack your bum first. Shut up and look here.'

Mrs MacNunn looked at the headlines: 'HUNS' LAST CHANCE'. Her eye wandered off to a nearby advertisement for a patent ointment, boldly spaced.

The Hun Looked For

THE DAY

Britain said: 'You will Want

ZAM-BUK

The Day After.'

'Wonder what will happen to them Huns,' she said, 'when it's all over? I hope they mow 'em all down with a machine-gun.'

'They're just people,' said Jerry. 'Like you and me.'

'Never!' said his wife. 'Can't see you and me bayoneting helpless babies in Belgium. And all them other things.'

'Matter of fact,' said the Nun. 'You got German relations. My oldest sister Eva married a farmer name of Linz. Lives in the big valley up above Ghinni Junction.'

Mrs MacNunn gaped. 'You oughta told me, Jerry!'

'Go on,' said the Nun. 'I mentioned Eva many a time.'

'Not that she married a Hun. You ought to of told me. Beforehand, I mean. It never entered my mind that your sister might have married a foreigner. Now you've given our Jackie Hun cousins. He'd never live it down if it got out.'

'Oh, shut up, you silly old tart,' said Jerry, losing patience. 'The Linzes aren't proper Germans, anyway. They come from a place called Bohemia long ago. Drove out, they were, by bishops or someone who wouldn't let them have services in their own church. Far as I know, this farmer old Eva married is a decent hard-working joker, grows fruit, prosperous by now I wouldn't be surprised.'

'You should of told me,' said Mrs MacNunn obstinately.

'I didn't tell you hardly nothing,' commented Jerry. 'Want me to start? Well, when I was fifteen, and I'd just come outa Borstal . . .'

'You liar!' shrieked his wife, hammering him, and amid grunts and groans of laughter they rolled on the floor, collapsing in an amorous heap of kisses and tickles and squalls of: 'I can't, I can't, I'm too hot, I'm boiling!'

'You know what?' said Jackie, rushing in. 'Cushie Moy's been sent home from school because they've all got mumps. What you doing down there on the floor?'

'Exercises,' said the Nun, rising calmly. 'Well, I'm going to see the cowboy picture. Who's coming?'

But it was too hot to enjoy the picture. Jerry went out at half-time and stayed out, smoking, looking at the stars, wondering about things, feeling the old pain in his leg like a red-hot coal. Yet he was content to bear it, feeling it a hostage to happiness, a small price to pay for his satisfying life. He thought of soldiers in distant countries, hoping that this should be the last night of the War, longing for home as he had longed for it on the veldt in that unreal experience of his youth.

'Be a bit cooler tomorrow, with a bit of luck,' he agreed with the first of the patrons tramping out before 'God Save the King'.

But November 11 was one of the hottest days in Kingsland's history, the town laid out helpless before the sun's fury. In the MacNunn kitchen the ice ran out of the ice-box. In the shop the cheese oozed drops of grease.

Jerry felt sick with pain. The shrapnel had moved, the doctor had told him, re-seating itself amidst muscle tissue and sinews. They'd have to have another shot soon at digging it out. Painfully, he lowered himself to the back step and got out his tobacco.

All the world was covered with fine dust, like peach fur. The vinous sunset was full of it. At eight in the evening the sun smouldered motionless behind bloody cloud-wrack that promised no coolness for the morrow.

In his best suit, of a cloth rigid as cardboard and, because of the War and the lack of good dye, of a purplish navy, Jackie trailed his mother home from Benediction. In common, their feet hurt excruciatingly, Jackie's in glittering boots and Mrs Mac-Nunn's in her Christmas shoes, which her husband had been kind enough to buy in advance. Mrs MacNunn's striped zephyr dress ended four inches above the ankle; her natural straw hat, ornamented by a bunch of stiff blue quills and a gilded lump of glass, transformed her into what she inwardly described as a vision.

But in spite of her stylish appearance, Mrs MacNunn felt high-strung to tantrum point. The thunder in the air made the roots of her hair turn in their sockets. For another thing, the War was about to end.

For a week Kingsland had waited on tenterhooks for the news of the Armistice. Still, it was hard to believe that peace was nearly here after all the dreary years. Mrs MacNunn found the prospect unreal, even though she had already inspected the huge woodstack in the park, ready for the Armistice bonfire. In the bandstand, too, had reclined several coarse effigies of the Kaiser and his son, Little Willie, ready for hanging from the flagstaff.

Kingsland had been decorated for peace ever since the false alarm which, a few days before, had thrown sophisticated Sydney itself into an hysteria of celebration, with screaming, jigging crowds doing their best to shove in the plate-glass windows, and hordes of hobbledehoys trying to turn trams arse over tip.

Jerry had strung the shopfront with Union Jacks, filled the shop window with pictures of the War leaders, and enriched the fascia board with a swag of tri-colour bunting. But his competition, the Chinese General Store, had gone one better by erecting a victory sign in fireworks.

'Hell, I can't go another step!' whimpered Mrs MacNunn, hobbling onwards nevertheless.

All day long Kingsland had been intermittently electrified by rumours that the Huns had signed and it was all over. A large crowd shifted restlessly outside the telegraph office, which had, without precedent, remained open for news. The operator and his assistant, now the most important men in town, made the most of it – appearing mysteriously at the window, scribbling notes, putting on grave looks, and refusing to answer the crowd's chiacking.

So it was justice, the Kingsland people felt, when the northbound express brought the news before it was confirmed by telegraph.

Jackie and Mrs MacNunn were near the bottom of Church Hill when they saw the express go through, blowing cock-a-doodle-doo on its whistle, the windows crowded with yammering passengers. The train had stopped for refreshments at Ghinni Junction: now a shower of white railway cups and saucers shattered on the station platform; a drunken soldier with a rifle scored a near-miss on the

43

water-tower; and the Kingsland stationmaster collapsed under a barrage of mailbags erroneously thrown from the van.

'It must be over, it surely must be over!' cried Mrs MacNunn, and she pressed Jackie's face into her stomach, releasing him to cry jubilantly, 'What a night we're going to have! Clear away home now, and get into your old duds, for you'll want to be comfortable for all the rumpus!'

The church bells began to ring; from the shunting yard sounded something like a collision; and the clamour of kerosene-tin drums split the air over a dozen back lanes. Behind the western cloud-bank was a gasp of light.

'Ah, God,' said Mrs MacNunn aghast. 'It wouldn't rain on us!'

From the veranda of the big house in Edward Street, Cushie Moy heard the hullabaloo.

'Mama!' she cried. 'The War must be over! Look, Mama, look!'

A rocket, invisible in the late sunset, exploded over the Chinese General Store, its smoke hanging in the air like a flock of cotton-wool doves.

Mrs Moy felt strange, tremblingly excited.

'I'm glad, aren't you?' ventured Cushie. 'Oh, Mama, could I go to see the bonfire? For a little while?'

Mrs Moy recalled her mother and father dancing half the night through at the Relief of Mafeking. Australia, her eldest sister, was 'out' then, but she was pro-Boer and remained in her bedroom, sulking all through the celebrations. She even hung a black flag out the window, till her father sent one of the servants to drag it down.

For Mrs Moy there was no chance of leaving the house. Olwyn was unwell, querulous and half-choked in a tent filled with the fumes of a bronchitis kettle. Mr Moy was away in a neighbouring town on Bank business, and there was no one available, on such a night, to sit with Olwyn even for an hour.

'I could, Mama!' said Cushie eagerly. 'You go and have a look at everything, and I'll look after Olwyn. And when you come back, perhaps I could go. Please, Mama!'

But Mrs Moy hesitated. Olwyn was always fractious with

Cushie, nasty-tongued and recalcitrant. She could work herself up into a fit of suffocation after ten minutes alone with her sister. Mrs Moy shook her head.

'But I don't like your going by yourself, either,' she said. 'There might be hooliganism, goodness knows what. Intoxication,' she added with restraint.

'Mama!' cried her daughter in an agonised tone, 'I might never have another war!'

A manic din on the firebell commenced. A long spiral of smoke ascended from the bonfire, prematurely ignited.

'They're going to hang the Kaiser! They're going to have fireworks and I won't see any of it!' begged Cushie. Mrs Moy hesitated, but before she could give the child a reluctant refusal, Jackie Hanna bowled through the gate, seesawing excitedly beneath the veranda.

'Mrs Moy, Mrs Moy, can Cushie come and watch with me and Dad and Mum? Oh, it's grand, Mrs Moy!'

'Mama, now I may go, mayn't I?'

To Mrs Moy there was something uncannily simian in the way the boy bent forward and looked upwards, tilting his large head back horizontally on a delicate neck. She marvelled that Cushie was not repelled by him. But the girl was flushed with excitement.

Suddenly Mrs Moy became indifferent. It was only the kind of vulgar tribal celebration to be expected in this dreary town.

'Stay with Jackie's parents,' she instructed her daughter. 'And don't stay out too long. Jackie, if people become rowdy, you must promise faithfully to bring Dorothy home immediately.'

Mrs MacNunn was pleased to see Cushie. She had a simple fondness for the child she had known since a toddler. The child was plump and rosy, perfect, yet the astute instincts of the woman recognised the anxiety or uncertainty behind the doll-like face. Now she squeezed her cheerfully, saying, 'Thanks be there's a girl to look after me, because I tell you straight, I'm going to be a wild woman tonight. I'm going to take a nip or two, no matter what his lordship over there says about it.'

She gave Jerry a roguish look.

'You'll get home by yourself if you keel over, I'm warning you,' he said. 'I'll not be seen with any drunken old biddy and that's flat.'

Jerry's leg was giving him jip.

Yet he grinned with spontaneous pleasure to see his wife capering about the kitchen, overflowing with high spirits not because of the War's end but because it gave her a chance of a bit of a shindig.

'Wear your new hat, love,' he said. 'You look a treat in it.'

From afar came the halting sound of half a band. Seven of the younger players were marooned in Ghinni Junction, staying over after the cricket match.

'Run along, you kids!' cried Mrs MacNunn. 'You don't want to miss a skerrick of it.'

She pinned on her dress the Nun's service medal from the Boer War.

'Someone's got to wear it on a night like this,' she said. 'And I'm proud that you went and did your bit, young devil that you were.'

The Nun smiled. 'You go on ahead with the youngsters, Peg,' he said. 'I got to scrape off the whiskers.'

As he shaved, he kept sipping at a medicine glass of painkiller beside him. Some said it was laudanum. All Jerry knew was that it sometimes euchred the pain in his leg. To help him get through the evening, he filled his pocket with Hean's Tonic Nerve Nuts, which promised nerve health for threepence a day. They couldn't do him any harm, he supposed.

As he left the house he noticed how bright everything was. People had left all their lights turned on. The Salvation Army marched past, all six of them. Their one lassie was a stout old duck who'd been a naughty barmaid in Sydney in her youth and had repented it ever since.

Jerry was astonished that his little town had so large a population. The main street was so crowded that no one could move. They fought, wriggled, fainted, screamed, cursed, amongst growing clouds of dust. A hysteric sentimentality prevailed. The mayor, sunset-faced on the hastily assembled official platform outside the town hall, inaudibly prayed, condemned, thanked, and was cheered to the echo. The half a band played 'Boys of the Dardanelles', 'Rule Britannia', 'The Old Hundredth'.

There was liquor everywhere. The publicans of three of the hotels had rolled out barrels of free beer. Quickly emptied whisky bottles passed amongst the crowd. The Nun, even as he drank, hoped that his old woman wasn't getting stuck into too much of it.

In the park, closely watched by the Fire Brigade, the flames licked up the post where the effigy of the Kaiser hung, his withered arm pinned across a chest heavy with jam-tin-lid medals. People threw things, clods, potatoes, dried horse manure, at the smouldering figure. Jerry, though he felt foolish and shaky with goodwill, thought it was an ugly scene, and he was glad when some moron hit the dangling dummy fair and square with a bottle of kerosene and the whole thing exploded in a pillar of fire. Some were burned, some knocked off their feet by the hoses being dragged here and there. Jerry was glad to see his wife's blue hat, now askew above a flushed face, well back in the crowd, and Jackie and Cushie on the very edges of it, dancing with excitement.

He pushed his way to them. 'Keep away from these boneheads,' he advised. 'You're likely to get wet to the skin.'

But of course the Fire Brigade didn't dare put the bonfire out, in spite of the captain's bellowed threats. They would have been mobbed if they had.

'You mind you look after Cushie, now,' Jerry said to his son.

Father Link went past, looking friendless, though there were many of his parishioners amongst the crowd. He had soft ginger hair like wool, a mouth pulled down into a strange shape as though it had been paralysed in the very act of saying 'Pip'.

'Poor lonely bugger,' thought Jerry. He wrung the priest's hand, said, 'Great night, eh? All over.'

Then he gave him a nerve nut. It must have done Father Link good, for some time later Jerry saw him moving self-consciously around in a circle, hand in hand with the blacksmith on one side and Mrs MacNunn on the other, singing:

> In the sweet by and by
> We shall meet on that beautiful shore,
> In the sweet, in the sweet, in the sweet by and by.

The Nun thought he had better sit down somewhere. The combination of whisky and Hean's Tonic Nerve Nuts had sent him into a curious languor. His fingertips were numb, and his bad leg in limbo, the pain having changed to a long-distance kind of pins and needles. Half-sprawled in the plushy dust near the Gallipoli memorial, he enjoyed a blissful melancholy.

The figures that staggered and jerked about the bonfire were all known to him. A few were friends, many were customers; but they were more than that. They were members of the Kingsland tribe, split up into septs and families, his tribe now, their involved folklore part of his own life and history. They were all part of the poor silly bloody human race, pitiable, mindlessly stomping around in the dust, off their heads because some other silly bloody humans had been killed, pauperised, bereaved, humiliated, beaten.

In his god-like drunken remoteness, Jerry felt nothing for them but impersonal affection.

'The Huns, too,' he thought. His wife found him. A beatific smile was fixed on her face as though tacked there. It stayed there even when tears began to trickle down her cheeks.

'God, you're a sloppy old bint,' he said. 'What's up now?'

'I was thinking,' she babbled. 'I was thinking of Piper Nicolson. His boy and all. Gawd, I been hard.' She burst out, 'I want to go and see him, Jerry. Tell him I'm sorry about Baillie.'

'Better not,' said Jerry. 'Come on now, you sit down here and forget it. You've taken too much aboard, not being used to it.'

She appealed to Jackie and Cushie, standing interestedly by.

'That's the decent thing, isn't it, kids? Make it up, comfort poor old Piper, the Christian thing to do. Holding grudges all this time, it's wicked.' She broke down and sobbed copiously.

'All right, all right, I'll take you,' said her husband.

Slowly and uncertainly they moved towards Edward Street. The main street was so carpeted with confetti that in places it was as soft underfoot as a lawn. Outside the post office the Salvation Army band continued to play between two carbide lamps.

'Wait, got to give them something,' mumbled Mrs MacNunn. She pressed a shilling into the elderly captain's hand. 'Goo' man,' she sobbed. 'Peace now. All brothers, goo' will to men. Play "Faith of Our Fathers" for me now.'

Cushie noticed that the light in Olwyn's room was still lit. She hesitated, thinking she should go home.

'No,' said Jackie authoritatively. Cushie started. The two began to giggle.

'Got to pee,' announced Jackie's mother majestically. Jackie and Cushie's giggles rose to an uncontrollable pitch.

'Ought to be ashamed!' said the Nun in mortification, and angrily he bundled his wife away. Jackie and Cushie waited in silence until the Nun reappeared, sheepish, but dignified.

'She's passed out,' he reported. 'Better put her into bed, best place for her.' He scratched his head. 'Don't know that she didn't have a good idea about the old Piper, though. Think I'll go along with you and ask him to come and give us a blast of the pipes, just to mark the occasion.' He said shyly, 'She's not really shickered, you know, she just isn't used to the drop she had.'

He propped an arm against the lintel, feeling his bad leg give, his head swim disagreeably.

'You two walk along towards Mr Nicolson's place,' he said. 'I'll catch you up in two ticks, soon as I've put her ladyship into her bunk.'

'Is it all right?' whispered Cushie anxiously.

'Of course it is,' said Jackie firmly. 'I'll look after you till Dad catches up.'

They turned towards the older part of town. A gas lamp lit the deserted street, a faint bluish nimbus. Conic shadows lay beneath each tuft of grass, each pebble.

'Do you remember when we went to find the dwarfs?'

'We were only little then.'

'The eagle in the rabbit trap. I was scared. Poor thing. I hope it got away from the Chinaman.'

The huge sky was dark. In the west over Paddy's Range the lightning stammered, deep within a cloud. A low bear-like growl rolled around the sky.

'Are there really dwarfs in our hills?'

'I don't think so,' said Jackie. 'But they're somewhere. Otherwise what are all the books about?'

Darkness was all about them, and a smell of ruin and antiquity. Here, on the fringe of the town, the settlement of Kingsland had been born as the mining camp of Paddy's Leak. Here the first cottages had been built, and the stone bank, police station, and chapel raised at the end of the corduroy road that led to the diggings. But within thirty years Kingsland had moved away: like all towns it had been drawn magnetically to the railway line. The old settlement, disowned and poverty-stricken, floundered at the hem of the modern town like a beggar.

'I'm scared,' whispered Cushie.

'No, you're not,' said Jackie. 'Come on.'

But she hung back. 'We'd better wait for your Dad.'

They waited near the fallen silvery fence of a derelict shack. It was built of overlapped narrow scantling patched with bits of tea chest and flattened kerosene tins. The yawning door showed a shuffling darkness. Cushie turned her eyes away from it, clutching Jackie's hand. She jumped as bricks fell in the ruined Gold Office across the street.

A few drops plopped in the dust. Mutely the lightning pulsed in the cloud.

'Come on, Cush,' said Jackie. 'Your mother will be mad if you get wet. We'll go and shelter with Mr Nicolson, and wait for Dad there. Come on, I know a short cut.'

Reluctantly she followed him.

'Does Mr Nicolson live in a broken-down old house like this?'

'No, he lives in a church.'

Cushie laughed in surprise. The rain swished across their path in a sudden wavering spurt. She cannoned into Jackie, who had stopped running.

'Ssssh! Listen!'

A low muttering drone suddenly rose to a wild yell. Jackie felt the hair rise on his head; Cushie almost jumped out of her skin.

'It's the bagpipes.'

Fascinated, they went closer. The air shivered. The music was inhuman, terrifying, a great voice of unassuageable sorrow. To Jackie it was as if the rocks sang. Vibrating with primitive excitement, the children crept through a gap in the church wall, blinking in the dim light, slowly distinguishing this feature and that of the comfortable rats' nest into which Piper Nicolson had converted the tumbledown chapel. The floor was spread with newspapers, an oil stove gulped below a steaming kettle, a straw-stuffed tick lay on a pew seat.

The piper himself marched slowly up and down the central aisle. In him Cushie could find no trace of the towering red-eyed figure that had ridden the steamroller three years before. John Nicolson was a stout little man with a crannied face and hair like wolf-skin. He turned to them blue eyes so ruined by the booze that they might have been looking through smeared glass.

Like a man coming out of sleep, he squinched at the two children huddling in the gap in the wall. The pipes died in a long squealing sigh.

'Well! What are ye after?'

'It's me, Mr Nicolson,' said Jackie. He ventured forth so that the man could see him clearly. 'Jerry MacNunn's boy.'

'Aye, I see that.'

'Did you know the War's over, Mr Nicolson?'

'I did. I heard the row from the town. But it's nothing to me.' There was a painful silence. Jackie heard the rain fingering the tin roof. Uneasily he looked about at the gapped walls, the pyramided arch of a window, which retained a slab of yellow glass, thick and lumpy as toffee.

Cushie nudged him. 'What your Dad said!' she whispered.

'Dad wanted to ask you if you'd come and give them a tune on the pipes, just to mark the occasion.'

'I'll gi' them a good kick up the fud, that's what I'll gi' them,' said the Piper. He took the kettle from the flame and made tea. The children, left to themselves, did not know whether to go or stay.

'Will you have this muck in your tea?' asked the elderly man, holding up a tin of condensed milk. Into his own he poured whisky.

'I shouldn't drink it; my liver's turned into cement,' he said, sitting before the oil stove. 'We'll wait for your Daddy then.' Cushie was uneasy, fearing that they could be marooned in this dusty stone ruin for ever. She pressed closely to Jackie.

'Did ye hear what I was playing as you come along the track?'

'Sad,' said the girl, inaudibly.

The piper sucked his tea, was silent, and then said, 'It was MacCrimmon Oge's "Lament for the Children". All his bairns died in a month from the plague. 'Tis great music, very suitable for this day.'

The children waited what seemed a long time, but there was no sound of Jerry sloshing through the wet. They watched the rain falling beyond the holes in the wall, lit waterdrops in the darkness, like strings of radiant seeds. In the brief intervals of the rain, night crickets purred. The piper ignored the children, who became restless, wanting to get away from this strange, half-drunken man, back to the bonfire and the excitement.

'Aye, I'll come,' he said at last. Stiffly he put on his coat, and began to comb his sparse hair before a speckled glass. He looked as old as a rock.

'I was the grand lad once,' he said. The children, watching, were unable to believe he had ever been anything but old; but both of them understood his woe. Jackie sensed a wildness in him, a silent scream. He was like a lion seeking what he might devour. But there was nothing, for he had no teeth any more.

Cushie whispered, half tearful, 'Mama will be angry with me. Oh, where's your father got to?'

'We're going now. Don't worry, Cushie.'

Mr Nicolson picked up the pipes and marched out, leaving the lamp to gutter, the wind to explore his dwelling. The rain had stopped.

'Come on, quick! Maybe we'll get back to the fire before it goes out!' cried Jackie.

The rising shriek of the pipes ripped through the moist darkness. Cushie's ears drummed. Her head filled with a mad excitement, and she rushed after Mr Nicolson, stumbling beneath the dripping pear-trees. The steady oceanic breathing of the drone worked in her blood like a tide. She heard Jackie laughing, shouting beside her. The piper paced majestically along the dark street away from them.

Cushie, overcome with excitement, began to cry. Something wondrous and terrible, something unendurably powerful, had filled her soul. She wanted to scream, or dance, or melt into the ground like a raindrop. She felt different, and everything looked different, the air diaphanous, the distant lights fuzzed like thistles.

'Don't cry, Cushie,' said Jackie. 'I'll get you home. It's not your fault Dad didn't come.'

'It's not that,' choked Cushie. 'It's just everything.'

'I want to kiss you,' said Jackie. She bent down, felt his warm face, smelt a dusty, puppyish odour in his hair. So that she wouldn't be taller than he, she slid down in the grass. Held in the boy's arms, feeling him tremble, she experienced an intensely concentrated awareness of their profound knowledge of each other. Yet it was only a small part of what could be known.

They stayed like that for a little time, exchanging darting, bashful kisses, each mostly conscious of the warmth of the other's body. For the first time in her life Cushie felt at peace. The long hunger for love that had eaten secretly at her self-confidence, her faith, her pride, ceased to be felt.

'We'll get married when we grow up,' said Jackie.

'They'll never let us.'

'They won't be able to stop us when we're big.'

All they wanted was to remain close together in the grass for ever. But the grass was wet; in between the splatters of rain the mosquitoes bit them; the piper was far away, the tense scream of the pipes almost lost against the tumultuous sounds of Armistice night. The grinding roar of fights, the smashing of glass, was an obbligato to the clamour of the kerosene drums. Jackie was abruptly awakened to his duty.

'They're all getting boozed. I promised your Mum I'd bring you home if they did. We'd better run, Cush.'

They went first to Jackie's home. The Nun was fast asleep, sprawled on the kitchen sofa, dead to the world. Cosy snufflings sounded from the bedroom. Abashed, Jackie said, 'They've both passed out.'

They hurried across the street. The big house was still lit up, and Mrs Moy was on the veranda, waiting.

'You're terribly late,' she said. 'And look at your dress, wet and filthy! And your stocking's torn!'

'I fell over,' said Cushie. She took the scolding with a dreamy, abstracted air, looking at the floor. The gaslight on her golden hair seemed to Jackie to be the most beautiful thing he had ever seen, the sheen of her flushed cheek unearthly. But so that the mother would not guess his feelings he looked away into the darkness. The Moy house was filled with the scent of pine oil and menthol. Ever afterwards Jackie associated it with the total absorption of his passion for Cushie. To smell it put him once more into a state of grace.

'I'm going now,' he said. Cushie smiled at him with such confidence that he marvelled her mother did not guess, accuse. He went away, running, floating, he did not know which.

The Nun had vanished from the kitchen; somehow he had got into bed. Jackie, as he had done when a little boy, climbed out along the fig-tree bough and into the treehouse. He sat amongst the drifted dry leaves and thought about the events of the night, going over and over them with marvelling pleasure. Sometimes home-goers passed along the street beneath, singing, staggering, nagging. Looking down at these revellers, Jackie felt older and wiser than they.

He smelled his hands and the front of his shirt, where it seemed to him that the mysterious fragrance of Cushie's touch still lingered. He put his fingers to his lips, felt their shape for the first time. Had she found them soft, or hard, or strange? Her own mouth had felt like a petal, faintly warm, unresponsive and yet magical.

Cushie, Cushie! It was like the murmur of a dove.

He lay amongst the leaves on the floor of the treehouse, curled up like a snail, as though to keep all memory warm in the centre of his body.

Far below his joy and exaltation, he was conscious of something else, an ominous feeling as though he had had some unspoken revelation. He felt he had reached some peak in his life, that he had left his childhood behind.

Long after he had gone to sleep, long after the rain had blackened the bonfire, and the last light in Kingsland had gone out, the piper still marched up and down the main street, a solitary rooster crowing over God knows what, until someone finally doused him with a bucket of water from the pub veranda.

Jackie Hanna

1924

2

In the winter of 1924 James Jackaman, head of the wealthy newspaper family and brother of the statesman Sir Lewis Jackaman, was knocked down by a tram as he crossed Pitt Street to his office. So, outraged and reluctant, he died, being still alert, healthy, and a mere seventy-five. It was only natural, in spite of the long estrangement, for his daughter Isobel to attend the funeral, taking with her her two daughters, Dorothy, seventeen, and Olwyn, the frail younger child.

The children's father, Bede Moy, had also been invited to the obsequies by the sorrowing widow, Mrs James, but being a man of sensibility he found himself unable to get away from the Bank. He wore a black silk armband and tie, and an expression of courageously controlled distress; but in his heart he was jubilant and anticipatory. Now, surely, Isobel's share of the Jackaman fortune would come to her in a lump sum. Her husband had long decided in which securities he would invest it.

At the same time, Mr Moy frequently found himself with a bitter taste in his mouth. He was jealous. The Dockers' Union had buried his own father; a shilling a week insurance had disposed of his poor mother. Isobel's father, son of a Cockney ragman, would be laid away as though he had been a king.

On his way back to the Bank, after seeing his wife and daughters off on the train to Sydney for the funeral, he saw the little dwarf, the Hanna lad, swinging along whistling like a blackbird.

'G'day, Mr Moy,' he said, with what Mr Moy considered an impudent jauntiness. He scarcely came up to Mr Moy's middle, and yet he was probably as old as Cushie. Growing up! Mr Moy made a mental note to prevent Cushie's seeing the little fellow any more. Further friendship was not quite the thing between his Dorothy and the grocer's son.

The boy was wearing a navy serge suit as though he had been to some business interview. It must cost MacNunn a fortune to have the lad's clothes specially made. Even in the stiff, well-brushed suit, the short massive legs with their slight angular peculiarities above and below the knees were noticeable. Yet the face with its pugnacious features and retroussé nose was humorous and intelligent. Mr Moy, feeling charitable because of James Jackaman's death and its consequences, asked affably, 'How's the job situation, my boy?'

Jackie's face continued to look up at Mr Moy with apparent optimism. 'No luck yet, but Dad says it's just a matter of waiting till something suitable comes along.'

'Very wise,' said Mr Moy, and with a smile scarcely more than a dropped lip he gave the boy a nod and went on his way.

'And bugger you, too,' thought Jackie. He resumed his whistling, but the man in some way had dimmed the day. A soberness foreign to him, but these days not unfamiliar, settled over his spirits like dust. He turned away from the town and went down to the river, where he mooched along, his hands in his pockets, his cap pulled down over his eyes. Jobs! Bloody, bloody jobs! The place was full of them in this boom year, and yet no one seemed to have one for him.

Sometimes he awakened sweating in panic that he'd never get one, that he'd spend the rest of his life delivering groceries, being cheery, firing blandishments at customers, arranging lemonade bottles or apples, or pumpkins in pyramids in the window, and 'doing the books' which his mother, and to a lesser degree his step-father, regarded as a task both difficult and grave.

The river was low, running between banks bearded with silvery weeds. A smell of burning leaves hung in the air, bitter and melancholy. The oppression of the last half-hour suddenly opened into full-blown despondency.

To distract himself he tried to recall, to experience once more, the ironic amusement he had felt only an hour or so before at the Dairy Co-Op. manager's attempts to get out of engaging him as an assistant book-keeper. Jackie was an old hand at rebuffs. He knew them all, from the lightning-fast 'Position's filled, I'm afraid,' to the brusque 'Afraid your physique's not suitable for the work.'

The eyes, dozens of them, under grey hair, bald foreheads, through gold-rimmed glasses, pince-nez – eyes embarrassed, stupid, resentful, because by merely applying for a job he had put their owners in an awkward position.

But this one, quailing, pussyfooting, had said, 'Your references myumm are excellent, yes, myumm, Mr Moy of the Bank, Father Link . . . I'm sure your qualifications, myumm, quite suitable. But it's your myumm delicate health, you see, the work perhaps too myumm much for you.'

'I've never had a day's sickness,' said Jackie.

'Really, myumm? I was under the impression that well, myumm no matter. My secretary will let you know, myumm. Good-bye then, delightful day myumm, is it not?'

Jackie, aware that he was being dismissed, that never would he sit on a high stool at the Dairy Co-Op. office, had committed the conversation to memory, and was looking forward to entertaining the Nun and his mother with it.

'Exacting work myumm couldn't be done by anyone under myumm six feet tall. Our stools myumm, would be much too short for you, don't you agree, myumm?'

But the joke wouldn't work; it had no fun in it any more.

'Poor silly old cow myumm,' thought Jackie drearily.

He was past seventeen and had never succeeded in getting a position yet.

'And maybe I never will.'

The thought struck him with a frigid horror, as though a doctor had told him he had some terminal disease. Maybe he did, as far as the labour market was concerned. What did his brains matter, his energy or industry? All they saw was a funny little sawn-off fellow they felt they couldn't cope with. His body was odd, freakish, so his mind and abilities had to be the same way.

Ah, God, for mediocrity, ordinariness, legs the same length as everyone else's, a head that would fit in a felt hat, a brain to match!

Yet at the same time he rejected this idea. He was himself, no one else. 'Be proud of it,' his mother had said. 'You're special. Never forget it. Never let yourself down.'

And he hadn't. Not until now.

'But I haven't let myself down,' he reminded himself, even in the depths of his unhappiness. 'I'm just being tempted to, that's all.'

'Dad,' he had once said to Jerry, 'when you were young, did you ever feel that everything had stopped and was never going to get moving again?'

'Damned right I did,' said the Nun, 'for years on end. Stuck on that stinking farm. Cows. I still hate bloody cows. I can't stand 'em even cooked with onions.'

He smoked, remembering his desperation, despair. At Jackie's age he had been no better than a convict, chained to an endless round of filthy, meaningless, unpaid tasks. He remembered the times he'd thought of tying a rock around his neck and drowning himself in the dam, or taking a dose of Lysol. It sounded crazy now. His father! The memory of him gave him indigestion, so he never thought of the old reptile.

Then the Boer War came, his chance. He ran away and joined up. And by the time he was invalided home his Pa was dead, and the farm resumed by the mortgagee, and all that part of his life was finished.

He told some of this to Jackie, knowing what the boy was feeling, and at the same time realising that he wouldn't be believed. Who amongst the young believed that older people knew what they were talking about?

He said, 'You never got to think that today's all there is. There's kind of patterns in life, like currents in a river, swirling around. Sometimes you're far out from the bank, then in a little while you're near the shore, and maybe someone's waiting for you.'

Jackie could see by the reminiscent smile on his face that the someone who had been waiting for Jerry MacNunn had been Peggy Hanna.

'Yes, all right,' said Jackie then; 'but a person can't be sure that will happen.'

60

'Will it happen to a person who is as different as I am?' he thought.

'Me old Jack,' said the Nun, knowing this, 'you can be sure.'

The female voice of the wind in the desiccating trees made him think again of his mother, looking at him in simple amazement one day, discovering he was fourteen and nearly grown-up.

'Where does the time go to?' she said. The years had been happy ones for her. Looking back on her time with Jerry all she could see was a kind of warm golden mist. She was well and hearty, the shop was more prosperous than it had ever been.

Kingsland had begun to grow. English migrants had swelled the population; two small factories had opened. Trade had increased, and Jerry had bought a modest, second-hand lorry for deliveries and fetching freight from the railway station.

'We'll get a wireless one of these days, too,' he said. 'Don't see why not. Things are getting better every month. The old country's coming to life again.'

Timorously, he opened a hardware section in the shop, tools and gardening materials. He wanted to stock a lawn-mower, a poultry incubator or two as well, but he funked the outlay of capital.

'We'll just go quietly,' he said. 'I don't take to gambling.'

When he was young, Jackie had believed he could talk to the Nun about anything, and he did. But some time after he was twelve or so he discovered that there were a number of things for which there seemed to be no words.

It took him a year or more to realise that he wasn't the way he used to be, and even then he couldn't understand which way he'd changed. When he was a child life was all of a piece. There'd been moments, like Armistice night, when at the sound of the pipes he'd seemed to be seeing sideways, through a crack, into a real world of terror and splendour. There'd been some times too when he and Cushie had glanced at each other, and he'd felt on the verge of learning something astonishing and wonderful. But mostly he had been a complete person with hard edges.

And then, without his noticing, he had split up. He was full of pieces going different ways, and most of them were troubling, or wildly miserable, or madly happy.

Cushie had none of his powerful, inquisitive questing after comprehension. She was so docile, so gentle, that when she was wounded or baffled by people, or happenings, or life itself, all she could do was to cry. As though she were an angel, or a changeling, she was ill-equipped for earth. Yet Jackie, who knew her as no one else did, understood that she was experiencing the same change as he; that she had discovered that beside the world on the outside of her, there was another – unmapped, mysterious, unexplored – on the inside as well.

Jackie himself felt that he – whatever *he* was, his self or his soul, a small speck of awareness and nothing else – was the swinging door between the two.

He tried to explain this to Cushie. For a moment or two her blue eyes shone. She said, 'Yes, that's it.' Then her mouth drooped, and she added, 'But so small, so powerless, no wonder it dies.'

When he was fourteen he had wanted to leave school, but his mother had said she'd knock his block off first.

'Brains like yours!' she said vigorously. 'The reports you've had! And what Sister Leo said at the prize-giving!'

The Nun, in his serene way, put a brake on her enthusiasm.

'There's always the shop,' he said. 'A nice secure thing, a shop.'

Mrs MacNunn shook her head. 'No, I never fancied that for Jackie, with his brains. It's different for you and me, Jerry. Why, I was taken away from school when I was in fourth class to look after my mother. I'd hardly got up to long division. It was different when you and me was young, Jerry. We've done quite nicely, but Jack's meant for better things, I've always thought.'

At the time Jackie hadn't an idea in his head what he wanted. He wriggled around, discomfited, bursting with energy, thinking of football, from which he was now barred, for he was too old for the junior teams and too light for the seniors.

They discussed trades, and the Nun even went so far as to inquire about the prospects in some of them. But Jackie's lack of stature made most impossible. Others were scorned by Mrs MacNunn.

'No, my Pa was a plumber and gas-fitter, and it was terrible heavy, dirty work. Jackie's not going to be a plumber, no fear.'

62

'I wouldn't mind being an electrician,' said Jackie, thinking of shinning up ladders and working out-of-doors in the sunshine.

'There's a future in the electric all right,' said the Nun thoughtfully. 'It's going to wipe out gas altogether. Maybe even electric cars and lorries before long. You sure your mind's set on that now, me old Jack?'

Jackie didn't care two hoots as long as he could leave school.

The Nun went around to the three or four electricians in town, but none of them cared to apprentice Jack. They gave no reasons, and the Nun felt he wasn't in a strong enough position to demand them. It was Jackie's first rejection in the world of labour; but although the Nun was disconcerted about it, Jackie and his mother were easy.

'There, you see?' said Mrs MacNunn victoriously. 'He's meant for a profession. And this afternoon we're all going up to see Sister Leo to ask what she advises.'

The upshot of that interview was that Sister Leo, a masterful and intelligent headmistress, arranged for Jackie to stay on at school and do a business course, book-keeping and letter-writing, banking, and what was known as 'office procedure'.

'We'll keep up his English, too, and do some elocution, and smarten up that accent,' she said. 'Telephones are coming in. Soon every office will have a telephone, and Jack will need a well-modulated voice if he's to impress clients.'

Jackie could have died. To be a book-keeper – ledgers, pens, and figures – until he was an old man! He could feel the walls closing in on him.

'And book-keeping will always be handy in the shop as a last resort,' said the Nun, but he said it to himself.

Jackie saw the boys who had been in his class, those who had been in senior classes, gradually being absorbed into the Kingsland community, working on the railway, driving tradesmen's vans, going on the land. A few vanished to boarding-schools in Sydney; some went to Ghinni Junction and attended the high school, boarding out and coming home for the weekend.

Jackie envied all of these boys in different ways, the railway apprentices for their uniforms, the money in their pockets; the Ghinni Junction high-school boys for their world of cricket, their solidarity, their knowledge of a wider milieu than that of Kingsland.

After a while Jackie got used to being the only one of the gang still at school, and found enjoyable his status as a half-grown youth who was not treated as a pupil except in the matter of tuition. Father Link, faded and brindled and still pathologically shy, gave him the run of his library. Through books he discovered that the world of the mind was almost without limits, and that a determined traveller might cover a great deal of it before he died.

'Astute and perspicacious,' commented Sister Leo to the nuns at recreation. 'If his family had been in better circumstances he would have been sent to a university, given a profession. As it is, what will happen? Wasted, poured down the drain. One can see it coming.'

So here was Jackie Hanna now, half-educated, with a brain full of bees of discontent, resentment, and honest consternation. The idea of going home and telling his mother and father that he'd missed out again made the languid hopelessness in him rise like a tide.

But he had to go and face up to their disappointment. The Nun would want him to help load the afternoon deliveries.

'So, you understand,' said Jerry, later that day, 'I was writing to old Eva, and it just came over me to inquire like whether they could use you for a few months in the orchard.'

Jackie, who knew that the Nun would rather walk on hot coals than set pen to paper, kept a straight face. He read his stepfather like a book, could almost reconstruct the conversation that had taken place in bed between him and his wife.

'Not good for him, love, feeling no one wants him. Almost anything would be better than nothing. He's dragging his tail a bit, haven't you spotted it? Feeling as though luck's got a down on him. Now, there's Eva – you know, the one that married the German farmer, up above Ghinni. They might be able to give young Jack a start, maybe in the picking season. What say I drop her a line?'

The compassion of the man was hurtful to Jackie's vulnerable, uneasy spirit, and he cursed the circumstances that made it necessary for Jerry to be kind to him. But he kept a look of attentive interest on his face as Jerry struck a match on the seat of his trousers and lit a cigarette.

'Well, I thought, maybe the picking season. It would be as good as a holiday for Jack, out in the sun all day, fresh air and all. But Eva when she wrote back today says no, we could do with an extra pair of hands right now. What do you think of that?'

Jackie said, 'Do they know? About me?'

'Yep,' said the Nun.

Jackie grinned. 'Right.'

The pleasure on Jerry's face increased the boy's genuine interest in this offer of a job. At the same time he felt deeply relieved that he would have to suffer no more knock-backs in Kingsland for a few weeks or months.

He would have liked to write to Cushie, tell her of his luck in getting a job, which might lead to some other opportunity as yet unguessed. But he had no idea of her whereabouts in Sydney, and he would not ask Mr Moy.

After the funeral, he supposed Mrs Moy would take Cushie directly to Mount Rosa, where the girl attended the Duchess of York Annexe, a finishing school for those girls whose families could afford the transition from the academy. These young ladies had many privileges – longer vacations, private dances, training in the more delicate social graces and the grosser snobberies. A few of them married from the annexe; others were taken for their final year to London or Switzerland to receive the ultimate polish.

But in spite of all their privileges, the Graces, as they were called by the junior school, were not allowed to receive letters from young men.

So Jackie could not write to her there, either. He contented himself with asking his mother to be sure to tell Cushie where he was, when she came back to Kingsland for the summer holidays.

He was interested and curious about this courtesy branch of his family.

'Foreigners!' said his mother forebodingly.

Mrs MacNunn was doleful, sniffing above the frying-pan as she thumped the chops about.

'First time away from home! How will you manage?' She fretted.

But Jackie had recovered his optimism. Something was going to happen, something positive, active. First time away from home it was, and he couldn't wait for it.

'It'll be great!' he said to the pleased Nun.

Three days later he took the train to Ghinni Junction.

When the Nun saw Jackie off at the station he was both genial and half apologetic.

'Don't you go worrying now, boy,' he said. 'This is what you might call a temporary expedient, just to keep you going until something better turns up in your own line. And it will, never you fear!'

'Jackie won't get his tail down!' asserted Mrs MacNunn, but with a quaver in her voice that indicated hers was down already.

Jackie kissed her wet cheek as she bent towards him. Their loving fear for his welfare made him put on his cockiest look.

'Don't you worry, Mum. I'll be amongst friends. Cheer up now! What's that long lip for?'

The Nun brightened. 'Old Eva will look after him like the Christmas duck. He'll be one of the family, and that makes a difference your first time out on your pat malone.'

On the way down to Ghinni Junction Jackie's high spirits remained constant. He felt as he had when younger, ready to take on the world. He exerted himself, as was his habit, to be sparkling, a bit of a comic, clowning a little to make his fellow-passengers laugh, and make them forget his lack of size. He was constantly abashed at his instinct to do this.

'What am I after?' he often said to himself. But he knew very well. It was to let people know that dwarfs didn't mind being as they were, that there was no real disability in being under four feet high.

Two of the passengers had their homes in Ghinni Junction and knew a good deal about the fruit farmers up in the hills beyond the town.

So he learnt that in that hard, cobby hill country there were good pockets of farm and orchard land, which had been taken

66

up by German or Scandinavian immigrants two generations back.

'They was running away from some war or something,' said the elder passenger. 'Germans, surely, wasn't they? That old bloke Sturm never spoke a word of English; and Vogt, wasn't there a Vogt?'

The other passenger remembered the Vogt.

'Which family did you say you were going to visit, son?'

'Linz,' said Jackie. 'But my auntie, Mrs Linz, she's Australian.'

Yes, they both knew of the Linzes, big men, five or six of them. Never seen Mrs Linz. But that was characteristic of the High Valley fruit farmers. Close as hell about their own affairs, very tough on their womenfolk, it was said. The sons stayed close to the farm, too, brewed their own peach cider, only came to town for stores.

Jackie, sensitive to nuance, had the impression that the High Valley people were still regarded, after half a century, as foreign, full of dark old hates and unacceptable ways. He reassured himself by the thought of his stepfather's sister, not a foreigner at all, a softer, womanly replica of the Nun.

There seemed to be no one to meet him at Ghinni Junction, and he stood disconcerted for five minutes or so until an engulfing shadow fell across him, and a resonant voice said, 'I am Linz.'

The speaker was in his late thirties, a slab of a man, gumbooted, heavy-coated. His ponderous features were marred by a long scar that dented the left eyebrow and dug into the cheekbone below a milk-glass eye. As he saw Jackie's gaze irresistibly fly to this blemish, his lips opened in an ironic smile.

'They call me Blind Hof,' he said.

Abashed, Jackie reached up and had his hand swallowed in the giant's grip. 'I'm Jack Hanna. Pleased to meet you.'

Behind Hof, Jackie now saw another burly figure, which in spite of its obesity gave an impression of sinister strength, a blue-eyed, carnation face wobbling with smiles, a sunny blond head with hair shaved up to the level of its ear-rims; a figure which now burst into enormous mirth, amidst which Jackie could distinguish the words:

'My God, if you could see yourselves, the long and the short of it!'

Blind Hof said briefly, 'This is my brother . . .' He said some name, but Jackie could not catch it above the laughter. Anyway, he never thought of this second Linz as anything but the fat brother. In due time, the fat brother heaved Jackie onto the back of a lorry as though he were a sack of onions, while Blind Hof picked up two other brothers, men in their late twenties, one of whom was puking drunk, and the other lean and sallow. While the drunk brother was laughing helplessly at Jackie, the dark one stared, grinning, and this seemed to Jackie to be more offensive than anything that had gone before.

So they rattled out of the town, the drunk brother rolling around, helplessly spewing over the various stores and packages that crammed the back of the truck, the dark brother staring and picking his brown teeth and sniggering, and Jackie gradually becoming more and more savage until at last he blurted, 'Well, you got nothing better to do than to stare?'

'Nope,' said the dark brother. 'Never seen such a comic cuts before, so I'm taking my fill.'

Jackie, red as fire, his eyes glaring, poised for a spring; but the dark brother snatched a spanner from the deck and clonked it rhythmically in the palm of the other hand, saying, 'You watch it, monkey man. Give me no trouble and I give you none.'

Jackie subsided, boiling; not afraid, but biding his time. His main emotion was bewilderment. In a kind of a way, these four men were his cousins; yet, with the exception of Blind Hof, they treated him with contemptuous ribaldry. He was perplexed. Seeping alarm about his prospects made his self-confidence dwindle. He turned his back on the dark brother and the snoring drunk and surveyed the countryside.

Jackie felt high in the air, isolated. The very wind that blew from the bush smelt different; larches, birch, and sycamore grew amongst the lemon orchards; the masts and spars of leafless Lombardies pierced the sky. North Europeans had settled these hills and valleys; their marks were everywhere.

The road was abominable; the scrub pressed in on both sides. Streams flung themselves down towards it, drummed underneath in rough culverts, and spouted out the other side white as soda water. The lorry moaned upwards around the bends, and Jackie was nauseated with travelling and hunger. But the journey continued, one hour after another, and he slept intermittently leaning against a bag of pollard that smelt of the drunk brother's vomit.

He awoke when Blind Hof's iron hands seized him around the middle as though he were a doll and dumped him, kindly enough, down on wet paving where dogs circled warily, men's legs were illuminated in lamplight, and smells of food gushed through a kitchen door.

'Wake up, lad,' he said. 'We're home. Go into the kitchen and make yourself known to your Auntie Eva.'

He took no further notice of the boy as he stood uncertainly there, but effortlessly began dragging the load off the lorry deck, first the heavy sacks, then the drunk brother's lolling body. A hand fell on Jackie's shoulder, and a new, halting voice said, 'You must be Jack. 'Ow are you? I'm Ellie.'

He looked up to see a frail, girlish-looking boy about his own age. He had a pretty skin, and blue eyes which, through diffidence or a habit of evasiveness, did not meet Jackie's. His left foot turned in at an uncouth angle, as though the ankle were deformed. But his voice had been friendly, and Jackie was grateful.

'I've got a bit mixed up,' he said. 'All these new people.'

'Yeah, I reckon so. I'm Eldred Linz. I'm the youngest of the litter. Come on in. Ma's got supper ready waiting. Come on, you must be perished. Maida reckons you're a cousin, is that right?'

And before Jackie could ask about this new name, he was escorted into a huge cavernous kitchen with a coved, sooted ceiling, hanging brass-roofed lamps, a black cooking range that filled even the far corners of the room with a comfortable warmth. The smell of food was so good, so strong, that Jackie felt quite dizzy. So it was in an equivocal, distracted manner that he met his Aunt Eva, an old woman with hair like dirty cottonwool and a small bowed frame, a woman so unlike her brother that their relationship could not be believed for a moment.

'Maida, sit him down next to you. Maida, carry the broth to the table; the boys will be in in a moment. Maida, take Jack's coat; it's too hot in here.'

Jackie was aware that a silent, sad-faced little girl obeyed all these requests. She slipped by him, taking his coat as she went; was back in a moment with a heavy tureen of soup, which she placed at the head of the table with its ladle.

'Sit here,' she said. Her long fair hair was tied back with a bootlace; she wore an ugly dark blouse and a skirt of unusual length. Jackie saw that she had unobtrusively placed a thick cushion on his chair.

In his heart a profound mortification struggled with appreciation of this young creature's motherly thoughtfulness. He thanked her quietly, and she bowed her head, flushing.

The brothers took their seats, Hof at the head of the table in a round-armed chair that Jackie assumed was their absent father's. In some manner the drunk brother had been restored to a facsimile of glassy-eyed sobriety. The fat brother, still shaken by snickers whenever he looked at Jackie, ate finickily. He complained of everything – the turnip in the soup, the rabbit in the stew.

Mrs MacNunn, had she been the cook in that household, would have sprung up and clouted him; but Jackie's Auntie Eva, ducking her small unkempt head ever closer to the table, replied not a word. At last Ellie said, half under his breath, 'Leave her alone, you cow!'

The fat brother bawled, 'I'll give you the flat of my hand, you bloody crip!' He went on abusing the lame boy until Mrs Linz began to cry, putting her hands over her frail, dried-up-looking ears, and snivelling, 'Don't say them things to poor Ellie!'

In all ways it was a painful meal for Jackie. No one asked him about his journey, his family; he might as well have been a dog. He was so baffled and angered by the behaviour of them all that he scarcely liked to look up. So he was astonished when he observed, sitting beside the fire in a rocking-chair, his feet in a basin of water, a newcomer to the scene, an old man, eating a hard-boiled egg which he occasionally dipped into a saucer of brown salt. He looked so placid, so entirely at ease with his surroundings, that the boy took heart.

The old man was the original farmer Linz, who had come from Bohemia long ago, in his velveteens, his iron-studded boots, his poverty and resolution. His name was Martin Linz, and he was

Maida's grandfather. In his old age he had forgotten his English, and because amongst the younger Linzes only the older boys could speak a Hottentot German, he led a dumb, lonely life. His wife had died thirty years before; he had become a stranger in his world. It was days before Jackie knew he was a member of the family at all.

At night he sometimes came into the barn where Jackie slept, lit another lantern, and with slow, methodical movements worked away at some carpentry. The first time this happened the boy, awakened by the long sob of the saw, gave a startled grunt. The old man, eyes hidden by round, silver-rimmed spectacles, jowls gauzy with stubble, seemed like a figure from a fairytale. Jackie lay back in his shadowed pallet behind the kerosene drums pretending to be asleep as Martin Linz came towards him and, with the lantern raised, examined his face. Jackie bore it as long as he could, and then impishly snapped open his eyes and winked. The old man, surprised, emitted a sharp quack of laughter. He dropped one knotted hand almost caressingly on Jackie's head, and said, '*Glück*.'

After that Jackie welcomed the half-dreaming interludes when he was roused from his exhausted sleep by the aromatic whiff of new-cut wood, the comforting ancient sounds of a workman about his business.

'What is he making, your granddad?' Jackie asked Ellie, and the boy answered, with his scuttling glance and half-stammer, 'His coffin.'

Maida did not like to talk about it. She was afraid of mortality. But Jackie thought it was dignified and good that the old man should thus round out his long life of usefulness. Sometimes, before he went to sleep, he looked at the coffin, the interior painted with tar and already half-lined with coarse, bleached fabric like sailcloth. The lid, which had been finished with three grades of sandpaper, was satisfying to touch. The old man had already carved his name and date of birth. There was space for the death-date, which Jackie supposed one of the grandsons, Hof probably, would fill in. A cross came before the inscription, and after it was a decorative bird, which Maida told Jackie was called a *Distelfink*. It was the sign of Martin Linz's distant village.

Jackie had been outraged and indignant when he had been first taken to the barn by the fat brother, who threw his baggage on a stretcher and said shortly, 'You sleep there. The hands are called at six. Late, your wages get docked.'

Later, when he saw the rough conditions of the bunkhouse in which the transient hands and the pickers slept, he was thankful for the privacy of the barn. The pallet was clean and dry; his bedding was regularly replenished by unseen hands. And, also, for some unknown reason, he was left alone there. The larking and teasing that kept his days in emotional turmoil never followed him to the barn. It was as though they wanted him to recover his equanimity for the next day's ordeal. So he began to look upon the barn as his only place of peace and shelter. And indeed, long afterwards, he would be able to close his eyes and reconstruct the barn's rustic interior as though upon a dark screen, the horse-collars on spikes, the saws in sheaths, hames, rabbit traps, fence posts, explosives in a metal box on a high bracket, harness on pegs, boxes of staples, barrels of nails, poultry food, potatoes in bins and onions in nets, wooden hayforks and part of a harrow that glinted like a row of sabres in the moonlight. There was the smell of oats, the drier smell of chaff, and now and again the acid whiff of excrement from the litters of wild squirming kittens, creatures of the shadowy loft high up under the eaves.

He slept so exhaustedly that when Ellie awoke him the next morning he had no memory at all of the fat brother's violently shaking him twenty minutes earlier.

'You gotta be quick,' Ellie said urgently. 'Ma's covered up for you, but you don't want to be picked on for being late the first morning. Have a sluice at the trough and come up the back way for breakfast. Quick!'

And he lurched away with his unexpectedly agile gait. Jackie followed him in a mad scramble. Somehow Ellie's nervous trepidation had communicated itself to him. Outside the world was dark except for large home-going stars that wavered in a fuming sky. Everything was starched white with frost. Jackie, his lungs stabbing, realised that the clothing he had brought was far from being warm enough. He ran for the kitchen door, which showed a sharp knife-line of orange at its foot. The air was full of a strange pungent smell of burning oil, and far away, suspended in air, was an unidentifiable pink glow.

The kitchen was full of interlaced shadows, and the scarlet tongue of the fire waved intermittently through a stove-hole as Mrs Linz moved a cooking pot. The little woman did not speak or look in his direction. She and Maida must have been up for far more than an hour, for the table was covered with food – platters of steaming fried potatoes, hot scones, fish stew, mountainous steaming dishes of chops and steak patties. Jackie saw that other men were at the table, overalled strangers who kept their heads down to their plates and shovelled in food as fast as they could, sibilating around it to cool it as they did so.

'You want to eat up, Humpy,' advised one of them. 'It's a long morning.'

'Don't call him that!' hissed Maida suddenly from behind Jackie. 'He's not a hump-back.'

'All right, then, Lofty,' said the man amiably. 'How come you're so short? You sure could walk under a log.'

'He's one of them dwarves,' said the dark brother, fixing Jackie with a serpentine eye. 'That's why he'll only get half a man's pay.'

Jackie ate in silence. Ellie, Maida, and the mother flew around, replenishing dishes, the huge teapot, the milk-jug. Even alongside that prodigious blue enamel milk-jug Jackie felt himself dwindle. Everything about this place, these people, made him feel small and insignificant. His spirits, vulnerable since yesterday, sank lower still.

Now and then he stole a look at Maida, illuminated intermittently by kerosene lamp or firelight. About her face there was something flat-planed, almost medieval, that made Jackie remember the Dutch pictures in his dwarf books. Now and then she gave him a speaking glance. It may have been only to ask him if he wanted more tea, but to Jackie it seemed to cry to him for help, rescue, solace. Her little wrists, as she bent across him, seemed to be those of a child. The odour of her body reminded him of Cushie's, a little milky, a little soapy. Her hands were already hardened, with split weeping chilblains and the long brown of a burn across one thumb.

One by one the other brothers stamped in, engulfed food. There was no conversation except for grunts, an occasional half-sentence thrown out as though it were any dog's bone.

Hof was red-eyed, coughing, his face and clothes grey with soot.

'What time you start lighting, Hof?' asked one of the hands.

'Three. She ain't bad. We got down to one degree. I got the full fifteen hundred smoking, though.'

'Forecast says fine and warm,' put in the dark brother.

Hof grunted. Nothing was explained to Jackie. He tried to be composed, in spite of the stares, nudges, and grins amongst the other men at the table. But as he left the kitchen, and he had to jump for the door knob and swing on it to open it, there was a wholehearted bellow of laughter. Quick as a flash Jackie whipped around: 'You'll get used to it,' he said. 'You've got used to the sight of your own ugly dials in the shaving-glass, so nothing's beyond you.'

Out in the dawn light, where a red veil sparkling like mica hid the mountains, the man who had first spoken to Jackie caught up with him.

'Sorry I put me foot in it back there,' he said. He held out his hand. 'I'm not such a bad bugger when you get to know me. Name's Cockie Bailey. What's yours, Lofty?'

'Lofty will do,' said Jackie, for the man's diffident smile was engaging. 'Jack Hanna is my name, though. I come from up the line – Kingsland.'

'Well, Lofty, look on me as a mate if you need one,' said Cockie. 'I been here in the valley on and off every year since I come out of the home, and I'm twenty-six now.' He spat out an anonymous knot he had fished out of a hollow tooth with a split match. 'You lucky, Lofty, you know that. If the old man were here we'd have to work twice as hard. I never met such a slave-driver as Remus Linz. And tight! A duck's bum ain't in it.'

Jackie guessed that Remus Linz was the father of Maida and the boys.

'He spends most of his time now away from High Valley,' said Cockie. 'He's a blacksmith and wheelwright, travels around the countryside mostly. A booze-artist, and the most brutal hound you could ever hope to find dead in a ditch. I seen him break a calf's backbone with an axe. And he belts the old lady worse'n a dog.'

'That old woman?'

'The story is that's why Ellie's foot is crooked. He gave her a slamming while the kid was still in the bag.' He dropped his voice. 'Hof is the best of a bad lot. If there's anything you want to be tipped off about, I'll drum yer.'

There was a bull's bellow from the kitchen garden: 'Cockie, you and the new man douse the pots.'

Martin Linz, long before, had taken up a selection of four hundred acres in the almost inaccessible and intractable High Valley. He packed in his equipment and stores on a bullock sled that was set not on wheels but skids. He cut the track as he went, and he and his wife were a month on the journey. It was in Queen Victoria's time; there was no train through Ghinni then, and the hills swarmed with goldminers. Linz had no interest in gold.

His first house was a tin one, brought in sections from Bohemia, bolted together and set up on log runners in the first clearing he made. There Remus Linz had been born in 1869. There were others, daughters, but they were dispersed or dead long ago. Maida was named for one of them.

Martin Linz had planted fruit-trees from seeds and rooted slips brought in pots from the old country, and these immigrants had been the foundation of the Linz orchard. Plums, cherries, apricots, and nectarines had followed. Some time in the early years of the century the farm had gone over entirely to stone fruit; cauled Cape gooseberries fruited in sheltered hollows, red and black currants thicketed between the vegetables of the kitchen garden. Oranges, limes, grapes, and almonds, grew farther down the hillsides. Olive-green stands of native bush sheltered this fertile valley.

It became apparent to Jackie that the darkness hanging over the mountain valley was half smoke. In the orchard men carried lanterns, and their faces were as grimy as if windows had been cleaned with them. Amongst the trees a sullen humidity lingered like a low cloud. The stench of the burning oil was like that from guttering lamps.

'I don't get it,' confessed Jackie. 'What's it all about?'

'Frost-fighting equipment,' said Cockie briefly. 'Jump to it, son! Fuel's expensive, maybe eightpence the gallon. Hof says douse 'em, we douse 'em, quick. You take that row, I'll take this one.'

Many of the smoke-pots between the fruit-trees had already burned out. Jackie, fleet as a rabbit, had doused the remainder and was waiting at the end of the row by the time Cockie panted up.

'How long does the smoke hang around?' asked Jackie.

'Maybe four hours or so. Cars going down to the Junction have their headlights on a good part of the way. It's not good for the town; the smudge seeps through doors and window cracks when the wind's blowing that way. But what can you do? Ghinni lives on fruit-canning and the juice and jam factories. And fruit's got to be protected against frost. There's upwards of thirty thousand pots up here in High Valley alone. We ain't the only orchard in the valley, you know.'

By smoke-oh time the smog had drifted away in huge soiled cumuli towards Ghinni Junction. Through them Jackie discerned the muted colours of the landscape. A dry winter had left the countryside bronze, sepia, malachite; the walls of gorges showed as grey as skulls; the shrunken creeks, awaiting spring rains, licked sleek islets of sand.

'You'll be real good, Lofty,' said Cockie Bailey. 'For a little fella you got plenty of muscle.' He added, abruptly, 'Don't you let them big squareheads poke too much borak. A man's got his right to respect.'

But the Linz brothers were like a ring of animals, not fierce feral beasts, for they were too easily amused for that, but something mischievous and derisory like monkeys.

They never let up for a moment. Each remark carried ill-concealed mockery. All the banter seemed to be directed at Jackie's appearance, the shortness of his legs and arms, the size of his head, his probable virility. The small contrivances by which he lived and worked as normally as possible sent them into fits of inexhaustible laughter. The sight of Jackie hopping up on chairs; swinging nimbly on door handles; jumping up and snatching what he needed, like a cat; carrying around a little box so that he would be high enough to work at a bench – these things were precious to them. They waited and watched so that they would not miss anything.

They had also little personal ploys of their own. The drunk brother liked to snatch off Jackie's cap and put it on to demonstrate how much bigger Jackie's head was than his own. The sight of his half-mad eyes peering out from under the brim never failed to send the rest of them into roars.

And the dark brother, whom Jackie detested most of all, because in his hatred he discerned apprehension, had a habit of leaning an elbow on the top of Jackie's head, as though by mistake, and then apologising extravagantly: 'Thought it was the table, I swear I did, or the work-bench, or the top of a stump.'

Ah, Jackie could have murdered the dark brother. When he thought of him, a vicious tremble began in his diaphragm.

Though as a child Jackie had been no stranger to teasing, he found this new situation so alien he had no idea how to deal with it. He could not believe that mature men could enjoy for so long such baiting. Only in later weeks did he understand that the teasing arose from a peasant humour so simple it was almost innocent. Before that realisation he made many errors. Pushed willynilly into the role of court fool, he stood on his dignity, glared, answered back, became sullen.

In the back of his head he could hear Jerry MacNunn saying, 'They're only waiting for a bite. They want to know they've stung you where you live. Ignore the bastards.'

But he could not. The joke went on too long. And yet it concerned small things: for example, the fat brother, at breakfast, stealthily taking food from his plate whenever he looked away, the tiny petal lips pursed in a smile of delighted expectation, waiting for the reaction.

'Ask the tub of lard if he's still hungry,' advised the Nun in Jackie's head. But instead the boy leapt up, shouting, 'Why don't you take the frigging lot?' and shoved the hot plate of food down the front of the fat brother's shirt. He heard Maida's cry of alarm, Ellie's hysterical burst of laughter, and then he was slammed against the door by a back-hander from the fat brother.

'I'll murder the freak!'

The man looked like a charging elephant. Jackie slipped under his fist and behind him, leapt on his back and tried to throttle him. He wanted to feel his hands sunk in the yielding flesh, the eyes gouged out, warm blood gushing. But instead he was plucked off the fat man's back by the drunk brother, as easily as if he were a bug, and amidst lacerating laughter he was borne outside and hung on a peach bough by his braces. He cursed, spitting with rage and frustration, and at the same time he knew coldly that his limbs were moving with the foolish ineffectuality of a fly on flypaper.

'Leave him alone. You asked for it, Kurtie,' rumbled Hof, restraining the carmine fat brother. And, growling, he lifted Jackie down. The rescue was as galling to the boy as the quarrel, and he wished he were dead.

The woman, his Aunt Eva, took a curious attitude. To Jackie she was still, after a week, an ambiguous personality, sometimes cringingly friendly, but brusque with him when her sons were in hearing. He thought she was hateful. He couldn't stand the sight of her soiled scalp through her sheep's curls. He hated the way she carped and whinged at Maida, as though, having been bullied all her life, she was now getting in for her cut. She had a word or two to say to Jackie, too, after the peach bough episode.

'You don't want to be a bad sport,' she said. 'The boys don't mean anything; it's just their liveliness. Look at Ellie there, he don't bite like a shark when the boys call him gammy or dot-and-carry-one. Ellie knows it's all fun.'

Jackie wanted to retort that the brothers never seemed to chaff Ellie, except for the outburst of the fat one at the table. He refrained; and he could see that the old mother was very protective of Ellie. He could not make Ellie out at all. Backward and shy, keeping close to the kitchen and the home garden, for which he seemed responsible, he snuggled around his mother like a child. The older brothers ignored him, except for a churlish sentence tossed his way now and again, but Maida, too, was loving with him. The only time Jackie saw her laugh was when she was with Ellie, her arm over his shoulder, their faces close together as though they were children.

Meanwhile, as though it were a part of his growth he could not control, Jackie's hatred for the brothers became obsessive.

Reason left him. He hungered for revenge. Each morning as he awoke he was sensible of a cold lump in his belly. It was created both of dread for the new harassments the day was sure to bring, and of undigested passion.

He longed painfully to go home, to tell these clowns to stuff their job, to set out walking for Ghinni Junction and freeze on the road rather than put up with the torture any longer. Yet something iron within him forbade it. To give in, to run away from such yahoos!

The weather became colder. Nearly every morning the world was sugar-white, becalmed, so silent that Jackie jumped when his footstep crunched the ice webbed like glittering hair in the interstices of the earth. Under the sun's heat the hills raised green helmeted heads from the immaculate landscape; but in the gullies from day to day the puddles remained irregular plates of obscure glass, and mushy mud-ice clogged the watergrass in the bogs.

By night birds collected in complaining, fluffed-out rows along the rafters under the barn eaves. There were always three or four dead and fallen in the morning.

The Linzes were morose, quarrelsome. Strange undertones and cross-currents of emotion seemed to run in the house, like artesian streams. Jackie saw the drunk brother, without warning, trip the dark brother as he crossed the veranda and, when he was down, hammer him unmercifully. He heard his Auntie Eva, several times, cry out as though someone had struck her. And he saw Hof, always slow to anger, slam Ellie across the head so that the boy sobbed piteously.

Maida was often red-eyed. But, through shyness or backwardness, she would rarely speak to him, though he longed for conversation with one as young and unhappy as himself. He knew she did not dislike him and was not repelled by his abnormality. She put good food on his plate, anticipated his needs at the table, and sometimes he caught her gazing at him with her long narrow eyes that were the most beautiful slate-blue. He remembered, too, how she had come out of her humble silence to defend him that first morning, when Cockie Bailey had thought him a hunchback.

The uneasy bad temper that seemed to prevail amongst the Linzes did not make Jackie's life any easier.

'They're leery about losing the crop,' said Cockie Bailey. 'Their old man would give them hell. He can still lay about them with his fists, even Hof. They just stand there like dummies and take it, you know. It's their way back in the old country or suthink. Bloody loopy, all these foreigners. Any Australian would chuck the old devil down the well.'

The fruit was now marble-sized; it could withstand the intense cold scarcely at all. For three weeks now Hof had had rigged up outside the room where he slept an electrical contraption powered by a battery. It was set for frost of one degree, and when the temperature sank to this lethal level the circuit was broken and a bell squalled out an alarm. Hof went to bed in his clothes; in a few moments he was into his sheepskin coat and down in the orchard.

Jackie was grateful when Hof told him that in future he would be one of his offsiders in these arctic awakenings. He was glad because that meant he would be allowed to sleep till the midday dinner, and so avoid the abrasive company of the other brothers for a portion of the day. And he was glad, too, because the orchard on frosty nights had a theatrical beauty unlike anything he had ever seen before. To see, in the countryside's Babylonian darkness, suddenly bloom the rolling clouds of smoke, the serried trees like dancers, rose-red, mysterious! Even Hof was a pleasure to the eye, a black phantom revealed as a delicately flushed half-human creature, pink running across his moist whiskers, ebbing and flowing in his one half-seen eye.

And the other orchards along High Valley were each a rosy galaxy, a Magellanic cloud of ruddy fumes. Jackie would have liked to stand and gaze at them, but there was never any time.

Each tree now had its own pot, a five-quart lard pail of crude oil, which would burn for four hours before needing refuelling. Thus, from the third hour, Hof and Jackie patrolled the orchard constantly watching for guttering pots. The other offsider, who was frequently changed, for the men hated this freezing, dirty, pre-dawn job, watched the trees on the lower slopes.

As soon as Hof called Jackie, after the alarm had sounded, the boy scurried into a heavy coat, pulled a sack over his head, and lit the asbestos wick of a kindler, a long-beaked can holding an inflammable mixture of petrol and kerosene. The first few nights the mixture splashed out past the wick in fiery gouts, burning Jackie's shoes and sometimes his hands. But he soon learnt to be fast and deft, running from pot to pot, passing the long spout quickly round the inside of each, till the oil was heated to combustion point. A chain of brief whuffs followed him as the smoke arose, coiling and swelling like a malodorous genie.

It pleased Jackie that he was more skilful and faster than either Hof or Cockie. There were some things in which he excelled, and he hoped frankly that Hof would mention it at the table, let the others know that in some ways the half-man was better than a full-sized one. But Hof never did. Still, a kind of speechless, vegetative harmony had grown up between them, and Jackie was content with that.

He wrote once to his mother, telling her he was well, and could cope with the work. He said nothing about his Auntie Eva except that she was a good cook, and kept turkeys as well as hens for laying.

But even writing home was disturbing, so profound was his longing to be there. So he did not write again.

He longed for Cushie, the golden princess who loved him as he was. When he returned at six or seven in the morning from the orchard, chilled to the bone, a frozen stick in a frozen bed, he often dreamed that Cushie was there to twine herself around him, soft as velvet, warm as a kitten or a puppy, smelling so sweet he could have wept at the memory of it. For the two friends were familiar with each other's bodies. Step by step, in a natural, secret unfolding since Armistice night, when Jackie had kissed her and the piper's music had sent her half-way out of her mind, they had become in the highest sense of the word lovers, though they had not yet possessed each other.

Since they had grown up there were not the opportunities for privacy; but there was a transparent delicacy between them. They had always, by some unexamined empathy, each reflected the other. Jackie was aware, though they had never broached the subject, that Cushie was not ready for this final intimacy. The time had not yet come, though both knew it would, as the seasons would change.

During the period of Jackie's severest loneliness and dejection, he felt he could not get through the day without the memory of Cushie.

'I love you, Jackie.'

'For ever and ever?'

'Ever and ever.'

One night about three the sky clouded over, the temperature rose, and Hof barked at Jackie: 'No frost tonight. Going to rain. Get to bunk. I won't need you until smoke-oh.'

In the barn the air was tainted by a recently extinguished oil lamp. Jackie knew that the old man had been working on the coffin. When he set down his own lantern, he smelled appreciatively the fresh varnish Martin Linz mixed himself. It had the odour of new-felled trees. Jackie dragged off his muddy boots. He took a child's size, and it was hard to get boots heavy enough for his work. These were already splitting soles from uppers, and his feet were miserably sodden and chill. He left on his flannel shirt; though damp, it was warmer than anything else he had. He scrambled under the blanket, but could not get warm. He lay there wretchedly, and listened to the night birds' repining double-call, joyless, maundering, as though they hated the dark, but were doomed to it for ever. And while he lay there, shuddering, drowsy, but too afflicted with cold to sleep, he heard somewhere in the barn a sob. It came again, from high up, where the wild cats littered.

'Who's that?' said Jackie, sitting up in the darkness.

There was silence, and then he heard again a smothered sound of a child's misery.

'Ellie, is that you?' he called. He lit his candle, looked around amongst the swollen shadows.

There was a scramble amidst the straw above. He lifted the feeble light and saw bare feet coming down the loft ladder, a nightshirt of brown stripes, and a long plait of colourless hair.

'Maida! What's the matter?'

She was silent, hanging her head. He saw that blood streaked her forehead and cheek; tears had bedabbled it pinkly on her nightgown collar.

'Have you hurt yourself, Maida? What is it? Has something happened?'

She seemed to him the distillation of all that was forsaken, her mouth half open and turned down like a distraught child's, her eyes swollen into slits.

'Maida! Will I get your mother or Hof?'

With that she seemed to come alive, as though threatened, and looked at him aghast.

'Oh, Jackie, he beat me and pushed me outside and locked the door.'

'Who? Who? Not Hof?'

From her tear-bubbling outburst he caught: 'No, no ... Con did it ... Con ... he was angry with me. He hit me with his belt; he said I could sleep in the outhouse or freeze to death for all he cared.'

Con? Con? Which one was it? The formidable dark brother with his inexplicable caprices, his sudden rages? The half-daft drunk brother? A cold sweat broke out on Jackie. He jumped out of bed, made Maida sit down, huddled the blanket around her. Her hands felt like stone.

'But what for? What did you do? He must be mad!'

She only shook her head dumbly.

'I'll go and give Hof a call. Hof will let you into the house.'

But at that she wept hysterically. 'No, no! No more trouble! It's nearly morning. No, no! Conrad would be all the angrier if I complained to Hof. You don't know what he's like.'

'Then you'd better get into my bed, or you'll freeze.'

Unresisting, she let him pull the bedclothes over her. Her little feet, stained at the heels, muddy-toed where she had run from the house to the barn, seemed to him to be pitiful. He could see now where purple welts were raised on her shins and calves. There was a swollen bruise across her hand, another coming up glossy blue in the hair above her forehead.

'I could kill him,' he said. 'I could kill the scum.'

She did not look at him, but turned her face further into the pillow.

'Jackie – you can't stay there – it's too cold. Come and hold me.'

The boy's teeth clenched. The gall and wormwood of his sojourn with the Linz family seemed to be concentrated in this moment, when he burned passionately to avenge this ill-used girl, and knew he was impotent to do so.

'I can't, Maida. Your mother wouldn't – want me to.'

She gave a woebegone cry, began once more to sob. 'What does Ma care . . . she wouldn't open the door to me.'

Jackie blew out the candle. For a while he waited for the girl's hysteria to subside, but it did not. The rain suddenly fell upon the barn roof in a torrent; he heard it thrashing the loft windows, gulping down the orchard paths. After a time he got into the bed, drew the girl close. She was shuddering uncontrollably.

'Go to sleep,' he said. 'I'll warm you.'

She was so thin, so frangible, he was afraid to draw her close. But eventually her sobs diminished to hiccups; these in their turn ceased and with a sigh she slept, her arms about his shoulders, her knees drawn up in some way so that they cradled his feet. From the hairy fabric of her nightgown a faint scent arose. At first he thought in his innocence that it was from her body, that all girls' bodies were fragrant in themselves, for Cushie, too, exuded a phantom sweetness. Then he became aware that Maida had a little bag of herbs around her neck on a string, and he was touched at this fastidiousness in one whose life was so isolated and austere.

In exquisite contentment that was dreamlike even before he slept, he inhaled her warmth, her softness, her very breath, and so for the first time experienced the strange naturalness of sleeping with a woman. Sometime before dawn he awakened, and almost without his own volition, entered her body. She responded with silent passion, fiercer even than his. He fell back exhausted, not sure if he were still dreaming, and the odour of the nosegay about her throat mingled with the green fresh aroma of the varnish on her grandfather's coffin.

When, at the sound of the breakfast triangle, he awakened, she was gone, and for some time he could scarcely discern whether it had been a fantasy. But the syrups that had dried on his body reassured him; the faint stains of tear-diluted blood on his pillow brought him wide awake. Shaken and yet filled with irrational elation, he rose and dressed.

During this time he did not think of Cushie. He did not think of Maida. He, himself, filled all his thoughts.

It was still raining; the world was muddy, the ducks sailing over the fringes of their overflowing pond. In the turkey-yard, half-sheltered under the chestnut-trees, the gobbler, inflated and purple, strutted and swanked. Jackie looked at him for a moment.

'Yep,' he agreed.

Remembering Maida then, protectiveness rushed up in him.

Yet he was doubtful about what he should do or say. Conrad, dark or drunk, should not be allowed to get away with his brutality, though Jackie had no doubt that it, too, was part of 'their ways', like standing submissively while the father hammered them with fist or boot. Still, his present jubilance bore him up, bade him wait and see, and almost debonairly he entered the kitchen, to find that the portly Kurt and his two younger brothers had already left for Ghinni Junction. It was Saturday, and it was their habit to go to the town for stores and stay overnight, returning by starlight on the Monday morning.

'How they'll make it through the mud I dunno,' said Mrs Linz. 'All them slips, and the washaways. But they would go, chains round the wheels, and spare parts for everything. Nothing won't set them aside when they've got their Saturday due.'

Maida was stirring porridge at the stove, Ellie was sitting beside it with his swollen face tied up in a black stocking.

'He's got toothache, poor dear,' said his mother. 'I've had that stocking full of hot salt on it for an hour, and it ain't done a skerrick of good. But the boys will bring home some painkiller for it, and some gutta-percha to stop up the hole. But I know they'll be late – poor Ellie.'

Her small defeated face was screwed up as though she herself were suffering her child's pain. She could hardly keep her hands off Ellie, so intense was her compassion.

Maida, even paler than usual, clearly bore the marks of her beating. The bruises showed through her coarse stockings; the bump on her head was like half an egg. Yet nothing was said about this. Jackie presumed that it was Linz custom to ignore such signs of familial disorder.

He sat alone at the table. Hof was still sleeping, it seemed. Jackie was overcome by a diffidence that entirely silenced him. As Maida gravely brought his plate to the table, he forced himself to look at her. Unobtrusively she gave him an eloquent look, a beam of such sweetness and acceptance that he felt something melt within.

'How did you get in?' he murmured.

'Hof left the door unlatched when he came up from the you-know-what,' she whispered.

In the week after that, she came often to his bed. It was like madness. He was obsessed. He could think of nothing else. To resist was unthinkable. He accepted her with frantic joy, looking forward all day with unbearable impatience to the possibility of her silent appearance in the barn. He became almost impervious, as though deaf and blind, to the tedious persecution of the brothers Linz.

She had come to him when he had most doubted himself; he was flattered and grateful for her mute passion, and never queried it except once. And that time, satiated and peaceful, an idle curiosity had made him ask her if she loved him.

She had turned and hugged him fiercely.

'I've got to have someone,' she said. 'You don't know how I feel.'

But he thought he did, and was tender and delicate with her. Her whole body cried out for kindness; she was like a greenhouse flower, folded gently, white and sunless.

She did not know even that she was lovely in his eyes, and looked stricken when he told her, as though he were teasing her. And later in the week, when the brothers were marooned in Ghinni because of the bad roads, and when Jackie climbed through her bedroom window, he saw why. In the chilly, ill-shaped room with its immensely tall walls and damp-blotched ceiling, there was only the bed and a skimpy chest. But upon the chest stood a mirror that showed the gazer as blanched, crooked-eyed, with hair coloured like a dirty bone.

Jackie, clinging to the edge of the chest, looked at himself and said, 'Is that how you think you look? But it's a lie. You're a lovely girl, beautiful.'

But she did not seem to believe him.

Jackie had been reluctant to go to Maida's room. He felt distaste, as though he were vulgarly invading the privacy of the Linz household. Their joyful grapplings in the barn, lit by moonlight or in deepest darkness, surrounded by the artless rural odours of timber, stock-feed and machine-oil, seemed inevitable and natural. There Maida had been a wraith, a creature of dreams, come to assuage him. But in her bedroom she was a girl with a bed of her own. He could not think why she had wanted him to see it.

But she lay warmly curled about him, saying, 'Go on, tell me a story. Tell me about Kingsland, the train, everything.'

She listened to him as though he were describing something magical. She had never seen a moving picture, been to school or church; she had visited Ghinni Junction only three times. Once, when she was six, a cousin of her grandfather's had come to stay, and he had taken all the children to a circus that was in Ghinni. She remembered everything that had happened as though it were engraved on her brain.

'Did your mother go, too?'

'No, Father wouldn't let her. I think she was having a baby. He said it would be not proper. But the baby died, anyway.'

He wondered if the old woman had had many dead children.

'Yes, four, five maybe. Father buried them up beyond the peach-trees. My mother sometimes said that he killed them, but I don't know . . . perhaps she was just talking. I remember when I was little, and she used to go there and cry and Ellie and I had to kneel in the wet grass and say Gentle Jesus for them. But that's a long time ago.' She added, as though it were connected in some way, 'Father made Hof blind, you know. He hit him with a tool, I don't know what, down at the forge. It was hot, and all the water-stuff came out of Hof's eye, and then he was blind.'

Talk of the absentee Remus Linz made Jackie feel queer, as though Maida's father were some dread mythical creature. Over the weeks he had even developed a certain dread of the unknown man, and Remus often slipped unbeckoned into his mind – swollen to an immense size like a smoke-genie. Sometimes he had the fat brother's satiny skin and hair like thin straw. Mostly he took on the venal yellow lineaments of the dark brother, but big, monstrously big, reducing Jackie to a manikin.

Maida wished to talk more about her father, but he would not listen. And so they fell once more into the blissful folly. As Jackie lay half asleep between her thighs, he saw the almost imperceptible luminance of candle-light draw upon the dark the crack beneath the door.

'Your mother ... someone ... out in the passage,' he whispered.

She started from her drowse. They heard shuffling slippers.

Jackie knew there was no lock on the door. If the old woman were up seeing about Ellie's toothache, she would awaken Maida to redden up the fire for hot water.

'Maida, I've got to go ... quick!'

She seemed paralysed with fright. Her thighs clamped on him like pincers.

By pressing down on her shoulders he dragged himself free. With a gasp, she seemed to come to her senses. He grabbed up his clothes, threw them out the window, and scrabbled over the sill after them. As he dropped, something growing below, a raspberry or rose cane, raked him from ankle to groin. Hideously cold, yet scalded with mortification, he shuffled on his clothes, seeing the window above him glow dimly as Maida lit her candle. He heard her call out something to her mother, but by then he was deep in the dark below the water-laden trees.

Half-way to the barn, he thought he would have to vomit. His humiliation was even greater than his alarm and anger. It lay in his belly cold as fog.

It seemed the last straw that the barn's clerestory windows showed the glimmer of Martin Linz's lanterns. Jackie cursed the old man's industry. He tried to compose his face, and, still trembling with emotion, climbed through the little slip-door in the barn's massive wagon-gates. The old man was stitching the lining of the coffin with a curved needle. He wore a sailmaker's palm.

'Good night!' said Jackie.

Martin Linz ducked his head politely. His glance lingered on the boots in Jackie's hand, lowered to his feet, black with mud; observed, Jackie was soon to be sure, the blood drops from the thorn scratch that had oozed through his light-coloured trousers.

The boy went straight to his bunk, undressed, blew out his candle, and flung himself between the blankets. Through the stacked bags of chaff he watched Martin Linz clean and put away his tools, each in a worn red leather sheath. Then the old man sat on a nail-keg and rolled and smoked a cigarette with shaky deliberation.

'Go! Clear out! Damned old fool!' thought the boy furiously.

When Martin Linz had finished his smoke, he put the butt in a small tin which he returned to his pocket. Then he came over with the lamp and for a while looked at Jackie, who feigned sleep.

After he had gone away, Jackie thumped over onto his face and tried to sleep. But a new wave of dismay submerged him. Suppose the old man voiced a suspicion to Remus Linz, or even one of the brothers?

'Ah, get away,' he assured himself. 'The old chap's gaga. He can't even remember people's names from one minute to the next. Who'd believe him?'

He could not sleep. The rain had ceased its spattering. He heard the grandfather clock in the homestead parlour strike three and then four. They'd belt the truth out of Maida, the father would thrash her half to death. As the hours passed, his sense of imminent danger increased. The father would murder Maida, shoot her partner in sin. Jackie had a delirious vision of his dead body lying in bloody mud, with the Linz brothers standing around roaring their heads off with laughter. And it was true, that corpse looked ridiculous. If Hof died and collapsed in the mud there would be nobility about him, like a fallen tree. But Jackie Hanna would look like a crumpled doll.

At six Jackie fell asleep, to wake half an hour later, head thick, eyes sandpapered, when Ellie shook him into consciousness.

'Hof's crook,' said Ellie. 'He's got a bad back. Wants to know if you can deal with things till the rest of 'em get back from Ghinni.'

Jackie nodded. He rose and washed. The day was bright; the sun as yellow as a dandelion. His terrors of the night had retreated. The old man Martin had not in fact acted differently from his usual manner; the prospect of his and Maida's recklessness being discovered was small. Yet a deep sense of shame at his own precipitate flight remained.

As he went into the kitchen he was self-conscious and crestfallen, diminished some way, hoping against hope that Maida were not there, for how could he even look at her?

Only Ellie and his mother were there, chatting, eating their breakfast.

'Poor Ellie's toothache is better,' said the old woman contentedly. 'But he was up in the night with it for hours.'

'Where's Maida then?' asked Jackie.

'Rubbing Hof's back with embrocation. Suffers agonies with it, he does.'

'Was it the War did it?' asked Jackie.

'No, Hof didn't go to the War. He wasn't allowed by the authorities. He had to stay and help his father, because the farm was producing food, you see. But the next two went. Called themselves Lindsay because of the name, you see. The authorities thought it best.'

'For a while they thought they'd intern Grandpa,' interjected Ellie with a laugh.

'Lot of silly rot,' said Aunt Eva. 'Been here for fifty years almost, his family all born here. Cut this orchard out of solid bush he did, him and old Grandmudda. Australian as any of us.'

'There was plenty of ill-feeling in Ghinni though,' prompted Ellie. 'People calling Hun and Squarehead after Dadda.'

'Both my boys were ruined by the War,' Aunt Eva said. 'Never been the same since.' She sighed.

'Poor Kurtie, you shoulda seen him when he was young. You remember, Ellie, don't you? Pretty as a little cupid. Colour! You'd a thought he painted. And you never seen anything like his hair, yellow as corn-silk. I dunno. Don't seem right. And then, after the War, after he came out of hospital, he blew up.'

Jackie was bewildered.

She said tersely, 'His wound.'

Ellie, with a sly grin, fluttered his hand downwards towards his crotch.

Maida had come in, smelling of wintergreen. Jackie was aware of her out of the corner of his eyes as she stood warming herself by the stove, but he was too self-conscious to look towards her.

He was glad that the old woman was prattling on. It was probably a change for her not to be told to shut her silly mouth.

'. . . a silver plate in his head,' she was saying. 'Oh, it'd turn you up to feel this hard thing through the scalp. He shouldn't be drinking the way he does. He gets into fights, and the doctor said one tap on the head would finish him off.'

'Gee, Ma, it's why he drinks,' said Ellie impatiently. 'He's always hoping to wake up dead. And it's a pity the bugger doesn't.'

'Oh, Ellie, you mustn't,' said Aunt Eva in a weak, servile tone, and Jackie felt a sudden spurt of compassion for the melancholy, half-crazy drunk brother, and contempt for Ellie, his mother's pussy-cat. Looking suddenly at Maida he saw that she, too, was gazing at her brother with the nervous protectiveness that so often marked her attitude towards him.

'Jack,' said Maida. 'Hof wants a word when you've finished breakfast.'

'Right,' he mumbled, not looking at her. He refused more tea, brushed past her. But a few steps down the passage he looked back, to see her looking snubbed and stricken the way she looked when her brothers were boorish towards her. Ah, and pale and haggard too, for while he had turned and trembled in his bed during the night hours, she had run here and there to do the bidding of the doting mother in attendance upon her spoiled youngest.

'Maida,' he said softly, and her face lit up as though the sun were behind it. He went to see Hof, feeling better, thinking how beautiful she was, how alone and pitiful. The thought crossed his mind for the first time: how would she get on without him, seeing, as she had said, that she needed someone?

For he knew now, without making a conscious decision about it, that he was going to leave. These people were too complicated; he could not understand them and did not want to. The Nun would be disappointed; his mother mad as a meat-axe. She would say that beggars could not be choosers and any port was good in a storm, and what other kind of job had offered itself to him? But he could not help it. The world of High Valley was unlivable for him.

He intended to tell Hof when he saw him, but the man was

in such obvious distress it went out of his head. Hof was trying to dress himself, all crooked over like a newborn grasshopper. His pants were around his ankles.

'Give us a hand with me shirt, Jack,' he said.

Jackie hopped on the bunk and eased the grey flannel shirt over Hof's head. Hof had a red flannel bandage, soaked in wintergreen from the smell of it, pinned around the small of his back.

'Pull me strides up. I can't bend.'

Jackie did this, and Hof leant forward a little, groaning under his breath, so that Jackie could catch the leather loops of his braces and hook them over the trouser buttons.

'Thanks, Jack.'

He eased himself back on the bed, reached for his pipe, in which he had a cigar butt sticking up like a chimney, and lit it.

Bristles along his haggard jowl had a silvering upon them, though he was probably not yet forty. Jackie looked diffidently about the veranda room, so bare, with a masculine stink of dirty socks, old dungarees, machine oil. There was no personal sign of occupancy except a comb full of dusty hairs. Not even the picture of a racehorse was tacked to a wall-stud.

What was Hof interested in? Who knew, who cared?

For the first time Jackie felt a pang at this man's withering life. He was alone in a houseful of scorpions, and he did not seem to know they were scorpions.

The man on the bed said, between puffs, 'I wanted me duds on before the boys come back from Ghinni. They get a bit frolicksome. Think you can make out all right today?'

'No worry,' said Jack. 'Take it easy. What I don't know, Cockie will tell me.'

Hof seemed strained; his blind eye was sunken like a little piece of grey wood.

Jackie said, 'You all right, mate? Anything I can get you.'

'No. I ricked me back few years ago. Wet weather catches it, that's all. Right as a bank tomorrow, more'n likely.' He paused in what seemed to be embarrassment, and Jackie waited.

'Chance to have a word with you.'

Jackie felt his heart trip. The old grandfather had said something after all. The frightful consequences of his relationship with Maida loomed so large that he did nothing but gape at Hof.

'You could do better than this, your education and all,' said Hof. 'Why don't you clear out, try for a better job?'

'You're . . . you're not satisfied with me?' blurted the boy.

'Sure I am,' said Hof irritably. 'Not saying that. Saying that a smart joker like you could be in a desk job somewhere. Figures. Accounts. Not slaving your guts out on a fruit-farm. That's for bullocks, like me and the boys.'

'I haven't complained,' said Jackie. Relief and confusion made his voice sulky.

'No, but you've had plenty to put up with. I ain't blind in both eyes. Just saying, you want to clear out, no hard feelings. If you don't, that's your business.'

Hof sounded short, somehow upset. Jackie felt that the older man had made an overture unusual and difficult for him, and he had not responded the right way.

'Thanks, anyway,' he said, but Hof did not answer.

Jackie worked throughout the morning, his thoughts elsewhere. During this time he did not think of Maida. His fright of the early morning seemed to have brought him back to his senses. He felt dissociated from her; she had once again become one of the Linzes.

Towards midday Ellie ran out, jubilant.

'Lorry's coming!' he called. Jackie could hear, in the mountain silence, the grinding and snoring of the vehicle somewhere down the slope. Ellie had been up on a high place watching it.

'It's all over the road,' he chuckled. 'The boys must be drunk as stoats.' His fair skin was flushed with excitement.

'Thank Gawd I'm near knocking-off time,' said Cockie Bailey. 'I'd rather face a mad bull than them blighters when they're grogged up. Take my advice, Lofty, lie doggo till they sober up.'

He put away his tools, grabbed his coat and went.

Jackie worked doggedly on. He felt a vague sickness in his belly. It was apprehension. The wasp-like whine of the truck came to him intermittently, louder each time, more threatening. He wished he had the honesty of Cockie Bailey, to clear out until the storm was over. He was afraid, he admitted it to himself, but would not allow himself to show it by going to the barn, or even to yarn, ostensibly, with Hof.

The lorry clamoured up the home track. Its radiator cap was off; the tank geysered scalding steam. There was a rending crash as a tree tore away the left fender. The drunk brother, leaning out flaccidly to see the damage, fell on his head in what seemed to be slow motion. Jackie could have sworn the truck ran over his legs as it jerked forward, but there he was, getting up, spouting bile, swaying after the vehicle like a blown leaf.

'Gee, Kurtie's driving,' cried Ellie, reedily thrilled. He seemed to palpitate with anticipation. 'Hey, Ma, you and Maida'd better lock yourselves in. Con must be in the DTs.'

Maida put a hand on Jackie's sleeve, tugged. 'You come too, Jack,' she said urgently. 'You come with Ma and me.'

Jackie dragged his sleeve away.

'What do you think I am, a kid? Like hell I'll hide!'

'Make him, Maida!' wailed the old woman. She seemed to be almost hysterical with fright.

'I won't,' said Jackie. 'Go on, clear out. Leave me alone.'

Maida pulled the old woman away. As they disappeared, he heard the girl crying to Ellie: 'Go and tell Hof, quick, Ellie, tell Hof.'

'Lot of bloody garbage,' said Jackie. 'Anyone would think they were murderers.'

But he did think they were murderers, in desire if not in fact, and as he stood on the veranda he was so afraid his mouth was dry. He stood there, feeling colder and colder, watching as the lorry stalled, roared, kangarooed forward, gathering in the corner of the fowl-yard, as it did so, trailing wire-netting, blood-soaked hens, uprooted shrubs, a clothes-line still hung with socks and woollen underwear. At last it came to a halt, its front wheel having shorn off the corner of the red-painted wooden steps below the veranda.

A wan croak of lonesomeness and protest came from the drunk brother, floating haphazardly up the track. His face was unrecognisable with mud and blood.

The fat brother flopped out like a toad from behind the wheel.

He blew out ham-coloured cheeks at Jackie, his eyes twinkled like sapphire chips. His skin was translucent as though he had a light within. Jackie could feel heat radiating from him as if he were a stove. The boy stepped back involuntarily to give him room, and the little mouth pursed in an infant's beam.

'Scared I might tramp on you, cockroach?'

Instantly Jackie knew he had been a fool to stand there, inviting drunken horseplay against which he had no hope of defence. He cursed himself for a big-headed mug. His cousin Maida had been right. He knew almost nothing about men like these. He saw the impatient appetite in the bloodshot eyes of the dark brother, as he approached, drawn, sour-breathed, but far from being in the DTs.

They began to push him from one to the other. He leapt from the veranda and in mid-flight knocked down the drunk brother, feebly dog-paddling towards the steps. The drunk brother broke into plaintive cries.

An iron arm across Jackie's throat held him down. The dark brother, mysteriously transferred from the veranda, showed Jackie laughing teeth from six inches' distance.

'Here, don't you know better than to tackle poor Theo? Theo's got a silver plate in his loaf, a fall might kill him. Kurtie, you reckon this frigger has killed poor Theo?'

'Uncalled for, that's what it was.' The fat man's voice was grieved. 'Poor Theo, he wouldn't hurt a fly. Ought to be learnt a lesson. What you say, Con?'

Meantime Theo's thin hand had shot out and encircled Jackie's ankle with the inhuman grip of a crab. As the boy was lifted, he had a brief glimpse of Ellie's face bulging from a bedroom window; he tried to shout to him to fetch Hof, Cockie Bailey, anyone. But a hand slapped his mouth shut.

The dark brother was full of novel ideas for chastisement, all of a donnish finickiness, but the others outvoted him. So, after ill-aimed and cursory punching and kicking, Jackie was stripped, flypaper was wound around his genitals, kerosene poured on his hair, and he was tally-hoed into the duckpond by the dark brother with a twist of lighted newspaper.

It must have been all over in the space of minutes, but to Jackie, in a stupor of helplessness, it seemed half an hour. Then, as he shivered in the water, trying to wash the kerosene off his face and shoulders, the fat brother, bearing aloft a barrel, waded in, and with one flawless movement dropped it over him. The bottom rim sank into the mud; he was as effectively trapped in a claustrophic dark as a beetle under a glass.

The barrel had been used for making plum brandy. Choking fumes were all Jackie had to breathe. In crazy panic he yelled, struggling to get his arms up to lift the thing off his head, to fall over so that air would rush in at the lower edge. But he could not move. Lights reeled around him, his ears roared, he knew he was suffocating. Then there was another, more thunderous sound, and he became unconscious.

He came to himself on a stretcher before the kitchen fire. Except for Ellie and Hof, the Linz brothers were not visible. Hof leant on a stick near by. Maida, not in tears, but with a frozen shocked face, tried to press Jackie's lips to the rim of a glass of brandy.

'Oh, God no, not that stuff.' He could scarcely bear to think of the fumes in the barrel. He sat up.

'I'm all right. What happened, what was that noise, like a gun?'

'It was a gun all right,' said Ellie merrily. 'Grandpa came with his old shotgun and fired in the air. The boys thought he was blasting at them; you shoulda seen them go!'

He sounded like a child who'd visited a circus.

'Cockie went in and pulled you out,' said Hof. 'Silly bastards, mad with the booze; didn't know what they were doing.'

Cockie, standing near by, hair standing up in wet tufts, said, 'Bloody near killed him. Ought to be reported to the John Hops.'

His kind, stupid mouth worked around his missing teeth. He was roused to fury at last. 'As for that other business – dirty, low-down trick, ought to be ashamed.'

Maida's face flushed faintly. Her glance caught Jackie's wild one for a moment, and her eyes filled with tears. Jackie was aware that the flypaper had been removed somehow, that he was stinging as though most of his pubic hair had been pulled out. 'I've had enough, Hof!' he blurted out. 'You can give me my time.'

'Going meself at the end of the month,' said Cockie, 'and if I was half a man I'd go this minute.'

Hof turned his ponderous head towards Jackie.

'I'm real sorry, Jack. It won't happen again, I warrant.'

'You're a bit late, aren't you, you stupid heap?' yelled Jackie. 'Why didn't you get up off your great cement bum and stop them before this? They've been at it in one way or another since the moment I first saw them. I'm clearing out. I've had the flaming lot of you.'

He became aware that someone was yelling even more loudly than he, in a high-pitched squeal, and that it was his Aunt Eva, who was jumping up and down and beating at the air in a rabbity hysteria, shouting, 'Don't let him go, Hof! What will we do if he goes? He'll tell my brother Jerry and Jerry will think hard of us.'

'For God's sake take her away,' said Hof gruffly, and Ellie and his sister half-dragged the skinny little figure from the kitchen.

'Aunt Eva never did anything to me,' said Jackie. 'Nor Ellie or Maida. And I've no complaints of you, Hof. But I'm going.'

'The truck's out of action,' said Hof. 'But Ellie and me can get her working by tomorrow afternoon. We could get you to Ghinni in time to catch the night express.'

'I'll bloody well walk, then,' said Jackie. He heaved up, wrapped the blanket around himself, and marched out. At the door he had to wait for Cockie to open it, otherwise the blanket would have fallen off as he jumped. This seemed the last humiliation.

Cockie helped him roll his few things in a swag. He kept shaking his head and saying, 'You'll freeze stiff on the road. Don't do it, you silly bastard.'

But in obsessive rage and mortification Jackie left, saying to Cockie, 'Tell Hof to send my wages after me. I got enough for the fare home.'

As he passed down the track under the overhanging trees he thought he saw Maida looking from the parlour window, but could not be sure. Damn her then. There were a lot of things he should have done, like thanking old Martin Linz. He hadn't thanked even Cockie, or Ellie for fetching him. Too late now. They were all of a piece, a nest of bull-ants, and the best thing to do was to get as far away from them as he could.

There was rain muttering about in the sky, the mountain gullies were filled with gauze. Orchards were everywhere, a sweet-smelling diapering of the long hillsides. Far below streaks of light, like spilled salt, showed the courses of creeks running again after the rains.

Ten miles down the road Jackie sat and rested, looking at the hills. They were not savage, lunar hills like those of Paddy's Range, but ruminative and placid, lying down around the landscape like pensive animals. His eyes stung at the sight of those mild unfortified hills, which in some irrational way reminded him of Maida. Or Cushie? His memories of the two girls, their butterfly softness, their defencelessness, rushed together. He began to shake with delayed shock. His anger evaporated, his insides vibrated, his legs seemed filled with water. The landscape quivered, and the trees detached themselves from the earth and stood in the air.

Before very long the Linz truck groaned down the hill. Jackie would gladly have fled into the scrub and hidden until it passed, but he was unable to move.

Hof could not lean from the cab. He jerked his head stiffly and ordered: 'Get in. I'll take you to the station.'

So Jackie returned to Kingsland, arriving at one in the morning and having to awaken his parents to let him in. His mother, mop-haired, flushed with sleep and alarm, could not be temporised with.

'Something's wrong, what is it?' she kept asking stubbornly. 'Have you been sacked? You gotta tell me, Jackie!'

'Can't you see the boy's just about knocked out?' protested the Nun. 'Let him sleep. Whatever it is, it'll keep to the morning,'

Reluctantly she agreed, going back to bed, pretending to sleep.

She jabbed an elbow into the collapsed form of her husband.

'You! Nerves of steel! You great vegetable!'

Jerry turned, threw a leg over her, pinioning her to the bed. His snores took on new life, resonant, majestic. She lay there, steaming with anger and anxiety, thinking. By the time morning came she had worked it all out.

'They been chiacking you, haven't they? Them squareheads!'

She stood foursquare in front of him, flushed and moist with love and accusation. She still wore her greying hair long, skewered into a lump rather than a bun. She looked, all of a sudden, a little shapeless and floppy.

'Don't you lie to me, John Luke Hanna! Tell the truth and shame the devil.'

During the dark, cold journey back to Kingsland Jackie had indeed plotted out some sort of story about his precipitate return home. But before his mother's observant eyes it fled from his brain. She struck at once at his hesitation.

'I knew it! What did they say, what did they do to you?'

After a while he answered, 'I don't want to tell you, Mum, so I won't.'

She raged, wept, abused Jerry's sister and her children. The Nun listened, disturbed and silent. At last, when she stopped yelling and gulping to look at him helpless and smeared, he put an arm around her shoulders. 'I'm real sorry it's turned out like this, love, but it's not the end of the world. Jackie will tell us about it when he's ready.'

Going early to bed that evening, Jackie was amazed to see Cushie's window light up. Surely it was not possible that she should be home? Eagerly he watched, and saw her fair head illumined by the gaslight as she pulled down the blind.

'What's Cushie doing at home?' he asked next morning. His mother said impatiently, 'I don't know. Think that high and mighty mother of hers talks to me? I heard she was home to study for her music examination or something. I don't know ... Jackie – was you sacked? Because, no shame in that if you was. But talk about it, will you? Say something!'

'No, I wasn't sacked,' said Jackie. 'I left. And I don't want to talk about it, so get off my back, Mum.'

Her squawk of indignation coincided with the postman's whistle. The Nun entered the living-room.

'Well,' he said, 'here's a letter from my sister Eva.'

He sat down and read it in a leisurely way. Jackie felt that if Aunt Eva had described the extent of his mortification he would never be able to look his parents in the eyes again.

'Aren't I going to read it?' burst out Mrs MacNunn.

'I'll read it out to you both,' said Jerry placidly.

Jackie could hear Mrs Linz's nervous, placating tone in every sentence. She was all apologies, all concern for the poor little nephew of whom she had been so fond. She admitted that the boys had come home drunk and had manhandled him because they thought he had punched poor Theo, who had a silver plate in his head. It was all a misunderstanding; Jackie was so touchy, things being as they were with him, and he had taken it all too seriously. The boys were only skylarking. Hof was very keen for him to come back, for Jackie was such a willing worker. If Jerry would wire, they'd be real pleased to meet the train. And she concluded with inquiries after Margaret's health and fond good wishes to everyone.

'Was that it?' demanded Mrs MacNunn.

'More or less,' said Jackie.

'Them big coots,' said Jerry, relieved. 'I don't suppose they know their own strength. Made it a bit too willing, did they?'

'I'm not going back there.' Jackie glared defiantly at Jerry.

Jerry was troubled. He had not seen his sister Eva for many years. He could recall her only as a young woman, thin as a white-bait, with scared, shifty eyes.

He was about to say that they ought to forget all about it for a while, let things simmer down, when without warning his wife let fly.

'Not going back, my foot!' she cried. 'Jobs aren't that plentiful that you can afford to throw one away.'

A customer rang the shop bell and, swearing under his breath, the Nun went to attend to him.

Mrs MacNunn splashed out a cup of tea for herself, and sat down to read Eva Linz's letter. Jackie waited in dread and defiance to hear her comments, for she was working up to something, he could see it in the very way she breathed.

'What's she like, your Auntie Eva?'

'Little. Skinny.'

'But she was all right to you, like?'

'I guess so,' said Jackie sulkily. How to explain to his mother the sneaking meannesses of his Aunt Eva? It would be like trying to explain a cat to a dog.

'And this girl, Maida?'

'You pronounce it like Mida,' said Jackie. 'She's all right. Shy. Fair hair, tied back.'

'Bugger her hair,' exploded his mother. She looked at him imploringly. 'Jackie, you've got to go back.'

Jackie began to say, 'Like hell I will', but she rushed over him with words.

'This is the first time you've ever given up on anything. A few years ago you'd have died rather than be licked, driven out of a place the way you've been this time. All right, so they picked on you . . .'

Jackie tried to interrupt, but she was volcanic.

'You been picked on many times, and you always stood up for yourself. You had self-respect. That's what your Dad and me have been drumming into you all these years. A wee fellow can have as much self-respect as a big one, and by God he needs it more!'

Jackie jumped up, face crimson, banged his big forehead on the top rail of the chair, cried, 'Will you shut your mouth, for Christ's sake?'

'Your Dad and I raised you to be a young bull,' she said. 'And here you are, run away home like a baby.'

'Will you mind you own business!' he shouted.

'Since when haven't you been my business, then, Jackie?' she asked.

He felt as though rage had placed a garrotte around his throat. He croaked, 'You've not an idea of what they did to me!' and was glad of it, for he could never have told her, or the Nun either come to that. The things that had been done to him were no likely to have been done to anyone of ordinary size: That was the shame of it, that was the wound. He leapt past her and tore upstairs, slamming his door as he had never slammed it in his life.

The Nun, who had returned from the shop, gazed at her flabbergasted.

'Well,' she blazed, 'what are you gawping at me for, like a dying duck itself?'

Then she wailed, 'Oh, Jerry, it's come over me all of a sudden that if we let him give in this time he may never have the guts again to fight the world. God knows what them Linzes did to him . . . but he can't be allowed to go on feeling that they've won, don't you see?'

'Does he feel like that, Peg?'

'Of course he does, you bonehead. Haven't you eyes in your head? Oh, I could kill him!'

The Nun regarded her quietly.

'You're not half a one for waterworks,' he said. 'Pints you must have spouted this morning. Will you knock it off and have your breakfast like a dear woman? Then you'll feel better and we'll talk some sense.'

'You will talk about it with me, then?' she snuffled.

'Sure I will,' he said temperately. 'Now go and wash your face. It looks like an ape's behind and I can't put up with it for another minute.'

'Ah, God love you, Jerry,' she said. 'You're a blessing to me, and I couldn't live five minutes without you.'

Jerry sat down and rubbed his leg meditatively. There was something in what she had said about Jackie. He was reminded keenly of the young soldiers, mere pups they were, deafened, blinded by shellfire, not wanting to do more than cuddle together at the bottom of a trench with their arms over their heads, and that sergeant punching, kicking, screaming, cursing . . . 'Get out there, you effing baboons, or you'll still be here when the Boers come to cut your throats . . .' and a lot more of the same. And he'd got them moving, too, and into safety somehow, though he'd got killed himself by a sniper.

But he thought he'd wait a day or two, till the boy cooled down, saw things straighter, more sensibly.

Deep in Jackie's soul there was a burning desire to let the Linzes know they hadn't driven him out, that it took more than a gang of half-baked hillbillies to take the sting out of John Luke Hanna. He knew perfectly well, in spite of Auntie Eva's letter, that this was what they thought. A mad rage seized him at the phantom sound of their laughter; he could have ground his teeth. He wanted the farmhouse to burn down, an epidemic disease to strike the whole damn lot of them except Hof and Maida and perhaps that creep Ellie. And even while he was seething and spitting within his heart, he knew that whatever the Linzes said was right: they *had* chased the little man out, like a cur dog.

He had never hated anyone before. Hate made him sick; it buzzed in his ears like a disgusting insect. Because of it he could not hear what the world was singing. The spring shone all about, but the air inside his mind was still cold and sodden. He was tainted. That's what the Linzes had done to him, all except Maida.

He felt he had to see Cushie, to settle himself, get his mind up the right way again.

He knocked at the Moys' back door, angry with himself for being nervous. It was the anticipated appearance of Mrs Moy that disturbed him.

But instead of Mrs Moy, Cushie appeared, wearing a blue apron. When she saw him, colour rushed into her face.

'Goodness!' she said. 'I thought you were the egg man.'

'No,' said Jackie foolishly. They stared at each other. The sweetest expression illumined Cushie's face.

She said, 'When I came back home this time, and you weren't in Kingsland! The first time! I always had you to come back to, before.'

'I didn't like to write,' said Jackie, 'because of everything.'

'Yes,' she said. 'I know.'

'Where's your Mum?' asked Jackie.

'She's not here,' said Cushie. 'She took the opportunity of my being home for a week to go off to Ghinni Junction with Olwyn. The hospital's got some new inhalation machine, and she thought it was a chance to try it. Nobody's here, Jackie! Come inside, come on.'

Cushie led the way up the Turkey-carpeted hall.

'We're not going to the drawing-room!' protested Jackie. 'She wouldn't like it, Cush.'

'Nonsense,' said Cushie with bold airiness. 'Daddy's at the Bank, there's no one here but me, and I'm the hostess.'

She took off her apron and skidded it down the hall.

'I've been keeping house for Daddy,' she said, 'and it's been fun.'

She flourished open the drawing-room door; its odour of brass polish, lavender furniture oil, and Mr Moy's occasional Turkish cigarettes, rushed out at Jackie. He hung back, but Cushie plumped upon the faded seagreen velvet of the sofa, spread her white arm along its curving back, smiled at him.

He stood beside her, stroking the thick, amber door-knocker plait that hung down over her white radianta blouse.

'You haven't put your hair up yet,' he said.

It came to Cushie to say that her hair would be put up after the ball at which her Granny Jackaman had arranged she should be presented to the Governor-General and the world. Cushie was enraptured about the ball, but was even more pleased because her Granny had taken such a fancy to her at Grandfather's funeral. Cushie's open heart had met another in Granny; they had flown together like two birds.

But, as she drooped her head against Jackie's shoulder, she felt him trembling. It was no time to talk about outside things.

'Jackie, I heard you had a job down Ghinni way,' she said. 'Did something go wrong? Why are you back?'

Jackie poured it all out, not troubling to hide his chagrin and mortification, for with Cushie it was as though he were speaking to himself. While he spoke she slipped down off the sofa, and sat on the carpet, her head bent, her arms around her knees. Thus Jackie felt much taller than she.

When he had finished, her face was against his knee. He felt tears. 'The devils! The brutes! But you stood up to them, and if it hadn't been three to one, you'd have beaten them, too. Oh, I hope the police have arrested them, I hope they get *years* in prison!'

Jackie was astonished. 'But I didn't tell the police,' he said. He thought he would explain again about the Linzes being, however remote, still family, but she cried, 'You're much nobler than I am. I want them punished, beaten.' Her mild eyes sparked fiercely. 'To think of their hurting you like that, and for nothing, just for beastliness!'

'You mustn't cry, Cushie,' he said.

'How can I help it,' she said, outraged, 'when it's you?'

Her head bent on his knees, his hand that felt the skin slip beneath her thin blouse, her tears falling for the humiliation he had suffered ... all produced in Jackie a kind of despair. They belonged together, he didn't know why, but they did, as though nature itself had decreed it. She seemed to hold the secret of identity for him. She was reality. Yet how could they ever be together?

In an effort to distract himself, he looked around the drawing-room, its bay window shaded with slatted blinds. The cedar furniture, the tapestry chair seats, the bronze gasolier with hanging crystals, all appeared incalculably costly and rare to Jackie. Everywhere he looked there were signs of the Moys' superiority and prosperity – the glittering brass fender, the fire-screen of beaten copper, the glass-bellied cabinet full of lustre jugs and finicky figures in porcelain.

'What will we do, Cushie?' He couldn't help it; his voice came out as a groan.

'We'll run away and get married. While Mama is at Ghinni!'

'I haven't any money. I can't seem to get a job. It might always be like that because ... because I'm a dwarf.'

He looked at her in anguish.

'It was all just a kid's dream, wasn't it?'

'No.' Cushie's voice was husky. 'I love you, Jackie. Nothing matters but that.'

Something sweet, powerful and irrevocable filled both of them.

Cushie said, 'It's time, isn't it?' She gave a gasp of fright and joy.

'Are you sure?' said Jackie. He dared not look at her, but felt her nod.

It was like a dream, half-unreal, and yet more truly real than any other experience in life. Once Jackie, at the moment of climax, saw a small bird with a red crest alight on a bough outside Cushie's window, perch there with the sun shining through its crest, turning it to a small formless flame that was reflected as a gibbous pinkness upon the curtain. And it seemed to him inexplicably that he was the bird, the sun, the curtain, light itself.

And another time he heard a car-horn, far away, and instead of being just a car-horn it had become a long clarabella sound, like the wind amongst precipices. He was mesmerised by it, hearing it in his ear long after it had passed.

'What is it?' asked Cushie, afloat in joy.

'I don't know,' he said. 'I feel . . . all changed.'

'I know,' she said. 'It's loving.'

It was as though the time of year, fortunate chance, Nature itself, conspired to make it easy for them to be lovers.

There were auditors at the Bank, and Mr Moy left home early and returned late. Mrs Moy had stood down the cleaning woman and the gardener for the short period of her absence and Cushie did the negligible household shopping herself. No one ever came to the house.

Sometimes Jackie was over there by eight o'clock, to leap into Cushie's tumbled bed before she'd cleared her father's breakfast dishes away. It was as if a madness had seized them; they forgot all prudence; the world scarcely existed. They frolicked like fishes, nothing between them but bliss.

The delight that Jackie had in the girl's body was extravagant. Upon the back of his closed eyelids he could see its whiteness, its tallness, the indescribable texture of the skin. Could this have been the fat little Cushie, roly-poly, smeared and weeping, he had brought down from the hills that day they had gone looking for the other dwarfs? Now she was a goddess.

Looking upon this perfection, he had been cruelly conscious of his own physical misshapenness, and had said, 'Don't you mind? Don't you care that I'm like this?'

She said, 'Yes, I do.'

It was like a knife stuck in his heart.

Then she said, 'I care because you care, that's all. It has nothing to do with me, really. I love you, and you haven't anything to do with the way you look, any more than I have.'

But to Jackie Cushie was the way she looked. He was besotted with the way she looked. Once, lying in his arms, she opened those beautiful eyes suddenly and said, 'We'll be separated again soon, and it will be much worse this time. I can't be apart from you now, never! What can we do? We'll have to plan – something.'

'Not yet. Everything will come out all right. Anyway, you ought to be doing your piano practice. You'll fail.'

'Nobody fails,' said Cushie contemptuously. 'It's all rubbish. All pretence. It's disgusting. Still, I'd better do some practice, and you'd better listen. Isn't your mother suspicious about your coming over here so much?'

'I've turned into a lying rat,' said Jackie. 'She thinks I go off to sulk around the town, complaining of the Linzes to my old mates. Sometimes I say I'm coming here to listen to you practise, and she says she doesn't know how I can stand it, all that classical stuff.'

Cushie laughed. 'I can't stand it myself. I'd rather cook Daddy's dinner. I've loved being here by myself, keeping house. Well, come on, I'll do my exam piece, and you can suffer through it.'

The shop had been more than usually busy that morning. The boom brought such brisk trade that Mrs MacNunn thought it would never end. She and Jerry were seriously considering putting on a boy, a steady young fellow old enough to do the grocery deliveries in the truck.

'We got Jackie, you know,' said the Nun. 'The lorry gears could be altered.'

Mrs MacNunn thrust out her lower lip in an Irish bulge of obstinacy. 'He's going back to the orchard. You'll see,' she declared.

'He's gone after a coupla jobs here, you know,' said Jerry mildly.

'Yes, and missed out on them, too,' pointed out his wife. 'Gawd, there's that bell again!'

She took a last gulp of her scalding tea, clutched her throat with an expression of agony, and hurried into the shop, wiping her lips on her apron. Jerry emptied the teapot and sat down rubbing his leg, which seemed to be transfixed by a red-hot screw.

The faint sounds of 'In a Monastery Garden' drifted across Edward Street. Jerry supposed, with some uneasiness, that Jackie was over there keeping Cushie company. He was sure that Mr Moy didn't know Jackie spent so much time with Cushie, and equally sure that he wouldn't care much for it if he knew.

It struck him that he should, in all humanity, say something to young Jack. But how could he put it.'

'Course, I know you aren't getting any lovey-dovey ideas about young Cushie; you're just chums like you always was; but you got to remember that any time now an upper-crust young sort like that is going to be took to Sydney and married off to some rich squatter's son, or a lawyer or something. I mean . . .'

It wouldn't do. And coming straight out with it wouldn't do, either.

'Jackie, you got to remember you don't look like other fellows. The fact is, me old Jack . . .'

Not only did the Nun not know how to put it to Jack that romance for him might be a distant or unlikely thing, but there was too much compassion in him to do more than think about dropping a word in the boy's ear.

'Can't shove me oar in, really, not without giving the kid a knock,' he pondered. 'And what about them Linzes, eh? Maybe I should have written to old Eva and gone scone-hot about the way they treated the boy. But if I did, and young Jack goes back there, like Peg thinks, it might make things worse for him. Better keep me jaw clamped.'

He said that night to Jackie, 'Cushie going off back to college soon, eh?'

'Saturday,' said Jackie shortly. 'Her Mum comes back tomorrow.'

Jackie had already said good-bye to Cushie, and it had almost killed him. He felt as though his blood were running out the end of his toes. At the same time he was impartially aware of his awe at the extent of his bereavement. It seemed to him that it was incontestable proof that he and Cushie were more in love than anyone ever had been before.

'Which is bloody garbage,' said one side of his mind, sounding disagreeably like that of an adult making nonsense of a child's ideas.

The other side of him, the lover, the lingering child, wanted to go away and sob and scream. He even took to sleeping in the treehouse, that old shelter and fortress of his, curling up in his blankets, imagining that Cushie was with him, one with him in watching the ceaseless dapple of the moonlight on the floor, enjoying with him the faint oceanic movement of the tree.

But it was too cold out there, either to sleep or dream, and he had to scrabble back along the branch to his own bed, melancholy and resentful that childhood and its ability to bear hardship for the sake of romantic fancy was seeping away from him.

Half-heartedly he tried for another job or two. There were plenty of them, for in spite of immigration from Europe the work force had not recovered from its brutal depletion during the War. But he did not get work. This did not bother him, for privately he knew that he was going back to High Valley. He had boasted to Cushie that he was not afraid to return there, and he had lied.

'If I was as big and heavy as they are, I wouldn't be,' he said to himself, and this was true. 'But I'm not. I'm not full-sized. There's no changing that. I'd change it like a shot if I could, but I can't. But that doesn't mean I can't lead a full-sized life, and I will.'

So, after Cushie had been gone ten days or a fortnight, he said almost absent-mindedly to Jerry, 'I think I'll get back to High Valley at the end of the week. I expect Hof needs a hand with the spraying.'

Jerry was nonplussed. But he had sense enough not to ask questions.

'Right-e-oh, me old Jack.'

Peggy MacNunn asked guiltily, 'You really have made up your mind yourself? Because I'm sorry I flew off the handle like that back there.'

'No,' said Jackie. 'I thought it over.'

Mrs MacNunn was certain that Cushie had had a word with him.

'Good sensible little thing,' she said. 'Not one of your flappers, that one. Kids listen to other kids more than their parents. I'll bet that's what happened, Jerry.'

So once again the Nun took his stepson to the station in the old lorry. Jackie's mother said she couldn't face it again; she'd stay home and scrub out the shop.

Once again the Nun shook hands with Jackie through the train window. He didn't feel easy. He didn't like the look Jackie was trying to keep off his face.

'Ah, God,' he said. 'I hope things will go all right.'

There were other people in the train compartment, so Jackie closed his eyes and pretended to be asleep. He let his mind return to that day when Cushie, suddenly sitting up and thumping him lightly on the belly, exclaimed, 'Granny!'

She had suddenly thought of Granny Jackaman, that loving, rather common old puss who was affectionately discounted by most of her distinguished family, and had taken such a fancy to her almost unknown granddaughter.

'Granny will help us,' declared Cushie. The plan for their going to Granny Jackaman, explaining their love, asking her assistance to marry, sprang fully-fledged into her head.

Jackie listened incredulously.

'When I have to go back to Mount Rosa,' said Cushie, flushed with daring and triumph, 'I'll just continue straight on to Sydney. I'll go to Granny and explain everything . . .'

'But you're under age,' protested Jackie. 'Your parents wouldn't let you get married. Don't be mad, Cushie. You're dreaming.'

'Aha,' said Cushie, 'Granny holds the purse-strings now. Granny's wealthy as can be. She'd get around Mama and Daddy somehow. She'd be tickled to be mixed up in an elopement; she's as romantic as a flapper; she's gorgeous.'

Jackie thought Granny sounded as if she had bats in her belfry. He sprang out of bed and began to dress quickly. But Cushie was adamant. 'Look, you don't understand. Granny was just a poor immigrant Irish girl who worked in my great-grandfather's workroom – sweatshop, more likely. And my grandfather James ran off with her, and old Joseph Jackaman cut him off without a penny. Granny knows what it's like to be young and in love. Granny . . .'

'You've got to be practical, Cushie,' said Jackie. 'You're going on like a kid of ten. What about me, what about a job? If you have ideas about you and me living on your Granny Jackaman, then put that out of your head.'

'But there's the store!' cried Cushie. 'And my Aunt Australia owns it! She's Granny's favourite daughter; she'll make a place for you. There must be thousands of things you could do at Jackaman's.'

They had argued about it interminably.

'I won't have you saying that Granny's just a silly old lady,' she flashed. 'And if you think that her family can argue her out of anything she's got her mind set on, then you're dotty. Even Uncle Titus – and he's the only living son – can't make her change her mind. Anyway, he's in England with Aunt Laetitia. Oh, please, Jackie, it's our only chance. Just let's try it!'

'I haven't even enough money for the fare to Sydney,' said Jackie irascibly. 'I couldn't turn up penniless. A man's got his self-respect: you don't understand that.'

'I can give it to you,' cried Cushie excitedly. 'I've got a savings account at the Bank. I can tell Daddy it's for new clothes before I go back to college . . .'

She saw at once she had made a tactical error. Jackie put on a display of affronted pride, half spontaneous and half theatrical because he thought she would expect it of him. But all she did was to blush miserably and gasp apologies, which he accepted after a while. 'I wouldn't offend you for anything, Jackie,' she murmured humbly; 'it's just that I don't know these things.'

But the next day she broached the subject again. She was desperate, Jackie could see. She had no idea how they could ever be together unless this romantic Granny helped. And they had to be together.

'It's all right, for you, being a boy. You're free,' said Cushie. 'But I'm dependent on everyone. I haven't really done anything I wanted to do since I was born. But this is different. I'll die if I can't be with you for the rest of my life; I just can't bear to think of it.'

At last they decided that Cushie's plan didn't have to be put into effect right away. Perhaps at the end of the term, in early November, Cushie could go to see her grandmother, even with her parents' permission.

'And I'll go back to the Linz orchard and earn some money,' Jackie said.

Cushie was against that; terrified, obdurate. His protestations of lack of fear did not convince her.

'I'm afraid for you,' she wailed.

It had seemed half a lifetime away to Cushie then, and so it seemed to Jackie now, as he sat in the racketing, jolting train on his way to Ghinni Junction.

'Things will be different with the Linzes this time,' he thought. 'They've all got the dirt off their livers; they'll be more settled down about me. And it'll only be for a couple of months.'

On the reddish darkness before his eyes a face began to form, Maida's, frail, anxious. He realised that the thought of her had hardly crossed his mind since he left High Valley.

The fat brother met him at Ghinni Junction, beaming, jovial.

'Glad to see you, son,' he said. He leant down to shake hands with Jackie. Jackie involuntarily recoiled, expecting that his hand would be crushed in a sadistic grip, but instead it was enfolded as though within the cushioned petals of a warm flower.

'No hard feelings, eh?' entreated the fat brother. 'Let bygones be bygones? Con and me were as full as ticks. We musta been off our heads and you can't blame poor Theo – he's half a looney.'

Jackie nodded coolly, and vaulted up onto the tray of the truck with an easy swing of his powerful arms.

'Wouldn't like to meet you when you're out for blood,' said the fat brother. 'Strangle a man quick as look at him.'

Jackie looked him straight in the eye, for they were now level. 'You're not kidding,' he said.

The fat brother put on an expression of playful alarm, and climbed into the cab. The drunk brother was already lolling there, unconscious or asleep. Jackie looked through the rear window at the ruckled neck of the fat brother.

'What's this bastard up to?' he wondered.

The lovely spring had filled the sky with swimming light, napped the hills with milky green; the parched bronze scrub of his previous visit now showed raspberry-red tips and streaks. On the eroded hillsides, knurled and ploughed by rain and water run-off, like clay glaciers, little trees had seeded and caught, prickly vines, something close and clawed with a bony yellow bloom. Late blooming orchards were everywhere.

Jackie felt a deep love for this countryside, wordless converse between his spirit and that of his country. Yet he felt the same for Kingsland, and perhaps would for Sydney if he ever got there, which he would if Cushie's granny was the fairy godmother the girl thought her. He tried to turn his thoughts to Cushie, at her posh school, spending her days on trivia, bored to rebellion ... even Cushie, so soft and docile and easily scared. He longed for the time when he could be with her and look after her, and sleep in her arms every night in their own bed.

It was dark as the fat brother turned into the home track, dragging the wheel around to avoid the potholes. One of the lorry's headlights was smashed, the other a feeble lemon yellow. Jackie saw, caught in the one-eyed beam of the headlamp, a big old lizard, drab and dry as an uncleaned snakeskin shoe, with its hard, neat-nostrilled nose, and its pleasant, almost human eye fixed sideways on the light. The creature was grey, black, gravel colours.

'I'll get him this time!' Jackie heard the fat brother shout, and the lorry swerved and roared. Jackie was shot up against the back of the cab with stunning force, and the drunk brother helplessly hit the windowscreen with a crack that nearly broke his nose.

Jackie saw the lizard trundle hastily under a rock-lily clump.

'Are you crazy, you slob?' he yelled. 'What a half-wit I was to come back,' he thought, holding his stinging ear as the lorry ground up the familiar track.

The kitchen, the odour of food, the darkness coming down amidst the fruit-trees, the oil lamps lit – all was the same as before, except that this time his Auntie Eva dropped her spoon and, with a mouse cry, threw her arms about him.

'I'm so pleased you're back. I was that sorry when you went! Give us a kiss, Jack!'

Bristles poked his chin as she kissed him. He almost shuddered. Ellie was lurching around, looking pleased. He slapped Jackie on the back, took his suitcase, his coat, trying to tell him all the news at once.

'We got a bumper crop of peaches. The old bay mare fell over the bank and Hof had to shoot her. We fed her to the pigs. Con broke his thumb, but it's coming good now. And what do you think, our grandfather is dying. Took to his bed ten days ago;

he's just fading away. Want to have a look at him, Jack? He looks real funny, just like one of them mummies.'

Once again Jackie had a queer feeling that the boy was wrong in the head. He wanted to ask where Maida was, but could not bring himself to do so. She did not appear during the meal, and neither did Hof. Someone volunteered that the two of them were with the old man, washing him, attending to his physical needs.

'Hof can understand when he speaks German,' said Aunt Eva; 'and he likes Maida to clean him and fix him up.' She gave Jackie a meaning nod. 'He's like a baby with regard to certain things, you understand.'

He was given his old stretcher-bed in the barn.

'You don't mind, I hope, Jackie,' said his aunt. 'We got the bunkhouse pretty full with extra hands for the spraying.'

But Jackie was grateful to be alone. He looked at the coffin on the trestle; it was finished now. The clean antiseptic smell of tar arose from its interior. Jackie looked at the lid, at the deep-cut Gothic letters: MARTIN OTHO LINZ, 1846–192––

Someone had started to carve the upright stroke of a figure four. The workmanship made Jackie sure that it was Martin Linz himself. He had made up his mind to die then, even before he took to his bed.

A profound realisation of some kind struck Jackie. But he didn't know exactly what it was. Some time it would come to him. Whatever it was, disturbing as it was, it was neither evil nor tragic. It was just ... but he did not know what. All at once he was very tired and sleepy, and pulling off his clothes he fell into the narrow, familiar bed and in a moment was asleep.

Some time during the night he awakened briefly, and the thought 'A king ... he knows how to be a king' stood very clearly in his drowsy mind.

Next morning Hof greeted him gruffly.

'Your back better, Hof?' asked Jackie awkwardly.

He felt self-conscious and ill-at-ease, not knowing whether to refer to his departure and return or not. But Hof was just himself, grumpy, taciturn and somehow sad as winter.

'She's right,' said Hof.

They worked together all the morning, with very little speech between them. The frosts had slackened off, Hof said – a mercy, because they could do great harm to the fruit at this stage.

'I'll stay till picking, maybe,' said Jackie, 'if you need me.'

Hof did not look at him when he said: 'Shouldn't have come back, boy. You went while the going was good. Shouldn't have come back. You got a life of your own elsewhere.'

Jackie thought he might tell him how little life he did have, how few prospects, but there seemed no point in it.

'I'm satisfied enough here,' he said. 'if you can keep those brothers of yours off my back.'

Hof looked as if he had more to say, but moved silently away with his bucket and spray pump.

Several times Jackie had seen Maida at a distance. He half-raised a hand to greet her, but she turned and vanished through the door that led to the covered veranda where Jackie fancied the old man Linz had his sleeping quarters.

Jackie experienced extraordinary confusion at the sight of Maida. Shyness, awkwardness, a faint sense of regret, mingled with a fugitive desire, a sharp reminder of their rapturous hours in the barn so few weeks ago. He liked Maida, and his pity for her was intensified by her drooping figure and wan aspect.

Yet what could he say to her?

It had not occurred to him to speak about Cushie, however casually, to her. Maida, and indeed his life at High Valley, did not impinge at all upon what he regarded as his real life.

He found himself dodging her, and he was ashamed that he should want to do so. But what would he do if she came secretly to the barn? He knew very well that he would succumb once more to the old lure of lust. And he didn't want to. He had too many complications in his life already.

Then it occurred to him that perhaps she was ashamed of her falling from grace. Even worse, perhaps she was ashamed of having expended herself on a dwarf. Perhaps she was disgusted with herself for being so hard-up that at last she had to come to the bed of such as Jackie Hanna.

Then his good sense reasserted itself. It was the tense atmosphere of High Valley that was making him read into happenings what was not there. Maida had not come to his bed because she was on heat. She had been beaten brutally, thrown out of the house in the dead of winter. There was nowhere else for her to go. And he, after all, had called her down from the hayloft into his bed, and he had been the one who had taken her, half asleep. She had responded, it was true.

'And why bloody not?' Jackie asked himself. 'I'm as good as anyone in that department, and probably better than most.'

Like Cushie, Maida had never shown any repugnance for him; she had accepted him with joy and tenderness. Perhaps, he thought with unaccustomed humility, even with love.

So, when he met her as he crossed the kitchen yard, three or four days after his arrival, he approached her with hardihood: 'What's the matter? Don't you want to talk to me?'

She muttered, 'Yes, yes, I do, but Grandpa . . .'

He saw to his horror that one of her eyes had been blackened. The bruise was now a fading yellow, but it was plain what had happened. And a small sticky scab ran across one of her downy almost invisible eyebrows.

'They've been knocking you round again?'

Maida gave a nervous giggle. 'That's how Con broke his thumb!'

With a kind of outraged possessiveness Jackie looked at her arms, her legs. Her legs were so welted the ridges showed through her stockings. She had a festering scratch on her forearm.

'What for, though? Why on bloody earth would he want to . . .'

She said hurriedly, 'Jackie, I can't talk. Can you come after supper to Grandpa's room? He's asleep most of the time, and we can talk. Please, Jackie, I do want to see you.'

He nodded, and went on to the kitchen.

Cockie Bailey had gone to work in the jam factory in Ghinni Junction. Jackie knew none of the other men at the table. They must have been warned against chiacking him, for they kept their heads to their plates, mumbling an occasional word to each other. The brothers, too, seemed to be putting themselves out to be agreeable to him. The dark brother did not speak, except to curse when he fumbled his food, for his thumb was still in plaster and he found it difficult to eat. The only unpleasantness was when

Ellie pushed a spoon across to him, and the dark brother, seizing it with his left hand, shied it back at him.

'Watch it, you gammy bastard,' he growled, 'or I'll screw your knobs off for you. If you've got any.'

Ellie's childish face flushed as he bent his head towards his food. Jackie saw a movement which indicated that his mother had consolingly patted him on the knee.

Jackie thought, 'It's no good, I can't stand these people, not even for Cushie. I haven't been here a week, and already they're poisoning me. I could kill that prick Con. I don't just want to damage him: I want to murder him.'

He was glad to escape from the table. He went first in the direction of the barn, and then doubled back along the side of the farmhouse. Light from a louvre window showed where the old man was lying. He entered quietly.

The light was so dim he could scarcely see anything but the top of Maida's head, as she sewed or mended close to the lamp. She looked up with relief and welcome as Jackie approached.

'He's asleep,' she whispered. 'He hasn't woken up all day. He's had nothing to eat now for more than a week.'

Jackie did not like to look at the old man, stretched like a wooden figure under a red blanket. So still! It was as though he were dead already. A faint odour of excrement came from the bed. Perhaps it was the way old sick people smelt.

The change in the old man was amazing. His brown face was muddy grey; the skull was poking through the skin. The huge old hands, docilely protruding from the frilled ends of his nightshirt sleeves, showed the knuckles and the wristbones as cream-coloured bosses. A rosary, the beads black and carved so that they looked like casuarina berries, was wound around one wrist. The paper eyelids twitched and shivered constantly.

'Is he dreaming?' whispered Jackie.

'I hope so,' she said. 'Whenever he wake up he talks of Grandmudda.' She smiled. 'He thinks I'm her, when she was young.'

She took a cloth and softly touched the old man's forehead.

'He gets so clammy.'

Jackie hated being there; he was disturbed by the change in Martin Linz.

'What's the matter with him?'

'He's just dying,' she answered. The expression on her face was so candid, so accepting, that Jackie experienced a gush of affection. He put his arms around her.

'I'm – fond of him, you know,' she murmured.

She had returned to her seat. Jackie stood beside her, not knowing what to say.

He felt that old Martin was engaged in some profoundly sacred and important business. It was right that he should be allowed to get on with it, without all the alien business of doctors and hospitals.

'I'm glad you didn't send him to Ghinni Hospital,' he whispered.

'The doctor said there was nothing anyone can do, so he might as well be here where he feels at home. He's just made up his mind to die, and so he will.'

She took up her mending again, and drew a long, uneven breath, seemed to steel herself.

'Jackie, I have to tell you. My mother wrote that letter to your stepfather, persuading you to come back here, because I'm going to have a baby.'

Her voice was so expressionless that Jackie thought he had imagined what she said.

'You don't mean . . . you don't mean I did it?'

She looked at him sombrely. 'I don't blame you, Jackie. It was just as much my fault, maybe more, because I'm older than you.'

Jackie couldn't believe it. He wanted to laugh. He walked over to the window and indeed, to his dismay, a brief chuckle did force its way out of him. But he covered it with a cough.

'How do you know?'

Maida flushed. 'I missed just before you went away, and then I missed again this time. But there have been other things. That's how Ma guessed.'

Jackie felt his heart flop like a fish. 'Your mother . . . she knows?'

'Ma's had ten children,' Maida said. 'How could she not notice?'

She lowered her voice. 'Jackie, I'm so sorry. I know it's a terrible thing for you to come back here to.'

'My God,' said Jackie in consternation. 'But maybe you're sickening for something. People make mistakes, I've heard. Don't you think maybe . . .?'

Maida shook her head. There was something so despairing about the movement that the boy was chilled. He said hoarsely, 'I can't believe it; it's . . . it's a shock. I have to think about it.'

But as he said the words he knew they were foolish. There was nothing to think about. He hadn't an idea in his head.

Suddenly it crossed his mind that this was what Hof had meant when he chided him in such abrupt words for returning to High Valley. That equivocal look of his – half embarrassed, half annoyed.

'Hof knows!' groaned Jackie.

'Yes,' said Maida. 'Ma made such a fuss. She had a real bad turn. They all know. That's why Con thrashed me. And when he'd finished, Kurtie kicked me.' She shuddered. 'He said some – awful things.' She did not look at him. 'Kurtie's bad, Jackie. Bad, like something going rotten.'

'What will we do?' asked Jackie. To his own ears it sounded like the question of a child, dependent, gormless. 'I never dreamed . . . I thought we were too young or something. We must have been mad.'

'I don't know what to do, Jackie,' said Maida. She raised her face suddenly. There was terror on it. 'I thought I might run away, but I haven't any money. Where would I go? And they'd come after me. But if I stay here I'll get killed.'

She stared at him with an absent, mazed look.

Jackie snapped, 'Don't be silly. Who'd kill you? That fat swine?'

She rocked herself to and fro: 'No, no. They've sent for *him* because of Grandfather. You don't know him. Oh, Jesus, you don't know what he's like.'

The boy's blood felt as though it had frozen. He stammered, 'You mean your father? He's coming home?'

'They sent for him last week, and he may come any time. Oh, Jackie, he's like a devil. He always said he'd slit my throat if I got pregnant.'

Now she was standing up. She seemed to have gone to pieces. Jackie noticed how haggard and wild she had become. She beat her hands together, and he feared she was going to scream hysterically. He took hold of her by the waist, resting his head where, in his ignorance of biology, he imagined his catastrophic child budding in darkness.

He held her tightly, saying, 'Maida, we'll think of something. You've got to stay calm a bit longer. Don't make a noise; you'll wake up the old man. Sssssh, Maida, ssssh!'

'Ma knows, Ma knows he'll kill me, and her too for letting me out of her sight. Oh, you don't know what he's done, what I've seen him do, what he's got away with . . . and none of my brothers would lift a finger to defend me.'

It was like a nightmare. And in the middle of it a dry, broken voice said, 'Trink, trink'; or so Jackie thought. One of the old man's eyes was open, wide open, with a cloudy fixity. As Jackie watched with horror, the other eye opened, this one with a gleam of intelligence. Maida disengaged herself quickly, ran to the bed, slipped her arm around her grandfather's shoulders, and raised him a little.

Tears went on dripping down her face, but she held the old man steadily enough. Her expression was one of pity, such as Jackie had observed before when she looked at her young brother Ellie. She said, 'Yes, Grandpa, a little wine and water . . . just what you like.'

But the old man was unable to take more than a sip or two.

His wavering hand seized on Maida's firm young one, held it. 'Warm.'

'Yes, Grandpa. You're remembering your English, Grandpa. You must be feeling better.'

'Little girl,' he said. 'Good.'

His eyes wandered towards Jackie. A smile twitched his sunken lips. 'Lucky,' he said.

Jackie came nearer.

'Say something to him,' urged Maida.

Jackie could think of nothing, so he winked. A gurgle of a laugh came out of the irregularly throbbing throat. He said something Jackie could not catch: 'Good little man', was it? He seemed to

look from one to the other of them, tried to say something, but his eyes closed again, and his head sank on his chest.

She tucked the blanket about her grandfather, slipped in her hand to see if his feet were warm, and turned once again to Jackie.

'I'm sorry I came out with it like that. I've been that upset, not knowing what to do for the best, and then when Ma said that you were coming back I knew that they'd tricked you into it. I knew you didn't know, about me I mean.'

She took a step towards him. 'Don't look like that, Jackie. I know it's an awful thing to happen to a boy your age.'

He looked at her, ashamed. 'You're only a couple of years older than I am. And it's you that it's happened to. God, Maida, I don't know what to do. I never imagined . . . I thought girls did something.'

But as he said it he knew it was a melancholy improbability that even if there were something girls could do Maida would know anything about it. She was as defencelessly fertile as a hen or a cow.

And besides, he hadn't thought anything of the kind: His head had been full of nothing but appreciation of his own bliss.

He said, 'Don't you give way again now. We'll think about it. There must be something we can do. But we have to think about it.'

She nodded dumbly, and her expression of trust was unbearable to him. He went straight to the barn, lit his lamp, and threw himself on his bed. His head seemed full of a duststorm, everything whirling mindlessly.

'Me going to be a father – and I only left school last year!'

It sounded not only mad but ridiculous and disgusting, as though he'd all at once grown a white beard.

'She can't be right. She's made a mistake somehow.'

But it was not the memory of Maida's distraught face that told him he was lying to himself. It was the attitude of the rest of the Linzes. Auntie Eva, kissing him as though she really welcomed him, the pig Kurt with his gentle handshake and his 'bygones be bygones'. Poor old Hof, wanting to say something to warn him, and yet not liking to be clear about it.

Certainty stabbed Jackie like a knife.

'Of course they had to get me back here. They're going to lay a complaint to the cops. Carnal knowledge, something.'

He tried to think of the talk of his friends about such cases, but he could remember more dirt than facts. What happened? Did you go to jail? Did you have to pay the girl money – support the kid when it was born, was that it?

And Maida? Put into one of those sinister Homes to which certain girls in Kingsland had mysteriously vanished? Her child whisked away into an orphanage . . . drab uniforms, grim spinster ladies to look after it . . . beaten . . . bullied . . . scorned . . . a bastard.

He was in such a state that he couldn't remember whether he was recalling something he had read in *Truth*, or whether these things had been told to him as facts by people he knew.

He supposed that if he hadn't returned voluntarily to High Valley they would have put the police on to him. Sergeant Trivett calling at the shop, his mother red as a beet, the Nun saying it was impossible, a warrant out for his arrest.

'But I came. I came of my own free will, like the biggest mug that was ever hatched.'

Once more he had a chilling feeling that in some inexplicable way he had been manipulated by destiny. If Jerry's sister hadn't married a Linz, if he'd been able to get a proper job in Kingsland, if he hadn't been so bloody miserable that he grabbed Maida that rainy night, just to get a little surcease from his loneliness and aloneness . . . But now he was trapped. And Fate had done it again. If Cushie hadn't showed him that there was some chance of their getting married one day, if he hadn't needed money to get to Sydney, if there had only been some other way of getting it besides coming back to High Valley . . .

The memory of Cushie was like a blow. Cushie, his darling, his soft, loving other self. Distractedly, Jackie sprang off the bunk and walked up and down. What could he do? Clear out, and do it quick. Hof would help him some way. Hof understood how he had felt. Hof had sympathy with a man's desires and inbuilt sexual opportunism. Maybe Hof had been through it all himself, when he was younger.

What would he say to Hof?

'Right-oh, I've had the drum now. I'm going. You can help me get away down to Ghinni. You said yourself that I should never have come back.'

But Jackie's imaginary conversation with Hof did not end there. Unvolitionally it went on: 'I've given your sister a kid, but that's her lookout. Maybe your old man will kill her, as she fears. Or maybe she'll just get thrashed within an inch of her life, as she looks as though she's already been thrashed. And after the baby's born, what then? Maybe your old dad will turn her out, and she can starve to death, or kill herself or get work in the tartshop in Ghinni. But more likely she'll be kept here for the rest of her life, as a slave to all of you, kept out of sight, less than the dirt.'

Like her mother, in fact. And he thought of the old woman, helpless before her brutal husband, delivering all those children in blood and torment, not wanting any of them, seeing them only as symbols of degradation.

The illogicality of it was fantastic.

How could so much dreadfulness come from a few minutes of joy? It was like rings spreading in a pond from a tossed stone.

So he continued all night. Sometimes he sprang up and threw a few of his belongings into his suitcase, moving with frantic hurry as though there were not a moment to be lost. Other times he sat on the bed in a daze of horror and incredulity. It was like a frightful dream from which he could not awaken.

Once or twice he went to the barn door, gulping in the cold fresh air like an imprisoned animal. He saw then, though it was very late, the dim lamplight in old man Linz's room, and a shadow moving between it and the window. Maida, he supposed, devoted, kind and simple. Better than he would be, ever. How could he leave her to face whatever cruel fate was hers?

At last he fell asleep in a delirious exhaustion, and was awakened in broad sunlight by Ellie's shaking him. Stupefied with weariness and despair, he made pretence of eating breakfast, and went off to the orchard.

He came, at last, face to face with Hof in one of the peach avenues. Jackie had not done his work well; he had missed trees, and sprayed others in a half-pie fashion. He looked at Hof with guilt and appeal.

'I can't keep my mind on it, Hof, and I guess you know why.'

Hof inclined his grizzling head.

'Maida told me last night. I . . . I suppose it's looney to say I couldn't believe it, but that's the way I felt. I just . . . never thought of consequences, I suppose.'

Hof did not look at Jackie. He gathered up a handful of green velvet pebbles which were prematurely fallen fruit.

'Hof,' said Jackie. 'I have to talk about it.'

Hof sat down with his back against a tree, fixed a cigar stump in his pipe, lit it. He did not look at Jackie. His eye fixed itself in sober concentration on the red end of the cigar.

'The thing is,' said Jackie, 'I don't know what to do. It's bloody awful.'

'You could scarper,' said Hof. 'Most would.'

He puffed awhile. 'Wouldn't blame you meself. Maida knew what she was doing. Knew the risk. Drummed into her for years.'

Jackie did not know what to say to that. At last he mumbled, 'She was unhappy.'

Hof gave him an unreadable look. 'No fun being born a woman, I guess. Still and all, she has to lie on the bed she made.'

'You trying to let me off, or something?' demanded Jackie. 'Anything Maida did, I did too. For all you know, I forced her.'

'She said you didn't,' said Hof. 'She's real fond of you, you know. Said she'd gladly marry you even if it wasn't a case of must be.'

'Marry me!' Jackie felt as if someone had punched him, winded him. He could only stare at Hof like a fool.

Hof seemed as though he could not believe what he saw on his companion's face. He said, almost compassionately, 'Boy, what in hell do you think the old woman kidded you back here for?'

Jackie stammered, 'I thought . . . I thought . . . so they could get the police after me. Or . . . so they, your brothers, could beat me up.'

Hof shook his head. 'You poor little bastard, you're still wet behind the ears, aren't you?'

'I can't get married,' yelled Jackie. 'I'm just turned eighteen!'

How could he marry Maida, this girl he scarcely knew, when some day he was to marry Cushie Moy?

Though it was only half-way through the morning, he went to the barn, climbed up into the loft and crawled in amongst the hay.

'I've got to think, I've got to think,' he kept saying to himself, but not hearing his own words.

After a long time he heard someone climbing the loft ladder laboriously. A hand touched him timorously, a soft voice said, 'Jackie, you all right, Jackie?'

'Frig off, Ellie.'

He could hear the boy shifting restlessly in the straw. At last he said, 'Maida says, you don't have to marry her.'

'Big of her,' said Jackie bitterly. 'Well, you've delivered your message, so sling your hook.'

Ellie said haltingly, 'I don't see why you don't want to marry Maida. I reckon you ought to be proud. I mean, Maida's a lovely girl, and you're . . .'

'I'm what?' growled Jackie, sitting up and looking blazingly at the boy, who retreated a step or two, seemed about to run, and then for a moment, uncharacteristically looked Jackie full in the eyes.

'I know you're a decent bloke, Jack,' he said, 'but you got to realise not every girl would want to be tied up to you.'

Jackie cursed him savagely, ceasing only when he saw the boy's weak blue eyes brim with tears.

'Oh, God, Ellie, don't make it worse. Clear out, will you?'

He flung himself on his face in the straw, tried not to hear what the boy was stuttering.

'When we were kids we were always planning to run away and hide, some place, Sydney maybe, where my father would never find us. Once we did run away, and Kurtie found us, and Ma gave Maida a thrashing, not me. Maida's always looked after me. If I had any money I'd take her away and look after her and the baby too. But I haven't got nothing, I can't even read, I don't know what sort of job I could work at.'

When Jackie did not answer, he subsided into a sniffling babble, amidst which Jackie distinguished the words: 'If only you'd take her away before Pa comes home!'

He stumbled away, moaning and coughing. Jackie just lay there, holding his hands over his ears, not wanting to hear the sounds of the world any more.

Inside him something mourned: 'Cushie! Cushie!' and each repetition of her name was like a knife stuck in him.

'I'm giving up,' his brain told him. 'I'm going to do what they want.'

But twenty minutes later the stream of his thoughts was turbulently flowing the other way, and he had decided to clear out.

'I did it before,' he thought. 'I could have got to Ghinni by myself, but then Hof came along. But they'd follow me to Ghinni, that's what they'd do, haul me off the train. Well, I could cut across country, catch the train at the watering halt.'

Vigour suddenly filled his limbs once more. He saw himself slipping through other people's orchards, following cattle tracks, hiding himself somewhere near the siding until the express pulled to a stop. Tomorrow's express, or that of the day after that; it didn't matter, as long as he escaped from the Linz farm.

He pushed the thought of Maida to the back of his mind, refusing to allow pity or anxiety to deflect him. She had her trouble; he had his. If he had brought distress to her, she had brought it to him.

He thought, 'I'll go tonight, as soon as it gets dark. If there's a moon I can get a good way down the road before they miss me.'

He hurried down the ladder, halted. His Aunt Eva was standing beside his bunk. He had kicked his half-packed portmanteau beneath it, but he was certain she would have looked at it. There was nothing to do but to keep on walking towards her.

'Jackie!' she cried, false-faced. 'You didn't come up for your dinner, and I thought, now, where's that boy? That's not like him; he must be feeling crook.'

'No,' said Jackie. 'Sorry I'm late. I'll have a wash and come straight up to the kitchen.'

But as he turned away, she put her little claws on his shoulders and turned him round again. To his horror she darted down her head and kissed him on the lips. It was like being kissed by a mouse.

'There, I understand,' she said, squeezing a thin mist across her eyeballs. 'The others are mad as hornets, Maida having her whole life ruined and all that; but I say it's happened to a thousand other young people, and no real harm done once you're married. And Maida . . . oh, you've got a gem there, you know, lad. She's that handy with the cooking and sewing, a real willing worker.'

'And with my disability I'm not likely to find another like her,' said Jackie.

The old woman gave him a sharp glance, looking for mockery, but apparently did not find it, for she smiled with pleasure: 'Ah, you're a sensible lad. I might have known my brother Jerry would bring you up to know right from wrong when you see it.'

'I'll be up to the kitchen in five minutes,' promised Jackie. 'Want to change my socks.'

The moment Aunt Eva bustled out of the barn Jackie rolled up a few clothes, an extra pair of boots, his shaving gear, a few personal belongings, in his oilskin coat, made a swag of it, and crept out of the half-door at the back of the barn. All seemed quiet; everyone was at the midday meal. He crouched up the hill, submerging where he could amongst the flowering shrubs, the unmowed grass. He cursed his Aunt Eva bitterly. The old bitch knew he was going to make a bolt for it; she'd have the men alerted in no time. But they'd try the road first, he was sure.

He skulked in the bushy gully beyond the grassy patch where the dead Linz infants lay buried. Straining his ears for sounds from the farmhouse, he heard at last the lorry engine struggle into life, and the vehicle rasp off towards Ghinni Junction.

He intended to hide there until nightfall, and then cut down through the orchard and into the next property, following its fence until he emerged upon the Ghinni road. He felt too sick with agitation to analyse his emotions; all he knew was that for the time being he had escaped. Couched in the warm grass like a scared rabbit, he watched the clouds forming their illusory landscapes in the sky, tried not to think, and so, after a while, fell asleep.

When he awakened, darkness had come. A lantern blazed in

his face. He wriggled out of snatching hands, escaped, floundered down the hill towards the pink glow of the orchard and, somewhere along the seething radiant aisles, was seized by the fat brother, who had been lighting the lamps.

He was beaten so badly that next day he could scarcely move, and Hof, returned from Ghinni Junction where he had failed to find Jackie, feared that his nose and cheekbone had been broken.

'Ain't you got sense?' he growled. 'Don't you see that's what they were waiting for, specially Con? I'm sorry, but. And if I'd been here it wouldn't have happened.'

They put Jackie in a disused storeroom near the kitchen, where there was always someone to keep an eye on him. The place smelled of sourness and dirt, like a forgotten cheese. A basket of mummified potatoes mouldered in the corner.

For the first few days Jackie could not speak intelligibly. The pain in his face was so bad that he was glad when people went away and left him alone. He closed his eyes as well as he could – the left one seemed as though there was a line of felt between upper and lower lids – and sank deep into his own head.

He felt different, but did not know how. At first the pain was oceanic, noisy. It allowed him no time for thinking or even feeling. He longed only for it to stop.

The huge conflict of the past two weeks had gone, but he did not know why or how. An apathy that was almost tranquil took its place. Had the physical savagery he had suffered broken his spirit? He felt honestly that this was not so. The whole mythos of his childhood was studded with tales of people and animals who had dropped their bundles . . . men beaten by drought, turning their faces to the wall, dying by their own will. Great horses turned into shivering victims that bowed their heads and fought never again after they had been brutalised by the breaker. Women who lost one child after another and at last just sat there, silent, unweeping, unmoving – docile, perhaps, but absent for ever.

Jackie knew that the beating had not touched him, wherever he lived. And though he felt a profound shame at his abandonment of Maida, it did not gnaw at him. The abandonment had been made in self-defence. He was ashamed, but not guilty.

No, what he felt was something darker, less explicable in human terms. It was fatalism.

'I've run out of luck,' he thought.

Some would have thought he'd been born without luck, but he had never felt that: his parents had seen to it that he didn't. But now he saw his luck as of an almost hallucinatory tenuousness, a thread beside which the spider's was a rope, and it seemed to have frayed through.

From time to time people came to look at him. His Aunt Eva: 'Fancy running away! What a thing to do with poor Maida in such a fix, I would never have thought it of you, Jack, I thought you was a decent boy.'

Through a squinched eyelid he could see the greedy vindictiveness on her little face. Someone else getting it rough! Jackie couldn't stand the sight, closed his eye, pretended to be deaf or dead.

Later came Maida, hand soft as a dove upon his face.

'The swelling's going down, Jackie. Does it feel a bit better? Can you speak, Jackie?'

He could mumble a few words.

'I'm sorry, Maida. I wasn't running away from you. Just . . . everything.'

'I know.'

And then one day a week or so later, when he was out of bed, and his face was looking almost human in shape once more, Hof came with a letter.

'This'll cheer you up. From Kingsland.'

Jackie took it apathetically. His mother's writing belonged to some other world which he had forfeited for ever.

'Aren't you going to open it, boy?'

'I will directly.' To his helpless shame tears came into his eyes. Hof sat down, put his head in his hands.

'Jesus, it's a mess, ain't it? This life ain't fit for a dog.'

After a while, he said, 'Don't want you to think I went after you to bring you back. Thought I might give you a lift somewhere, and no one any the wiser.'

'What about Maida?'

Hof shrugged.

'One way we got both of you miserable, the other way only one. Anyway, women . . .'

Jackie said, 'Supposing I married Maida, what then?'

'Room here,' said Hof, 'but you wouldn't want to stay here.' He added, 'I know where there's a job going, on a cream boat on the Dovey River. There's a cottage goes with it.'

'Yeah?' said Jackie indifferently. He watched the disappointment momentarily relax the other's wooden face.

'How's the old man, your grandfather?'

'Sinking. Asleep nearly all the time. We been wiring our father everywhere, but it's hard to know where he is, being a traveller.' Hof rose.

After Hof had gone, Jackie opened the envelope, holding the letter listlessly before unfolding it. A thousand miles, a hundred years seemed to stretch between him and his home and family.

News. The Nun's bad leg. Business. Somebody dead, lovely funeral. Hope you're settling in better this time. Cushie Moy off to Sydney. Morning train, Thursday, perhaps you could make it your business to see her at the Junction as it passes through. She'll be looking out for you, always so fond of you and all. Hope you will make all effort to see her.

Jackie looked blankly at the underlining of this. He came to himself again as though someone had given him an electric shock. His apathy vanished, his face began to hurt as though a horse had kicked him. Cushie sprang alive before him, yielding, beckoning, like a lovely mirage. Hope filled him. Cushie had news for him; perhaps she already had contacted her grandmother, perhaps all the problems were solvable after all.

He continued to say to himself, bracingly, 'My luck's not out after all. Doesn't this prove it?'

But he didn't believe it.

Still, he had to do what he could. If opportunity was there, he had to give it its chance.

He put on his boots. As he went out into the daylight he thought he saw Ellie scurry away around the corner of the barn. Keeping an eye on him, no doubt. A moment later the dark brother lounged into sight.

'Going somewhere, little man?'

'I want to see Hof.'

'Got ideas, little man?'

'Where's Hof?'

The dark brother looked at him consideringly. 'Next time it might be for keeps, have you thought of that?'

'I've thought of it.'

Jackie stepped around the dark brother and went on to the orchard. Some of the hands looked at him furtively, looked away quickly. He found Hof.

'I have to go to Ghinni Junction tomorrow. I want to be there when the southbound express goes through, there's a friend of mine on it.'

Hof looked dubious.

'I'm not asking you, Hof,' said Jackie. 'I'm telling you, I have to see my friend.'

'Bloody little rat,' said the dark brother, half admiringly. 'See green in our eyes, do you? I can just see you hopping on the express and going into smoke.'

'One of you come with me then,' said Jackie indifferently. He waited. 'Well, what about it?'

He could see the doubt in Hof's face, a candid struggle with God knew what simple plans he had made as a solution to this crisis. Jackie thought, 'Poor bastard!'

He said, 'I'm telling you this: if you don't agree to take me to the train tomorrow, that's the end. I'll never marry Maida.'

'We'll see about that, Shorty,' said the dark brother.

'Yes, you'll see,' said Jackie.

'Got to have a word with the others then,' said the dark brother, oafishly baffled. 'Go on, get out of my sight, you bloody abortion.'

Jackie stood where he was. 'I want to leave early. I don't want to miss the express.'

As he turned, he caught the queerest look on Hof's face. It struck him afterwards that Hof was going to work it somehow that he could leap aboard that train. Was that what he himself wanted to do? He didn't know. He just wanted to see Cushie once more, as a man about to be blinded might want to see the sunshine.

Later that night the dark brother looked briefly into the room where he lay, and said, 'Sun-up, then. Hof will drive and I'll go along to keep an eye on you.'

'Right,' said Jackie, and turned over to face the wall. He sensed the man's standing there, his ravenous desire to punish, but he forced himself to lie motionless, and after a while the dark brother went away.

'My luck's changed, my luck's changed,' repeated Jackie to himself. 'And whatever opportunity comes, I have to be ready to take it.'

At sunrise the dark brother awakened him, waited while he dressed, escorted him to the truck.

All the silent way to Ghinni, Jackie tried to keep his hope steadfast, thinking, 'My luck's changed, my luck's changed.'

But he didn't believe it, and he was right. The truck broke down eighteen miles outside of the town, and though all three of them worked on it, they did not get it going until too late. Though Hof pushed the old vehicle until it shuddered and steamed, they did not reach Ghinni Junction until the express was pulling out.

Jackie leapt monkey-like to the platform, ran after the train as it gathered speed. Amongst the faces that stared from the carriage windows, he could not see Cushie's.

He yelled, 'Where are you? Where are you?'

As Hof and the dark brother caught up with him, he thought he heard her voice calling his name, but it was lost in the brattling roar of the train.

He stood at the end of the platform, his head bent. Tears fell down his damaged face. Hof picked him up like a child and carried him to the truck. Like a melancholy cry sounded the whistle of the express as it rounded the curve, a cry that lingered, mourned, wept in his ears, long after they had returned to High Valley.

Cushie Moy

1924-1925

3

Cushie Moy awakened one morning and knew she was pregnant. Though she had listened to so many whispered discussions on the theme after lights-out in the dormitory, Cushie had never contributed anything; she felt she had nothing to say. And nothing was expected of her, for at Mount Rosa she was looked upon as a mild-tempered nonentity. Yet the conversations themselves left her uneasy, as if there were a world outside herself and Jackie and their love for each other – a world harsh and ribald.

A large number of the girls in Cushie's dormitory believed that one could get pregnant only after marriage. They were dismayed and outraged when others, who knew without possibility of error that wretched servants in their family households had, whilst still unmarried, got into trouble, informed them snubbingly that they'd better sharpen up.

Until she turned fifteen, Cushie had been one of this ignoramus group, and had been jeered at by the more sophisticated pupils. But where could she have found out? It was unthinkable that she should ask her mother. Once, when small, Cushie had inquired, 'Where did Olwyn come from?' and the answer had been, 'God sent her to be a darling little playmate for you.'

The mistresses at Mount Rosa shied like frightened horses from any mention of the body or its functions. In all the college's venerable history no girl, as far as was known, had dared ask for an elucidation of the facts of life.

'If you do,' was the legend, 'you are expelled at once, and taken away in a black van.'

As each pupil neared her time of maturation, she was called to the matron's office to listen to a terrifying speech full of incomprehensible phrases about the sacred burdens of womanhood. She was then given a small blue-wrapped parcel which contained a packet of sanitary pads and a copy of a booklet entitled *Jane's Twelfth Birthday*. After that she was allowed at regular intervals to skip physical education on the grounds of having a headache, known amongst the girls as 'visiting Jane'.

There was, in fact, no way of finding out the truth about anything except by listening to the girls, who were obsessed with guilty curiosity and fear. Some, bolder by temperament, or blessed with parents more broadminded than the rest, spoke out indignantly:

'What a lot of utter rot it all is! All these filthy things have to happen to us, and we can't even talk about them!'

Cushie said, 'Having a baby can't be filthy.'

'Oh, shut up, Moy! What do you know about anything, Dotty-Dot? Go on, Valerie, tell us about your sister having a baby.'

'My sister says having a baby is beyond description. She said she'd jump over South Head before she had another one. Not only the pain and everything, but all the blood and stuff.'

Stuff? The blood of the younger listeners ran cold. Yet, their hideous curiosity remained unsatisfied, their panic unsoothed, as Valerie dropped her voice, spoke only to the girls on either side of her, so that the darkness remained fraught with secrecy, shame, and dread.

None of this had ever worried Cushie. Her animal innocence remained undisturbed. Even when she knew what could be the consequence of making love with a boy, she found it impossible to believe that it could happen to her. It was something that belonged to grown-up people, like money troubles, or dying, or having superfluous hair grow on your top lip.

For Cushie still thought of herself and Jackie as children. Almost imperceptibly they had passed out of playing childish games under the willows or in the treehouse to lying in each other's arms. The contented joy of one was no less continuous than the rapture of the other. What was between her and Jackie was something suspended in time, unrelated to any other fact of existence, part of her private world, where all was natural, and secure, and cherishable.

So when she awakened and recognised that something had happened to her she was thunderstruck. Yet never for a moment did she doubt it; the change in the way she felt was too novel. She went around in a daze, constantly in trouble for absent-mindedness and carelessness. In a fortnight there was the first confirmation of her belief, in six weeks another. It was incredible.

As the brief term ended, and she realised that she would soon be home under the critical gaze of her mother, the full horror of her circumstances rushed upon her. She had no desire to confide in any of the girls. Wrapped up within herself, she did not even think of Jackie and his part in this catastrophe. This extraordinary thing had happened to her, not to Jackie. Her one thought was to hide it – for a little time, while she thought out what to do. Beyond that her helpless imagination could not take her.

When she arrived home half of her went on as usual, tried to please her mother, played with and even quarrelled with Olwyn, went to afternoon-tea parties and docilely showed off her pretty Mount Rosa manners. The other half gibbered with terror and dismay. Her ignorance was terrible. She did not even know when her body would change so that her mother would notice. But there was one way she could postpone discovery: she could grow fat.

This solution seemed to Cushie to be very sensible. It would give her more time, perhaps even until Jackie returned from Ghinni Junction. And before then she would have found enough courage to speak about her predicament to Jackie's mother.

The one silver-framed photograph on Isobel Moy's dressing-table was of her sister Laetitia, Lady Broome – whom she disliked rather than otherwise – smiling a frail, imperialist's smile from beneath some rajah's spider-like fringed umbrella. Laetitia, Papa's 'rogue', did more than anyone to keep alive in Isobel's heart her implacable contempt for her husband. And contemptuously she watched him now, as he methodically prepared for bed, keeping well away from the window.

Submissively, Mr Moy served a great many superstitions. He

avoided sitting beside an open window in case someone shot him; he shunned the sea, whether below or around him; and he was convinced that the occasional Puss Moth that chugged above would fall on him, his house, or the Bank.

He was still handsome. But Isobel's Papa had been right. That was all there was to him. Under that gem-like exterior was a soul as big as a bean.

Perhaps he was considering a little dutiful dalliance tonight? For as he pulled on his pyjama trousers he gave her an arch look. Reflectively she stared at his belly, a firm melon of unreal white substance. Not flesh. Fish perhaps – one of those inedible river cod. No, she had it. It was nougat. She was spellbound by the likeness. The texture, colour, everything was perfect. What, no cherries, no almonds?

There, her fascinated gaze had put him off his stroke. Now he'd go and have an enema instead.

To think she had thrown herself away on this trash! She could scarcely believe she had once hated her father because of his opposition to the marriage. He, who had given her everything else her heart had ever desired, had irrevocably forbidden it, and rightly so. In six months she had become a creature of bitter precocity, fully aware of the trap into which she had so wilfully marched.

'Mother should have locked me up, sent me over to Adela in India, disabled me in some way, rather than let me do what I did.'

Ah, she could have been great with a strong, dynamic husband to inspire her, as her sisters had been inspired! She knew she had within her volcanoes of energy like her elder sister Australia, to whom their diabolic grandfather, Joseph Jackaman, had left sole control of the emporium in Sydney. She knew that, like Australia, she was made of steel; better than that, of hard, hard diamond! She had the capacity to glitter, as Australia had never had. But her light was hidden by a bushel, this smug ninny, whose very limit of ambition was to be a Bank auditor.

Even her children were unsatisfactory, one of defective health and appearance, and the other gauche, flinching, often glum – and, what was more, getting fat. Cushie had always been a hearty eater, but these last two weeks she had become a gluttonous one as well. Two helpings of dessert, endless slices of bread and butter smuggled up to her room, and heaven knew how many chocolate wrappings secretly sneaked out to the rubbish tins. But the daily woman, inquisitive like all her class, had spied them and made it her business to remark that some lucky young ladies had more pocket-money for such tooth-rotting fiddle-faddle than honest working men had to feed their families on for a week.

She, Dorothy, had been so shy and awkward at her Grandpapa's obsequies that her mother had scarcely been able to bear it. Her lack of poise, after all those wickedly expensive years at Mount Rosa! And Olwyn had been little better, showing off, becoming ill, coughing and spluttering all through the service in the cathedral. She had seen the glances of her sisters, especially Britannia, or Anna, as they called her now, who had married a wealthy military bachelor late in life and had turned into an extremely thin, iridescent sort of woman like a mosquito.

'How on earth did poor dear Belle produce such a pair of goblins?'

Isobel's fine nostrils stiffened. She could hear Anna's high-bred whine in her very ear. Venomous creature! She had never liked her sisters very much, and had scarcely known her only surviving brother, Titus, who had been sent off to be educated in England when she was still young. But now! The thought of Titus was so disturbing, so darkly exciting that ever since her father's death she had been turning over and over like a pebble her memories of Titus's face, voice, his bad, bold eighteenth-century eyes.

Isobel sat up in bed. She could have sworn she had heard the stealthy opening of a door downstairs. If it was Cushie again, stuffing herself, she'd know the reason why!

Silently, the mother descended the stairs and stood outside the kitchen door. Through the crack she saw Cushie at the icebox, cramming into her mouth handfuls of cold potato. The girl gagged, her hands clenched; she looked as if she were going to vomit. Then, resolutely, she filled her mouth with the cold soggy stuff once more.

The strangest sensation of fright filled Mrs Moy. Was the girl insane? For while she was cramming this atrocious mess into her mouth, tears were spilling out of her eyes.

'Dorothy! What on earth are you doing?'

Cushie's eyes flared; her face blanched. She jumped to the

kitchen sink and vomited. Half-way between disgust and terror, her mother ran forward.

At the end of the paroxysm Cushie began to weep with panic. 'I'm sorry, Mama; I'll clean it up. I'm so ashamed.'

She looked quite mad to Mrs Moy, off her head with terror, yellow as wax.

The mother's eyes were watery, dazzled, as though staring into a strong light. A preposterous thought had come into her head. In a moment it had become certainty.

She said, 'You're in trouble.'

Cushie cringed against the evil-smelling sink. She wanted to say something, tell some tale, some lie. Nothing came out of her mouth. Only her big eyes fixed themselves on her mother's blanched face.

Mr Moy, thoroughly reamed-out as to body, and feeling in consequence absolved, lightsome, spiritual, strolled out of the bathroom just in time to hear from the darkened ground floor of his house a scream that chilled his blood. He thought instantly of burglars. His wife . . . attacked . . . some villain disturbed while rifling the silver-drawer . . .

He rushed back into the bathroom for a weapon. There was nothing but the lavatory brush. Wait, his cut-throat razor! Holding a weapon in each hand, he hurried down the stairs, hearing the screeches growing louder, more piercing. He burst into the kitchen, too alarmed to be cowardly. The place stank like a drain; his wife lay collapsed in a chair; his daughter Dorothy was screaming and running round and round the room, hammering her fists like a lunatic against the kitchen window and the cupboard door. She didn't see him standing there, petrified, with his lavatory brush in one hand and the razor clutched in the other. She just shrieked in as fearful an attack of hysterics as he had ever seen in his life.

At first he thought Isobel was dead; she was so pale, so limp. He roared at the girl to be quiet, think of the neighbours, get a grip on herself! He threatened her with the lavatory brush, and then, feeling ridiculous, dropped it.

His wife opened her eyes, gasped, 'She's been seduced . . . Dorothy . . . somehow. She's expecting!'

Mr Moy's ears buzzed. He thought he had heard wrong through all the commotion. But the girl had to be stopped. She might well be heard as far as the main street. The Bank!

In self-preservative panic he caught Cushie as she charged past him, grabbed her by the front of the nightgown, and slapped her on the face with his open hand. The nightgown ripped, showing tiny pathetic breasts. Mr Moy almost fainted with horror.

'Stop that noise, stop it this instant!'

Out of the corner of his eye he saw Olwyn at the door, ferret-eyed. A terrible dumb anger seized him. Scarcely knowing what he did, he cast Cushie from him, then chased after her, as though regretting his action. Accidentally his hand struck her face; her nose began to stream blood.

'Oooh, Daddy, you punched Cushie!' squealed Olwyn, thrilled and outraged.

Cushie lurched through the door. He heard her running up the stairs, banging her head against the wall, still screaming.

'Quick, quick!' urged Isobel. 'She might try to kill herself. Anything!'

But Cushie did not think of killing herself. In a frenzy of fury at herself, her parents, life itself, she rubbed her bloody hands along the wall, tore into her mother's room and dripped blood all over the lace counterpane carefully folded across the chair. She smeared blood on the mirror, opened the wardrobe, and bled over as many of her mother's dresses as she could reach.

Then all at once there was silence.

Mr Moy approached her timidly. Pity and disgust struggled in him. With blood all over her, she looked like some hapless, mal-treated animal.

The girl said in a calm, genteel voice, 'You won't let her get me, Daddy, will you?'

'No, of course I won't. You're not well, you're overwrought. I'll take you to your bedroom.'

She seemed like a sleepwalker awakened, looking at the bloodied dresses with quavering cries.

'I've done some dreadful things, and I don't know why. I don't know what came over me. Oh, Daddy, she'll kill me, and I deserve it!'

She felt boneless and alien in his arms as he laid her down. Her eyes were glazed, her blood-smeared face that of a lifeless child. With no trouble at all he got her to swallow some Veronal.

He sat beside the bed a long time, numb with consternation, and remembering irrelevant things, like Cushie's slippers when she was four. They were furry, and made her feet look like animals' paws.

His misery and bewilderment were so great that he could feel his very face changing, his cheeks falling into empty folds, the ligaments of his neck softening. He felt his mother's old worn face taking over his own. Something profound and inexplicable was taking place in his heart: pain, pain!

With difficulty he rose, went downstairs.

Mrs Moy had cleaned up the kitchen, sponged the blood from the walls and floor, got Olwyn back to bed.

'Warm milk and a spoonful of brandy,' she said.

And she had done all this before the first neighbour had plucked up enough impudence to knock at the back door and ask was there anything wrong.

'I said Dorothy had cut herself badly and had become hysterical,' she explained.

By some magic she had become firm. Her face was composed. She had risen to the occasion. But Mr Moy, bowed and trembling, sat down at the kitchen table, an iron band across his chest.

'Are you sure, Belle . . . what you said?'

'No; but I think she herself is sure.'

'The Bank. If it ever gets out. A man in my position.'

'It will not get out. Somehow we will work things so that it never gets out. I'll think of something.'

'But what, what?'

'You can take it for granted that what I shall say will be believed,' said his wife disdainfully.

'But who?' he muttered. 'Who could it be?' How could it happen at the Duchess of York? It's eighty guineas a term! And they watch the girls like hawks.'

His wife's silence made him falter.

'You don't mean . . . you can't think . . . not the little fellow across the road?'

'I fear so.'

'But I never thought . . . I didn't think it was possible with such . . . I mean . . .' He hid his face. 'How *could* she, our daughter, a refined, well-educated girl, a *lady*? Oh, God, then the child might . . .'

She thought he was going to break down, so she quickly brought him a glass of brandy. A dry competence had taken possession of her.

She accepted the crisis, and she would see it through, as her own mother, sentimental, bumbling, Victorian wifey-woman, should have seen through the ruinous infatuation of her daughter Belle.

She made herself speak quietly, soothingly. 'Everything now depends upon our acting quickly. It may not be too late to have something done.'

'But that could be dangerous, to Cushie, I mean.'

He saw her stiffen.

'You mustn't be too hard on her,' he muttered. 'She . . . she is so scared.'

She dropped a hand on her husband's beautiful black Celtic hair. 'Nothing more for you to do, Bede. Go upstairs and try to sleep.'

They lay motionless, side by side in the bed. After a while Isobel leant over and dispassionately looked at her husband's face in the moonlight, greyed over like an old plaster cast. She rose and stood at the window.

Silence, Kingsland asleep, only the moon's polished face to gape at her. Controlled and still, she faced the crisis that was as great for her as it was for her daughter. This could be the end of what had been in the back of her mind since the funeral. It could be, but it would not be. When after nineteen years of exile she had entered her mother's drawing-room, and smelt once again heavy silks, cigars, wine, *eau-de-Portugal*, fondly cared-for flesh and hair, she had known that her opportunity had come.

She was determined to salvage something of her life, and she would do it, even burdened as she was with the ailing Olwyn and now the almost insupportable blow of Dorothy's idiot delinquency.

At her father's funeral Olwyn and Cushie had let her down, but she had carried off the reunion with her family like a princess. Her sisters, smart, prosperous, had been dismayed at her matured but untouched beauty; she had seen envy and consternation written all over their faces.

'How could it be?' She could sense their thoughts. 'Married to that person ... no servants ... living in that disagreeable little town.'

All except Australia, still sharp-chinned, pared in manner and personality; Australia with her abrupt ironic glance that perused her younger sister, understood, and discarded.

In spite of her present state of nervous exaltation, Isobel again felt the peevish astonishment she had experienced when her sister Australia, after an indifferent sentence or two, had turned away to have a long and apparently interested conversation with the blushing Cushie.

She turned her mind to Titus, a tall stranger with a gentle English voice, his clothes subtly different from those of the husbands who stood around the room with their sherry and their stuck-on expressions of gravity or grief. Titus was five years older than Isobel, and had once been married. His wife had died in a boating accident that had had a hushed air of suicide about it. He had no heirs.

Their eyes had met as though they were man and woman, not brother and sister. They had talked a little.

'Are you going into Papa's business, Titus?'

'No, dearest, my interests are quite other. I shall leave the newspaper business to my worthy cousins and brothers-in-law, and be content to draw my dividends from a safe distance.'

She felt dismay. 'You're ... you're returning to England, then?'

'Indeed I am. I have been away from this country so long.' He smiled. 'I no longer feel antipodean, if indeed I ever did.'

He took her hand, turned it over, looked at it curiously, returned it softly to her lap.

'Why did you do that, Titus?'

'Our hands are so alike – and so unlike the navvy hands of our dear sisters. I wonder why? Do you suppose that our beloved grandpapa, Joseph Jackaman, could have been the byblow of some London beau?'

'Undoubtedly.' She smiled faintly.

Without preamble he said, 'Come back to London with me, Belle, and be my chatelaine.'

She tried to laugh. 'I, Titus? But you forget –'

He shook his head smilingly. 'No, dearest, I remember. Bring the goslings with you, if you wish. Think what advantages for them, their colonial corners rubbed off, handsome marriages. I assure you that our sister Laetitia will do all she can for them. She is under certain obligations to me, is pretty, imprudent Tish.'

The fearful longing that swamped her at his words made tears come into her eyes. He surveyed them with ironic comprehension, and turning without haste to his mother, soft, weepy old puss sitting in her big chair with a sodden handkerchief clutched in her plump hand, said, 'Poor sweet Isobel, so sad for her that she could not farewell dear Papa before Providence called him. Please comfort her, Mama.'

'Oh, Mama!' said Isobel mechanically, and so was pressed to her elderly mother's duck-like keel, her cheek hard against the dry limestone-coloured hair, that a gush of daughterly emotion shook her.

'I've missed you, Mama. Letters aren't enough, are they?'

'Poor, poor James,' blubbered Clara. 'He was so *angry* about dying. I'm sure it was no way to meet his Maker. Oh dear, and he did so grieve about you, Belle, my pet. Wasted, wasted, wasted. That's what he always said. And yet he could not bring himself to make the first step towards reconciliation; he was too proud. Oh, Belle, if only you had come home, thrown yourself on his parental affection . . .'

'You forget, Mama, I am Papa's daughter. Stiff-necked, I fear.'

Clara smoothed her hair. 'But it's all right, you know. In the will, I mean. And he has provided handsomely for the girlies, too. Dear James, so generous, so upright, never a harsh word to me all those years . . .' She dissolved again, and one of the other

145

daughters, Adela, fortunately home from India at the time of her
father's unexpected death, gave Isobel a vexed look and led her
mother to her boudoir.

Isobel, behind a classic mask of courageously borne
bereavement, accepted a cup of tea, sat in the bay window, bent
her golden head under the small swathed black satin hat, softly
answered the inquisitive questions of her sisters, their husbands,
their fashionable offspring in their looped, belled, handkerchief-
hemmed clothing, most of them not even in mourning.

What did she care for them? London. Wealth. Visiting my sister, Lady Broome . . . Cadogan Square. A French governess for
Olwyn, the best doctors. Dorothy licked into shape in Switzerland
perhaps. And Titus. At the thought of Titus something cloudy
and enigmatic stirred. Fear, excitement, a sense of peril – whatever
it was, she wanted it.

'And I shall never come back,' she said to herself.

She did not want to lie down again beside her snoring husband,
but there was nowhere else for her to rest. She lay there, staring
into the moonlight.

There was no question of taking Cushie to either of Kingsland's
doctors. Doctors could be trusted, nurses and receptionists perhaps
not. Mrs Moy slipped away by train with her daughter to a
northern town and, under cover of an alias, had Cushie
examined.

The girl was unresisting. Her predicament seemed so insoluble
that she could do nothing but lean on her mother. No matter
how her mother raged at her, how condemnatory she was, there
was no one else upon whom to lean. Humbly she accepted all
that was done and said to her. She felt unsealed, her integrity
gone, not because of Jackie, not because of her mother and father,
the curt doctor, the superior nurse . . . but because something that
was private and divine had been soiled.

'I must tell Jackie,' she said with desperate boldness.

'You will tell no one,' commanded the mother.

'But Jackie will marry me. We could go away. He loves me,'
cried the girl.

'Stop that absurd whimpering, and never let me hear such a
ridiculous suggestion again. You, the granddaughter of James

146

Jackaman, married to a shopkeeper's brat, a penniless labourer, and a dwarf at that. And the ages of you both! Scarcely eighteen. Love! Don't you dare speak the word. There is a great deal more to love than behaving like an animal, let me tell you. Six months from now you will thank your father and me for what we are doing for you now.'

'I want Jackie! I have to tell Jackie!'

'Listen to me, Dorothy. You have done the worst thing any girl can do. There is nothing, *nothing* that is worse. If it ever became public, your father's professional life would be ruined, Olwyn and I would never be able to hold up our heads again.'

'Why is it so bad, why?' blubbered Cushie. Her mother took no notice.

'No one must know. No one. Are you listening? And if, through your stupidity, that creature or his parents ever get to know about this, then I am finished with you. I shall not lift a finger to help you. Do you understand me, Dorothy?'

Inexorably she kept on and on at Cushie until the girl's sobs became cries of terror.

'I want your word of honour, your sacred word, that you will not communicate with the Hanna boy, or try to get a message to him in any way. You hear me, Dorothy?'

Tearfully, Cushie promised, for what else was there to do?

'What will happen to me? I don't know anything about being like this.'

Mrs Moy had a pang of compassion for her shrinking, shuddering daughter, but she steeled herself. The girl had to be frightened into complete obedience.

'Some parents would send such girls as you to special places, homes of correction, where your disgrace could be hidden and you would have no opportunity to corrupt others. Other families would cast you out on the street, disown you, and well you would deserve it.'

'No, no, what would I do, where would I go? Mama, help me! I'm sorry; I didn't know it would all end like this.'

'Your father is now in Sydney making arrangements, at great cost and anxiety to all of us, I can assure you. There are surgical treatments that can, if it is not too late, prevent such an unwanted thing happening. No, ask no questions. What right does your wickedness and vulgar irresponsibility give you to query anything your father and I decide?'

Cowed, unwell, utterly without resources, ignorant as a young animal, Cushie did as she was told, keeping to the house, speaking to no one. But she prayed for Jackie, and his return, his protection. Wild appeals, those prayers were, like messages thrust into a bottle and cast into the sea. And she prayed for forgiveness for the trouble she had brought upon her parents, for whatever she had done wrong.

What had she done wrong? It seemed to Cushie that it was not that she had made love with Jackie, but that she had become pregnant. But she hadn't expected that to happen. She hadn't meant to do wrong, if this was what was wrong.

She was not stupid, but her values were not those of the world in which she had been reared. What it believed romantic folly was something she could not change: the innocent opulence of her own ability to pity and love.

Observing that her sister looked sallow and unwell, Olwyn was not only envious, for it was her privilege to be the delicate one, but inquisitive. Mrs Moy coped with her briefly.

'It's just growing-up,' she explained. 'And it will happen to you by and by. But it is not to be discussed by little girls.'

Cushie's disturbed appearance did not go unnoticed by others. Mrs MacNunn, giving the bedroom windows their annual clean, saw Cushie dawdling in the garden across the road, and something clutched her heart.

'There's something the matter,' she declared to the Nun. 'I'm worried, Jerry, I'm telling you straight.'

'Yeah? Go on,' he said, lowering the newspaper.

'She's got that look about her. I was thinking . . . she and Jackie always so thick, ever since they were babies.'

'It's always on the cards,' said Jerry. He eased his aching leg.

'Our Jackie wouldn't. He's a decent boy.'

The Nun gave her a look.

She burst out, 'I just got to know, Jerry! I mean, if it's true . . . that poor kid! And that mother of hers has a lemon for a heart.'

The matter troubled Mrs MacNunn deeply. She spied intermittently from the upper windows, hoping to get some clue from Cushie's appearance as she walked briefly amongst the garden trees. But all Mrs MacNunn could sense was an intuitive feeling of change. The girl looked downcast, pallid, distrait.

'If it happened, it musta been when Jackie was back from High Valley that time he cleared out. Wouldn't be more than six weeks or so. Ah, God, I'm shook to know what I ought to do.'

'We could drop young Jack a note – ask him straight out,' suggested the Nun.

'Oh, I couldn't! Never! I couldn't bring myself to it,' declared Mrs MacNunn. Tears sprang to her eyes. 'Such a dear little girl she was, too. Confiding-like. I always felt for her.'

'You want to put it out of your head, Peggy,' said her husband. 'Been no gossip around the town, has there? And you know what this place is like. If Prior's pig is in pod, they know it before Prior does.'

Still, Jerry kept his ears open. He learnt that Mr Moy of the Bank had taken an unexpected week's holiday and gone to Sydney for family reasons. He learnt, because he was a drinking mate of the station booking clerk, that Miss Moy, who hadn't been too well, was shortly going through to Sydney to stay with her wealthy relatives over Christmas.

He reported this to his wife. 'Now, old hen, maybe we're doing the right thing and maybe not, but I think you ought to send young Jack a note and tell him he can maybe see Cushie when the train stops for coaling at Ghinni Junction.'

'I'll do it!' cried Mrs MacNunn excitedly. 'And that leaves it up to Jackie and keeps our noses out of it, if they ought to be kept out.'

But Cushie was not being sent to the wealthy Jackamans.

'If they should ever know!' said Isobel. Her eyes flashed; her pride stabbed her husband in his newly sensitive heart. '*That* would be the last straw, to have my sisters crowing over me in such a sordid matter.'

Cushie was being sent to her aunt, Claudie List. Isobel had always detested her, resenting Bede's faithful attachment to this pretty sister who had been a wild devil during the War, and had rightly come a cropper.

Mr Moy was the eldest of his family. The three girls who

followed him had gone early into service. He scarcely knew them, and certainly never spoke of them. Skivvies! Best forgotten. The other sister, Virgie, considerably older than Claudie, had disappeared from view in some sordid scandal. Cushie and Olwyn did not even know that they had an Auntie Virgie Moy.

It was an insufferable thought to Cushie's mother that in this family crisis she had to rely for help on the despised Claudie. But there was no one else. And Claudie would be paid well for her silence, out of the trust Papa had left for his granddaughter Dorothy.

'You're not being fair to her, you know, Isobel,' complained Mr Moy. 'Claudie's always had a good heart. And even if she did make a mistake during the War she came out of it all right.'

'At least she has the right connections to help Dorothy out of her predicament,' retorted his wife cuttingly.

Mr Moy flushed darkly. Money would do the trick, as always.

It hadn't done so for Claudie, because the Moys had had no money behind them at all. Claudie, getting pregnant by an anonymous soldier while her husband Billy List was overseas with the AIF, had to have the kid in a charity home and have it adopted out quick smart. But, of course, some nosey parker let poor Billy know about it at once: 'Dear Digger, it breaks my heart to tell you this, but your wife has been playing around with every Tom, Dick and Harry and now she's had this bastard . . .'

Billy List, a decent country boy, straightway volunteered for a trench raid, and got a bayonet in the lower gut. For a long time Claudie had gone from man to man, blithe, wayward, always ready for a grog and a laugh, kicking up her heels, funny as a circus, really. But of course, Belle was right: she was common as dirt. But somehow, like dirt, *good*.

Mr Moy had even liked the woman she shared her little house with, a Mrs Iris someone. They were partners in a hairdressing parlour and seemed to be doing satisfactorily. Mrs Iris must have put up the money, of course. Claudie never had a sausage. But she'd been properly trained as a hairdresser: how their poor old mother had scraped up the money to pay for her apprenticeship Mr Moy couldn't imagine.

'You mustn't look down on Auntie Claudie because she hasn't been educated to be a lady,' he said to Cushie. 'All the money to be spent on education in our family went on me and your poor Uncle Graham, God rest his soul. But blood's thicker than water, and Claudie will look after you and be good to you.'

'Daddy,' she whispered, 'I want to marry Jackie. He loves me, really he does. He'd come back to Kingsland tomorrow if only he knew about me . . . about this.' She said imploringly, 'Mama made me promise not to communicate with him; but you could, Daddy, you could send him a telegram. Oh, please, Daddy!'

'My dear girl, he's under age; his parents would forbid the marriage,' said Mr Moy. 'For goodness sake be sensible. The thing's quite impossible. Outrageous! To think of my daughter,' he gulped, 'being married to that young scamp, that unprincipled seducer . . .'

'He didn't seduce me, he didn't!' cried Cushie, so wildly that Mr Moy had quite a *frisson*. 'If you want to know, it was I who suggested it, not Jackie.'

Mr Moy could not believe it. The shock was fearful. He had to sit down.

'God grant your mother never hears you say such words,' he said in a groan.

Sitting there, he felt himself shrink, like a snail with salt on it. The secret, ineradicable carnality of these young girls! Virgie and Claudie, gorgeously pretty, lighthearted and empty-headed, flashed across his mind. Tears, yells, shame, grief! It was insupportable what parents of girls had to suffer.

And yet somewhere at the back of his head there was a small pleasure: Cushie was a Moy, not a Jackaman. For who could imagine Isobel, or indeed any of her snobbish, affected sisters, getting into such a predicament? Too mean and too artful, thought Mr Moy in a rare burst of perspicacity.

'We shall say no more. I am more grieved and horrified than you can imagine. I ask only that you obey your mother and myself to the letter. You owe us something, you know, for all the shame and anxiety you have caused us.'

Cushie subsided into a spiritless melancholy. Even Olwyn's inquisitive questions failed to arouse her. The little girl – she now seemed very young indeed to Cushie – had become even more fragile, with a sallow, birdy face.

Cushie had never been able to get close to her sister, but now the reedy voice, the pathos of the illness-racked little body, gave her a physical pain in the chest.

Olwyn seemed to have changed. With some belated affection or anticipated loneliness, she kept bringing little things for Cushie to look at. Once it was a family album in which she had found a portrait of their mother as a young girl.

'Look, that's Grandmama Jackaman.'

Cushie looked at the light-eyed, Irish face under a frizzy, Queen Alexandra fringe. It was pretty, and rather mulish, not at all like the fat, crumpled old face that had smiled moistly at Cushie at the funeral of Grandfather James, twenty-five years later. Against her leant a little girl. Her fair hair was pulled back under a thin tortoiseshell bandeau. Her dress, adult in style, with a tiny bustle, was of fawn and blue shot silk.

'That's Mama. Her name was Isobel Jackaman. Her hair was really golden then.'

'It's still the same, Olwyn.'

'No, she keeps it that way with camomile wash. She hides the bottle behind the wardrobe.'

'You know too much, little snoop.'

'I know what's the matter with you, too.'

Cushie looked at her in fright. Olwyn continued, selfconsciously bold-eyed. 'I heard the servant talking to her daughter when she brought back the ironing. She said the young madam had got the curse, and the fuss she'd made would kill the cats.'

'If Mama knew Mrs Cartwright gossiped that way she'd dismiss her.'

'Oh, I knew before, about the curse. Some of my friends told me. But I didn't know it came out of your nose. I'm not looking forward to it for myself, I can tell you.'

'Oh, Olwyn, you have it all wrong. Mama will explain when the time comes. Come now, let's look at some more pictures.'

Mama and Daddy on their honeymoon, straw-hatted, stiff as pokers; Daddy lined up in a mummified group before the new

Bank building; baby pictures of Olwyn – and slipped in amongst these was a water-colour impression of Cushie, slapdash, too pastel, a blunt-profiled child looking downwards as though scolded. The likeness that Isobel had attempted and impatiently discarded indicated more wistfulness than the mother had ever consciously discerned in the real child.

'Oh, Mama!' said Cushie faintly. The tears cascaded down her face as though there were a depthless reservoir in her heart. Had the young mother who had drawn this three-year-old loved her?

Cushie's passionate desire to be loved was no less now than it had been then.

'Of course I love you,' she remembered her mother saying, over and over again. 'All mothers love their children.'

'But I want to be loved my way,' replied the little child.

It was all she really knew and comprehended about life. The rest of the world and its opinions were nothing to her. She was a trespasser. Deep and true in her soul she knew only that she believed in loving, and all denial of this was dishonour.

She became aware that Olwyn was pressing against her, a spiky, insect-like little being, smelling strongly of menthol.

The child was alarmed. 'Don't cry, Cushie. You'll be coming home soon. Why are you crying? Is it because you will miss us?'

'Yes, I'll miss you, Olwyn.'

The child was astonished. 'Goodness! I always thought you hated me.'

Kingsland merely stirred and turned over in its sleep as the early express went through. The air was chill, although the sun was up early, licking away the dew. The milk cans on the station ran with moisture; the half-washed porters wiped cold red noses on the backs of their hands.

'I'm glad Mama didn't come,' said Cushie, as her father took down her luggage out of his new motor.

She looked around her, at the brindled sky, the cloud shadows mousing over the blighted hills. The poplars had their curdy new leaves; the leafless jacarandas would soon bloom. But finality was in the air, as though a tune had ended.

'It's funny. I feel I'll never see all this again.'

'Don't be fanciful, dear. And please hurry. The train's in already.'

Mr Moy was more nervous than he had anticipated. His daughter's pale face swam a little before him; he itched with desire that she should be gone, and at the same time longed that she should stay. 'Do hurry, dear. I want to see you settled comfortably.'

The train was snoring intermittently, giving tiny jerks back and forth. Steam clouds, smelling strongly of rust, burst from amongst the wheels. There was no one in Cushie's non-smoker compartment except a black bundle in a corner, an elderly woman still asleep after her night's uncomfortable journey.

Mr Moy said with awkward kindness, 'Everything will be all right. Auntie Claudie will meet you at the Travellers' Aid restroom. Don't worry, dear. It will soon be over.'

'Oh, Daddy!'

He could see she might cry, so in haste he kissed her and hastened from the carriage. A whistle, a bell, and then to his horror he saw the grocer woman, Mrs MacNunn, uncombed hair jammed like sofa stuffing under a hat, an old coat around her shoulders, running up the platform. She saw him at once, came at him with a smile like a clown's, crying, 'Just one word with Cushie before she goes – oh, I'm that out of breath!'

What could he do? He froze, his ruddy face turned purplish, not with anger but indignation. For he saw at once that the woman, determined as a terrier, was going to speak to his daughter.

'Mrs MacNunn,' he said in his Bank voice, 'I'm just seeing my daughter off. Really ... family occasion ... my wife ...'

'Oh, get away, or I'll give you such a puck in the chest,' she said, jocosely. 'Cushie and me's been friends since she was three months old. Give us a kiss, pet' – and she stuck her face through the train window and made a succulent sound somewhere in the direction of Cushie's face, saying almost simultaneously, 'Look out for him at Ghinni Junction. I've sent a letter.'

Jerking her head back out of the window, she hit Mr Moy painfully on the chin with it; and what with her apologies and loud laughter, and the train whistle blowing, and the porters slamming the doors, and the clouds of steam, Mr Moy had scarcely time to say farewell to his daughter, or do more than pant a few steps along the platform to see the last of her face under the blue summer hat as it disappeared for ever.

For ever, for ever. The words were like hammer blows on Mr Moy's heart. He had to sit down in the waiting-room to recover. It was only because of the curious looks of other travellers, huddled over the surly coals in the eight-inch grate as they were waiting for the local, that at last he went out to his motor.

His mother had known when the crane dumped the bale of goods on his father at the docks, dropping the spoon with which she was stirring the soup and giving a bawl that made the hair of every person in the kitchen stand on end.

'Dead, dead, me Pat's dead!' she had shrieked.

Now Mr Moy felt the same way. He felt he had seen his daughter for the last time; that she would die with that abortion, and it would be his fault that he had not stood up to Isobel. It was the first time he had entered the august country of grief and he was taken with a huge bewilderment.

Though he had prudently put the old rug over the bonnet of the motor, the engine was cold. He cranked ineffectually for a while until some hanger-on at the station – blue trousers, dirty striped cuffs, a porter perhaps, Mr Moy really didn't see him – jovially slapped a brutal paw beside his and with a couple of tremendous heaves got the engine going.

'Thanks, much obliged,' Mr Moy muttered, and gave the man a shilling.

He was half-way home when a coldness seized his chest and ran down his left arm. He managed to pull over towards the side of the road before the urbane sky shot upwards and vanished from sight.

Mrs MacNunn's appearance had been like a miracle. Cushie wanted to pray, to sing a *Te Deum*. But it was not the place for either; so carefully, as though it were a sacred ceremony, she took off her hat and pinned it in the large brown paper bag thoughtfully provided by the Railway. She was saved. At Ghinni Junction the nightmare would end.

The old sleeping woman had awakened, and secretively fumbled her teeth back into her head. She was like a little toad, speckled with liver-spots, yellow and cream with fatigue.

'Soon be there,' she said vaguely to Cushie.

The morning landscape looked half-painted. It had been a droughty year. The pastures were greenish-blond, like worn plush, but around the permanent way, elevated above the long swamps, coarse grass shone translucent and livid in the heightening sun. The drainage project, abandoned because of lack of public funds during the War, had left islets of white sand where navy-blue, tail-less waterhens dabbled amongst the pigface and river hyacinth. Pink dirt roads keeled down to disused sidings; derelict wooden farmhouses, toppling barns, stood amongst ashen trees.

Everything had failed since the gold ran out, everything except the canned fruit and jam factories at Ghinni Junction.

The little toad had got up. 'Going to freshen up,' she explained to Cushie. 'More'n two hours to Ghinni, but we can have a cup of tea and a bite there.'

Cushie slid the door aside for her and she hobbled into the corridor. With the old woman gone, the mysteriously compact world of the train closed about Cushie.

Saved! Saved! Somehow Mrs MacNunn had guessed, that warm, motherly woman, and had told Jackie something was wrong. Cushie wanted to laugh, shout. She knew very well that if she let herself go even for a moment she would begin to cry with relief, so she concentrated on the world beyond the windows, where the mountains of Paddy's Range ran in towards the line, grey as spiders, and swooped away again, dark blue.

The express stopped nowhere, ripping through dog-box stations with a deafening snarl. She caught glimpses of paintless, veranda-ed shops, market gardens, streets that began in desolation and ended five hundred yards farther in a dusty paddock. These villages were all old goldmining towns, built on the banks of gravelly creeks called Breakfast, Shadowgraph, Jump-up. Sparsely vegetated mullock dumps were everywhere.

Suddenly Cushie was starving. She felt electric, scarcely able to sit still in her seat. When the old toad came back she shared her sandwiches with her.

'Over our homesickness, eh?' said the old woman. 'Don't take the young ones long.'

She said she had come from the Queensland border to visit her daughter south of Sydney, who had a lump in her breast – God knows what, they had to hope for the best; but there were the four children to be looked to, and a husband who had to be fed and got off to his work regular.

So passed the two hours. As the train pulled into the busy junction, Cushie scanned the crowds that drew together, scattered, rushed in and out of the train. She saw Jackie nowhere. But knowing what to do, she left her luggage where it was and hurried to the telegraph office to see if a message had been left for her. There was nothing.

She stood at the office door, her heart beating painfully. Dazedly she sought Jackie's face in the crowds.

Nothing amongst the dreadful happenings that had gone before was worse than this moment. She felt that she had got off a ship in the wrong country. She rushed in again, besought the telegraph clerk, 'Are you sure, are you *sure*? The name might have been spelled wrong, Foy, or Hoy. Please, please, look again.'

Nothing. Whistles were blowing, porters shouting, people scampered on board the express with slopping cups of tea and thick slices of bright-yellow madeira cake. The telegraph clerk, touched by the girl's distress, said kindly, 'Better get aboard, miss. Ten to one your wire's been sent on to Sydney. Cheer up! That's where it'll be.'

She scrambled aboard the train, to find the four empty seats filled.

'Thought you'd fallen in, dear,' said the little toad, cheery with tea.

Cushie threw up the window, leaning out as the train gathered momentum. She saw running down the platform a grotesque little figure, its face darkened, disfigured in some way, waving its short arms, pursued by two tall men, one of them laughing.

She screamed, 'Jackie! Jackie!' He struggled against restraining arms, seemed to see her frantically waving hands.

'Here, little lady, want to fall out? That's enough of that!' One of the newcomers to the compartment pulled her back onto the seat and, with an authoritative air, slammed down the window.

She turned her face into the faded velour of the seat. She knew they were all looking at her, so she pretended to be asleep.

She had missed him – but he had tried to see her. Her disappointment was terrible, but it was not irreparable. He loved her, he cared about her. A kind of numb peace filled her. After a while the flitting patterns of sunlight across her eyelids ceased, and she slept deeply.

For half an hour they had been running into Sydney. Clicking gently over the points, slowing down after its long urgency, the train slid through Victorian suburbs of soiled brick, carrot-red roofs; drear or handsome terraces painted ochre or greasy white; Town Halls and schools stiff and spiked as crabs.

'Better rinse your face, dear,' advised the little toad. 'It's all over smuts.'

In the juddering washroom Cushie washed her face, tried to comb the soot out of her hair, put on her new hat and pinned it. She felt unreal, with fatigue after the night's journey, already tormented with dread of what unknown Aunt Claudie might say to her, thus fleeing in guilty disgrace to the city. But she still knew a rising hope that waiting for her at Central would be a telegram from Jackie. He had seen her at Ghinni; she was almost certain of it. Jackie would know what to do.

Almost lightheartedly, she reeled back to her seat, and greeted with anticipation the grey waste of platform, the dark vaults of roof that, when the hoarse breathing of the train ceased, echoed with clangs, bursts of steam, and rolling thunders.

Away she went behind a porter, not noticing the shabby man who met the little toad, or the old woman's painful, scanty tears.

At the inquiry counter there was no telegram for Miss Moy, no message of any sort. She stood there dumbfounded.

'Miss, do you want to check your luggage? Miss?'

She gave the man two shillings to take it to the right place. He pointed out the clean, pleasant room of the Travellers' Aid Society. Cushie stood for a while in the huge arched cavern of the station, staring blankly at the lurid advertisements, the bitumen floor patterned with submerged cigarette ends. She was aware of a huge smell of burned cabbage from the tea-rooms, a cleaner in a semi-uniform languidly pushing a broom around her feet, his dustpan a cut-down kerosene tin on a long handle.

At last she moved to the Travellers' Aid waiting-room, answering the attendant's questions, refusing a cup of tea, sitting down at last beside women with babies, opposite a young girl who stared around with scared eyes and picked her nose in between times.

Why hadn't Jackie wired? Because those men had prevented him. But who were they? Not policemen. So her thoughts scurried round and round while this stranger and that came to collect the other people. A sombre man with a black band on his coat-sleeve met the nose-picker, and pushed her out the door with inexplicable vehemence. Sick with agitation, Cushie tried to concentrate on these comings and goings, until at last there entered a strongly-built short woman about the age of thirty-five. She looked around the waiting-room, and came straight over to Cushie.

'Miss Dorothy Moy?'

Cushie nodded. The woman thrust out a capable hand and shook Cushie's.

'You're – you're Auntie Claudie?'

'Not me.' The woman smiled. 'This is too early for Claudie. I'm Iris Pauley, her partner. You can call me Auntie Iris or plain Iris or whatever you like. Buck up, Dorothy! Nothing's as bad as it looks at seven in the morning.'

Iris had a direct, pleasant smile. She had thick bobbed black hair, very light eyes, and a pale skin freckled lightly like a bird's egg. She led the way to the left luggage, got a porter scurrying with a handcart.

'I must go back to the inquiry desk first,' said Cushie desperately. 'I've been expecting a telegram.'

There was no telegram. Iris eyed the girl with half-cynical, half-sympathetic understanding.

'Come on,' she said and, as though Cushie were half asleep, led her out of the reverberant confusion of the crowded station. Fleetingly she patted the girl's hand.

'I know this must seem ghastly to you, but it will be over soon.'

Cushie looked uncomprehendingly at this kind, meaningless stranger. A lump blocked her throat.

'No,' said Iris firmly. 'Don't start crying yet. When we get home you can bawl all day if you want to, and Claudie and I will bawl with you. But not now. You'll frighten the tin lizzie.'

Cushie was hustled into a car with a tiny engine and tall square body. They were off through the city, which was as noisy as if it had been awake for hours. It smelled sweet, stale, and different. Near the railway a huge circus tent stood on a vacant allotment, and there was a whiff of lions and mouldy straw.

'Not far now,' said Iris. 'We live at the top end of Elizabeth Street. Strawberry Hills, it's called. No strawberries and few hills. But it's convenient, and the salon is just across the road.'

The street was narrow and hilly, but there seemed to be an astonishing number of lorries and big horse-drawn wagons in it. Shabby factories, their chimneys smoking, were mixed up with cosy, sluttish little shops, and small cottages and terrace houses. The taxi pulled up outside one of these, painted a nasty hay colour, with a frangipani in a front garden nine feet by three. Its door was so blistered and repainted that it looked like a slab of melting toffee.

'I'll bet it seems foul to a country kid,' said Iris; 'but, never mind, it's a roof.' She hammered on the front door with the flat of her hand shouting, 'Claudie! It's us! Open up.'

The door flew open and Cushie saw her Auntie Claudie for the first time, posing there in a blue kimino.

'Poor, poor little Dorothy!' she cried. 'Welcome!'

'Oh, cut that out, you lunatic,' said Iris, pushing past her, 'and let me get the kid's luggage inside.'

Cushie found a silky head under her chin, a small compact body in her arms.

'Poor little thing!' said Auntie Claudie. She had a sweet, plaintive voice. She gave Cushie a small shake of what was apparently sympathy. 'Poor deceived little girl!'

'Oh, quit it, will you, Claudie!' said Iris, banging down the stairs and shoving past for another fistful of luggage. 'And if you've cooked breakfast, give it to us. I'm as empty as a boot.'

160

Cushie had always thought of her Auntie Claudie List as a huge flaxen doll, handsome but vulgar, run to beef. This was the way Claudie had come through in Mrs Moy's rare references to her. But she was a very feminine woman, with a bulging baby forehead and a long frail throat with a bump in it. Her fair hair was parted in the middle and held by a broad black velvet band that disappeared at each side under coiled earphones. She had large grey eyes with a glassy shine. Cushie recognised with a tiny thrill of disapproval that not only were her aunt's eyelashes darkened, but her thin smiling mouth was brightened with lipsalve.

A photograph of the blonde giantess, the very Claudie of Cushie's imagination, was on the chiffonier in a seashell frame. Cushie's eyes fixed on this, couldn't move away, for the pretty plump lady was clothed only in a swathe of gauze from which her bottom protruded. The model looked backwards over her shoulder, a finger to her delicious chin as though to say, 'Gracious, there's my what'sname, how did *that* get there?'

'That's your Auntie Virgie,' said Claudie. 'Isn't she adorable?' She picked up the photograph and kissed it. 'Only eighteen she was there. What an art model she made! Oh, my darling big sister!'

She cradled the picture to her bosom. 'I suppose Bede – Daddy – never speaks of her?'

Cushie shook her head, and Claudie put on a tragic face.

'For God's sake, Claudie!' expostulated Iris. 'You know you can't stand a bar of her. Stop bunging it on, will you? We want food. What about it?'

'Oh, rats!' Claudie flounced off, and shortly afterwards brought breakfast to the table. Cushie discovered that she was starving. Gratefully she ate sausages and fried tomatoes. Claudie gave her a patronising glance.

'You haven't had morning sickness then,' she observed.

'Only at first,' admitted Cushie with shy reluctance.

Claudie said proudly, 'When I fell I was as sick as a dog – Chuck-chuck-chuck all day, all night, for the whole nine months.'

'You be quiet – you'll turn Dorothy off her feed,' said Iris. 'You know she can't have anything more to eat today.'

She nodded consolingly to Cushie, and pushed the toast across to her. 'Because of the anaesthetic, you see. We've fixed up the arrangements for tonight.'

Cushie's hand froze on the butter-knife.

'God, you're brutal, Iris!' cried Claudie. 'Now you've gone and scared the poor kid. As though she hasn't enough to put up with, deserted and left to bear the brunt of it all by that young hound.'

'Jackie isn't a hound,' fired up Cushie. 'He doesn't even know. Daddy wouldn't let me tell him. Jackie's . . .' her voice trembled, 'a good boy.'

Everything Claude did was agile and unexpected. She flew up out of her chair, threw her arms around Cushie, snatched the toast from her hand, cried, 'You're going to have one of Auntie Claudie's magic pills and spend the day in bed. She's just worn to a thread, Iris, anyone can see that.'

Iris shrugged, lit a cigarette, put a long yellow holder between her teeth. 'As you like. I'll do the early appointments. What's on?' She began to turn over the pages of a large day-book.

As her aunt insisted on supporting her, the staircase seemed even narrower and more dangerous to Cushie than it had from the front door. They emerged on a landing with two attic rooms opening off it.

'This is Iris's,' explained Claudie. 'No, not a word about inconvenience or anything. She's bunking in with me and doesn't mind a scrap.'

Cushie, beyond words, saw a tidy bare room with a steeply sloping roof and a deep dormer window splitting the wall with sunshine. The recurrent hum of traffic came through this window with an agreeably sociable air. Cushie's luggage was lined up against a wall.

She swallowed the tablet and glass of water her aunt offered her, and undressed mechanically. The bed was hard, monkishly narrow.

'Sleepy-bye now,' cooed Claudie. She pulled the curtains over the window and was but a shadowy figure as she said, 'The diddy's downstairs, through the kitchen door right at the back.'

She kissed Cushie on the forehead. 'Don't worry, pet. This time tomorrow you'll be smiling. But I know how you feel. I've been through it. Unfair, that's what it is.'

Half-way through the day Cushie awakened and stumbled downstairs to the lavatory. The house was empty. A note propped up against Auntie Virgie's behind said: 'At salon. Home at five. *Don't eat or drink a drop.*'

The backyard was minute, the bottom of a brick well. Chill, oozing bricks floored it, a feeble vine struggled up a string suspended from a hook above. The blue sky glared down upon Cushie. The lavatory and a lean-to converted into a laundry formed the end of the yard and, judging by the voices Cushie heard from the lavatory, a back alley ran behind that.

It was all like some bad dream. The very smallness of the house seemed unnatural, as though Cushie had, through some unkind spell, been made huge and lumbering in an ordinary-sized house.

The sleeping pill had made her feel queer, with buzzing ears and dry throat. She crept up the stairs again.

She was still groggy when they took her to the doctor after dark. Iris had hired a car. Afterwards, Cushie could remember seeing little but a bottle of red wine, drawn in electric lights, and a wine-glass that jerkily filled, the two of them hovering in the dark.

Coming home, packed in towels, with a dull pain in the pit of her stomach, and a sore arm where needles had pricked it, she mostly remembered Iris cursing as she tried to get the car into gear, and Auntie Claudie, her arm protectively around Cushie, saying, 'Can't you drive more gently, Iris? We've got a poor sickie girl here.'

Cushie couldn't believe any of it. Had she really been going to have a baby? Whatever it had been, there was no baby now, only blood and wounds. The pain in her abdomen was nothing compared with the ache in her heart. It was all over, that dream-like time with Jackie. Jackie had vanished somewhere; her life at home, at school, all had gone. She felt that she had climbed to the top of a hundred-foot pole, and there was nowhere left to climb.

Yet her body quickly convalesced. The dumb, suffering thing

163

renewed itself, became hungry, slept. But inside her mind it was different. She felt all to pieces, one moment helplessly agitated, the next precariously calm. Everything that had been stable had proved itself quicksand.

Every day she waited for letters, from her family, Olwyn, even Jackie. It was a week before she realised that he could have no idea of her address, that even Mrs MacNunn wouldn't know. She imagined him tortured with anxiety about her, his mother trying to get Auntie Claudie's address out of her father and failing.

But the old doubt was back; perhaps Jackie wouldn't want to know. The many glacial remarks her mother had made about him, about all men who had tricked foolish girls – ah, they were unforgettable!

Profoundly painful, as well, was her homesickness. She yearned for her mother, even her mother unresponsive or condemnatory. Anything, anything, thought Cushie, as she lay sleepless upon Iris's hard bed.

Saying good-bye to her in the kitchen that early morning, her mother's hair in a thick plait, her blue dressing-gown smelling of Olwyn's inhalant.

'She was sorry for me . . . worried . . . I know she was! She was trying to be brave, for my sake, and Daddy's.'

Isobel's words: 'Remember, on no account contact your grandmother. She would be horrified; it could kill her. The disgrace . . . Grandmother belongs to another generation. This burden would be too great. Promise me, Dorothy.'

Then her father's face came before her, as she had seen it at the railway station, somehow pinched, diminished from its usual waxy perfection.

'He loves me. He doesn't hate me because of all this. He couldn't. He's my father.'

Iris understood something of the girl's emotional disorder. But Claudie tried only to establish a kind of freemasonry with her niece.

'We've been little devils, and we've paid for it, and now we're going to have a good time, aren't we?' was her theme. Inquisitively she probed for the details of Cushie's love affair, how the mother had found out, what she had said, how it had been kept quiet.

But Cushie was unable to speak of it. It was her secret and Jackie's. Give the playfulness, the tenderness, the delight to this woman? To anyone at all? Her sullen silence offended Claudie, who huffed away, feeling rejected.

The external Claudie was a mingled reflection: Half was that of a titled lady drunk who had patronised Claudie's first place of employment and, after some theatrics, tried to puncture her throat with the scissors. Claudie, at fifteen, had admired the lady's scratchy fashionable voice, her hand-tossings and toe-pointings, and had imitated them tirelessly until her mother handed her a sharp one over the earhole. But, like a ghost, the lady drunk still twitched, tossed and tensed in Claudie's persona. The other half of Claudie was a film actress's rendition of a gay, reckless madcap, a role which had been highly successful during the Great War.

The real Claudie was, like all the Moys, uncertain and insecure. She was given to tears and depressions and, like Cushie, needed approval and encouragement as others need food and drink.

Rebuffed by her niece, she assumed a brusque attitude: 'No, Iris, you needn't smile. The quicker she wakes up to men the better for her. Treat them like dirt, that's what she has to learn. Love 'em and leave 'em, with their money in your garter and no regrets.'

'There's my way for an alternative.' Iris put her arms round her friend, rubbed her nose gently against Claudie's baby forehead. But the other woman pulled away absently, saying, 'Mind you, Iris, there's a lot of her rotten mother in her. She's a bit stuck-up about her fancy education and all. And under the circs she's got no call to be looking down on *me* – all I've done for her and her little mistake!'

'For fifteen quid a week,' Iris said dryly.

A beatific smile irradiated Claudie's face. She jiggled a dance step or two. 'Isn't it peachy?'

Iris never asked questions of Cushie. In spite of her tomboyish speech, she was a housewifely person, seemingly content to sit companionably with Cushie, cleaning silver or darning stockings to the accompaniment of the gramophone.

When Claudie went out in the evenings Iris often expostulated with her, though in a low voice, so that the girl would not hear.

Cushie supposed it was because Claudie so often had a headache the next morning, or was too tired to go to the hairdressing shop until ten or eleven.

Claudie had no qualms about Cushie's overhearing their conversation, and often her sweet, querulous voice would rise: 'You don't own me, Iris. I've got to have a little fling now and then – goodness knows I'll be pushing up daisies soon enough. Oh, Iris! Stop being jealous, don't be so dippy. I'll do what I damn well like!'

And she would rush down the stairs in a jingle of beads and swish of fringe, saying, 'Ta-ta, kids. You be good and I'll be careful', sometimes poking out her tongue mockingly at Iris after this enigmatic adieu.

Usually quiet after Claudie's whirlwind departures, Iris now uttered an exclamation of impatience.

'That Claudie! She'd forget her own head . . .'

She took a letter from the sideboard. 'Claudie had this today from your mother. She meant to give it to you to read.'

Cushie was alarmed. 'Is . . . is everything all right at home?'

'Well, no,' said Iris. 'Your Dad isn't too clever, as a matter of fact. But Claudie said you'd better read the letter for yourself and get the picture.'

The sight of her mother's firm, dainty writing made Cushie tremble. Why hadn't the letter been written to her? 'My dearest little girl, don't worry about anything any more. We'll forget everything. Daddy and I love you so much . . .'

But the words were quite different. '. . . regret to have to tell you that Bede has had a little upset in health . . . chest condition, and must rest for a few weeks. Fortunately, the Bank . . .'

Cushie rushed down another few lines. 'If it would be convenient for you to keep Dorothy with you until after Christmas . . . The financial arrangement would continue as at present.'

'Would you mind very much?' asked Iris, who was watching the girl's face.

Cushie, sick with disappointment, shook her head.

'If you liked,' said Iris, 'you could help in the salon, giving shampoos and so on. It might fill in the time for you.'

She saw the girl read to the end, looking for some affectionate mention of herself, turn over the page, find nothing, quickly make her face blank. That devil of a woman, thought Iris.

Cushie was anxious about her father. Never had she known him miss a single day from the Bank through illness. Her distraught mind fixed on this new trouble almost with eagerness. She wrote her father an extravagantly loving letter, pouring out her sorrow for having worried him, hoping he would soon be better.

'Please let me come home, Daddy. I could help to look after you,' she pleaded.

She sat up writing it, absorbed, while Iris, neat as a sailor, sewed new straps on Claudie's silk vests, cleaned her own shoes with white spirits, took up a hem an inch.

'They say skirts will be around our ears before long,' she observed.

'Could I post this tonight?' asked Cushie, not listening.

Iris folded up her sewing.

'Yes. If you feel fit enough. I'll walk down to the corner post-box with you.'

A roiling red cloud hung over a nearby factory, and a pungent stink of salt and putridity drifted into the street.

'Never eat frankfurters,' said Iris. 'Get that smell, will you? They're just seasoning the dead cats ready for the morning shift to start work on them.'

Scarcely anyone was about. Lights shone under the gables of a house here and there. A crumpled derelict blew up against the sequined backdrop of the city and passed them, singing, exhibiting a mouthful of graveyard teeth.

'It's just past the church, the pillar-box,' said Iris.

The church was on the corner. From the dormer window in Iris's room Cushie had looked down on its iron-coloured walls, its chained gates and doors, locked like a fortress. Its small yard had not a blade of grass or ivy; it was a church to freeze the heart of Christ.

Yet someone had got over the gate.

In the small porch, where notices in the Welsh language hung, two figures bumped and shuffled.

'Giss a bit, come on, giss a bit,' blurted a hectoring male voice.

'Ay might and Ay mightn't,' replied his companion, in an accent of extreme refinement.

Iris grabbed Cushie's arm and hurried her past. Not daring to look at her, Cushie posted her letter, and with bowed heads they retraced their steps past the church. Grunts and titters were still coming from the church doorway.

'That sounded like . . . but it couldn't have been,' blundered Cushie when they had regained the small lighted cave of the house.

'Oh, shut up. Go to bed!' snapped Iris. She was an ugly colour, her freckles ragged and noticeable.

Cushie retreated up the stairs. Her heart walloped; her throat felt dry. That man – Aunt Claudie – they *couldn't* have been, could they? She stood there, her hand over her mouth, and felt the very expression of her mother under the hand, shocked, nauseated.

'It wasn't like that,' protested Cushie. 'Jackie and I were never like that.'

But her mother had thought of her and Jackie behaving like that. Cushie pulled her mind away from the memory of her mother lying collapsed in the kitchen chair, and undressed quickly.

'I won't think of it. I won't think of it.'

As she put on her dressing-gown she heard a key in the front door. Aunt Claudie's face and its probable expression flashed before her like a vision. Scared, but impudent, putting a good front on things. And Auntie Iris, with her fierce blind look, so different from her usual impersonal calm.

Auntie Claudie must have seen Iris waiting for her, for there was a small silence before Claudie spoke:

'Ay don't see why you are staring at may in that tone of voice, Ayris.'

'You tart. You absolute, stinking, unmitigated tart!'

'Oh, what a mood we're in, to be sure.'

Cushie heard one of Claudie's shoes hit the floor. The other, thrown by an erratic hand, broke glass or china.

'Oooh, sorry, Ayris. Ay'm a teeny bit tiddly.'

'He got his bit, I've no doubt, that swine.'

'Maind your own business. You're so common and vulgar, Ayris, a maind like a drain.'

'I can smell him, all over you!'

'Oh, rats.'

There was the sound of glasses being knocked over, a slammed cupboard door, and Claudie's petulant voice: 'Haven't we anything in this bloody house to drink?'

'You might be interested to know that – she, upstairs – saw you in the church doorway with your tomcat.'

'Oh, fency! And Ay suppose she doesn't know more than her prayers?'

'You'll be less cocky when she writes and tells that smug brother of yours, and he takes her away. You'll miss your fifteen smackers!'

'Shut up, shut up, shut up, you awful bitch, Iris! She's a naice kid, she's not a mean-minded perv like you. Kindly get out of mai way. Ay'm going to bed.'

There was a sound of a scuffle, hoarse cries, weeping, a blow.

'Now you've done it, you beast. That will be black tomorrow.'

Claudie exploded into genuine sobs, and charged unimpeded up the stairs, Iris following, agitatedly weeping. Cushie could not believe it. Iris weeping?

'Oh, Bubby, I didn't mean it; it was an accident. Bubby, say you know I didn't mean it.'

A door slammed, cut off the rest. Cushie crept out onto the landing. The quarrel broke out again behind the bedroom door. There were thumps; something tipped over with a frightful crash.

An intermittent banging on the front of the house began. Cushie ran back into her room and looked out the window. A man was leaning across from the neighbouring dormer, belting whatever he could reach with a broom.

'Let a man sleep, willya? Oughta be ashamed this hour of the night. I'm on early shift – you hear, your drunken cows?'

Cushie hesitated a moment, and then went to knock timorously on the door of her aunt's bedroom. She called, 'Auntie, there's a man . . . swearing . . . the man next door. What shall I do?'

Claudie uttered a short muffled squeal.

'Ay'll fix the old baboon. Hang on, dear. Let me go, Ayris.'

The bedroom door flew open. Claudie barged out, clad in

knickers and an embroidered camisole badly torn at its square neck. One of her earphones was off, and the other hanging by a hair or two.

'False hair!' thought Cushie, amazed.

Her aunt's black eye was already puffed to closing point. She shoved past Cushie and into the other bedroom. Hanging perilously out the window, she seized the broomhead from the pro-testor's unwary hand, and heaved on it.

'Why don't you fall on your bloody empty head!'

The neighbour let go the broom just in time. Cushie heard him yelp to someone behind him, 'The damned bint tried to pull me out! Tried to murder me!'

Victoriously Claudie slammed down the window, turned to the awed Cushie, and said in a queenly tone, 'Go to bed. You're sup-posed to be sick. Never mind him next door, he'll be quaiet for the naight, you'll see.'

She weaved away to bed.

Cushie tried to sleep, but she could not. Shocked giggles escaped from her involuntarily, so that she hid her face in the pillow to stifle them.

The unaccustomed activity had renewed the bleeding. With aversion, she rose to attend to it, as though her body were a stranger's. It did not like what she had agreed to have done to it, so it bled. Remembering Jackie's admiration for her body, she looked at it wonderingly. The belly seemed slack, her breasts were still sore. The texture of her flesh was different, yielding, ready to expand and enfold. But there was nothing to enfold, and per-haps never would be again.

She heard soft whimpers from her aunt's bedroom, a soothing murmur, and imagined Claudie woebegone, sorry she had drunk too much, and Iris sitting beside the bed, holding her hand for-givingly. Cushie felt an almost unbearable longing to have someone hold her hand until she went to sleep. The endless, wear-ing procession of thoughts began once more: Daddy ill . . . What were those men doing to Jackie? . . . What will become of me, what will become of me? . . . Mama loathes Auntie Claudie, and yet she wrote to her rather than write to me . . .

170

A sullen wrath filled her heart. How could Mama do such a thing? I would never do that to my daughter, never. Her rage was against the idolised mother, the adored father, life itself. She punched the pillow in a blind fury and all of a sudden fell into exhausted sleep, to dream of a baby, faceless, nameless, yet familiar.

She awoke with an uncanny sensation that the little creature was asleep next to her, its head on her pillow. The feeling grew stronger. She was afraid to look as she rose and dressed. Her unsettled mind had seized on the thought obsessively. She tried to recapture her feeling of anger, but it had gone. The baby stayed in her mind, crying, playing. She could hardly drive it away long enough to concentrate on what Iris was saying to her as she set off to work, glum, almost silent.

'Take Auntie Claudie a cup of tea, will you? She's not the best this morning,' she tossed over her shoulder as she hurried out into the radiant heat.

Cushie had never seen beyond the door of her aunt's room, nor did she wish to. Reluctantly she knocked.

Claudie was sitting up in bed, smoking. She had a hangover and a black eye, and a puffy, satiated face. The room was thick with the smell of Turkish cigarettes, rosewater, and an unemptied chamber-pot under the bed.

'Ta, dear. You're a good kid. Oh, gee whiz, my head feels like a hive of bees.'

Claudie had an extraordinary look of slyness and silliness that filled the girl with embarrassment. It occurred to her suddenly that she disliked her aunt profoundly.

'Suppose you're wondering about last night.'

Dumbly, Cushie shook her head, dropping her gaze as she did so to avoid her aunt's sidelong glance. She saw that the carpet was patterned with big pink cabbage roses like babies' faces. They looked at her upside-down, sideways, right into her eyes. It was terrible. She began crying helplessly.

'For God's sake don't, or I'll start, too. Stop it, will you?'

But Cushie couldn't stop, couldn't explain, and at last Claudie crawled from the bed, impatient, petulant, crying, 'As though it's not enough to have the mother and father of a hangover, I've got to have a potty niece as well', and trailed downstairs to get a strong brandy for herself and a weaker one for Cushie.

'Here, wrap yourself around this.'

Claudie toppled into bed, wreathed her head in smoke. Cushie gulped down a mouthful, choked.

'You're not the only girl who's had hard luck, you know,' said her aunt. 'Ever think what would have happened to you if you hadn't a good, kind father? What happened to me, that's what!' The expression of an older, drier, sourer woman flashed across her face. 'Yeah, I had a baby, in a charity home, with the cruellest, most sanctimonious bitches in the world looking after me. A little boy, it was. I often wonder how he's grown up. He'd be nine now.'

'Didn't his father . . . didn't he want him?' ventured Cushie.

Claudie shot her a narrowed glance. She said shortly, 'No, 'course not. Well, this won't get the paddock ploughed.'

She sprang out of bed, winced, tottered to the glass to examine her eye. 'That rotten Iris! One of these days she'll go too far. Go on, hop it, sweetie. I gotta get the glad-rags on.'

Cushie went. The brandy had made her feel better, harder. The anger against her mother rose in a steady and invigorating glow. She wouldn't have treated Olwyn like that; she'd have written to Olwyn. She'd be with Olwyn right here in Sydney, taking care of her. But anything does for me. All right, I promised I wouldn't write to Jackie, I gave my sacred word, but I'm going to break it. I love him and he loves me, and I'm going to write to him.

With uncharacteristic resolution she wrote to him, stamped the letter, took it to the pillar-box, and was not sorry. How long would it take the letter to be picked up by Jackie's employers, delivered to him, answered? She resolved to wait for ten days without fretting too much. She would be patient, try to be friendly to Claudie and Iris, she'd put herself out so that fate would reward her with a letter from Jackie, perhaps even a visit from Jackie himself.

Claudie, peevish, banging around in childish tantrums, disguised her black eye as best she could, and made her ostentatiously feeble way across the road to relieve Iris at lunch-time. Cushie was glad to have the excuse to accompany her. The baby was back in her head and she wanted to lose it.

Iris looked harried and fatigued. She was wearing oilskin gloves sooted over with dye. An elderly woman with hair as black as a bowler hat looked at her grotesque reflection and smiled doubtfully.

'Ten years younger if you're a day,' said Iris, taking off the protective cape, brushing the woman down, accepting her money, all with a false, admiring smile.

'Me old man will go scone-hot,' predicted the woman. 'We don't care, do we?' But Cushie, expert in fear, knew that the poor fright was all a-quiver with trepidation.

Iris said brusquely to Claudie, 'There's a shampoo waiting.'

Claudie made a pathetic face at her. 'Oh, Iris, I'm not up to it, really. Bending over the basin, I'll heave, I know I will.'

''Ere,' said the shampoo customer, uneasily.

'Only teasing,' said Claudie instantly, and Cushie was faintly ashamed to see that the potato-faced client got the same coquettish smile that Iris received when Claudie wanted something out of her.

'This is my little niece from up country,' prattled Claudie, whipping off her blouse and putting on a pink overall. 'She's going to help her poor overworked little auntie, aren't you, precious?'

'I've something for her to do first,' said Iris firmly. She beckoned to Cushie.

'How do you feel this morning?' she asked. 'Not too shaky? Because if you feel you're up to it I'd like you to sit on this stool and dry this water-wave for me. You wouldn't mind, would you, madam? Dorothy is recovering from appendicitis. Now then, Dorothy, you hold the hand dryer like this, and move it over Madam's hair like this . . .'

Cushie timorously took the dryer, the customer emitted a sharp hoot, and Iris unostentatiously moved the blast of hot air from cheek to snail-curled head.

'Call me at once, madam, if you're not comfortable,' she said, retreating to the next cubicle for a cigarette and a cup of tea. Gratefully, Cushie knew that Iris was keeping on eye on her. She uttered timid monosyllables in response to the woman's encyclopaedic recountal of all the appendicitis operations of which she had ever heard. Her arm ached unmercifully, she found the small job long and tedious. Before it was finished, Iris appeared, took the dryer, said, 'Mrs List would like your assistance, please, Dorothy.'

Claudie had disposed of her client and was sitting on the lid of the lavatory puffing a cigarette between snivels.

'Whatever's the matter, Aunt Claudie?' asked Cushie with dread.

Claudie made a loud tragic sound.

'I'm just fed to the back teeth with washing these dirty old muffs! That one was chatty!'

'My person talked a lot too,' offered Cushie.

'You've sure led a sheltered life,' snapped her aunt. 'Chats are lice. And I'm sick of them. God, am I sick of them!' She threw the cigarette in a nearby heap of hair cuttings. At once it began to smoulder.

'Hell!' screamed Claudie, scooping up the stuff and jamming it down the WC. She dragged at the chain, but the cistern only hiccuped and groaned. Evil-smelling smoke seeped out around the lid. The two women looked at it in horror for a moment or two, when there was a subdued hiss. Cautiously Claudie looked into the bowl.

'Uggh,' she said, bursting into laughter, at the same time wincing and holding her hand over her black eye.

'Oh, bust it all,' she said. 'I'm bloody down today, I can tell you, kid. I'd go down to the pub for a hair of the dog if it weren't for Iris.'

Iris appeared round the curtain. 'If you want to sneak off to the pub, damned well do it, and don't bother coming back.'

Claudie sniffed dolorously. 'You're holding a grudge, Iris. And how you can, when you know how miserable it makes me, I simply don't know!'

Iris sighed. 'Go and have a spot, Claudie, go on.'

'If that's the posish, then,' said Claudie in a trembling voice, 'I'll go, as invited!' And she pulled on her hat, snatched up her fringed bag, and flounced out of the shop.

'Hungover as a bedspread,' said Iris. She grinned at Cushie. 'Poor little beast. She'll be back, all jam and kisses. But I'm sorry about banging her in the eye. It was an accident.'

She added: 'You could be a bit more friendly to her without putting yourself out.'

Cushie said sulkily, 'I don't really know her, do I?'

Iris shrugged. 'Right!' She thrust the long holder between her teeth, spoke around it. 'I must be off my chump trying to make an infant like you understand anything about an older woman.' She glanced around. 'Now then, fancy dusting out the window, rearranging it? I've a perm due in a few minutes, so I've just time for a puff out back.'

Cushie took the feather-duster, thankful. that now Iris would stop talking. She slid back the flap at the back of the window and carefully began dusting the many exotic objects the little showcase contained. There were two busts of ladies cut off under the bosom, with stiffened muslin swathing the plaster. One wore a short, wavy, chestnut wig, and the other a blond buster-cut with the edges turned forward on the cheeks in cat's whiskers.

But, as though to let more conservative clients know that long hair was still dressed at List and Pauley's, the floor of the window was lavishly scattered with long-toothed tortoiseshell combs, hair-pins, nets and boudoir caps, hair-tidies and bristle brushes, and the wall behind tastefully hung with long plaits, switches like horses' tails, small coronets of curls, and little earphones similar to those Aunt Claudie wore. A price card announced: Shingling, 2s.; First Shingle, 3s. 6d.; Water Waving, 1s. 6d.; Bleaching Henna, 15s. 6d.; Permanent Waving, Full Head from £1. 15s.

While she was rearranging the window, Cushie saw her Aunt Claudie almost running up the street, looking frightened. She shot into the shop, fell into a chair.

'Oh, Iris, you'll never guess! I saw Virgie!'

Their voices rose and fell, and Cushie caught a sentence here and there.

'Went into the Ladies Lounge. Small port. Before it came saw this huge fat . . . Couldn't believe my . . . Drunk as a . . . Sitting in the corner, hair like a rat's nest. Dress undone down to *here*! Nearly died. Of course I recognised her. But she's . . . oh, Iris! My own sister. A derelict. Oh, Iris!'

Iris said matter-of-factly, 'Did she see you?'

'Oh, God, I hope she didn't. Imagine if she came here!' gasped Claudie. 'No, I just got up quietly, even before my port came, and went like the wind. Oh, my heart, just feel it, Iris! I think I'm going to have a funny turn.'

'No, you won't,' said Iris sharply. 'And keep your voice down. That perm will be arriving any moment. You just go out back and have a cigarette and calm down.'

'But it was *Virgie*,' squawked Claudie. 'I always thought she was dead, you know I always did. All these years . . . and then to see her sunk so low!'

'Shut up!' hissed Iris. The next customer appeared in the doorway, and Claudie stumbled off behind the curtain. Cushie, dumbfounded, went on dusting. A young workman stared into the window, grinned boldly at her until she looked away in confusion.

Iris went on working composedly, talking pleasantly to the customers, occasionally calling Cushie from the window to fetch dry towels, sweep hair cuttings, brush madam down.

After twenty minutes or so Claudie appeared in her overall, pallid and absent-minded but apparently restored to calm.

Iris said to Cushie, 'Thanks. You've been a great help. Don't know how I would have managed without you.'

Cushie blushed, pleased.

She knew that Iris and Aunt Claudie did a lot of talking about Virgie. Occasionally at night she heard Claudie's voice rise emotionally: 'You don't know what Virgie was to me when I was little. And then when she went away – of course I loved her, you stupid thing, more than anyone. And then I hated her, oh, I could have killed her. But I forgave her when I thought she was dead. Well, fifteen years since anyone's heard of her, Iris! We just took it for granted . . . Oh, shut up yourself, you've got no sympathy, you're hard as nails . . . And the same to you, with knobs on.'

Cushie was not interested. She just waited for a letter from Jackie. She began to feel well again, more cheerful, though her wounded anger at her mother did not diminish. Her mother knew how anxious she would be about her father, yet wrote her no word of reassurance.

She wrote to her father again, asking for a line on a postcard, if he were well enough, expressing again sorrow at giving him and Mama so much sadness and trouble. 'I love you, Daddy,' she concluded. 'I miss you. Don't hate me. I couldn't bear it.'

After many days a letter bearing a Kingsland postmark was delivered. Dizzy with joy, Cushie snatched it from the doormat and flew off to her bedroom. But the envelope was addressed in unfamiliar handwriting. Dreadful fear seized her. Her father was dead. The letter was from the doctor. Her mother was too distraught to write, Olwyn too young. Her heart palpitated. No, no, they would surely have telegraphed Auntie Claudie? It couldn't be that.

She stared in terror at the letter for several minutes before she could bring herself to open it. She looked quickly at the end of the scrawled sheets. Margaret . . . Margaret who? MacNunn! Mrs MacNunn! Then something had happened to Jackie?

The letter which it had cost Mrs MacNunn so many tears and so much trouble to write was read in a few moments. The girl could not believe it. She thought she had misunderstood. She kept going back to the most horrifying sentences and trying to make something else of them:

Dear Cushie,

Your letter was sent on by them people Jackie worked for at High Valley. I don't know if I done right to open it, but both me and Mr MacNunn thought it might save you sorrow and grieving to hear the news from us.

Jackie got married, we didn't know about it until it was all over. He married a young girl of the family at High Valley, and they have gone away to Dovey River where Jack has a job.

I know this will be a terrible shock to you, you having your trouble and all, though thank the good God that you miscarried. Only good thing in a sad mess. We both feel very ashamed about Jackie. We wouldn't have had it happen for the world. I hope you will find it in your heart to forgive and forget. I hope you will not be hurt too much. Try and forget, dear.

No one will ever know from me or Mr MacNunn what has happened, so do not worry. Sorry about your poor father so ill. It's a cruel world. Don't be too bitter against Jackie, dear. Marrying so sudden, I mean. A good, sweet girl like you will find someone better and more with your own background, and you deserve it, too. It may be all for the best in the end. God keep you and bless you, dear little Cushie. Your sincere friend –

MARGARET MacNUNN.

Cushie sat still, dazed, until she was aroused by the tidal roar of the five o'clock traffic. She felt stiffened in all her joints. Yet at the same time she was aware that something mysterious had happened to her. She had been a creature in a chrysalis, and now the chrysalis had split up the back, like the seam in an outgrown dress, leaving her exposed, feeble. More than that, different. She did not know in what way. That had yet to be proved.

Jackie married. Jackie gone away to the Dovey River with a girl, his wife. No name, just his wife. Mrs Hanna of Dovey River.

'I love you, Jackie,' she said aloud, as though that would change things. 'And you love me, too.'

She remembered the look on his face as he came flying down the platform at Ghinni Junction, looking for her, distraught, frantic. Sharpened by pain, her memory painted in the bruises on his face, the swollen eye. He had been hurt, perhaps by those two men who overhauled him with such ease, and held him as though he were a child.

How long ago was it? It must have been about the time he was married. There was some connection there – those men, his damaged face. But it scarcely mattered now. He was married, gone beyond her reach for ever. So many cruel and corrupt things had happened to her, and now he would never know about them, as she would never know what had really happened to him after he went away to the Dovey River.

When Claudie and Iris came in Cushie saw that they had had a drink or two, for Claudie looked puffed and pale, like a blown-out paper bag, and Iris's voice was a little louder and more precise, her swept-back cheeks faintly reddened. She gave Cushie a shrewd look.

'Hullo,' she said. 'You look like something the cat brought in. Didn't get bad news from home, did you?'

To Cushie the women's voices sounded slightly muffled, as though her ears were full of cottonwool. She turned Iris's question over in her mind and after a while replied, 'I haven't heard from home.'

Claudie gave her a hug. 'No news is good news! I know, let's all have a little drinkie. Pep us up. Dorothy too, poor little pet, so pale and peaky.'

'Oh, no you don't,' said Iris. 'A youngster like that!'

'Oh, rats,' said Claudie. 'She had a brandy and water with me a few days ago and it slipped down nicely, didn't it, love? Don't be such a wet blanket, Iris.'

'Her father would have a fit, you know very well, Claudie,' said Iris. 'Don't you be a chump, Dorothy.'

'Yes, I should like a drink, thank you,' said Cushie. She took the glass, sipped it. It tasted filthy, but she kept her face straight in the best Mount Rosa tradition. Little trickles of warmth ran here and there in her body.

'Let's all have another,' said Claudie, smacking her lips.

Cushie remembered eating dinner, washing up, going up the stairs, hearing a nagging squabble between Claudie and Iris and the sound of a slap. She awoke late at night. There was still an argument going on in her aunt's bedroom. She was now quite sober. Memory brought a recurrence of pain that lapped her from every side. Was it pain or sorrow? Mrs MacNunn had used the word grieving. That was right. She grieved. She was bereaved. She was bereft of everything, love, home, family, future.

She rose and went silently downstairs to get another glass of brandy, stronger this time. After a while she heard the quarrelling in Claudie's room as no more than the altercation of seagulls on a distant beach. A soothing hum in her ears deafened her to the sounds of the city, the faraway rattling of the trams, the trains whistling, a band's loud music. She slept for a little while, and then awoke. She felt that she was flying to pieces, going mad. She sat up in bed and screamed and screamed, unable to stop when Claudie and Iris came running in, when Iris slapped and shook her.

'What's the matter, what's the matter?' Iris repeated.

'He got married to someone else,' said Cushie.

The neighbour next door was hammering on the wall. His shouting drowned the girl's voice. Claudie cried, 'What did she say?'

'She said he got married to someone else. The boy who put her in the family way, I suppose.'

'Of course he did. Don't they always? Bastards!' cried Claudie – and she put her head out the window and yelled, 'I'm going to ring the police and put you in, you pest. How dare you use such language, effing and beeing all over the place, you ought to be ashamed, and in front of respectable women, too, not to mention a young lady visitor.'

Iris pulled her inside the room, closed the window. Cushie lay limply, her eyes unseeing.

'Do you think she's all right?' asked Claudie anxiously.

'If you ask me, she's as tight as a tick. And it's your fault. Giving a kid like that brandy. She's probably never had anything stronger than cocoa in her life. Look at her. She's sloshed, I tell you.'

'Hang on – how'd she come to hear about the boy getting married?'

They looked in the drawer beside the bed. They read Mrs Mac-Nunn's letter with exclamations of compassion.

'What did she expect? Girls! Mad as rabbits.'

'Well, were you and I any better at her age?'

'But Iris, what will I do if she starts to go to pieces like this? I mean, she might have a breakdown, or do away with herself or something, and Bede would blame me.'

'Write to him then, and tell him to make other arrangements,' said Iris, looking with pity at the sleeping girl.

'You know that stinker Isobel would read the letter,' said Claudie vexedly, 'and *she'd* make other arrangements like a shot, and then what about my fifteen smackers?'

'God, you're a stingy little article. I don't know how I put up with you.'

'Who said you had to?' snapped Claudie. More cheerfully, she said, 'Probably it was the grog, as you say.' She returned Mrs Mac-Nunn's letter to the drawer. 'Men,' she said.

'Well?' said her friend smilingly. Claudie fended her off.

'No,' she said. 'I'm going to bring the big chair in here and keep an eye on her. Suppose she jumped out the window or something? All right you shaking your head, Iris, but she was in a real state. And she is my niece, anyway. My one and only, unless Virgie tripped up. Oh, God, Virgie! The worries I have!'

Iris shrugged, and returned to bed.

Claudie huddled under a rug in the chair. The girl lay like a statue. The cars swished past, each pair of headlights throwing an arm of lemon light over Cushie. Sometimes she looked quite yellow and drawn, so that Claudie amused herself by imagining that each time the traffic illumined her Cushie became older and older, like SHE in the moving picture. Thirty, wan and disillusioned, forty-two starting to melt, to run down into folds and flab, like Virgie.

Claudie shuddered.

'I don't want to think about Virgie,' she pleaded with the dark, with her memory. The bad days after her father's death came swarming back, like hornets.

Claudie was four when her father, Pat Moy, was killed, flattened under a cargo sling that broke. She remembered her mother and elder sisters howling, her big brother Bede there, bossy, grown-up, herself crouching in the furthest dark corner under the table with Graham, the baby brother, and Virgie crawling in to sit with them there, to hold them in her arms, saying, 'It's all right, I'm here.'

Virgie at twelve was a fierce, motherly child, glowering at the world. She had left school, and, too young for factory work by law, she laboured much harder as a boarding-house slavey.

After Pat Moy's death, his wife turned melancholy, sitting all day in the kitchen smoking and crying. The big girls, all in good places, all three courting, were reluctant to come home to look after things. Selfish lumps they were. But, give them their due, their mother had not treated them to much affection. Pat Moy's wife had not cared for her children: she was too much besotted with Pat. The children were the price she had to pay for his love.

Virgie left her situation and took over the house, bullying, worrying, working, trying to make out as best she could on the mother's widow's pension, and the minute income from the father's compo. Bede helped too, Claudie supposed.

The mother couldn't bear the sight of Claudie and Graham. Change-of-life children they were, and perhaps the mother begrudged the time they had kept her away from Pat's embraces.

Claudie hungered for the mother's love. She was always hanging onto her skirts, clutching her leg. Once the mother hit her on the face, moaning, 'Get away from me! You're like a leech, a bloodsucker. I don't want *you*, I want your father. Take her away, Virgie, take her away!'

Virgie was everything to Claudie, shelter, mother, protector. She took her to school, threatened bullying kids, punched up a schoolteacher who had thrashed the child over the head with a cane.

Virgie, when Claudie was seven, carrying her on her back to the hospital, cursing a strange man in the street who was reluctant to help, yelling, 'My sister's dying! It's her throat, all clogged up. You gotta help, mister.'

Claudie half dead with diphtheria in hospital, Virgie looking at her, crying, 'Her back there, saying the rosary and watching you choke to death – she ain't a mother's toenail.'

And then suddenly Virgie grown beautiful, blooming overnight into something so queenly, so peach-like, that it seemed impossible that she had sprung from the pitch-dark terrace house on the steep street above the Woolloomooloo docks. The fellows were after her like flies. The mother screaming at her; Virgie shouting; Bede leaving home, boarding somewhere; then Virgie clearing out.

'Leave me and Grah?' wailed Claudie. 'But who's going to look after us?'

'I don't know,' wept Virgie. 'But you got to try to be good, look after yourselves, don't cross her too much. I'd stay if I could – I would, Claudie, true.'

Mad with fright, Claudie flew at her, punched her, kicked her. Virgie just held her off, saying, 'You don't understand, you're too little. I'd stay if I could. I'll come back some day, I promise, Claudie.'

A voice retreating, fading like an old gramophone record. Claudie throwing herself on the bed, bellowing, scratching her own face till the blood ran, wetting herself, bashing the sleeping Graham till her mother ran in and smacked her half-silly.

The grown-up Claudie supposed that Virgie had been pregnant, had run away to spare her mother and clever, respectable Bede the scandal. But that did not excuse her.

'She could have taken me,' said Claudie, hardening her face.

'And she never did come back, in spite of her promise.'

So Claudie, eight years old, was left to the depressed woman's mercy. In her orphaned desperation she had loved her more than ever. Mrs Moy had been a small-boned woman. Even now sometimes when Claudie looked in the mirror she caught a spectral glimpse of her mother, looking through her eyes as though through windows. And then her heart jumped with longing, as if the years between did not exist. The years she had spent, seeking, seeking, being rebuffed, being outrageous so as to have some notice taken of her! But the mother never had loved her. Even when she had come back to herself, she had preferred Graham.

Virgie was not mentioned in the family again, even when her photograph began to appear in the smut shops in the arcades. Graham had swapped his pencil-case and a comic book for a post-card that was being passed around at school. The pair of them, Claudie and her young brother, looked at the 'draped pose' with frozen horror. One of the subject's breasts was bare; she had nothing on her legs at all. But she was even prettier than the children remembered her.

'It can't be her,' whispered Claudie. 'She wouldn't.'

'The fellas say it means that she's a low woman,' explained Graham. 'No better 'an a fourpenny touch.'

'How could she, showing herself off like that?' Claudie was almost in tears. Then she cried in fear, 'You never said she was our big sister?'

'Think I came down in yesterdee's shower?'

Graham, like his brother Bede, had his head screwed on the right way.

Later on Claudie discovered that for a brief period Virgie had been mildly celebrated, a favoured nude model, an occasional glimpse of whom was seen in classic poses as Victory or Renunciation behind a gauze curtain at the Alhambra.

Claudie, grown up, became furtively proud of Virgie, so saucy – naughty but nice. She bought a photograph of her and often looked at it.

But in her heart Virgie, as sister, remained unforgiven.

'She was all I had, and she went away and left me, *abandoned* me.'

183

What was the meaning of it all? Virgie's face, sagging over the pub table, dissolute, swollen, ugly as hell.

'Serve her right for leaving me,' thought Claudie. 'Serve her right.'

When a hand touched her shoulder she jumped.

'You're nearly asleep, ducks,' murmured Iris. 'It's after one. She'll be all right. Come to bed, Bubby.'

'I'm miserable, Iris,' said Claudie dolefully. She rose and put her head on the taller woman's shoulder.

Drooping against her friend's strong arm, she left the room.

Christmas passed, intense heat, so that the tiny house was like an oven. Claudie and Iris, worked off their legs at the shop, tottered home late at night with bits of Belgian sausage and potato salad from the ham and beef shop, Claudie crying because her feet were so swollen and sore, and Iris with tart tenderness bathing them, powdering them, gently rubbing them, till Claudie went to sleep on the settee, saying drowsily, 'Virgie used to do that when I had a toothache . . . poor Virgie.'

Cushie had a five-pound note from her father, with a scrawled note wishing her a happy and holy Christmas. She wept over his handwriting, so feeble, so bloodless. She had longer letters from her mother and Olwyn, full of Kingsland chatter, her mother hinting at a lovely surprise that the New Year would hold for them all.

Cushie wondered what sort of Christmas Jackie had on the Dovey River. Jealousy sharp as a spear went through her heart. But now she knew how to make herself feel numb to such pains.

One later afternoon, Iris took the brandy bottle from the sideboard, shook the dregs and asked her friend, 'Hey, have you been hitting this stuff behind my back?'

'Not me,' sang Claudie, swinging her beads and jazzing up to Iris and back around the table again.

'There was half a bottle there on Monday,' said Iris. 'My godfather, you don't think our star boarder has been blotting it up?'

The two women looked at the bottle and each other. Claudie said thoughtfully, 'Well, she's certainly spent a lot of time sulking in her room lately.'

'Sulking, my eye! That kid's turning into a cupboard drinker.'

Claudie giggled. 'Oh, lord, just imagine Isobel bitch's face when her darling daughter gets on the grog and drops the teapot on the vicar's family treasure.'

Iris scowled. 'Funny, funny! It's no joke, Bub. That girl's in a bad way.'

Claudie shrugged, began to jiggle once more. 'Well, she can jolly well pull herself together like anyone else. Going on like a bloody big softy. It's not the first time a girl's been let down by a boy.'

'You'll have to speak to her about the brandy, damn it,' said Iris.

Claudie put on an impudent face, danced past. With a sudden spurt of anger Iris seized her by the shoulders and shook her.

'Are you seeing him again tonight? You are, aren't you?'

'Maybe and maybe not. Mind your own business. Honestly, Iris, you give me the pip.'

She hissed at her friend like a cat, one hand raised to strike.

'Don't you push me too hard or I'll clear out. You just remember that.'

Iris said under her breath: 'You just do it to make me jealous, don't you?'

'Don't flatter yourself,' said Claudie, a soft, teasing smile relaxing her drawn-back lips. Her eyes were once again a doll's eyes.

Iris muttered, 'Don't do it to me, Bubby.'

Claudie glanced at her enigmatically, danced away.

Iris replaced the bottle by a full one, but by the middle of the week it was three-quarters empty once more.

'Are you going to say something to Dorothy, or aren't you?' demanded Iris. Claudie looked helpless.

'Oh, sweetie, I wouldn't know what to say, honest. Besides, does it matter? The odd spot doesn't hurt anyone. Don't be a wowser, Iris!'

That evening, after Claudie had gone out, Iris said mildly to Cushie, 'I don't care about the brandy. I just care about a baby like you trying to drown your sorrows with something that never drowned any.'

Cushie said stiffly, 'I'll pay you for it. It's just that, as I'm under age, they won't sell it to me.'

Iris was shocked. 'Girl, what are you trying to do to yourself?'

'I don't want to talk about it, Mrs Pauley.'

Iris pleaded, argued, reasoned. Cushie stood with her head bent, like a child, a yellow strand of hair falling beside her cheek. When Iris paused for breath, Cushie said, 'May I go now?'

The older woman said compassionately, 'Oh, Dorothy, whatever you feel now – he wasn't worth it.'

'Yes, he was,' said Cushie.

Claudie came home early, irritable, restless, snapping at Iris.

'Stood you up, did he?' murmured Iris maliciously.

'No, he didn't,' shouted Claudie. Then she dropped her head in her hands. 'Oh, God, Iris, I saw her again.'

'Drunk?'

'She was standing with the Salvation Army at the corner of Hay Street. Singing hymns.'

'Well, gee whiz, that doesn't sound so bad,' said Iris. 'What's the matter with the Sallies?'

Claudie burst into tears. She cried with her mouth open, like a child, her eyes squeezed shut, and tears tinged with eye-black spurting down her cheeks. Cushie saw that her aunt was pale; she seemed genuinely distressed. She rose, saying to Iris, 'I'll go to bed. It's time, anyway.'

But Claudie turned to her blubbering: 'Your own Auntie Virgie, and looking so dreadful, clothes hanging off her, and her hair . . . her lovely hair. And so fat. You can't imagine. Like a balloon or something.' Suddenly she blew her nose, wiped her eyes, and glared fiercely at Cushie.

'And that's exactly how you're going to look, you silly mutton, if you don't stop sneaking booze and making a fool of yourself.'

Cushie felt that she had been slapped in the face. She gaped at her aunt. A fearful indignation, such as she had never felt before, rose in her. A vulgar, glittering spate of words rushed to her tongue: Mount Rosa had never heard the like. With physical effort she choked them back.

'Don't you dare speak to me like that,' she managed.

'Why shouldn't I?' yapped Claudie. 'I'm supposed to be looking after you, aren't I? Your father entrusted you to me when you were in a nasty fix, and I've done my very best to be kind and sympathetic to you, with mighty little encouragement, I might say. Not everyone would have taken you in, the way I did.'

'Don't you preach to me, you, you common thing,' cried Cushie. 'Do you think I haven't heard you come in drunk yourself? You can talk! And as for being kind and sympathetic, you've been well paid for it. Fifteen pounds a week! Why, my father doesn't earn half that at the Bank!'

Both Iris and Claudie were gazing at her as though hypnotised. Furiously Cushie went on: 'I shouldn't have helped myself to your liquor, but I'll pay you for it. Then you won't have anything to complain of about me.' She paused to draw breath, seeking some epithet both cutting and ladylike, but before she could think of anything Claudie ran wailing into the kitchen and slammed the door.

Iris let out a long breath. 'Well, all I've got to say is, there's more to you than meets the eye.'

'She shouldn't have spoken to me like that,' mumbled Cushie, cold and shaken.

'Maybe not,' said Iris. 'Just the same, you shouldn't have set her down like that. There's no harm in Claudie.'

The girl said defiantly, 'I've written to my mother asking if I can go home.'

Iris nodded. 'You've done right. You're a fish out of water here. And at least when you're at home you won't be able to get at the booze.' A softer expression flitted over her face. 'Or perhaps you won't want to, you poor little chump.'

'Kindly mind your own business,' said Cushie. Her voice sounded peculiarly familiar to her ears. After a little she realised that she had perfectly reproduced her mother's freezing tone when she was displeased. In some unexplained way this upset her.

Iris said, 'Cushie, this isn't you. Don't be like this.'

In spontaneous kindness she put out a hand to touch the girl. Cushie jerked away.

'Don't you call me Cushie. That's for my family and Jackie.'

She rose unsteadily and went up the stairs.

'Damn you, Jackie,' said Iris. 'Damn you, and all you Moys.'

She went to the kitchen. Claudie was leaning against the sink, sniffing, blowing her nose angrily, talking to herself.

'She made little of me, Iris,' she snivelled.

Iris held her comfortingly. 'Well, you should have been honest. Never mind, she's written to her mother asking to be allowed to go home. Yes, I know, you'll miss the money, but at least we won't have the bother of her. We'll be alone together once more.'

Claudie began to bawl.

The postman came early in Kingsland. Mrs Moy had scarcely bathed and dressed before she picked up the letters from the front doormat where they had fallen. She listened at the foot of the stairs, hearing the day nurse moving around in her husband's room, his washed-out whining voice. Olwyn, whose health had improved lately, was chirruping to the daily woman as the latter washed up the breakfast dishes.

Mrs Moy went into the morning-room. She felt thin, brittle; the mirror over the fireplace showed her face as gaunter and more set than usual. She sat down, still erect, though her aching back longed to bend. She riffled through the letters. Titus! His bold black handwriting prowled across the thick envelope. It so resembled Titus's personality that like a young girl she raised the envelope to her lips, kissed the paper his hand must have touched.

'Oh, Titus, save me! Help me!'

She read his letter quickly. Life flowed back into her body. She put up a hand to her severely brushed back hair, loosened a hairpin or two, pulled a wave out over her forehead. Her body relaxed, her breasts felt heavy. She had a sensation as though her blood sparkled.

... Hurry up, Belle, darling. I long to see you sitting in the drawing-room, wearing a delicious teagown from Molyneux, enchanting all the old aristos and making Laetitia mad with envy. What does it matter if your husband is ill? Do be a sensible girl. What are hospitals for? Or bring him with you, and he might subside into a wheelchair, like poor Broome. I promise you, dearest, sister Tish had no such qualms after the old bart. had his stroke. A wheelchair, a strong manservant, rooms on the other side of the house. Just the thing for what's-his-name. Come now, make up your mind, don't be naughty, I shan't wait for ever, you know.

Isobel went to the glass, passed her fingertips over her face. Her beauty was clouded, the skin above her eyes a little puffy, her hair had a look of straw rather than silk. She was perfectly aware that without her beauty Titus would not look at her twice. But this dimming was a temporary thing, caused by all the broken sleep she had had since Bede had his heart attack. In spite of the night nurse, she was not able to get proper rest. She would have to have professional beauty treatment before they left for London.

'And I will go to London, I am going to London, I will arrange it somehow.'

She returned to her chair, rejected the temptation to read Titus's letter again, and looked at the others – one from her mother, bills, the Bank, Cushie's unformed hand. It looked like a child's careful, round-lettered writing. Was that all Mount Rosa could do for her?

'Mama, please let me come home. I am perfectly well now. I don't like this place. It's very nearly in a slum, and Aunt Claudie and Mrs Pauley are quite common. I worry and worry about Daddy. Please let me come home.'

Mrs Moy's hand clenched on the page in a frenzy of irritation. Olwyn ran in, something almost like vivacity enlivening her narrow face. She was plain. The Jackaman nose, so impressive on the menfolk, stuck out like a beak in that countenance; the child's jaw also had grown too large for the rest of her. The eyes were Clara Jackaman's wan, blue, protuberant eyes. Why the devil couldn't Bede have passed on his matinee-idol features to his child? Mrs Moy's heart filled with love and compassion for Olwyn. London doctors would cure her, a long sea voyage, a change of climate . . . She might yet turn out a beauty, who could tell?

'Is it all right if Mrs Cartwright teaches me how to bake a sponge, Mama?'

'Of course. Only a sponge, however; no other dishes, except a trifle, perhaps. I don't like to think of my little girl in the kitchen.'

'Oh, you've a letter from Cushie! Read it out, Mama.'

'Presently, dearest. I must read it to Daddy first. Do you feel well this morning?'

Olwyn lingered. 'What does Cushie say? Does she miss me?'
'Of course. Run along!'

Isobel, her face firm, returned to Cushie's letter. The rest of it was as ineptly phrased as the first page, a passionate plea to return home, assurances of good behaviour, love, helpfulness.

'You wouldn't need a nurse if you had me, I could look after Daddy, truly. I would be so willing.'

Mrs Moy neatly folded the letter. Power had come back to her fatigued body and mind. She felt it running, bright as electricity, in her veins. She sat quietly, conserving this now rare energy, thinking about Cushie.

What would be the advantage of having the girl at home? She could imagine Dorothy's distress when she saw the change in her father – tears, sobs, oh, darling Daddy, great soppy outbursts. Upsetting Bede, who was, God knows, hypochondriac enough, worrying about the Bank, his job, every twinge in his chest, his pulse, the late arrival of the doctor, the fussiness of the nurse. He had even seen the priest, and now kept a rosary under his pillow. After all these years of estrangement from his Church! She could not help a twinge of distaste. Holy water next, she anticipated.

No, Dorothy would not be good for Bede. There was also the danger that the Hanna boy might come home. The idea was intolerable.

The crisis of the girl's condition had been solved. She was temporarily in good care, and even if Claudie List and her friend were vulgar it would make Dorothy appreciate her own home, education, and refined background.

No, Dorothy must not return. In fact, it might be better to leave her in Sydney until they all went to that city to take ship to London. London! Isobel closed her eyes, a tremor went through her, her cheeks flushed. For an instant she looked like Belle Jackaman, dazzling Belle.

At first she had seen Titus's invitation as a possible avenue of escape to her old life, the rich, dignified life to which she had been born. But now she saw it as a certainty. Bede's illness had seemed a fatal blow to her hopes; but perhaps in its way it was a blessing. He was frightened and submissive. She knew that if she played enough on his apprehensions he could be wheedled into retirement. Going to England could be presented as a means of restoring him to health: the restful voyage, the finest medical care in the world, Harley Street ... she could imagine his dull, anxious eyes lighting up with the importance of that famous name. She smiled. Bede would be no trouble.

And if he should die? The doctor had said there was a grave possibility. Well, she did not wish her husband dead, but if he should – Isobel did not trouble to prevaricate. It would be the simplest way out of a predicament, and the girls were young enough to get over their bereavement quickly.

No. Cushie's intransigence was a barrier to be removed. She would stop this homesick wailing and whining once and for all, by writing a letter of some asperity. Cushie was too soft, vacillatory: in truth, a real Moy. She had to learn her lessons the hard way.

The days during which Cushie waited for a reply to her letter were uncomfortable ones. Claudie did not speak to her, but treated her to an entire repertoire of looks – haughty, wistful, heartbroken, and innocent. Yet Claudie had other things on her mind: she seemed obsessed with the reappearance of Virgie, and did not go out any more in the evenings in case she met and was recognised by her sister.

'I just couldn't manage, Iris,' she said pathetically. 'Whatever would I say to her? Oh, why did she have to turn up again; it's just too awful.'

When her mother's letter finally arrived, Cushie opened it with hope and gratitude.

To someone other than Cushie it may have seemed a little brusque, no more.

> ... You must understand that Daddy has been very ill. It is likely that he will have to retire.
>
> You must cease this nonsense and pull yourself together. I am happy that you have recuperated so well from your illness, but this is all the more reason why you should understand my present burdens and co-operate with my plans for us all.

You are now eighteen, my dear Dorothy, and I expect from you the support of a grown-up daughter. Remember that you have brought upon yourself this separation from your family. You must bear your troubles with fortitude, as indeed I try to do. Olwyn, too, has been brave and helpful, though not at all well.

Of my plans for Daddy's convalescence, more later. In the meantime, I expect you to behave like a lady, and my daughter, even though your circumstances may not be entirely to your liking. These people have not had your advantages. You must make allowances at all times.

Cushie, examining the letter, could see where, now and again, the fine nib of her mother's pen had dug into the paper.

She's still angry with me. She doesn't want to see me. Yet I've been away so long!

She read the letter over and over again, and the words stabbed into her heart. How long, how long? Grown-up? She felt no different from the way she had when she was twelve, except then she had been happy and now she was wretched. She longed for relief from this nagging pain and emptiness. But the brandy bottle was almost empty.

'I have to have something,' she thought in desperation. Something to help me stick it out till things get better. What does it matter if Mama wouldn't approve? There are so many things she doesn't seem to understand.'

Vividly she recalled her mother's disdain of the drunken men who sometimes lurched along the streets in Kingsland – spew on their chins, their eyes unseeing, faces varnished crimson.

'It's because they wanted to shut life out, Mama. They couldn't cope with life somehow. Like me, Mama.'

She went downstairs. Iris was preparing a meal.

'Well?' she said. Cushie knew Iris had noticed the letter from Kingsland arrive.

She said, in as indifferent a voice as she could produce, 'She wants me to stay here. My father seems more ill than I thought. But I suppose if you and Aunt Claudie want me to go . . . if you write . . .'

'Neither of us wants you to go. We're just sorry you haven't been happier here.' She turned down the gas to a ring of azure dots, sighed. 'Have you thought of going to your other relatives, your Grandmother Jackaman?'

Cushie shook her head. 'My mother made me promise not to let them know I was in Sydney, and I truly don't want to worry Granny.'

Iris nodded. 'Well, let's sit down in the dining-room and try to sort things out. Yes, come on – you can't dodge everything, damn you!'

She seized Cushie's arm and propelled her into the little room, sat her down. 'Sit there and shut up. And don't come the little lady with me. A drunk is no longer a little lady, and that's what you're promising to be.'

Cushie flushed, tried to speak, hung her head.

Iris continued. 'You think I can't possibly understand how you feel, about your boy especially; but I do, and so does Claudie. It's just that we're old enough to know that nothing lasts, not even misery, or the feeling you've been let down and nobody loves you and the end of the world has come. By the time you're twenty you'll have forgotten all this.'

Cushie shook her head.

'I'm telling you that's the way it is. You kids never listen, that's the trouble. No matter how bad you feel, time marches on, and the day comes when you won't even be able to remember Jackie's face.'

Cushie gazed at her in dumb misery.

'It's hard to believe, isn't it? It's more romantic to think you're the centre of a tragedy, like someone in a play, and that your whole life is finished. But life isn't like that. It's self-mending, if you let it be. Claudie's had her troubles, worse ones than you know exist, and so have I. I was married once, and my husband left me. And I had two little boys who both died in one week during the big 'flu in 1918. Eight and six they were. I took a dose of chloral, but it didn't do the trick, and I'm glad now. And then I went into hairdressing, and I met Claudie, and I began to feel happy again.'

'You're not happy,' said Cushie abruptly. She looked straight at the older woman, saw her eyelids flicker. Then Iris grinned.

'Well, it doesn't matter about that: contentment, happiness, who knows the difference? I just want to tell you nothing's worth drinking yourself silly for. Sure, booze deadens your troubles for a while, but it cures nothing. And it'll ruin your looks and your health, sure as eggs are eggs.'

She put out a hand and gently lifted Cushie's chin. The girl did not pull away, and looked fleetingly at the woman – a glance of such sad incomprehension that Iris sighed.

'Ah, girl, I'm not even alive for you, am I? Just an older woman, butting in where I'm not wanted, embarrassing you, and all for nothing.'

'I know you mean to be kind,' muttered Cushie, hanging her head. 'And I'm sorry about the little boys. I didn't know.'

Iris nodded. 'Well, no more then. But promise you won't hit the bottle any more? Word of honour?' But before Cushie could answer she said, 'Anyway, Claudie and I have agreed that not a drop more of the stuff will come into the house while you're here: so you're euchred, kiddo.'

'But that will mean that you and Aunt Claudie won't be able to have a drink if you want it.'

'Do us good.'

'Liar,' thought Cushie.

She knew that Claudie at least would not go without alcohol; it would be hidden somewhere around the house. The frequent quarrels between her and Iris were sharpened and precipitated by drink. How quickly Cushie had learnt to recognise it in their voices! She did not care how things were between the two women, but she learnt from the nagging, the complaints, that Claudie was fed up with everything, wanted to go away for a little fling. Yet Iris was desperate that Claudie should not go away. Why? Cushie could not think of a single reason why a sensible, self-sufficient woman like Iris Pauley should want to continue an association with the flighty Claudie.

The protests of 'You're smothering me, Iris!' made no sense to Cushie.

Cushie was clumsy and speechless in the hairdressing shop. She got on Claudie's nerves so that at last she couldn't bear the girl's doing anything but sweep away hair clippings or make the tea.

But Iris did her best to keep her occupied, sending her on errands here and there to fetch supplies, to get scissors and razors sharpened in queer eyries at the top of crumbling buildings in Pyrmont and the Haymarket. So she began to learn a little of the city that lay, like a lump of irregular, time-worn stone, on the palm of a huge hand that was the blue-fingered Harbour. It was a city she had not guessed existed. On her brief holiday forays with her mother and Olwyn they had shopped only in the fashionable streets, with a cab waiting at the shop doors, the cabman ready to dart forward to take their parcels. Then afternoon-tea at Quong Tart's, and back to the Metropolitan Hotel with its palm-shadowed drawing-rooms. Cushie, sweating along precipitous back alleys, up flights of hollowed stone stairs, in and out of warehouses so tall and narrow they seemed to totter against the clouds, could have laughed at the child's idea she had had of Sydney.

The warmth and squalor of the unknown town appealed to her strangely; she felt almost happy sometimes. Perhaps this was because she often managed to have a small drink before she left. In the older women's absence she searched the house – the kitchen cupboards, under Claudie's bed, amongst the garments in the wardrobe. As she did so she was amazed at herself, her lack of shame.

She was very crafty at taking the smallest amount from the bottle when she found it, and putting things back exactly as they had been, so that Claudie or Iris could never be sure whether the bottle had been touched. And it seemed that, with care, in spite of what Iris had said, an intelligent person could manage to keep a thin veil of alcohol between herself and the sharp corners of life. It was probably what Iris and Claudie themselves did, in spite of Iris's preaching.

The boom after the War that had raised gorgeous cinemas and cast up huge skeletons of electric posters everywhere, that had put plate-glass windows on shops, and tramlines where none had been before, had not changed the Victorian character of the city. A flood of new cement-rendered cottages, gaunt as bones, had washed up to the feet of tall old schools with bell-towers and pillared porticoes; terra-cotta Town Halls decorative as jelly moulds; churches with crocheted spires filled with silent, rusted bells. Along beaches white as sugar, jerry-built follies had sprouted.

The city was rich, bursting, coarse as old sacking, a sandstone city that seemed to have cast up stalagmites of its own substance, coloured with the sun. Its traffic clanged like beaten bronze, and its heart, lying athwart an entire block like some vast beached vessel, was Jackaman's Emporium.

Once or twice Cushie had gone there, almost timorously. The place was like a city in itself, full of clatter and light, the pneumatic change-carriers whizzing above the customers' heads on a network of electric wires centred above the cashiers' ornate brass cages. It was hard for the girl to realise that her great-grandfather had created this incredible monster, and that her own aunt Australia Jackaman had built it into a store larger and more modern than anything in the southern hemisphere.

One boiling January day, during the autumn sales, she did indeed see Australia, in a costume of grey linen and a brimless hat with a veil pinned with a diamond, hasten across the ground floor, glancing sharply at this and that, and throwing an occasional comment to a man secretary who made notes on a pad.

Cushie, fearful of being seen, shrank back into a rack of house-dresses, turning her face away. And a woman beside her said excitedly, 'Did you see that? That was Miss Jackaman, who owns the shop. They say she's worth millions. Skinny thing!'

The sight of her Aunt Australia reminded Cushie of her grandmother, her sagging face, her fat, liver-spotted hands. Grandmother lived in Balmain, near the water, in a house she would not leave, though the district was running down and becoming industrial. Often Cushie longed to see that loving, commonplace old Grandmother Jackaman; the very thought of her was comforting, healing. But how could she put her burdens on that old woman?

Some deprivation or distress must have shown on her face, for the woman who had spoken to her of Australia Jackaman looked at her suspiciously and then moved away quickly, an extraordinary expression on her face.

When Cushie caught sight of herself in a mirror she saw that

196

her top blouse button was undone, and her hat was crooked. She tried to pull herself together, but her fingers felt numb. She had drunk too much of the bottle of port wine she had found hidden in Aunt Claudie's wash-jug, and now she was going to disgrace herself in public. Cold sweat ran down her back. That woman must have smelt the wine on her breath.

Who could have guessed that wine was so intoxicating? Her father had a small glass of it every night after dinner, for medical reasons, and it had seemed to have no effect on him. The sheer horror of her situation rushed upon her. Her fingers would not do up the button; she could not even feel the button. Could she get to the ladies' retiring-room, hide herself in a cubicle until she felt better? She took a few steps towards the lift, and the sight of it whizzing up and down in its enclosure of whorled and twisted gilt wire made her head rock. For a frightful moment she thought she was going to be sick right there on the parquet floor.

Somehow she got to the doors; they swung in and out at her, mahogany inlaid with bright brass, waving in blasts of noise, gusts of heat, people. A voice a mile away said, 'Do you feel faint, miss?' Cushie pulled away with a feeble anger; she was terrified that someone else would smell the wine, say, 'That young lady's drunk. Did you ever!'

Her one idea was to get home to Claudie's house, hide herself. Deep inside her brain there was a small sober centre that knew just what to do to be unobtrusive, ladylike, decorous. But her body no longer took orders. She felt her hair fall down, her skirt placket split. One shoe seemed loose, as if the lace had broken. Inanimate things had turned against her. It was like black magic, or a bad dream.

Fifty yards from the shop, the late afternoon sun hammering down from a steely sky, she knew she could not do it. She could never climb on a tram, and she could never walk such a distance without collapsing. The small sober centre was screaming with fright.

Some time elapsed, full of noise, faces, people who appeared and disappeared. She became aware that six inches in front of her nose were three sweating bricks in a herringbone pattern. They were part of a wall. Roaring in her head drowned out most of what a voice was saying in her ear. With difficulty she slid her eyes sideways and saw a strange face hovering near by. It wore an expression of sentimental concern that did its best with features so curiously marked with dirt and a harsh life that it resembled a piece of crocodile skin. Cushie looked blankly at it, but it did not move away. She felt a certain remote relief that it was female. At last she thought that it might be the courteous thing to say something, so she muttered, 'I'm not at all well.'

'Course you're not, love,' said the face.

'I want to go home,' said Cushie. She thought she had better give the woman the address, but it would not come out.

'And so you shall,' said the woman. 'But first you'd better come with me and have a nice lie down. Oh, you don't look at all clever.'

'It's the heat,' said Cushie, docilely stumbling along the lane with the strange woman, who was small and decrepit, and kept glancing back over her shoulder as though the girl were a prize that someone might dart out and grab. She fell into a narrow dark passage, smelling of gas and food, and realised that she must be in the woman's house.

She said, woebegone, 'I have to go home.'

Panic rose in her; she saw a yellow old man, half-naked on a tossed bed in a room as big as a cupboard, and a young boy appeared from nowhere, picking his nose. But the panic did not last; she was not able to keep her attention on anything. It whirled away vertiginously, and so did she, with rushing watery sounds. She heard herself moaning, like a cat crying, far, far away.

At some stage she felt someone touching her breasts. She whispered, 'Jackie!' but it was not Jackie. A strange face with topaz teeth and bulging eyes leant over her, grinning. There was the sound of a blow, laughter, a yell of, 'Can't trust you a minute, you ratbag!' And then someone, the woman perhaps, was hoisting her to her feet.

When she awakened she was paralysed with cold, the sky was full of diamonds, and a policeman was shining a torch in her face.

'Come on out of that, you poor little devil. My God, what a mess you're in!'

198

She was wearing only a bodice and waist petticoat, her feet were bare, her hair fell over her face, tacky with vomit and dirt. Everything had gone, her handbag, her hat and dress, her silver chain and the watch that it suspended, her silver link belt, the white gloves and kid shoes, even the tortoiseshell clasp from her hair.

'Sleeping it off, were you? Well, a lane's no place to do it in.'

She was bundled into a vehicle of some kind. There were lights, other people; and then she was wrapped, with what appeared to be rough kindness, in a blanket. Thankfully she turned her face against a clammy stone wall and slept.

They kept the lights on all night in that place, glaring bulbs set into a concrete ceiling. Cushie woke up, lay for a while, the thin harsh blanket up to her chin, not sure whether the nightmare was continuing. She thought, dumbfounded, 'I think I'm in jail.' The following thought was, 'No, it's not possible – I'm dreaming or I'm mad.'

She kept her eyes shut, pretended to be still asleep. Meanwhile her hands travelled stealthily over her body. She wore no dress, and her chemise front was wet and smelly. Oh, God, then she had been sick, in public! She could remember nothing, except Australia Jackaman's grey hat, a lavender veil caught with a small diamond brooch. She began to sob, pulling the blanket over her head.

After a little while a hand twitched away the blanket.

'Feeling crook, dear?' inquired a hoarse voice.

A hand smoothed the matted hair from her face. 'That funny old cow Thompson is on duty: she's not too bad. You just try to stick it out till she comes around.'

Cushie did not answer, cringing in the blanket, afraid to look out. The room was filled with a confusion of sound, faintly reverberant as though in a dream. Cushie listened, trembling. The noise divided itself into strata. At the top was a muted blare of drunken singing, shouting, snoring. Then came a layer of belching, moaning, subdued intermittent chatter, punctuated ever so often by an obbligato of thin cursing, like someone dribbling. At the bottom was a faint, wretched whimper, and Cushie discovered that she herself was producing it.

The girl felt ill and wambly; her head hammered. But otherwise she seemed physically normal. If indeed she was in jail, then she had hit bottom. The daughter of Bede Moy, of the Bank, picked up half-naked, filthy, in an alley. And what had happened before that?

'I must have gone mad. Perhaps I have, perhaps this is a mental hospital.'

This freezing thought made her pluck the blanket away, sit upright, her mouth open to scream. The room was full of women, none of them taking any notice of her. It was a huge concrete chamber, like the inside of a tank, painted green, with dazzling peepholes of light in the high ceiling. It smelt of phenyl, urine, and old wet flannel. A low platform ran around the wall; women snored there, wept, lay as if dead. Near Cushie two women sat, both wearing similar bashed-in hats, chatting away, it seemed, in a mild, social manner. But after a moment or two the girl realised that each was talking to herself, droning drunkenly.

'I never missed first prize for me melon and lemon,' said one.

The other took out her dental plate, looked at it fastidiously and said, 'I got it at Paddy's Market, but it don't fit. There's knobs, lumpy bits.'

In the middle of the room a tall, fat woman, architecturally large, wearing a green tennis eyeshade and a man's khaki shirt, was sweeping the floor. She was aggressive about it, beating the broom around the limbs of lolling bodies, occasionally giving some sleeping hump a brisk crack with the handle.

The melon and lemon woman got her eyes focused momentarily said, 'That Virgie Goldsmith, real house proud, ain't she?' Ever since she moved over to this side of town she's been at it. I s'pose we ain't as posh as Darlinghurst. Regular as Epsom salts she is. Jugged every Friday, got the place spring-cleaned by Monday morning. I even seen her yell for a bucket and brush so she could do the double-you.

'Me son could bail me out, he's nicely fixed, but he won't,' said the other one, and a tear ran down her nose. She had a sick, oleaginous face with a huge dent in the middle of her forehead. A finger could have been laid in it. Cushie wondered how it had been done. It looked like the result of a hatchet blow in infancy. But the woman seemed all right. She turned puffed eyes on Cushie saying, 'Feeling better, love?'

'Yes, thank you,' whispered Cushie.

'Pretty little thing. New to the game, are you?'

Cushie, not knowing how to answer, withdrew into her blanket. She watched the woman sweeping, sweeping, a redoubtable figure with pink arms like legs of pork. She was a mammoth, exemplifying the nightmare unfamiliarity of this place. The inhabitants were all freaks, and so was Cushie Moy, or she wouldn't be there.

The melon and lemon woman said thickly, 'That Virgie Goldsmith, I wouldn't cross her. Not for JC himself. She's got a temper like a tiger. Six years she spent in boob for manslaughter. And look at her, going on like Mother Hubbard. You'd never guess it, would yer?

'I got a heart, you know,' she added vaguely. 'Quack at St Vincent's said I gotta take care, and I do.'

She suddenly folded up into a heap of old clothes and began to snore.

Cushie shrank away, relieved to see a stocky woman in a dark uniform enter the room through a barred door, which she locked after herself. She seemed on familiar terms with most of the inmates, chiacking this one, shaking another to consciousness, exchanging a few remarks here and there.

'You here again, Virgie? Why don't you make it permanent?'

'Aw, it makes a nice change, Tommo,' answered the large woman. 'So I'll stick to me own routine, thanks.'

'Matron,' called the scarred woman in a placatory tone, 'the new girl's come to, poor thing.'

The police matron came over to Cushie, and the large woman came too, leaning on the broom and regarding Cushie from under her eyeshade.

'What's your name, lass?'

Cushie was silent, panic-stricken.

'Don't you give matron a made-up one, now,' cautioned Virgie Goldsmith. 'Only make it worse for you. They're bound to find out, noses like ferrets, ain't that right, Tommo?'

'Butt out, will you, Virgie?' replied the woman. 'Come on, love.'

'Dorothy Moy,' whispered Cushie.

'And your age?'

'Eighteen.'

'Got anyone to bail you out?'

Cushie looked at her uncomprehendingly. In her pleasant middle-aged face was no scorn or disapproval, nothing but slight impatience.

'Better than staying in the tank all night, love,' put in the woman with the scar. 'A kid like you gotta have someone, how about your Mum?'

'There's Mrs Pauley whom I live with,' said Cushie. She gave the address in Strawberry Hills, and the police matron noted it.

'I'll mention that you need clothes. Might be a little while,' she said, moving away. Virgie remained behind; her formidable shadow fell across Cushie.

'Moy, you said your monicker was?'

Cushie made no answer, but lay down and pulled the blanket over her head. A large hand rolled her back to the light.

'Let's have a gander at you.'

Fingers hard as wood forced up her chin.

'There's a resemblance all right. Would you be Bede's kid?'

At the sound of her father's name tears filled Cushie's eyes. Instantly she knew she had given herself, and him, away. She could not look at the grotesque face bent above her, the eyes shadowed, the glossy little red mouth stuck amongst a wreath of cheeks and chins.

With one sweep of her arm, Virgie rolled the sleeping woman off the platform. She fell in a boneless heap on the floor. The scarred companion scuttered off hastily.

'Where's your dad that he's letting you get into trouble like this?'

'Kingsland,' whispered Cushie. 'But he's sick, and I'm living here in Sydney with my Aunt Claudie, Mrs List.'

'Claudie, eh?'

Cushie, hardly daring to look, was aware that the woman had pushed the tennis shade up on her head, revealing a tangle of dirty straw, and was mournfully rocking from side to side. Her neck was covered with scabs.

'Claudie, eh? Chris'sake!' The woman blew a long breath, both sad and foul. She was silent, humped over like a collapsed haystack. Cushie stole sideways looks at her. Amazing to think that she was probably about the same age as Cushie's mother. She could see no signs in her of the girl in the saucy photograph. The creature was a travesty of any kind of woman.

At last she stirred. 'I'm your father's sister. Virgie Moy's my name.'

'Yes, I know now,' whispered Cushie. 'But I never knew . . . I mean, Daddy never mentioned . . .'

'Always was a mean bugger, Bede,' said the woman. She gave a startling bellow of laughter, shouting out: 'Hey, what do you think, this kid here's my niece. And here we are, together in the same tank.'

'We all go the same way home, Virgie,' cackled a voice.

Time passed. Virgie said things. Cushie tried not to hear. She wept helplessly. Then the police matron called Cushie to the door. Unsteadily she made her way there, aware of the Stone-Age faces that stared or glared at her, Virgie following after, dragging her broom.

The redoubtable woman seemed agitated.

'No, you can't go yet, you ain't answered my questions. I got a right to know, haven't I? Graham, what about my young brother Graham?'

The door opened, and the matron took Cushie by the arm. She turned to say, 'He got killed in the War. Gallipoli.'

She did not see Virgie's face. The matron took her into her own office. She had one of Cushie's own dresses, a pair of shoes and a jacket.

'Put them on. There's a Mrs Pauley here to take you home.'

While the desk officer completed the formalities, Cushie did not look at Iris, but idly stared at the floor. She was stupid with fatigue. If Iris had turned on her with a torrent of furious words, she would just have gone on staring at the floor.

'I've a taxi waiting outside,' said Iris. 'Come on.'

Without a word between them, the two women were driven to the house in Strawberry Hills. Claudie, face swollen with tears, met them at the door.

'Oh, Dorothy, how could you? If you knew what we've been through, Iris and me, hospitals, police stations . . .'

'Just shut up, Claudie,' said Iris. 'Go to bed. No use having kittens at this hour of the morning.'

'Well,' said Claudie, shrilly, 'she has to have a bath, with plenty of Lysol. She might have picked up crabs in that awful place.'

'I'll attend to it,' said Iris.

At five, as dawn's raspberry red streaked the sky, Cushie fell into bed, subsiding into sleep as into a pool of oil.

She awoke in the early afternoon. She heard Iris or Claudie padding quietly around the house, the soft clink of china, a broom's whisper over the linoleum. She lay there for a while, forcing herself to think of the previous day. The memory of it made cold sweat come out on the palms of her hands. But she kept her attention fixed on what she could remember. It was shameful, abhorrent, squalid, but it had to be faced. Otherwise she would do it again, as those women in the concrete room did it again and again, and would continue to do it until they were found dead in a city gutter amongst the Mintie papers.

She was aware that there was a subterranean residuum from her experiences, shame, horror, disgust, something like hysterical amusement at the sheer unlikelihood of what had happened to her, These memories would grate like boulders in a dark stream, and every now and then, perhaps to the end of her life, their frightening sound would rise to humiliate her, even if it were only in dreams. But at the moment she was still numb, and able to think objectively.

Lying there, her body purged, feeble, cold, her eyes fixed unblinkingly on the yellow flicker the breathing blind threw upon the wall, she surveyed as if from a height her behaviour since she discovered that she was pregnant. She had, in effect, co-operated in creating this misery and degradation. She had used neither ingenuity nor intelligence.

To be innocent and trusting was sheer stupidity, she could see that now. It was spiritual clodhopperism. Her mother's shocking statements returned to her: they had implied, in refined words, that relations between human beings were all deceit, cruelty, self-seeking; that all humans were lice, sucking each other's blood, and that the one who dropped off before he could be squashed was the smart one.

'Iris and Claudie are like that, perhaps, and maybe my mother and father. But I'm not, and Jackie isn't, either.

'The moment I got back to Kingsland from Mount Rosa I should have gone and told Mrs MacNunn how I felt. She would have had Jackie back there as fast as lightning, and she and Mr MacNunn would have helped us to get married.'

It seemed to Cushie now that the same kind of manipulation that had put her where she was had probably been used on Jackie. He had found himself doing things and agreeing to things that were not his choice at all.

Iris glanced into the bedroom. Finding Cushie awake, she entered and stood beside the bed. She was uneasy and gruff.

'How do you feel?'

'I'm all right now. I'll get up soon.'

'You silly galoot, you had a real bun day, didn't you?'

Cushie nodded. She asked, 'What's the procedure now? With the police, I mean.'

'Nothing. Just forfeit your bail. My God, you're cool enough about it.'

'Yes, I am now,' said Cushie.

Iris seized the hand mirror, thrust it into her hands. 'Here, look at your face.'

Cushie looked. Her face was covered with a gravel rash, as though she'd been dragged along a pavement.

'You might have been murdered as well as robbed,' said Iris. 'You could have been raped even.'

Cushie looked at Iris, who quickly shook her head. 'No, I'm sure you weren't. I had a good look at your underwear before I washed it. God, we've made a rotten job of looking after you, Claudie and I.'

She looked at Cushie forlornly, angrily.

Cushie said, 'You tell me off if you want to, Mrs Pauley.'

Iris snorted. 'I'll leave that to your Aunt Claudie – she's as mad as a meat-axe. She'll eat you, bones and beak.'

'Well,' said the girl, 'you were right, anyway. About drinking, I mean. That's the end. I'll never have another drink in my whole life.'

'Ah, kid, I wish I thought you meant it.'

'I mean it. You didn't see those women. Or –' she hesitated, 'Virgie.'

Iris subsided on the bed. 'Virgie was in the tank?'

Cushie told her. Iris's face was pale and glum.

At the end she said, 'But still, even though she realised you were his niece, she doesn't know where you live.'

'I mentioned Aunt Claudie's married name,' confessed Cushie, shamefaced.

'Oh, God, why?' groaned Iris.

'It just came out,' said Cushie, and, dreading the look she knew the words would bring to Iris's face, she said, 'And she was standing next to the police matron when I had to give your address.'

'Damn you!' yelled Iris, and she rushed out of the room.

Ten minutes later, as Cushie was creeping feebly into her clothes, she heard the front door slam. When she hobbled downstairs to make herself a cup of tea, she found a letter from her mother propped up on the sideboard.

Her mother said that because Daddy's condition had not improved, she had made up her mind to sell the house in Edward Street and accept Uncle Titus Jackaman's wonderful invitation to live indefinitely with him in London. Olwyn was so excited, was packing already, and looking forward to all the fun of the month's voyage. Cushie was to remain with her Aunt Claudie until the family came to Sydney.

Cushie put aside the last pages. She began at once a letter to her mother:

> I don't want to go to London. For one thing I hated Uncle Titus, and for another, if Daddy is as ill as you say, I don't think he ought to be dragged off on such a long trip. I'm old enough now to have a say in these things and not be treated as if I were eight. So I won't be coming with you, and neither will I remain here with Aunt Claudie. I am going to Grandmama's house to see if she will allow me to stay with her. I am sure I can be useful to her, and I like her almost better than anyone. I know I promised you, Mama, but things have changed. And please don't call me Cushie any more. My name is Dorothy.

As she sealed and stamped the letter a strange cold pain seemed to strike her heart, as if she were her mother reading it. For a second her hands hovered over the envelope as though to tear it up. Then she thought, 'She won't care. It's not as if I were Olwyn.'

She posted the letter. As she returned to the house, she glanced over at the salon. It was closed, though usually open until six on Saturday. Somewhere Iris and Claudie were talking things over.

They had been quarrelling. When they came in after seven, Iris's cheeks were blotchy and her light eyes fixed in a stare of distress. Claudie was blazing, pushing chairs around, kicking off one shoe to the ceiling. Cushie stood up, as though she expected her aunt to fly at her, punch her with both fists. She felt the old pang of horror at hostility, then said to herself, 'She can't kill me.'

'What did you have to tell Virgie my married name for, you rotten little beast?'

'Oh, Claudie,' remonstrated Iris, 'she was squiffy. I don't suppose she knew what she was saying.'

'It just slipped out,' said Cushie. 'I'm very sorry, truly.'

'Sorry, sorry, sorry, my eye!' shouted Claudie, hammering the table. She had bared her lower teeth like a fighting cat; her glassy eyes glittered. 'You've meant nothing but trouble ever since you came here. Ohhhhh!' She gave a long wail. 'I don't want Virgie to come here, I don't want to have anything to do with her. She reminds me of awful things I want to forget.'

'Oh, Bubby, don't be so silly. She might not remember your name, or the address. And even if she did, why would she want to look you up?'

'Because she used to love me,' said Claudie. 'And she might love me again and I don't want to be loved by anyone, I just want to have fun. I keep telling you, Iris, but you won't listen.'

The older woman looked as though she had been stabbed.

'If she comes here I'm going away,' shouted Claudie. 'You've got to get it into your head, Iris, I'm not going to live anywhere where that great boozy wreck can come and pester me. I don't want anything to do with her, and I won't, either.'

'You're only using Virgie for an excuse, aren't you?' said Iris huskily. She covered her face with her hands and began to weep, hackingly, like an old woman. Claudie glared accusation at Cushie.

'This is all your fault, you stupid big lump.'

The sound and sight of her friend's tears brightened her at once. She put her arms around Iris, stroking her hair, making cooing noises. 'Of course I won't go away and leave Ikey, not unless nasty Virgie comes. You keep Virgie away from me, and I'll stay, I promise, Ikey.'

Iris nodded, her hands clenching. For the first time she seemed to Cushie not strong at all – an uncertain lost person, in spite of all her brisk ways.

On the Sunday evening Cushie left her aunt's house in a taxi.

Iris carried out the last of her luggage. 'Are you sure you have enough money? It's a long way to Balmain.'

Cushie nodded. Iris gave her hand a quick strong squeeze.

'I hope everything's all right for you. Be sure to drop us a line and let us know.'

'Yes, I shall.'

The cab moved away slowly down the narrow street, congested even on Sunday. The late sunset fell upon snail-grey slates and old brown bricks, turned them cinnabar and plum-coloured; the windows of a passing tram flashed like mirrors. Cushie put out her hand, and a rosy blob lit upon it for a moment, like a moth. It was like life returning to her hold.

Down near Central Railway she saw an immensely tall, immensely fat woman, drunk as a lord, shove a man out of her way. He stumbled a step or two, toppled like a falling log. Cushie saw other pedestrians scatter hastily. The woman's face was crimson, not only with the sunset but with glowering temper.

'Stop, stop!' cried Cushie.

'Can't stop here, darl,' said the driver. 'Use your loaf, dear.'

But he slowed down, creeping towards the kerb. Craning through the rear window, Cushie saw that Virgie was tacking up Elizabeth Street. For a moment she thought that she must insist that the driver turn somehow, go back, so that she could warn Claudie and Iris. But what good would that do? Virgie was not her problem. She began to shake. She could not afford to go through another dreadful scene; she had to get away while she was strong enough to do so.

'Come on, miss,' cried the driver, jumping in his seat with impatience. 'What you want to do?'

'Just drive on,' said Cushie. 'I think I made a mistake.'

4

Jackie Hanna

1924-1929

4

Maida and Jackie were married in a church full of angry light from a western window. There was a parson with a face of iron, a smell of sodden dust. The witnesses were the parson's downy-chinned sister and a woman who had been scrubbing the church. The latter could not take her eyes off Jackie, and at the end of the ceremony she shot out her swollen paw and touched him lightly on the back of the neck. Blind Hof, who had stood like a statue behind the bride and groom, struck her hand away.

'They say it's lucky,' she mumbled, and, frightened by the inhuman jerk of his dead eye, did not look at any of them again.

Hof had booked the young couple in at the Royal Hotel, which stood like a spectre on the waterfront. He himself had taken a room in a boarding-house somewhere.

'Leaving at first light,' he said. 'It'll be all the old lorry can manage to get me there in time for the funeral. So I'll say good-bye now.'

Maida said wistfully, 'Won't you just have tea with us, Hof? Seems funny, you going off like this by yourself.'

But he wouldn't. He stood there a moment, the huge gaunt man, as though wishing to say something but having no words for it. The opaque lavender eye twitched.

'Maida, you do the right thing now,' he said. 'You're lucky, you are.' Maida bowed her head. Tears glinted in her eyes, and Jackie realised that the girl, too, had left all that was familiar to her, was at his mercy, as the old woman was at the mercy of her brutal wheelwright and his brutal sons.

He said, 'I'm sorry about your grandfather, Hof. He was a good old man.'

Hof nodded abruptly and strode away. Jackie turned and took Maida's cold hand.

'We'll make a go of it, Maida,' he said.

She smiled. 'I know we will. It's just that – I hope Ellie will be all right, when my father gets there, I mean. He couldn't stand up to him if – ' She stopped, seemed to gain control of herself. 'Well, that's all behind me now. It's just you and me, Jackie, from now on.'

The bar and front parlour of the Royal Hotel were full of people peering through the windows at the pale girl and the queer little dwarf who stood out front. Greedily they pointed out to each other the fading bruises on Maida's face, the youth of her husband.

'But you can't tell,' said the knowing. 'Them dwarves look the same for years. He might be thirty, forty; there's no being sure.'

'Don't you think he looks knocked-about, too?' asked another.

'Been in a fight prob'ly. They got fiendish tempers.'

Most of these Duchess Bay people had never seen a dwarf before and were brazen in their curiosity. Jackie was used to stares, but the concentration of the Royal Hotel's habitués made him squeeze Maida's hand as they entered through the corner door, under the ceiling of embossed tin, and saw the heads sticking out the doors.

'Don't mind,' he said.

Maida's face flushed crimson. She lifted her head abruptly and gave the poking faces a searing stare, so that they retreated with subdued chatter.

She looked down at Jackie. 'Never you say that again,' she said. A certain power glistened suddenly in her sad eyes, and with amazement Jackie recognised it as anger.

The bedroom was a queer shape, with cut-off corners and deep recesses containing tallboys and wardrobes with wedges of yellow newspaper under their corners, and doors and drawers that wouldn't open. There was highly polished oilcloth with no pattern left, and an extremely narrow strip of dirty Turkey carpet. The bed was covered with a thin white honeycomb quilt, the blankets worn and harsh.

214

'I wish I could have brought you to a better place,' said Jackie, wistfully.

His wife sat down before the window, took the pins from her hair. Slowly she brushed it, it meanwhile turning deep yellow and ruddy in the ominous light from the west. To Jackie she looked strange and very beautiful, and he crossed to her and pressed his cheek against her cool one.

'Maida, everything will be all right, you'll see,' he said. 'We're young; we'll make a go of it.'

She undid her blouse, and put his hand on her breast. It was already swollen a little, warm and lush, waiting for the child. But Jackie felt a child himself, bereft of all he knew, desolate, and for the first time in his life afraid of the future.

As they went down for their evening meal, the cheerful male burr of voices from the bar faltered and stopped, and they were aware that thrilled eyes were noting every detail of their appearance. But in the cold, cabbage-smelling dining-room, the other guests, few, aged, and vague-looking, studiously stared at their plates. The waitress dithered, her eyes constantly straying from her notebook to rest greedily on Jackie's face and form. And although he had been through this ordeal many times before he realised that he cared more this time, for Maida's sake.

Ah, it was not only for Maida's sake! With doleful certainty the sensation the Linz Brothers had aroused in him – that his outer skin had been taken away, and he was vulnerable to the closest and most satiric observation – returned. He felt the eyes, the mutters, the smiles sharp as knives, and cold shock swept over him. Had it always been like this: the personality so lovingly nurtured by his mother and the Nun so frail and brittle that it could not last away from his familiar environment? He straightened up, ate his soup carefully, aware of the resentful stare Maida returned to their audience.

'Don't give them the satisfaction,' he murmured, and Maida nodded.

'Clods,' she said. 'A new dog in the town would be a sensation to them.'

That night, in their chill, disinfectant-smelling bed, she took him with silent passion, and he accepted it as silently, with humble joy. Yet he could not sleep, and after Maida had turned away into slumber he got up and went to the windows, which opened onto a small balcony littered with leaves and bird-dirt. The moonlight held all in bond, bleached and austere. Jackie could hear, far away, the flat sea plodding in and out, dragging its pebbles after it.

He tried to raise his spirits by telling himself he was at last near the ocean; but all the knowledge did was to bring back the last hour he had spent with Cushie, so long ago, it seemed.

'You know I've never seen the sea,' he had mumbled into her neck. 'I often dream of it, the sea,' he had said.

Once again Jackie saw, clear as a picture, those dreams where the water ran in long convolutions of mica upon wide sands that no one ever trod, not even ocean birds.

'We'll live beside it some day, won't we, Jackie? All by ourselves.'

'Yes, we will.'

There were a million things to tell Cushie. Even now he wanted to tell her about the Linzes, about Maida.

Though he had not seen her that fatal day on Ghinni station, his knowledge of Cushie was so complete that his imagination was as clear as a memory. As though he had indeed seen it, he could imagine her face looking out of the express window, borne away, growing smaller, vanishing. The puzzlement, the disappointment on that face! And as he realised that very probably he would never see Cushie Moy again a pure and particularised pain went through him. It was the pain of bereavement, of deepest loss, not only of Cushie but of his entire life until now; for both consciously and unconsciously it had been woven in and out of hers.

His eyes prickled; he felt as if his entire being were breaking up.

He clung to the railing, his little hands on the top bar, his forehead pressed against the second. The lights of a home-going car discovered him, and he saw down below on the street a man and woman patiently waiting, hoping for a glimpse of him, and now richly satisfied that they had caught him spread-eagled against the balcony rails like a monkey.

His mother and stepfather had taught him to be a person superior to misfortune, but it did not seem as though he were. The circumstances of the past few months had bundled him away from his desired pattern of life with the utmost ease, as though he were a child, or a helpless animal. Panic filled him. It struck him suddenly that all the delights of his past had likewise been imaginary.

But Cushie had loved him, there was no denying that. She had always loved him, and perhaps loved him still. Sooner or later she would find out that he had married, and at the thought of the pain and bewilderment inflicted on her defenceless heart his eyes filled with tears.

All his life he had taken her beauty for granted, her docility and kindness as though they were his due. But nothing was his due. Anything good that life ever gave him was a gift, and nothing else.

'But at the last I knew, Cushie,' he thought in bitter pain. 'I was beginning to know.'

Maida's shadow fell across the moonlight.

'Jackie, come to bed now.'

In bed she took him in her arms. 'Are your eyes red?'

Dumbly he nodded against her shoulder. 'Things will look better tomorrow and the next day. Go to sleep, now. I'll look after you, Jackie.'

Exhausted, he sank into the warmth of her arms and slept.

Some time during that night, it seemed to Jackie afterwards, his subconscious mind accepted the fate that seemed to be his, and he awakened truly Maida's husband. He looked at her sleeping face, and thought, 'Hof didn't tell me to do the right thing, but I will. I'll look after her and she'll never regret it.'

But he wished he were older, with more knowledge of the world, and men and women.

The morning awoke like a child, opening clear eyes that did not remember the night. Jackie watched the light falling like silk on Maida's clothes, hung on the back of a chair. He had been amazed at the coarseness of her garments, the calico bodice, black lisle stockings, a petticoat with home-made crocheted edgings. Out of these dowdy wrappings the beauty and fragility of her body had emerged – her white legs with blue veins showing, her wing-like shoulderblades, her child's elbows, a little grubby and callused on the points. These elbows, and her thin battered hands, touched Jackie.

He thought, 'Just as soon as we get settled on the Dovey, I'll send to Sydney for an Anthony Hordern catalogue, and she can pick out some pretty duds for herself.'

At the thought of her delight, he rubbed his feet up and down her knees, and blew softly on her nose. She awoke yawning, and he told her about the catalogue. She was wide awake instantly, ecstatic.

'Oh, Jackie, could we truly? And I could give my size and they'd send them in the colours I wanted and everything?'

He laughed. 'Don't you know anything, you little country bumpkin?'

'I don't think I do. You'll have to tell me everything.'

'Right,' said Jackie. 'Let's get up and have a look around this place.'

'I like it when you're bossy,' she said. For an instant her bosom was supended above him. He breathed her like a flower. 'I love you, Jack,' she said for the first time.

Now that Jackie's innate good humour had reasserted itself, the bedroom at the Hotel Royal seemed to him comical. Everything was immensely tall, and Jackie could scarcely reach a thing. He had to stand on a suitcase to wash his face at the basin. Even then he could see only the top of his rumpled hair in the age-darkened mirror.

When he sat in the armchair his legs stuck straight out and Maida had to tug him out of it.

'It's a room for giants,' Maida said.

'They must get a lot of giants,' he replied. Their stifled giggles disturbed the guest next door, and he banged sleepily on the wall, groaning, 'Shurrup. Shurrup! Gaw'sakes!'

They crept down the wooden stairs, past tall palm-stands filled with grimy paper ferns, sand, and cigarette-butts. The hall below had a dado of dirty handprints. From the kitchen came the sound of crockery.

'Early morning tea,' said Jackie. 'Let's get out quick.'

Duchess Bay had been a popular watering-place in Edwardian times, but the new highway from Ghinni Junction had left it to die on the beach. Their footsteps echoed in the empty, sandy main street with the beat of a funeral drum. Nobody was about except a milkman who drove past and almost fell out of his cart looking back at them.

They stood above the long beach that was like an empty esplanade. The hugeness of the sea awed them.

'I'm glad we're seeing it together for the first time,' Jackie said.

'I never dreamed,' said Maida. 'Not as big as this! And I thought it would be a different blue, like Theo's shaving mug.'

The waves pranced, light in their manes. They ran up to Jackie's feet and scratched at the gravel. The sound of a buoy away out near the heads was a crack in the silence, man's signpost. Weeds bellied in the water, anchored shadows.

'If I lived here,' she said, 'I'd be looking at it all the time. And that smell in the air!'

'We'll come back here,' promised Jackie. 'The baby will have to be born here, I suppose.'

Reluctantly they turned away.

'Guess we'd better have a look at the town before the cream boat bloke comes.'

Maida was impressed by the extravagant style of the buildings, with their cupolas, fretworked porches, windows shaded with wooden awnings in faded circus colours. They were all empty, scuttled, the cupolas streaked with white dribbles from seabirds, or red runnels from rusting nails, the windows boarded up or smashed, the porches filled with stinking hillocks of garbage, broken bottles, old bicycles, and wet paper.

Here and there smashed electric light bulbs spelled out half a word over a dangling door: Mon Rep ... Lingalonga ... Bellev ... Seavi ... Cr.ter.on.

'It's spooky,' said Jackie. Yet the sun blazed down, the sea wind was full of enlivening dampness, at the end of a side street gulls snow-stormed in a nervous spiral.

There was a pier slumping at the end of that street. It had been fenced off. There was a sign saying: 'Dangerous. Condemned.' But the fence had rotted away, leaving a gap, and on the end of the pier was a man cleaning fish and throwing the guts in the water.

Along one side of the pier were boarded-up booths that had sold fish and chips and gingerpop, a shooting gallery, a shoot the chute which had collapsed into a tangle of grids and twisted iron, a bathhouse whose scabbed wall bore the sign: 'Ladies Wednesdays and Fridays. Attendant.'

Stray cats sat around the man, hooking away a head or a fin, hoicking with flattened heads and convulsing sides over bones. The gulls screeched and battled amongst the offal in the water.

The man did not seem interested in Jackie's size. He nodded, saying, 'Heard you was in town . . . heard you was married yesterday. Funny place to come for a honeymoon.'

'We're going to Dovey River,' offered Jackie. 'We're going to be picked up today.'

'Duchess Bay's dead as a doornail,' said the man, ripping a fish from vent to gill. 'It's like a shipwreck, a mile of rubbish on the beach. Who's picking you up, did you say?'

'Mr Morgan,' said Maida.

'He runs the cream boat,' said Jackie.

'Know him well,' said the fisherman, putting his hand in the fish's belly and with one skilful tug taking out all that had made it live and breed. 'A bit sawney. Brought up on the Nelly Morgan Lighthouse. A real decent joker, Lufa.'

'I'll be working with him,' said Jackie. His spirits rose. He was joyfully relieved to think he'd be working with a decent joker.

About ten in the morning Lufa Morgan arrived in a rattle-trap Ford. He had left the Dovey long before daylight, he said.

Jackie liked the look of him at once. He was a young, turnip-coloured man, with sandy hair in tight crinkles over his skull. He wore a grey flannel shirt and his pants were belted with electrical flex. He climbed down from the truck, stretched, said, 'Well, there ain't too much of you, that's for sure. You got plenty of muscle, Jack? Because them cream cans ain't featherweights.'

Lufa saw Maida shyly standing amongst their luggage on the veranda of the Royal Hotel. He pulled off his hat.

'Didn't see you there, missus. How are you?'

'Very well, thank you,' said Maida. 'When do we start back?'

She gave Lufa a smile. Jackie could see that she liked him. Lufa squinted at the sun.

'Pretty soon. You folk ready? Hope the lorry ain't too rough for you, missus. The track's wicked, part of the way.'

There was room for all three of them in the huge crate of the lorry cabin.

Not three miles out of Duchess Bay the road became a dirt droving track, following long slow grades as though the cattle mobs had marked it out themselves. The country was so dry the road was the colour of dried blood; it was speckled by stones that gave off sparks and twinkles. It was the pyrites, Lufa said.

Redgums with barkless, glowing flesh leant over dry creek-beds. Here and there ravenous sheep clustered like flies about a clotted pond.

'We've had some bad seasons,' said Lufa. 'Squatters all whinging. But down on the Dovey there's good feed. You'll see.'

Jackie asked how it was that Lufa had agreed to give him a job on the cream boat.

'Well, it's a case of blood being thicker than water, you see. Mrs Jack here now, she's a Linz, right? Well, my old mum was a Schneider, and her mother was the eldest Linz girl, one of old Martin's heifers. So we're kind of cousins.'

'Did you know he died two days ago – Grandpa?' asked Maida.

'No!' Lufa pulled a face of shock and melancholy. 'That's too bad. Fine old fellow, so I've heard. Well, that's the way of things. Didn't wait for the funeral then?'

'Everything was all arranged with you,' said Jackie, 'and Maida's brother, Hof that is, thought we'd better stick to it. He drove us down from High Valley yesterday.'

At midday Lufa pulled in the lorry under an overhanging bluff of stone, saying, 'There's a waterhole here. We can freshen up. You two want to wander off, it's down that way. I'll get a fire going, and we'll have a drink o' tea and some tucker.'

Maida said, ashamed, that they could have brought food from Duchess Bay; but Lufa had a tuckerbox, and cheerfully said he could feed a football team.

The two young people went down the way he pointed, and found amongst casuarinas a deep green pool. The soft mud at its brink was marked with paws of wallabies, possums, even the small handprints of lizards. Jackie took off his clothes and leapt in. Maida took off everything but her petticoat. She was very modest, and Jackie had never yet seen all her body at once. She said of the petticoat, 'It'll dry on the bush afterwards. I'll put it on again before we leave after we've had our meal.'

The water was deep and cold, bubbling around their legs as they swam, welling up out of a crack in the earth.

Maida slicked back her wet hair, tied it with a ribbon from her bodice. She looked a child.

'Mr Morgan's nice, isn't he?' she said. 'He'll be good to work with. A change from my brothers.'

Jackie kissed her. 'I feel different somehow, as though everything will turn out all right.'

Lufa had a fire crackling, a billy over it on a green branch. He was holding a frying-pan in which eggs and bacon danced.

'I'll take care of that,' said Maida. 'You go and have a dip. It's lovely.'

'You got a real little bush girl here, eh, Jack?' said Lufa. 'I'll just have a rinse. Be back before the billy boils.'

In early afternoon they came in sight of the Dovey. It was a wide, bankless river, dawdling over the flats, spreading out into complexes of lagoons and swamps dappled with auburn and sallow green. Fuzzy, fawn-coloured grassland marked the cleared pasture, but the larger part of the countryside was still under bush. Scrub already delustred by summer stood in strongholds at the water's edge. Long sandy islands lay here and there in the Dovey, the diverted current showing as giant wishbones in the stream.

'Well, there she is,' said Lufa with pride. 'She goes right out to the coast, and if you look where I'm pointing you'll see the lighthouse at her mouth.'

'I do see!' said Maida. 'Tall . . . painted white!'

'Yep. That's the Nelly Morgan. Named for my mum, she was. That's where yours truly was born, in the middle of a storm, and a freighter straddled on the bar, and me dad trying to get the crew off on a flying-fox.'

'Tell us about it,' said Jackie.

'Nope. Some other time. I gotta concentrate on getting you people down to the river and settled in your shack before dark. Have to warn you, it ain't Buckingham Palace.'

He was a simple man; the world was small for him, but he was satisfied with it. Maida, sitting between him and Jackie, her legs disposed behind the gears, could see his flat leather cheek, marked with a thousand lines as fine as hairs. He gave off a good odour of sunshine, wood smoke, and a natural man smell of cleanliness and health. She gave a long sigh of contentment.

'Tired, missus, eh?'

'A bit,' she replied, 'and you better call me Maida.'

'Too right I will, if young Jack there don't mind. So you two only been married six months, eh?'

Jackie nudged Maida. 'How did you know that, Lufa?' he asked.

'Hof mentioned it when he wrote. He writes a good letter, the old Hof. Couldn't read it meself, course. Never got any schooling. But I took it into Keever's and Pop Keever read it to me. Keever's is one of our call-ins, Jack, for the cream, I mean.'

'I'm looking forward to working with you,' said Jack. 'When do you want me to start?'

Lufa slid a teasing glance sideways. 'Tomorrow at sun-up too soon?'

'No,' said Jack. 'Ready any time.'

In westering sunlight the truck drew up beside a toppling line of wire, an overgrown foot track that led to a small humpy with a tin chimney. A tarpaulin was pulled over the roof and weighted with stones.

'We sometimes get some big blows from the coast,' explained Lufa. 'But she's watertight at the moment.'

He bumped open the unpainted door with one of their suitcases, marched in.

'Phew, she's stale!' He opened a window by main force, propped it open with a sauce bottle lying near by.

'Now, don't get your tails down, kids. You'll get it fixed up to your liking in no time. There's plenty wood out the back, and a quart of kerosene. I cleaned and filled the lamps yesterday.

There's matches there.'

''You've thought of everything. Thank you very much,' said Maida sincerely.

'I done better than that,' said Lufa with delight. He threw open the musty meat-safe. 'I got sugar, and tea, and some condensed, and bread, and some tins of sardines and stuff.'

'You shouldn't have . . . oh, it'll be plenty!' said Maida. 'And we'll have to fix you up for all of that very soon.'

'Nope,' said Lufa. 'A little welcome like. And tomorrow when me and Jack call in at Wininnie Bend down the river he can get any extra stores you need at the general store.'

He took them to the door. 'See there now – behind them she-oaks, that's my shack. So if any bunyips come up outa the Dovey in the night, Jack, and scare the tripes outa Maida, you can give me a whistle and I'll bring up the rabbit rifle.'

They saw the truck grind away towards the she-oaks.

'Oh, Jackie,' said Maida, 'isn't he kind? I never met anyone like him.' She was silent a moment. 'But then I don't know any men except Father and my brothers, and the pickers and all . . . and I was never allowed to have anything to do with them.'

Jackie, too, was impressed by Lufa's naturalness and neigh-bourliness. He said, 'He reminds me of my dad. I reckon that if my dad had a son of his own, he'd have been like Lufa.'

The little cottage was cranky with age and weather. When Jackie held the lamp close to the wall, he saw that it was papered with old sheets of the *Bulletin*, most of them dated long before the War. The bed was of planks laid across a box-like base, the mattress stuffed with springy vines instead of kapok. Maida brought out their blankets, made them a nest.

'We can fix things up, just like Lufa said. Curtains. I'll make a rag mat. We can Kalsomine the walls. It'd take on that paper . . . Now let's have our supper.'

After the meal Jackie went outside to fill the kerosene-tin bucket with water from the tank. A gush of mud and rust, then the water ran clearly but reluctantly. He left it to trickle, straightening up and trying to still himself inwardly so that the natural voices of this new countryside should make themselves heard.

He heard the gruffly breathing ocean far away, miles away for all he knew. Closer he heard night birds, solitarily commenting on the late moon. There was also the secret sound of heavy dew dripping like sweat or blood. To the east the beam of the lighthouse fanned rapidly across the sky.

Contentment filled Jackie, something quite new and calm. This would do. It was better than what he had had since he left Kingsland so few weeks before. The turmoil would be over for a time.

He took the brimming bucket and went inside. Maida was undressing for bed, looking vexed.

'I left my petticoat!' she said. 'On that bush where I spread it to dry.'

'You won't need any petticoats here,' he said.

But she would not be comforted, and at last he said, 'Lufa goes into Duchess Bay sometimes. We'll tell him to look for it.'

She said, 'It was getting a bit tight, because of the baby; but I could have let it out. Well, never mind, perhaps it will still be there when Lufa goes back to the waterhole.'

They snuggled around each other, the baby between them. It was as if they shared the same air, the same life-warmth. They forgot where one's skin ended and the other began.

'We're just like two possums,' said Jackie.

'I never, never want to leave here,' said Maida. He felt her body tremble with her intensity, but he was too far gone in sleep to answer.

The place where they lived on the Dovey had no real name, but people round about called it Morgan's Clearing. There Lufa had lived since his mother died and his father went off into an old men's home down towards Sydney. The old man couldn't write, and Lufa couldn't read, so Lufa hadn't an idea in his head whether his father was still alive.

'But I guess so,' he said. 'Tough as old boots, like me.'

Lufa was a lone man, completely self-dependent, unselfconscious as a stone. He lived amongst the she-oaks in a ham-handed shack that had been built by the previous owner of the cream boat. In this dwelling everything was a fraction off true, with doors that would not open and windows that were reluctant to be shut. It was a frightful rats'-nest of old clothing, rusty tools, frying-pans full of congealed fat. Every so often even Lufa got sick of it, and he lived for a week or two on the cream boat, sleeping in a blanket on the flat deck, cooking on a primus, playing his fiddle, being himself.

Then, strengthened, he would return to the shack, jam the overflow of the rats'-nest into a sugar-sack, and dump it in the deepest part of the channel.

Lufa belonged to that enormous tidal river as a reed or a black swan might belong, and when the cyclic pulse of the sea sent its sheets of silk sliding above the slack current, sometimes to overlap the low, mangroved banks, Lufa felt revivified. The spraddling jetties, the raft-like islands of the delta complex, the farmhouses half-seen through river gums and casuarinas, were sufficient of the world for him. Though occasionally he had to go to Duchess Bay for petrol and stores, he hated it. The decaying hamlet made him uneasy; it was too big, too noisy.

He had no clock but a sun-mark scratched on a windowsill, a diagonal line pointing inwards from the edge. When the shadow of a certain redgum fell on the mark, he knew it was noon.

'But it only works in winter, and buggerall on a rainy day,' confessed Lufa. But he did not need a clock. He awakened automatically when the lighthouse was turned off at clear daylight.

That first night, after he had slept for some hours, Jackie awoke to find the cottage filled with gliding brightness. He rose and went outside. Darkness, darkness, absorbent as black blotting-paper, without a star or water-glimmer. Then suddenly the Nelly Morgan flailed its beam across the bush, the sea, the long reefs, brushing the clouds, the Dovey, the swarthy scrub, with swift light. It was a great wheel, spoked with light, turning for ever in the universal blackness, and its majestic regularity buoyed up Jackie's heart.

He thought, 'All right; so my life has changed. It's not what I planned. But here I am with a job, and a house to live in, a wife and even a baby growing. You wouldn't believe it.'

It seemed so comical to him that all these things had happened so quickly and unexpectedly that he chuckled, threw up his arms, and did a few steps of a jig, so that the next sweep of the Nelly

Morgan caught him capering. He leapt inside, still chuckling, hoping that by some mischance Lufa had not been awake to glimpse his new partner grotesquely hopping in the dark.

'Where have you been, Jackie?' murmured Maida. 'Is it time to get up?'

'Not yet. Go to sleep again.'

It was four o'clock, so he thought he would not sleep again. He lay there stroking Maida's hair, making plans, waiting for the dawn.

In a little while the window of Lufa's shack drew itself faintly on the dark, so Jackie rose, lit the lamp, and blew up the banked fire in the rusty stove. Half asleep, Maida cooked his breakfast, and by the time he had eaten a vinous flush suffused both sky and river, and Lufa's small eyes were beaming around the door.

'Well, Maida,' he said, 'think you're going to settle down?'

'I'm settled down already,' said Maida. She smiled. 'This is the right place for Jackie and me.'

In later years when Jackie Hanna looked back on his life on the Dovey, he felt that it had all been a dream. He forgot the grinding endless labour on the cream boat, and recalled an existence that seemed to have been an idyllic, perpetual picnic. Jackie shot rabbits, caught fish, sluggish big things that tasted of dirt. Until Maida became too cumbrous they often went eeling on the leaky, oozing islands, or into the bush where bogs stretched long fingers into the valleys. The scrubland was full of tea-coloured creeks, lakelets, swamps that dried up in summer.

The work, as Lufa had warned him, was extremely heavy, and during the first month on the cream boat Jackie ended each day in a stupor of weariness, too tired even to eat. But gradually his musculature began to develop, and his extraordinary natural strength to show itself. He thickened and put on weight, so that Lufa said, 'You'll end up as broad as you're long, Jack. I tell you, it's a moral.'

He and Lufa soon became known as the man and a half all along the river and the delta farms.

The river-flat people accepted Jackie as naturally as they would have accepted a man with a wooden leg, or a twenty-five-year-old cursed with premature baldness. His dwarfism made him different in appearance, and that was all. He couldn't help it, it couldn't be fixed, and it did not interfere with his capable handling of his job or his personal life. To most of them Jackie's minute stature seemed lovable.

'Sort of dinky, ain't he?' they said. 'Like a banty rooster. You can't help but smile.'

The fact that he was a dwarf passed completely from Jackie's mind. He was Jack Hanna of Morgan's Clearing, Lufa's mate.

The thirty-foot cream boat was one of a rapidly dwindling fleet of shallow-draught flat-decked vessels which from the seventies had moved up and down the Dovey carrying the dairy farmers' milk-cans to the co-operative factory farther up the river near the railhead. Lufa's boat chugged up tributaries and navigable anabranches, and in and out the delta islands, daily covering about fifty miles of difficult water maze.

'I can smell a mud-bank,' said Lufa, 'and I know the channels like the wrinkles on me dial. Dark mornings, winter like, or heavy mist rising, you gotta listen to the boat, sorta feeling her way along, dead slow. You'll catch on, Jack. You're real quick. I suppose that's what schooling does for a man.'

On Lufa's run the pick-up averaged seventy to eighty milk-cans, and he calculated that with the loading and the unloading he and Jackie lifted eight to ten tons a day.

'Yet that ain't nothing to what the old timers lifted,' Lufa said. 'Now, the late Mr Harry Tremlett, who died in the rats last October leaving me the cream run, as I told you, he went back to the old steam launch days, and he lifted fifteen ton or more each day. Ghost, he was a strong man. Could carry a man of my size on each shoulder. Always showing off. Tore a chube or somethink in the end and that's why he took to the plonk.

'Summer's hard – when I can't get the tub closer'n twenty-thirty feet to the jetties, and we got to manhandle them bloody cans over the mud and roll 'em up the plank. I seen this same river shrunk back to the channels, and cows grazing where we are now; but I ain't ever grounded the boat yet.'

His simple pride in his own craft was not new to Jackie. The Nun was the same, able to do certain things well and pleased that he could.

Lufa was a good mate to Jackie, kind and undemanding and helpful. He was like a good dog or a horse, and gradually Jackie fell into the habit of commenting on things that interested him, or had happened to him, as unselfconsciously as a lone man might do to such an animal, and Lufa listened with absorption, his nut-coloured eyes twinkling, until at last the young man was brought to himself by Lufa's slapping a hand on his thigh with a crack, and his yell of admiring laughter.

'By Ghost, you're little but you're shrewder than an abo. dog! Bet them old squarehead cousins of mine, them Linzes, was sorry to see you go.'

'Heart-broken,' replied Jackie.

At first he was more at ease with Lufa than he was with Maida. Her submissiveness sometimes irritated him, so that he said, somewhat brusquely, 'You don't always have to agree with me. I won't get cranky if you have opinions of your own.'

'But I'm your wife,' she said, with such a look of wonderment that Jackie remembered with a pang that she had known only one

So he stopped chiacking her and expecting her to explode into laughter and chase him round the room, as his mother would have done. She was different; he might long for her to aim a frolicsome clout at his head along with the kisses; but he was not Jerry Mac-Nunn and she was not Peggy. And looking at her sometimes, her long beautiful eyes, the European planes of her face, her fair hair coiled in a little net, he was humble that she loved him so unquestioningly.

Voluntarily, then, he accepted her for what she was: the solemnity where he would wish for playfulness, her mind that had been bullied and frightened along narrow, rigid ways, her superstitions and old-world beliefs, the fears and sorrows that sometimes shook her, especially as the child grew.

'It won't have the kind of bad life me and Ellie had, will it?' she entreated Jackie. 'No one will ever knock it around or lock it outside in the cold or hurt it like Father hurt us?'

'That couldn't happen, because I'm here to look after it, and you too.'

'I wish there was someone to look after Ellie,' she said wistfully. 'I miss Ellie.'

Sometimes she told Jackie long stories about Ellie and herself, their tiny excursions around the hills beyond the orchard, the Afghan pedlar who gave them a few sweets in a flimsy pink twist of paper, and how their mother threw them away lest they should be poisoned. They had been two against the rest of the family at High Valley, Maida always protecting the younger child, taking the blame, getting it even when she did not accept it.

Every month or so she wrote briefly to her mother, sometimes getting a postcard with two or three lines in reply.

'I wish poor Ellie could write,' she said. 'I miss Ellie.'

Weeks before the child was due, Maida became sickly and fretful. Sometimes Jack awakened to find her crying silently. He was exasperated, not knowing what to say or do, but contrived to be patient with her.

'I don't know what's the matter,' she said. 'I'm frightened, I suppose. Mama always had terrible times and she said I would too. If I died, Jackie, you wouldn't give the baby to Mama to look after, would you?'

Jack was so worried that he even mentioned the matter to Lufa.

'What you need is a good motherly old chook to look her over,' he advised. 'Tell you what, son. What say I bring up Pop Keever's missus from Wininnie Bend? She musta calved eight or nine times herself, knows all about it, and a real nice old biddy, too.'

Mrs Keever, from the family sixty years settled at Wininnie Bend, had all the characteristics of the river farming people. Reticent and dignified, she was a sensible countrywoman, plain and thin as a pole, who looked at Maida's gaunt face and swollen form consideringly.

'I don't know, dear,' she said. 'This is an iffy kind of time, especially when you're carrying your first. I think you should go into Duchess and let the doctor have a look at you.'

Maida protested; but Mrs Keever paid no attention.

'No, dear, I have to be firm. It's my duty as an older person and your nearest neighbour. If your mother was here she'd say the same as me. Don't you be silly now. You don't want to lose your baby prematurely. That's right, dear, you have a little weep while Jackie and me make the arrangements. Now then, Jack, first thing tomorrow, my boy Roley will bring the Mack truck around by the bush road, and him and me will take Maida into Duchess. We'll take it slow, and I'll be there to keep an eye on her. No need to worry at all. We'll stay overnight at my sister Enid's, and if the doctor says she's all right we'll bring her back next day. No trouble, dear. You just leave it to us and get on with your job, easy-minded.'

Maida went off, tearful and timid, and yet half excited at seeing Duchess Bay again.

The next day Roley Keever returned to say that the child had been born shortly after they had got Maida to the hospital. It had been a stillborn boy.

Though he had not felt very deeply about the coming child, Jackie was dismayed and distressed, more for Maida than the baby.

'I suppose he came too early to live, poor little beggar.'

Mrs Keever was soberly compassionate. 'Things sometimes happen this way.'

When Jackie arrived, Maida was depressed and querulous, hating the hospital.

'Take me home,' she begged. 'I want to be home just with you. I'll get better quickly there.'

'Did you see him, the baby?' Jackie asked Mrs Keever privily. 'I just wondered, if he was – like me. You know. Small.'

Mrs Keever said, 'No, I didn't see him. Don't think of it any more and try to keep your wife's mind off it, too. Nobody could help the baby coming before time, it's just fate.'

When Maida returned to the river she looked round the cottage with an intense and hungry glance.

'I wanted to be here,' she said, and suddenly: 'When I tell Mama that the baby was born dead, you know what she'll say? That it's a punishment to me for being wicked.'

She wept all night. In the morning she seemed calm, completely herself.

'I must look a sight.' She covered her swollen face with her hands. 'Don't look at me.'

'I always want to look at you,' Jackie said. 'I love you. You're my girl, aren't you?'

'Yes,' she said. She pressed his head against her still-sore breasts, rocked him gently, saying, 'You can be my baby now, Jackie.'

The years slid by, less marked by event than the river. They were the years of the big boom, of cities expanding and country towns turning their backs on the old traditional standbys of sheep and cattle raising, goldmining and grain-growing, and venturing into light industry. The railways veined the countryside, shipping increased. Crazy men like Kingsford Smith and Charlie Ulm talked about regular airmails, freight planes linking Australia with Home, carrying lightly chilled lamb, choice tropical fruits, wines for the luxury market. Lufa and Jackie agreed that these dreamers needed their heads read.

The farmers along the Dovey leased more land, burned and cleared bush, increased their herds, and the dairy factory raised more capital and built a new jetty and iceworks. Lufa could have bought another cream boat and put a couple of men on it, but he said he couldn't bother his head with it.

'Ghost!' he said, 'what would I do with more money?'

But Maida and Jackie saved a little. Maida had never owned any money in her life, and she never looked at their savings bankbook without glee. 'All that! Ours!'

'We could go for a little holiday if you like,' Jackie suggested.

'Oh, no,' she said, dismayed. 'I like it here! It's a holiday here all the time. You don't want to go away and leave it, do you, Jackie?'

Within a year Jackie could scarcely remember the Kingsland hillsides of faded green velvet which had filled his infant eyes with familiar security and his infant head with dreams of dwarfs and gold. Like Lufa, he began to speak of the river as an entity, and when the big blows came, the gulls snow-storming in to the bogs, the whooping wind full of salt that made frost-flakes on the window, he said, 'She'll be eating her banks tonight', feeling helpless and anxious as though this great brainless thing of water and sand were an animal bent on its own destruction.

During these blows, when Jackie and his wife learnt the value of the tarpaulin that anchored their roof till the whole structure seemed to crouch and cling to the ground like a limpet, the nights were full of awesome tumult, the bush booming forth its mighty mantra, ᴏᴍ ᴏᴍ ᴏᴍ, and the Dovey driven back upon itself by wind and tide, tacking from shore to shore with an antiphonal roar and rattle. On such nights the two young people made love with inexhaustible vigour, driven by the prodigal energy that filled the river, the sky, the whole dark world about them, until they felt one with each other and that dark world and all that it signified.

'I wonder if you'll keep on loving me?' Maida sometimes said as they lay together. At first this question had amazed Jackie. He himself had never thought of Maida's ceasing to love him. He was her husband, she was his wife, they liked being with each other, one day they would have children: that was all there was to it.

'I'll try,' he replied playfully, and was surprised and irritated to see a look of fright in her eyes.

After that the question was often forced out of her by some profound anxiety. And although he knew her recognition of love was uncertain, her faith in its durability shrivelled at birth, and understood the reasons for these things, he grew bored with her need for constant reassurance, and would escape to Lufa's artless tranquillity with a feeling of relief.

Still, he understood her need for patience and gentleness. He wished that she might become pregnant again, and in the joyful and all-needed love of a child find faith in her own lovability.

In the fourth year of his marriage, Jackie received a letter from his stepfather that filled him with trepidation from the moment it arrived. For Jerry never wrote letters; that task was left to his wife, who at long intervals overflowed into written words, and sent Jackie and Maida all the news, in a letter which invariably began, 'I take pen in hand to tell you . . .'

Jerry's letter, carefully reassuring, told Jackie that his mother hadn't been too clever for a long time now, something to do with the heart, the doctor said. No cause for alarm, but it would be tip-top if the young feller could take a few days off and come home and cheer her up a bit. After all, she was getting along in life.

Jackie was apprehensive. His mother had receded into the background of his life. He was content to know she and the Nun were well, doing a fair trade at the shop, putting away a trifle, all of which he had gathered from her letters, and having the fun of Cork whenever there was half a chance.

Maida was pregnant, blooming and tranquil, soothing him with her very appearance. She wanted him to see his mother.

'Look here, now, there's most likely nothing to worry about. But there's not a reason in the world why you shouldn't go to Kingsland and stay with her a week or ten days. She'd be so pleased it might give her the right turn in her illness. Tomorrow, now, you talk it over with Lufa. We've a few pound in the bank, and we can well afford a holiday for you.'

'Would you come, Maida?'

But she shook her head, smiling. 'No, no, it's you she wants; and besides, I wouldn't like the travelling to upset the little one.'

Lufa raised no objection at all. He said he would get the help of one of the farmers, or even two of them, seeing that it would take more than one good man to replace Jackie.

'Go on,' he said. 'Get off, you little scut.'

Kingsland station looked scarcely different from what it had been when Jackie left it five years before.

'We got the electricity on, though,' boasted the station porter as he welcomed Jackie. A few strangers stared at him covertly, but he ignored them. With a painful throb of pleasure he went forward to meet his stepfather.

'You old bastard!'

They wrestled each other around a little, beaming.

Jackie was taken aback to see how much the Nun had aged. He was not so old, in his early forties perhaps, years younger than Jackie's mother. Yet he was the same old Nun, brown-paper face inscribed with its ironic smile, unhurrying voice, leg a little stiff, though he said it was great, better than it had been for months.

'They're still digging for that broken bottle, or whatever it is,' he commented. 'Twice I let them have a go at it last year, but no joy.'

'Mum never mentioned it,' said Jackie.

'Stale news.' The Nun shrugged. 'Fact is, Jack, I come to prepare you for the way your mum looks. There's been a change since the dropsy set in, and she's that swollen up. It might give you a turn if you didn't expect it.'

'It's really bad then?' asked Jackie, feeling cold.

'It's the ticker,' said the Nun vaguely. 'But she could go on for years, maybe. Seeing you will be a tonic.'

She had become a thick, breathless woman, her hair coarse and brindled, cherry cheeks shellacked by disease. A mole had grown on her chin, a little black felt bobble, and her tender mouth now had no teeth in it.

The shock of this change struck Jackie such a blow he could hardly keep his face and voice unmoved. To think that this could happen in four years! Her body was immense, jelly-like, her ankles lolling like cuffs over the shoes.

'I tell ... you no ... lie,' she said. 'My bloody legs ... feel ... as though ... they've been ... put in ... upside-down.'

This was the way she spoke, as though her lungs could hold no more than a spoonful of air.

'I'll be ... better soon,' she said to Jackie, eating him with eyes black as ever, but lost in pouches of bruised flesh. 'Not too ... well today ... excited ... better soon.'

Jackie felt as if the air were full of dust, the familiar roof fallen in, the chimney dry and limey, crumbling. A wild prophetic imagination conjured up for him weeds on the hearthstone, a doorless cupboard full of nettles, his mother's chair fallen in the corner, pocked with dry rot.

'The sky takes over in the end,' remarked the Nun.

Jackie looked at him in terror. Then he realised that his stepfather had said something different altogether – something about Maida.

'She's expecting another baby,' he said. His mother was pleased. Her toy-soldier cheeks became more empurpled.

'A real good girl,' she gasped. 'You ... been lucky ... Good kind girl ... stick to you.'

The Nun and he sat up late that night.

'How are you going to manage, Dad,' asked Jackie, 'when she gets worse?'

'Oh, I got the district nurse coming in now to do what's necessary to keep her comfortable,' said Jerry. 'And Mrs Early next door, she's real thoughtful. Do you remember Mrs Early, Jack, and the way you used to skedaddle away from her into the treehouse when she was after you to give you a skelp?'

Jackie nodded, though he had almost forgotten.

'And I'm a handy bugger myself,' went on the Nun with some pride. 'Did you notice her hair? I curled it meself this morning with a clothes peg.'

Suddenly he pulled his lips tight, turned his face away and said, 'Another bad spell might send her off, the quack said. Ghost! I don't know what I'd do if that happened, I tell you straight.'

He pulled himself together. 'Well, better bank the fire and we'll get off to bunk, eh? I fixed up your old room. Your mum will be asleep. Them pills the doc gives her are like bombs. But the effect don't last.'

Jackie could not sleep. He missed Maida in the bed, and the sound of the ravenous sea running up the Dovey and knocking on the islands. Kingsland's night noises did not belong to his life any more: the long bray of the night express fleeing to Queensland, the rhythmic thump from the gasworks. He heard coughs and murmurs from his parents' room, and a few moments later heard Jerry go downstairs with extravagant noiselessness.

Jackie smiled. Good old Jerry. The best day in their lives when he stepped over the shop's doorsill. He heard the small roar of a primus below, and knew that the Nun must be getting a hot drink for his wife.

He awoke before sunrise, his first thought being of Cushie. She had been at the back of his mind ever since he knew he was to come back to Kingsland. Over the years he had never asked about her or her family; he knew nothing. Was she married perhaps? Gone away? He let his thoughts linger on her, waiting for the sense of deprivation that had stayed with him for so long. But it had gone.

From where he lay he could see the corner of the treehouse, unpainted, sagging a little. He thought he might get up and climb along the branch, see what it looked like now, that old refuge and castle of his. But he didn't really want to reawaken memories of his childhood, good though it had been. That night, Armistice

night, when he had kissed Cushie in the wet grass, and the mosquitoes had bitten them, and he had felt so strongly, so purely,
the first intimations of true love. That a kid could feel that way!
But he had, and so had Cushie. He couldn't doubt it for a
moment.

He got up and dressed quickly, putting the blind higher so that
he could look out at things starting to glisten, wet pebbles, grass
blades, tiny puddles like larks' eyes. Something was making a
thready sound under the big tree where he and Cushie used to
play houses.

'I won't think about it, it belongs to years ago,' he thought,
but just the same his eyes turned to Moys' big house across the
way. He knew at once that the Moys were no longer there. The
untrimmed hedge, toppled by its own weight, the gate-post
knocked out of alignment, the slate roof mended with a sheet of
unpainted corrugated iron . . . all spoke of the absence of those
superior, aloof people.

Jackie felt better at once. Had he been afraid or embarrassed
to meet Cushie? He didn't know, and he wasn't going to work
it out. He heard his stepfather going downstairs, and he followed
him, ready to turn his mind to other things.

Yet over breakfast he found himself saying, 'Moys' place over
the way is looking run-down. Lose their money, did they?'

'Gawd, no,' said Jerry, puffing the fire into flame. 'Come into
it, more likely. Thousands, I heard, when her old pa died. He
was lousy with it. Burn up, you cow!' He fussily laid a little nest
of chips over the wandering tongue of flame. 'That'll get her going.
Nah, it's a boarding-house now, the old house. Been so for years,
ever since the old man, Mr Moy that is, kicked the bucket.'

'I didn't know about that.'

'Mum didn't mention it in her letters, eh?' said the Nun, clumsily rising. He gave his knee an accidental clout and winced.

'Ticker went on him, I heard.'

Jackie remembered how Cushie worshipped her father; a
stuck-up swine, he seemed to be in retrospect. He couldn't have
been as old as all that, either. It would have hit Cushie hard.

He said indifferently, 'And Cushie and her mother and the little
kid, I forget her name, they still in Kingsland?'

'No; gone away to Sydney. Old Moy died while Cushie was

away at school, I think. Any old how, she never came back. And Mrs Moy and the young kiddy, they packed up and left like greased lightning after Mr Moy died. Get the cups and saucers out, will you, Jack?'

Jackie found it strange to be back. His life on the Dovey stood between him and Kingsland like a transparent but impassable curtain. The Jackie who had left the little town was a boy; the one who returned was a man. Yet he was uneasy. He was afraid that Kingsland would reassert itself.

His mother, sometimes for an hour or two able to speak without battling for breath, kept telling him what she called the news: how this one had died, that one had left the town in disgrace, how a marriage had turned out to be bigamous, who had gone bankrupt with gambling or the booze. And against his will Jackie found himself obsessively thinking about these people, once part of his life, and now blown away like thistledown to find random resting-places.

Tides of people, coming and going, in and out, and his mother soon to be amongst them.

'Don't go! Don't go!' It was his heart shouting.

But she had let *him* go, and he well knew what he meant to her, more than Jerry, more than life. She had found the courage somewhere.

It was bad coming back to Kingsland, and worse leaving it. For miles Jackie could still feel the iron grasp of Jerry's hand through the train window.

'Don't take it too hard, me old Jack,' he said. 'I mean, if I have to wire you in a hurry. It's the wheel of life; we got to accept it.'

Jerry gave him a wink and a sideways nod of the head as the train pulled away. Jackie stared blindly into the brightening day where the trees bent into right angles and whipped upright and away, stock-ponds caught the sunrise like mirrors, and emus and kangaroos fled across endless paddocks. He was glad he was alone in the compartment.

He became aware that the train was stopping at a siding to water. Boys were running alongside it already with the day's papers, and lean-faced country women with baskets of fruit, hot scones, homemade cakes, were waiting beside the line.

One of them smiled through the window. 'Lovely rock cakes, still hot from the oven! Like one, dear?'

As Jackie fished in his pocket for the threepence she said kindly, 'Going back to school, sonny?'

'Yes,' said Jackie. It seemed easiest.

Lufa and Maida met the service car at Duchess Bay. Pleased as he was to see them, Jackie was anxious for his wife.

'Coming over that rough road! It can't have been good for you.'

Maida hugged him. 'Lufa drove like a snail. I couldn't wait to see you. Besides, I wanted to see the doctor and arrange for my booking at the hospital and everything.'

'The doctor! You're all right?'

'Perfect.' She hugged him again. 'And I bought some baby clothes. Wait till you see them!'

Lufa scratched his nose. 'This going to be over soon, this Rudolph Valentino bit? Because I want to get home before dark.' He gave his slow smile. 'Plenty room in the truck for canoodling, if you don't mind me being there.'

In bed that night, Maida said, 'Must have been queer, seeing your old home again.'

'I don't live there any more,' said Jackie. He took her in his arms. 'I live wherever you are.'

As the summer months wore on, and the drought clenched on the country its fist of iron, Maida became gaunt, drooping with the heat. The river dwindled, dark amber with mud; dead fish convulsed, steamed, and stank on the sand-bars. At night there were unfamiliar sounds of battle on the banks as rabbits and other animals fought for water.

The shallow-draught cream boat moved sluggishly along the channel; Lufa and Jackie were often forced to lay planks along the drying mud-banks that separated them from the jetties, and manhandle the cans back to the boat. It was wickedly hard work even for fit men, and Jackie returned home each night saturated with fatigue.

He was anxious about his wife.

'Are you all right?' he asked over and over again.

'Doctor said I'm fine,' she answered with a smile.

But she looked taut and anxious, and oftimes in the night he found her awake, silently crying.

'Won't you tell me what's wrong? We're mates, aren't we?'

'Oh, Jackie!' Fiercely she turned to him and kissed him. 'Always, always.'

'Then tell me the truth. You're afraid our baby might be like me?'

'A little,' she said, after a moment. 'Don't be hurt, Jackie. It's just that, if it happened that way, he mightn't be as brave as you. He mightn't be able to manage the way you have.' Then she said, 'Now you're angry with me. Disappointed.'

'No,' said Jackie. 'My head's been full of it since you first told me you were carrying. But there's not much chance of it. When I was back home I read the books on dwarfism Mum got from the doctor long ago, and since then I haven't been worried. You put it out of your mind, Maida. Everything's going to be perfect.'

So he spoke to her, soothingly, like a father, stroking the hair already damp with sweat. The air shimmered in the window like burning water; the iron roof gave out kettle-drum cracks in the heat.

'You didn't worry like this last time,' he said.

'It never entered my head. We were such kids, silly as a tin of worms. And so many other things to worry about.'

Her spirits seemed to have lifted. She rose laboriously from their bed, coming back to kiss his forehead and say, 'You're my little tiger. What would I have done without you, Jackie?'

The child was born without trouble in the Duchess Bay hospital, a long-limbed boy.

'I'm afraid he'll top six foot,' said the doctor, pleased. 'Be bossing the pair of you around in no time.'

Jackie and Maida called him Carl. He was a blue-eyed child of great vitality. Jackie could scarcely believe that he had called into being this magnificent creature, this jewel-coloured, completely new human.

Lufa Morgan inspected him with wonder. 'Little beaut,' he said. 'Gawd, you got the knack of it all right, Jack. What a little ripper! What a friggen peach!'

Jackie was hit by fatherhood as a man might be hit by a tidal wave. He was lifted off his feet, unresisting. He was swept away into dreams, plans, and an ungovernable protectiveness. He knew he would tear apart anyone who hurt, even threatened, Carlie. His nostrils dilated, his fists tightened at the very thought of it. Maida laughed at him.

'Nobody will hurt him. He's got the look of luck in his little face.'

Maida was entranced with happiness. Her beauty returned.

'My whole life's been leading up to this,' she said.

Jackie wrote to his mother: 'Now I understand how you felt when I was born. Well, Mum, you did what you set out to do. I've got a job I enjoy, some good friends, the best wife in the world, and now Carlie, whom the doctor says will grow to more than six feet. I do thank God often, but most of all I thank you and Dad.'

Jerry wrote back of their joy in the grandchild: 'Your mum is hanging on,' he said; 'up and down, but she keeps her spirits. Times are not as good as they were. I don't know what the country is coming to. The meatworks are closed down, and I hear the jam factory in Ghinni is shortening staff. But something's better around the corner; we got to be hopeful.'

Jackie experienced the first six months of his son's life as a gift from heaven. Something had happened to him. All his life he had sensed that lightness, brightness existed in the corner of his eye, that sweet music breathed just outside the reach of his ear. Now he experienced these things. A passionate clarity informed his awareness of the world.

Yet the world was wicked and ugly during that half-year, the heat worsening, the stock starving. The earth shrank away from the surface, leaving rootless mats of dried grass and vegetation; rocks appeared where no rocks had been before, wreaths of gibbers, and long runnels of gravel ejected by the contracting soil.

The winter brought no rain. The pelicans wheeled over the

dying river, the sun shining pink through fishless throat-pouches. At twilight the desolate note of the black swan made Maida shiver, as the birds flew high overhead to reedy bogs that still existed in sheltered mountain coombs.

When Carlie was five months old, just having dragged himself with shouts of glee to a sitting position, Maida received a letter from her mother. Her attitude towards her mother had always been ambivalent; in the first months of her marriage she had often been homesick for her, cried for her when the first child was born dead.

'You don't know what she's had to put up with,' she said to Jackie, her words interspersed with long silences as though these memories were too hurtful to recall. 'She's had a terrible life with Father. Terrible.'

Gradually Jackie had learnt that his intuitive feelings about his Aunt Eva during his sojourn at the High Valley orchard had been correct. From the day he married her Remus Linz had systematically humiliated and ill-treated her, because this was his way with all things in his power. Most of his sons had followed his lead, treating her contemptuously, not afraid to give her the flat of their hands if she was reluctant or stupid.

'Hof was the only one to defend her,' said Maida. 'But Father belted him within an inch of his life. Then Hof got too strong for Father, and he thrashed him.' Her eyes shone with honest pleasure at the memory. 'Thrashed him! That's what made Pa go off to be a travelling blacksmith. But every time he came back he gave the rest of us a belting. To make up, I suppose.'

Her face softened. 'And Ellie is good to Ma. Like a little faithful dog to her he is.'

During the years of Maida's absence, changes had occurred at the High Valley orchard. The drunk brother had been found drowned in the duckpond. Hof had married a neighbouring widow with a grown-up family, and had left the Linz property to work his wife's farm. The dark brother, after a quarrel with the fat brother, had flung out and gone to Sydney, and no one had heard of him for two years.

When early summer was on the Dovey country, Maida heard from her mother that Remus Linz had been killed in a brawl in a far-west township. His travelling forge, his horse and wagon, had been sold up to pay for his funeral.

'Well, that's that.' Maida drew a long breath. She sat silent so long that Jackie said, 'You can't feel anything for him?'

'No,' said Maida. 'When I was a kid I prayed every night that he'd die and burn in hell. But that was when I was a kid. Now I don't care whether he's dead or not. He's nothing. But there's something else, Jackie. Ma wants to get away for a while, come and stay with us, and see Carlie.'

Jackie's heart sank, but he replied cheerfully enough, 'Well, it's no palace here, but we could make her comfortable.'

Maida put her hand on his. 'I don't want her to come, Jackie.'

Jackie felt her tremble. 'What's the matter, love?'

'I just feel bad about her coming. I don't want her to come. We can make some excuse.'

'It's only natural she'd want to see Carlie,' expostulated Jackie. 'And what could she do to upset us? She's just a poor old woman who's had a hard life. She wasn't especially friendly to me when I was at the orchard, but I suppose she had things on her mind.'

Mrs Linz, five years away, seemed to Jackie to be an exhausted, impotent creature. He could hardly recall what she looked like.

'I don't know why I don't want her here,' said Maida. After a little, she murmured, 'I'm frightened, that's what it is.'

'Of your mother!'

She looked at him pleadingly. 'I'm frightened she'll come between us some way. Do some damage. Please, Jackie.'

Jackie thought she was unreasonable. He felt, too, a certain guilt about Mrs Linz. Though he had guessed she had every reason to be cringing and demoralised, he had detested and despised her. Besides, she was the Nun's sister; he wanted to do something for Jerry.

But it was a week before Maida would agree to her mother's coming to stay on the Dovey for four or five weeks. Even then she was tearful, reluctant.

'You won't let her upset what we've got, Jackie? Oh, I suppose I'm being silly about it, but I'm scared. I can't explain it, but

I am. I just want you and me and Carlie going on the way we are, that's all.'

'How could anything change us?' said Jackie, kissing her. She had some secret way of knowing when he was likely to kiss her, and always contrived to be sitting or lying, so that he would not have to stand on tiptoe. Jackie could see that she thought he didn't notice her stratagem, only one of a gracious many she had devised to keep him from feeling small. So he kept her secret, and loved her the more for it.

Eva Linz had changed in the years since Jackie had seen her. Age had settled upon her like dust. Her hair was scanty, screwed up at the base of a meagre skull. Her neck and face were lined in an irregular mosaic, and she had frail little dried-up ears. From the small frame in its neat black dress came a voice that had diminished to a quack.

Mrs Linz set herself out to be sociable. She gushed over the baby and said that heat didn't bother her at all.

She lay in her bed that night deeply satisfied. First the death of Remus, at the thought of which a chuckle of delicious joy escaped her. So he would never be coming home again, never, never.

'God rest his soul,' she thought: at the bottom of the sea, or a volcano, under a million tons of hot mud.

She thought lovingly of Ellie, left alone at the mercy of that woman who was now housekeeper at High Valley, for Hof had brought his wife home when his father died. But she'd given Ellie a few tips on how to manage her, the upstart.

As for the rest of the world, she was going to give it something to think about. Her life had left her with an obscure ill-will towards all things living. Her heart felt like a lump of tin. Now and then a faint scratching sound came from it, but that was all.

She had seen at once that Jackie and Maida were happy and at ease with each other, and this filled her with unexamined resentment. As the days went past, and her daughter recovered from her nervous stiffness and relaxed into the gently blooming appearance that was now natural to her, the resentment slowly turned to a profound jealousy.

Mrs Linz sat and watched Maida feed her child. In spite of everything the girl had suffered, the unspeakable days of her childhood, this was how she could look, and all because a stunted, ugly little beast of a man had married her.

'So you're happy, dear?' commented the old woman.

Maida had flushed and turned her head, so that the pure flat plane of her cheek was all that her mother could see.

Knowing this, that the girl had found happiness, the old woman could not keep her hands off it. It was not that she hated Maida. Well she remembered when the infant girl was born, and she had wept with an objective compassion because this female child would no doubt grow up to have the same fearful life as she. Ah, yes, she had loved Maida then, and in a dark maternal way she loved her still.

But as a human being she bitterly envied her daughter's contentment, crying out in her heart: 'Why did it happen to her and not to me? I never did anything to be punished for. I wasn't no more than fifteen when that swine Remus got to me and Father made him marry me. I never done nothing to deserve the dog's life I got.'

And so, in between looking after the baby, helping assiduously with the housework, reading her prayer-book, and being pretentiously friendly to Jackie, she poked and pried into the girl's life, insinuating, dropping hints and criticisms, only desisting when Maida began to cry.

'But what are you crying for, dearie?' she would ask with a half-genuine concern. 'What did I say?'

'You know,' Maida replied, then lapsing into a long silence.

Over the cottage had fallen the most impalpable of grey shadows, the brightness dimmed, the contentment rendered paltry or fatuous. The child felt it, turning its face from its mother's breast, aware of her frightened heart. Jackie, returning to a house of silence and oppression, uneasily asked the reason.

'I don't like Mama being here,' was all Maida replied.

'But why, darling?'

'She's jealous of us.'

But Jackie couldn't see it. For him love was generous and all-enveloping, sharing itself with the beholder as well as its possessor.

He laughed and buried his face in her milky-smelling breasts, breathing her in like a garden.

'She's a spoiler. She just is,' said an almost inaudible voice above his head. 'She upsets me that much my milk's going off.'

As time went on a sense of mischief added itself to Mrs Linz's other simple but entangled emotions. To make Maida cry soothed her; to put Jackie at a disadvantage with innocent-sounding words was exciting. And he, who, since he left High Valley, had never felt his difference from othe men as a reproach or shame, now began once again to be self-conscious about his lack of height and uneasily avoid standing next to Mrs Linz, lest she should say he was a little button, or ask could she reach something down from the shelf for him.

She would also lean over the child in his cot, pretending she did not know she was observed, and shake her head wistfully.

'Ma!' said Maida, in a hard voice. 'That's enough.'

The old woman was momentarily startled by the look on her daughter's face, but she swiftly recovered, saying placatingly, 'I never meant you to see I was worried, love. But there, they do say boys always take after their mothers.'

'Mama! I can see through you like a pane of glass! You ought to be ashamed, trying to spoil what Jackie and me have got.'

A thrill of adventure stirred Mrs Linz's heart, and her eyes sparkled.

'You haven't got that much, then, my girl, if a few innocent remarks from your own mother can upset it. I don't know what's the matter with you, always taking me up wrong, reading things into what I say. You ought to be ashamed of yourself.'

She sat in the rocking chair, snivelling. 'So soon after your father's death, too. And that woman of Hof's messing around in my kitchen. How'm I going to manage with a strange woman there? It breaks my heart to think of it. I done my best for you, Maida, things being as they were, and I been hoping that now that I need help you'd offer it and not make me beg for it.'

After a silence Maida said in terror, 'What do you mean?'

'I got no real place of my own now, Maida. You're my only daughter. It's up to you . . .'

'You want to live with us – is that what you mean?'

Mrs Linz peeped up at Maida, whose face was dead white and set. 'I'm sorry, but we can't manage that. You'll have to go back to High Valley. There's no reason why you can't get on with Hof's wife.'

Her voice trembled on the last sentence, and Mrs Linz knew she had her.

'Go home, Mama,' said Maida. 'Leave us alone. Jackie and me, we're happy. Leave us alone.'

When Jackie came in from work, a little later, he found both women in a high state of tension, Maida crying, the old woman with red spotting her face, eyes sunken in her head.

'What's going on?' he said. He was exhausted, crimson-faced and grimy from the day. He took Maida's trembling hand and looked up at Mrs Linz, who faced him down with a glare compounded of defiance and excited triumph.

'I won't have Maida badgered,' he said. 'What have you been saying to her?'

'Send her away, Jackie,' stammered Maida. 'I told you it was the wrong thing to bring her here. Send her away now!'

She collapsed into a shaking heap. Her distress was so extreme that she made retching noises. Jackie was frightened and embarrassed.

'You'd better leave me alone with her for a little, Aunt Eva,' he said.

But his mother-in-law, excited and insolent, was out of control. Babbling and sobbing, she rocked, ramming the rockers of the chair hard upon the floor, in a repetitive, irruptive punctuation of her speech.

'Send me away! I wouldn't be the only one sent away if he knew. You wouldn't have sent me away a few years ago when there was nobody but me between you and disgrace.'

'Mama,' cried Maida in a strange, croaking voice, 'don't say any more.'

The child in the lean-to awoke and began to cry loudly, and the sound seemed to excite the grandmother further.

'Just as well the other one died before he found out!'

Jackie slapped her across the cheek. She stopped babbling instantly and said almost demurely, 'You'll be sorry for that, Jack.

You loony fool, you were taken in pretty as pie, weren't you, back there at the orchard? You were just as green as Kurtie and Con said you'd be.'

There she stopped, half-aghast, and rose hurriedly, muttering something about attending to the child.

But Maida, seeing Jackie's face, and the understanding on it, sobbed, 'Cruel old woman, you couldn't resist it, could you? You can't stand to see us happy in spite of everything.'

She suddenly rose from the floor like a swooping candle-flame, towering over her husband. Immensely tall he thought her in that moment, with a broken face and glittering eyes.

'It would have been better if I'd killed myself then,' she said. 'But I was afraid of dying. And –' she added almost to herself – 'I liked you, I wanted to marry you. I love you now; but I liked you then, I truly did.'

Jackie's throat ached so much he couldn't speak. At last, with a strangled cough, he blurted out, 'Who?'

'Ellie.'

Jackie turned right round and walked to the door. The air was so dry he felt the hairs on his arms turning in their sockets.

'Ellie,' he said, in a mild conversational voice that he did not even hear, so great was the roaring in his ears. Maida ran after him.

'Don't you understand, Jackie?' she wept. 'Before you came he was the one they teased, because of his foot. I was all he had, Jackie, I had to do something.'

'That explains it, does it?'

'It did for me,' said Maida. She looked bewildered, troubled. 'It did then. I – don't know what else to say. I had to help him any way I could.'

Her voice sounded a long way off. Jackie looked away from her. In some way her tragic face infuriated him.

'Let me get it straight,' he said, still conversationally. 'Let me get it straight. You were pregnant when I came to High Valley, and I was set up to save Ellie from a charge of incest, was I? I suppose Kurt and that other bastard had a great time holding it over his head.'

'Yes.' She added desperately, 'But we have been happy, haven't we? And we have Carlie, your very own baby. Jackie, try to understand.'

'Understand,' he said. 'I don't think I'll ever understand anything again.'

Then he added, 'But I do, in a way. Pity, that's what made you do it. Pity.'

He walked outside, under the trees, and sat down with his hands over his ears. The sun's last gilding on the topmost leaves flitted upwards through the blue, came to rest on high cirrus. Jackie looked vacantly at the mosquitoes spiralling over the mud-banks. To himself he said, once or twice, 'Pity', to try to get his thoughts moving again; but nothing happened.

After a while he was aware that Maida stood a few feet away. She said, 'Jackie, I'll go away if you like. I'll go away tomorrow and you need never hear of me again. But I have to take Carlie, because I'm feeding him and all. I don't want to go away but I will if you want me to.'

He shook his head, unable to speak. He shook it again, agitatedly.

Maida was silent. The mosquitoes whined about them, and a long time went by.

At last the old woman came to the door carrying the lamp.

'Baby's sleeping nicely,' she said in a scared, ingratiating voice. 'Shall I get the tea on, dear?'

Like an irresistible tide rage engulfed Jackie. It hung all around him for an endless moment in which he heard his heart gulp, his blood pump. It was like a breaker reaching up into the air, and he thought it would never fall. Then it suddenly exploded out of him. He was so helpless before it he felt that it spouted from his ears and nostrils. He heard himself shrieking curses at the old woman and her diabolical family; he felt himself jumping up and down like an ape, progressing towards her by stamping leaps.

Maida ran after him. Mrs Linz shrieked: 'He's gone mad, he'll murder the lot of us!' and threw the lamp at him.

It hit a tree near the house, threw oil in a shower, and exploded. The fire leapt simultaneously into the dry grass and up the tree in a windy rush. It vaulted from bough to bough in a yellow flash, a sharp crackle following it like a tail.

'Now see what you've done, you stupid old sod!' shouted Jackie, his frenetic rage dying on its feet and alarm taking its place. 'Quick, Maida, run and get some sacks, anything, and help me beat it out. Aunt Eva, hurry over and fetch Lufa, get a move on!'

But Mrs Linz was petrified, her hands over her mouth.

Jackie seized a branch and began thrashing at the serpents of flame that glided with astonishing speed through the grass. He did not come from bushfire country; he had had no idea of the almost instantaneous combustion that takes place in dry hot air. Until now he had never seen a tree nodding and lashing until it shook from its hair fragmented masses of fire to sail about and settle on nearby bush. In twenty seconds, fires blazed in four or five places.

As Maida ran back with a sack and a doormat, Lufa lumbered up the track carrying buckets.

'Seen the smoke. Cripes, you got a healthy one going there, Jack. Here, Maida, fill these, you and the old lady. We got to try to save the cottage. Keep throwing water on the walls.'

Maida ran back and forth. The river was so low she had to scrape the bucket along the gravel to get sufficient water. She sloshed it along the walls, and now and then over the men, whose shirts frequently caught alight from floating embers. Both were coughing and choking, eyes streaming.

'Help me, Mama!' she kept calling to her mother. 'You can take the other bucket.'

But Mrs Linz, white as death, could not move for fright.

The fire jumped into the tousle of bluegums beside the road; they heard it catch with a hiss, and then the trees turned into towers of tall flame.

'My God, she's well away,' panted Lufa, flicking out a cinder that had alighted in Jack's hair. 'Dunno if we can do any good, son. Still, you got to be in it to win it, so bash away.'

The smoke now churned all about them; as the evening drew on new blots of pink shone out, crawled and swelled in the under-bush, burst out with a roar. Further away crashing branches tossed out clouds of stars.

Out of the smoke dashed rabbits, wallabies; a tall kangaroo

erupted from the darkness in an effortless twelve-foot jump, and they heard it splashing out into the river.

The men had retreated to the west side of the house. Sixty and seventy feet between it and the fire had been burned out.

'A real good fire-break,' said Lufa. 'We might do it yet, Jack. Long as the wind holds she'll be jake. Maida, just to be on the safe side, maybe you ought to get the young fella and your Mum down to the river, eh? And anything else you want to save if it comes to the worst.'

The man was unperturbed as ever. His broken teeth and blood-shot eyes smiled in a mask of soot. 'Never say die, Jack,'

In the dark crimson light they began beating along the edge of the retreating fire. 'What about your shack, Lufa?' said Jackie, half-strangled with smoke. 'Hadn't you better get your stuff out?'

'No sweat,' said Lufa. 'Any old how I got nothing worth saving 'cept me fiddle, and blankets and that, and they're all on the cream boat. Nope, if the shack goes up all I'll lose will be the fleas.'

In the cottage Maida found her mother clutching the wide-eyed, astonished Carlie. The air was roastingly hot, and the child's face brightly pink. Mrs Linz was coughing and crying. During one of the spasms her denture flew out and shattered on the stove. This catastrophe seemed to bring her back to life and she cried, 'Me plate, me plate! See what you made me do!'

Maida shook her. 'Mama, listen. Take Carlie down to the river and put him in some safe place. Then come back and get your clothes, some food, the blankets, anything you can carry. Mama, did you hear?'

'Yes,' gasped Mrs Linz. 'Carlie down to the river. Blankets . . .'

'Quick, then. The men think the house won't catch, but this is just in case. Do it now, Mama.'

The old woman was galvanised into life. Looking over her shoulder as she dashed outside again, Maida saw her wrapping a blanket about the child. She herself took her place beside the men and beat along the edge of the fire.

So they worked for another ten minutes with an urgency born

of desperation. They could hear the fire chewing into the forested gullies, the gun-like reports of heat-cracked stones, the screaming of trapped animals. As far as Jackie could see, upstream and down-stream, the trees waved flags of flame, or swung and bowed in black silhouette against a wine-coloured sky. Lufa watched the smoke uneasily.

'I dunno, is she turning or not? What you think, Jack?'

All at once, it seemed, the smoke rolled over them in a cloud so dense, so massive that it obscured the fire and all they could see were mute twinklings under the roots of trees. Then a wild whipping wind blew towards the river, the fire snoring behind it, blowing out long fingers of flame that seized new areas of bush, dragging blazing boughs and twirling embers in its wake.

The roof of the cottage burst into flame. Fire from the ground climbed hand over hand up the west wall. They heard the window fall in, the one on the other side blow out before the heated air, and all, so it appeared, while they watched open-mouthed.

Maida screamed, 'I've got to see if Ma took Carlie all right!'

She bounded over the smoking ground towards the door, with Jackie after her. She had scarcely gone through the door before the roof fell in, a sheet of iron coming down like a portcullis half across the door. Jackie wrenched at the hot iron, while Lufa sped around to the window. Fire reached out of it with a curled tip. Lufa pulled off his shirt, wrapped it around his face and head and several times rushed at the window but he could not get within six feet of it. The blast from within was like that of hot iron. He thought he could hear Maida screaming, but the noise was too great, a deafening roar. Then he realised that it was Jackie screaming. Shouting, cursing, Lufa rushed back to Jackie, who was still dragging at the iron.

'It's no good, it's no good,' shouted Lufa, and he seized Jackie by the middle and one leg and dragged him away. The little man was like a madman. Lufa had to lie on him and subdue him by weight alone.

'You can't help, Jack. You gotta listen. No point in killing your-self too. Think of the kid!'

Jackie collapsed under him, moaning. The enormous torchlight of the burning house illuminated his hands, puffing up like cooked meat, the skin already shrivelling on his scorched chest. Lufa stood there for a moment, his head down. Then he picked up Jackie.

'We better get in the water, Jack. No use staying here.'

Jackie stirred, croaked, 'Carlie. Maida's mother took him down to the river.'

'Yeah, we'll find him. Don't you worry now, boy.'

He carried Jackie to a mud-bank. As the men approached, animals jumped off it in panic, paddled and scrabbled farther out into the stream.

'You put them hands in the water, Jack; it might help the pain a bit. Stay here now. I'll go and find Carlie and the old lady.'

'Maida, Maida,' he heard Jackie moaning as he turned back across the mud.

'Maida,' echoed Lufa in his mind. When he was out of sight of the man on the mud-bank he stood for a while, his head hanging, his hands hanging, trying to gather himself.

'I can't drop me bundle now. Gotta keep looking,' he said.

But the fire raging through the casuarinas and the river grass drove him back. He splashed up and down in the shallows, calling Mrs Linz, and the fire ate up his voice in its immensity of sound. He had to return to Jackie.

Half the night they searched, first on foot, stumbling in the crimson glare, calling, coo-eeing, and then in the cream boat, moving at a snail's pace along the channel, scanning the banks.

'They gotta be here somewhere,' said Lufa. 'That old lady now, she is a country woman. She wouldn't do anything silly. Maybe she's walked downstream in the shallows, maybe upstream, carrying the baby, but one thing you can be sure of is they're all right.'

'Why can't we hear the baby then?' asked Jackie. 'He'd be frightened. Hungry by now, too, he didn't get his ten o'clock . . .'

He went to sleep in the middle of a sentence, his blackened hands sticking out before him like boxing-gloves. Lufa gave up the pretence of searching. He anchored the cream boat in the channel, and lay down on the deck. Every inch of his body hurt in one way or another, and the dumb hurt within was more than he could bear. He grizzled a little, wiping away the tears with his hand and smearing soot and ash into grotesque marblings.

'It ain't fair,' he muttered.

The river leapt with reflected radiance. A fallen tree lay on the nearby mud-bank like a marine monster, its roots still breathing smoke. A strange sight, far away, drew Lufa's dull gaze. It was a powerline, severed by heat, a whipping, thrashing blue snake, inscribing swift S's upon the smoke.

'She was that beautiful,' he thought.

Before dawn Lufa saw upon the distant ranges the intermittent glint of lightning; when the light came he discerned a rainstorm standing on the hills. A shower moved faintheartedly over the smoking trees, then splattered across the cream boat's deck. It was too late to do any good, but he welcomed its soft chill upon his stiff, scorched skin. With dread he heard Jackie stir and mumble, and turned to face him.

'We didn't find them, did we?'

'No,' said Lufa; 'but you gotta believe me, mate, that's a tough old chook, your mum-in-law. What do you bet she paddled down to Keever's and spent the night in bed, her and the bub?'

'Yes, I have to believe that,' said Jackie. He heaved himself up on his hands and knees, flinching.

'I'll pump up the primus and get us a cuppa tea,' said Lufa. Jackie nodded.

'Thanks, Lufe.'

Lufa ambled aft. He sighed deeply as he went, long shuddering sighs that seemed to come up from his boots. Jackie buried his face on his knees.

Lufa had to hold the cup to Jackie's lips, trying not to spill the hot liquid on the young man's blistered chest. He had hardly finished drinking before they heard a hail, and a rowing-boat moved slowly into sight. It carried four men and one woman, Mrs Keever.

Jackie ran to the rail. 'Have you seen Mrs Linz and Carlie?' he shouted. The people in the boat shook their heads, glanced at each other uneasily.

'All right then,' said Lufa. 'So they went upstream. Don't worry, I keep telling you, son.'

Mrs Keever, as drawn and smutty as the menfolk, wordlessly

received the news of Maida's death. She had brought carron oil and torn-up sheets for bandages, and silently she offered to bandage Jackie's hands. But he pulled them away, saying, 'I want to look for Carlie. Now.'

After a short discussion, Jackie and the Webster boys went upstream in one boat, to search the banks for any sign of the missing Mrs Linz and her burden, while Gordie, the Keever stockman, stayed on land to search the ravaged bush in the vicinity of the jetty. Jackie realised that his neighbours wanted to remove Maida's body from the devastated cottage before he got back.

Lufa nodded at him, saying, 'You go, Jack. Better that way. No sense in making things worse.'

After the boat had disappeared round the bend, Lufa turned to Pop Keever who had volunteered to help turn over the debris of the cottage. Mrs Keever stood firm, having refused to go away from the site.

'No, she'd want another woman to be here,' was all she said.

She had been up all night. The fire had come up to the back of the hen-house and then cut away again. Her neighbours, the Websters, had fared better; the small fires ignited by drifting sparks on their island had been easily extinguished. There had been no other deaths in the locality except of stock in outlying paddocks. Most of Mrs Keever's layers had been killed by the heat, but that was to be expected in such a narrow shave.

Mrs Keever wondered how her two boys were managing. They had left the homestead before the boat did, in an effort to bring the old Mack lorry around by road to Morgan's. But the road would be blocked with fallen trees; it would be a long business.

She was not a religious woman. There was no comfort for her anywhere as she watched the men working in the unclean tangle of the cottage. It was still smoking, smelling hideously from the dawn shower. After a while Pop Keever dragged out a sheet of corrugated iron, and he and the stockman lifted something onto it.

Mrs Keever felt her inside begin to shake. She thought, 'I have to keep a good face. No help to go to pieces. I have to keep a good face for everyone's sake.'

She turned away, but all too soon her dread and fascinated horror made her take a quick glance as the men carried the iron past her to the river's edge. She saw a black mummified thing, shaped somewhat like a shoe, split along one side to disclose a scramble of discoloured bones. At the same moment Lufa Morgan, standing amidst the wreckage of the cottage, began to blubber.

'It ain't fair,' he howled. 'I didn't really believe she was dead until now. I tried and tried to get her out, didn't I, Pop? Eh, you believe me, don't you, boy?'

They sat him down, got some brandy into him.

'It's all been too much; everyone's got a breaking point. You just cry if you want to.' Mrs Keever pressed his filthy, snot-smeared face against her bosom as if he had been a child. 'There, there, it was terrible for you, but you did your best, we all know that, you and Jack. Poor little thing, it was just a frightful accident.'

'I loved her, you know that?' howled Lufa. 'I know I ain't much, I'm just a nothin', can't even read or write, but she was always so kind to me, mending me clothes, cooking me scones and things, never forgot me birthday . . . I would have done anything for that girl.'

'Gordie, lend us your hanky, will you?'

Mrs Keever wiped Lufa's face, made him blow his nose. She put his big bristled head back against her elderly breast and held it there.

'You did what you could, Lufa, and none of us here thinks any the worse of you for breaking down, do we, boys?'

There was a prompt murmur of denial. Lufa shook his head violently, his face still hidden. 'Feel ashamed,' he muttered. 'Big sook. Just the shock, that's all. Didn't believe it last night. Didn't sink in. Gawd, poor Jack. It started here, you know, the fire.'

Mrs Keever motioned for her husband to pour out a mugful of heavily sweetened tea from the thermos. As he drank, Lufa talked on. It seemed a comfort to him to be able to tell the others something they didn't know. His bleared eyes and grotesque mask became almost animated.

'Jackie said the old lady threw the lamp at him, and everything went up in a flash.'

'Ghost, what'd she want to do that for?' muttered Gordie.

'They had words,' said Lufa. 'Jack said so. And I heard meself the old lady sing out, "He'll murder the lot of us." That was just before I heard the lamp explode.'

His hearers glanced at one another. Lufa pushed away the tea petulantly. His lip began to shake, and he rose and went down river a little and leant against a tree with his arm over his eyes. Mrs Keever said, 'Better keep our mouths shut about this. Don't know the real story, after all. And poor Lufa is half out of his mind, anyway.'

The stockman agreed readily, but Pop Keever said, troubled, 'There'll be an inquest though, Mother. Lufa's bound to be called.'

'Well, we'll meet that when we come to it,' said Mrs Keever. 'Is Maida's body well out of the way so that poor Jack won't see it?'

They nodded, and went downstream to continue the search for Mrs Linz and the child. Lufa blew his nose and followed them, lurching with exhaustion. Left alone, Mrs Keever walked over to the debris of the cottage, musing sadly on the warped iron bedstead, on a silvery metal clot she recognised as a frying-pan. Near the stove a few brown teeth lay. Mrs Keever's heart bumped with fright, then she recognised them as the remains of a denture.

She thought of that quiet girl, her secrets. She remembered the dead child delivered at Duchess Bay hospital. Jack had thought it premature, and she, Mrs Keever, had never told anyone, not even her husband Pop, that it had been full-term.

An ash-smeared bird flew down and listlessly picked at something amidst the debris; it was an apple, half cooked, its shape miraculously preserved amidst the holocaust. It cheered Mrs Keever. She thought, 'It's possible Mrs Linz and the baby are all right. Stranger things have happened.'

She heard the Mack lorry labouring in from the road, and went to meet her sons and tell them the news. They were big grave men, graver as they looked about them. Hesitantly she repeated to them what Lufa had said. Roley, the elder, commented, 'Better let it go no farther. It's done now, anyway, whatever the cause.'

Pop Keever returned, picking his way amongst the pockets of hot cinders. In answer to his wife's call, he said, 'Yep, we've found 'em. Honest to God, it'd draw tears from a glass eye.'

When Jackie returned they let him look for a while at the body of his child, untouched, unburned in his soot-smeared nightgown. Carlie looked as if he were alseep, the little face shut up in a dream. Jackie touched the silky hair with a finger.

'Somehow it seems worse,' whispered one of the Keever boys to the other, 'Jack being the way he is.'

They had found Mrs Linz lying on her face over the body of the child. Her back was severely burned, but she did not look as though she had died by fire.

'Either she collapsed, heart attack or something, and fell on the boy and smothered him, or she failed to get to the river and tried to shelter him when the fire swept over,' said Pop Keever, trying to lead Jackie away.

They were otherwise silent, not knowing what to say.

They tried to get him on the lorry, take him away, salve his burns, comfort him, get him drunk.

He broke away blundering through the smoking woods, disturbed cinders sparkling and springing scarlet about his boots.

Some time after midday Pop Keever found him, a little red-eyed ogre crouched by a creek, which had begun to run meagrely again, fed by the splashing thunderstorms in the hills above.

'He was that black he looked like a stump or a burned-out beef carcass,' said Pop Keever. 'And them little half-blind eyes! His hands was dangling in the water, big as footballs, with the skin peeling off like gloves.'

Jackie did not speak. The men, fidgeting wretchedly, talked in mutters.

'Bloody shame. Enough to send anyone off their nut.'

Pop Keever said, 'Lift him onto the back of the lorry. Me and the boys'll get him to Duchess hospital; that's our bit.'

The others were glad to see him go, the truck lurching into the yellow nimbus of the smoke, the two Keever sons going ahead of it with axes and crowbars to move debris fallen across the road.

They drew straws for the task of wrapping the bodies as best they could and putting them on the cream boat. Mrs Keever tried to get Lufa to stand out, but he mulishly resisted.

'Gotta see it through,' he said. Compassionately, she saw him draw a short straw.

Those who won, quickly went off to see what assistance they could give on other parts of the river. Lufa remained with his head in his hands, but the stockman and the younger Webster, feeling the pouncing heat of the invisible sun, shook him into action.

'We gotta get moving, Lufe,' said Gordie. 'Can't bury 'em here, with the police wanting to examine them and that. Got to put them on ice till the authorities take over. Jesus, though. That little bub! I'll never forget it.'

Lufa insisted on taking the wheel, and the others fell asleep in exhaustion as the cream boat travelled sluggishly upstream to the dairy factory. Lufa, eyes bloodshot, face wan under the soot, alternately licked his burned arms and fingers and cried noiselessly in simple, weary misery. Now and then he uttered a quavering sigh.

For a long time Jackie huddled in the blankets on the lorry deck, eyes wide open and unseeing, like a dying animal. Every time the vehicle halted, Pop Keever came back to see how he was getting on.

'I think he's asleep with his eyes open,' he confided to his sons.

Jackie heard the laboured breathing of the fire as it died in the last patches of charcoal. The idling wind was full of ash and charred smells; now and then, like a breath, it brought the crude, hideous stink of burning fat. How could animals carry any fat on their strung bones after such a drought? Jackie wondered. At either side the devastated trees stretched in a grey and rufous sea; charred rocks, revealed by the fire, were like huge burned skulls. The road was littered with the carcasses of birds which, fleeing, had been licked out of the sky by tongues of boiling air.

His mind was inert. Nothing but the enormous pain of his hands concerned him. He concentrated on that greedily, but fell asleep, toppling over on the lorry deck like a shot duck. When they came to the edge of the burned-out area, Pop Keever and the boys were able to lift him to a stretcher without waking him.

Hundreds of fire-fighters were still at work on the edge of the smouldering, shrinking bush. Large breaks had been felled. There were cars and trucks everywhere, crowds of fatigued, blackened men.

'About five thousand acres gone, I guess,' remarked the police sergeant. 'Funny, all this bush was due to be cleared for pastoral development, but the Government decided against it, with the slump threatening and all. Well, they got it cleared now, the sods. Four dead.' He sighed, a stout man's asthmatic sigh. 'Wonder how it started, eh?'

'No idea,' said Roley Keever.

'Probably spontaneous,' said his brother, rolling a cigarette.

For a long time before Jackie came fully to his senses he was aware of Jerry MacNunn sitting beside his bed, at first a dream-figure and then for a moment or two a real man, with his hair spiking around every which-way, and his glasses pushed up to rest on his eyebrows. Jackie wanted to say something, but he was too drugged. So he just put his hand into Jerry's and left it there, as he used to do as a child during exciting movie serials, or when he awakened with a bad dream.

He felt comforted and secure, and went to sleep.

But when, a day or more later, he became fully conscious, he found that his hands were still immobilised in mummy-wrappings: he could not have touched anything or anybody.

'How'd you get here, Dad?'

'Come when I read it in the paper about the fire.'

'Mum?'

'She's apples, jogging along; not better but fair enough. Mrs Early moved in to look after her.'

The Nun wondered if he should say anything about Maida and the youngster, decided to wait until Jackie did. He remarked, 'Your hands will be good-oh, the quack said. Full use of them and all that. He's taking the heavy bandages off in a few days and you can leave hospital and just go back for dressings.'

Jackie nodded. There was a long silence. The Nun, fidgety with affection and anxiety, did not know what to say. After a while he muttered, 'Funny place this, all boarding-houses and all empty. Jack, maybe you could come home for a while, eh?'

'Could do that,' Jackie said. He tried to grin, but his face felt as stiff as a board. Perhaps it, too, had been burned.

'Dad,' he said at last, 'is the funeral over?'

The Nun nodded, not looking at him. 'Quite a while ago. You been in here nine days now. They been holding the inquest over.'

'Inquest?' asked Jackie in horror.

'At Ghinni Junction. I thought I'd get off the train there with you, see you through that business before I go home to your mum. I better not stay away too long.'

'Oh, God,' faltered Jackie. 'I can't, Dad. How am I . . .? I can't.'

'Gotta be done, boy. Some things gotta be faced up to, and anything to do with the law is one of 'em. It'll be straight sailing, all over in an hour or two.'

The young man nodded. The Nun, filled with compassion, looked for some place about Jackie that he could squeeze sympathetically, but he was defeated by the cast-iron hospital blankets, the bandages. He scruffed Jack's hair briefly, winked.

'On my way now, old son. Back this evening. You go to sleep now.'

Jackie pulled his apathy about himself, sank into it, and was asleep before the doctor came along to give him his injection.

The Nun, sitting by himself on a broken seat on the sea front, smoked placidly, looking out on the long grey sheets of ebb-tide, smooth and vacant as linoleum, with cloud shadows skating across them. Now and then he gave a little grunt, as though someone had unexpectedly struck him.

His head was full of worries. Duchess Bay was humming with rumours. Keever's stockman Gordie had told this one and that that Lufa Morgan had come right out and said he was in love with young Hanna's wife. There'd been more doing there than anyone realised, and if that poor old lady had thrown the lamp at Jack Hanna it might have been in self-defence, or maybe protecting her daughter. Lufa had said he heard her use the word murder. The story grew and grew like a genie from a bottle, Lufa's emotional outburst when Mrs Hanna's body was found was picked over and garbled and deplored. And, come to that, who knew whether the old lady had chucked the lamp at Hanna? There was only Hanna's word for it. Not even Lufa Morgan had seen it happen. Maybe Hanna bowled the lamp at his wife, having found out about Lufa and her carrying on.

'Ghost, they're like blowflies around a dungheap,' thought Jerry. 'Poor old Jack. As though it ain't bad enough for him.'

He plotted laboriously how to get his stepson onto the motor coach to Ghinni Junction without his hearing the gossip. He managed to get him seated, but a small knot of people pressed around the window outside. Jackie turned his face away, thinking they were staring at him because he was a dwarf. It was only when someone said loudly, 'Hope they stretch you! Hope you swing!' that he realised this interest in him was something altogether new.

'Aw, it's nothing,' said the Nun easily, as the vehicle ground away. 'You know people. Ideas in their heads. Mad as meat-axes. Forget it.'

'But what can they mean?' insisted Jackie wildly. 'You've got to tell me, Dad.'

Reluctantly, the Nun told him. Jackie shrank against his seat, sickened.

'It wasn't like that at all. And Lufa – I can't believe he said Maida and he were carrying on. The best mate any man ever had, and the decentest. If you could have seen him during the fire ... You don't believe that about Lufa and Maida, do you, Dad?'

'Never in a million years,' said the Nun. 'And all you got to do at the inquest is to tell your story straight like you told me.'

'But why didn't Lufa come to see me in hospital?' pondered Jackie.

'Jack,' said the Nun decisively, 'you gotta put all that crap out of your head. You know what happened. Not all the gossip and dirt-chucking in the world is going to change that. Now you just face up to this, like you've faced up to everything else in your life. Time goes on, and you'll feel better about everything sooner or later. No, you don't believe it, but it's true. Your mum and me, we're counting on you not to drop your bundle, and we ain't going to let you off that.'

'How'm I going to face talking about her to strangers?' said Jackie.

'Not all strangers,' said the Nun. 'I'll be there.'

There was a large crowd around the Ghinni Junction courthouse where the inquest was to be held, greedy faces bending down above Jackie, people jumping up and down to see over the shoulders of others. The Nun stalked through them, dragging his stepson behind him, occasionally halting to direct an icy glare at some heckler. Women clucked, said officiously, 'Oh, it's a disgrace to let him get away with it . . . something ought to be done . . . that poor young woman, that little baby . . .'

Once the crowd parted a little, and Jackie saw the tall, severe form of Hof, greyer than he remembered, accompanied by the shabby, drooping Ellie, pressing close to his big brother, darting terrified sidelong glances at the menacing crowd.

Jackie gazed at him with as little emotional reaction as if he had been a cardboard figure. It was impossible to believe that this crumpled, frightened creature had been responsible for so many disasters. Poor Ellie, thought Jackie involuntarily, that his first excursion into the world outside High Valley should be this.

Just inside the courthouse door, Lufa Morgan approached him.

'You better, Jack?'

'Pretty near. How've you been, Lufa?'

Lufa shrugged. Jack introduced the Nun, who shook his hand and said, 'I want to thank you for all you done in the fire.'

'Wasn't nothing,' said Lufa. He looked defeated, enfeebled in some way. 'Jack, you heard the talk?'

'Yes, but I know what to think, Lufa,' said Jackie.

Lufa nodded, fetched up one of his quavering sighs. He gave Jackie a small parcel. Jackie looked at it in astonishment.

'It's hers. Her petticoat. You know when she left it at the waterhole that first day. I got it next time I went to Duchess Bay, and I kept it. Nicked it. Told Maida and you it had blown away. Wasn't the right thing to do, but I done it. She was that nice to me, Maida.'

Amazed, Jackie scanned Lufa's face, but all he saw there was uncomplicated misery.

'She thought the world of you, too, Lufa,' he said.

Whenever Jackie faltered in his evidence he looked at the Nun, sitting in the front row in the public gallery. In effect he told his story of the fire to that familiar figure, its unrelenting eyes fixed upon his, daring him to falter or break down. In reply to questioning he said only that Mrs Linz had wanted to make her home with them, that his wife had objected, and there had been an argument. He was very angry at Mrs Linz's attitude towards his wife, and the old woman had lost her head and thrown the lamp at him.

At this point Ellie leapt up at the back of the court, jumped on his chair and yelled hysterically. 'That's not true! He killed my mother, a poor old woman who had just lost her husband! He always had a terrible temper. He attacked my brother Kurt and tried to choke him. He murdered my poor mother . . . my sister . . . and you're going to let him get away with it.'

Hof clamped a huge hand over his brother's mouth. The coroner, rapping furiously, ordered Ellie to be removed and, weeping and babbling hysterically, the young man was half-carried from the court. At the door Hof turned and said, 'He is upset. What he says is of no importance.'

'Indeed, sir,' said the coroner, outraged. 'This court can conduct its own business without your advice.'

Hof bowed his head and departed, amid an uproar of excited comment and speculation, which could not be silenced until after the third threat to clear the court.

Lufa, his hair sticking up, so bewildered that he looked half-daft, hung down his head and mumbled his evidence. He heard the report of the lamp, saw the smoke, grabbed a couple of buckets and ran. Jack Hanna was already trying to extinguish the fire. Mrs Linz was in the doorway looking a bit knocked. Mrs Hanna brought a doormat down to help fight the fire. He knew nothing about any argument, except what Jack Hanna mentioned when they were working on the fire.

He had never had a difference with Jack Hanna. He was his mate. There had never been any improper relations between him and the deceased Maida Hanna. She had been good to him, darned his socks, asked him to come to Christmas dinner every year. He respected her. He didn't know what he'd said when they dug out her body, he was upset and might have said anything. It was no good asking him and asking him what he said because he couldn't remember, he was that upset about poor Jack Hanna losing everything.

The verdict on all three deceased persons was death by misadventure. It seemed to kill Maida and Carlie once and for all, and Jackie, still numb, went out of the courthouse and stood blinking, half-dazed, in the sunshine. A few people still stood around. There were stares, whispers, stiff ostentatious shrinkings away. The Nun said, 'Come on, boy', and took Jack to the modest boarding-house where he had booked a double room.

'You want to talk or blubber, or punch me in the nose, you do it, son,' said the Nun. 'You got to get it out of you. Let it rip.'

But Jackie remained silent. There was nothing to talk about. The huge fact of his bereavement engulfed all else; it needed no comment. He thought that some day he would consider all that Maida had told him before the fire; at the moment it seemed irrelevant. So he went obediently to the hospital to have his hands dressed, ate his meals when Jerry bade him. At the end of four days he said to his stepfather, 'You'd better be getting on home to Mum, I guess.'

The Nun, uneasily remembering the giggling and nudging amongst the hospital staff, the women turning around and staring censoriously at Jackie in the street, said, 'Why don't you come too, me old Jack? After all, it's your home. And Mum and me'll be that glad to have you.'

'No,' said Jack. 'It'd be a step backward. I've had years on my own, with plenty of responsibilities, and I have to make my own way.'

The Nun nodded. 'Yeah. You're doing the right thing, son. But I'm a bit leery of you meeting too much rough stuff for you to handle. I mean, like you've had these past weeks.'

Jackie smiled. 'Well, Dad, there's no point in my changing my name. I'll just have to take it. But it'll all die down after a while.'

'Sure it will,' said Jerry heartily. After a moment he asked, 'You think you might go back on the cream boat? Real solid bloke that Morgan. Stick to a man, he would.'

'No,' said Jackie. 'I want to get away from the river. Find something else.'

'Times is getting hard; you might have a struggle,' said Jerry, anxious. Then he aimed a punch at Jack's middle. 'But you'll make out. Course you will, boy.

'Send us a line now and then, won't you?' he said at the train window. 'And I'll explain everything to your mum, never fear. I'm real good at getting her feathers smoothed down.'

Jackie walked slowly back to the boarding-house from the station. The town drowsed; the pepper-trees drooped; windows shot fire. There were numerous boarded-up empty shops, and an air of bedraggled apathy hung over all. The frightening events of the vast, incomprehensible world outside Australia cast long shadows, spectral glooms that the small Ghinni Junction businessmen could neither understand nor defend themselves against.

Jackie thought, 'Maybe I won't get a job. What then?'

But he did not care. He could not care.

He thought, 'If nothing turns up, I'll go on the track.'

He felt as though the world had stopped and he would never get it going again. This was not his place. His place was in the cottage by the Dovey, with Maida cooking tea and Carlie jumping up and down in his cot like a blue-eyed monkey. At the thought of Carlie hopelessness came down over him. He sat there and suffered dumbly like a beast.

The next morning he was dressing himself, a task of frustrating difficulty, so that he could go down the street to be shaved, when he heard shouting outside. He fumbled the last buttons into their buttonholes, crossed to the window. Ellie was swaying on the kerb, half drunk, bareheaded in the blazing sun.

Jackie went downstairs quickly. He said to the porter, 'I'll get rid of him, take him back to his brother.'

As he left the veranda a dozen people had already gathered to watch. He walked up to Ellie.

'Where's Hof, Ellie? He'll be looking for you.'

He had not really seen Ellie close during the fracas in the coroner's court. Strange things had happened to his face. It was still

266

a boy's undeveloped face, grown older, finely lined, like creased silk. His teeth were pocked with decay. Colourless stubble on the cheeks and chin gave his face a dirty, aged look.

'You killed my mother and my sister, you dirty little freak.'

'It was an accident.' Jackie spoke firmly. 'A bushfire. You heard the evidence.'

Ellie's hand came up. It had a stone in it. He threw himself on Jackie, wildly striking. The stone struck Jackie on the side of the head and came away bloody. Jackie grabbed the boy by a handful of shirt and pushed him backwards. He fell in the dust, screeching, 'I'll get you. I'll get you with a bullet in the guts.'

Jackie took the stone and threw it away. 'Never you do that again, Ellie. Come on now, you're pissed as a ferret. I'll take you back to Hof. Where are you staying?'

Weeping, cursing, Ellie permitted Jackie to support him back in the direction he pointed. The crowd followed at a safe distance. Before long they met Hof, searching anxiously.

'Just get us inside,' said Jackie to his brother-in-law, 'away from these bloody rubberneckers.'

In Hof's room, Ellie passed out, snoring, face tear-stained. Hof brought a wet cloth from the basin to Jackie.

'Just a bit of skin off,' Jackie said, dabbing. 'Nothing.'

Hof looked at him sombrely. Jackie could see the thoughts passing through his mind. He felt, out of his withdrawn, distant state, a faint emotion that he recognised as compassion for Hof.

'Don't worry, Hof,' he said. 'I knew all about Maida and why you were all so anxious to get her married off to me.'

'I was never for it,' muttered Hof. 'Never. I wish none of it had happened and that's God's truth.'

'Well,' said Jackie, 'if it makes you feel any better, we were happy. I had five years as happy as any man deserves to be. And Maida and I, we loved each other, right to the end.'

He had begun as a liar, to comfort Hof, but before he finished he knew that he was telling the truth. Some time in the future he would be strong enough to think of Maida and what she had done, but his conclusion would be the same as it was now. They had loved each other and been good to each other, and it was because of Maida that he had grown to be a complete man.

Pain pierced him. He knew he would have to get away at once.

'It's not likely that we'll meet again, Hof, so I'll wish you good luck.'

He shook hands with the big man, left the boarding-house quickly.

He hung around town for a few days, until the doctor said the bandages could be taken off his hands, and then joined a team of western drovers as offsider to the camp cook.

Jackie Hanna

1931

5

In the beginning of 1931 a three-months-old letter from Jerry Mac-Nunn caught up with Jackie Hanna. He went to the muster camp boss and said, 'My mother's died. I ought to get home to the old man.'

The leather man pushed up his hat, wiped the ivory white top of his forehead, said, 'Crook news, Lofty. Always hits you, don't it, no matter what? Well now, we can get you in to meet the store wagon at the Crossing, and you can bludge a lift to the Chipp Creek siding. That any good to you?'

'Thanks. Who'll take over the cooking?'

'Dad Wright. Getting past drafting. I was going to pay him off, anyway, at the end of the month, so this will give him a break. The company's putting off men everywhere. Only a matter of time before I get the axe meself.'

Jackie returned to the camp ovens where his bread was cooking. The ovens squatted on a bed of hot coals. The air above the embers heaped on their lids was smeared with heat. He pulled a box up to the trestle table under the dry, rattling trees, stood on it, and swiftly, absently, mixed a brownie for the men's midday meal. Rubbing the currants in a little flour so that they would not sink, he remembered watching his mother do this, and looked at his hands to see if they were the same as hers. But there was no resemblance. During the years on the Dovey River his hands had become broad and thick, looking too large for the short arms, appearing clumsy, but quick and agile in use. These strong hands resembled no one's except another dwarf's. They were scarred with burns and there was a slightly disabling tightening of the sinews in the left hand.

Jackie's face had changed. A burn had left him with a permanent bare spot in one eyebrow; there was a pitted scar across one cheekbone. He looked much older than he was.

'Mum's gone,' he thought. 'Hard to take it in.'

It had been so long since he had seen her, and even then she had not looked much like the mother of his youth. He found it almost impossible to comprehend that both the middle-aged lusty woman and the swollen old gasping one had vanished somewhere together.

He padded around the dusty track between fire, tuckerbox, and the drum of bore water which was his only supply, his own constellation of flies whirling with him wherever he went, his hand constantly brushing automatically before his face to keep them out of his eyes in the immemorial gesture of the outback.

The plains were scalped by summer; the lapis sky bore down upon it unappeasably. Like a quernstone the heat lay over the supine countryside, grinding the earth to granules, the granules to flocculent dust that the wind took away in willy-willies, glassy shapes spindling and bowing in the sky.

One would have thought no living thing could move here without being sucked dry. Yet on the horizon Jackie could see the dust-cloud that marked an approaching mob of stock. They would be here before two hours were gone. When he distinguished the barking of dogs and bellowing of cattle, it would be time to take the bread from the oven.

This was the third stock camp he had been with since he left Ghinni Junction nearly eighteen months before. Each time he had waited for a job that would take him deeper into the west, away from the coast and the tidal rivers. He could scarcely remember his first four months as offsider to a half-demented bushman whose life swung between dumb, morose periods of sobriety during which he was a 'poisoner' – a dirty, unbelievably bad cook whose fare reduced the men to endless gastric malfunction – and bouts of drunkenness when he talked non-stop in manic gaiety and cooked like a chef. Jackie supposed that the old man had been a professional cook on shearing circuits, tossed out on his ear for unmanageable drunkenness.

But that knowledge, if indeed Jackie had ever had it, had gone, blotted out along with the man's face and name. His agony of bereavement, delayed shock from his own experience and injuries, had cast around Jackie a wall of non-communication. He supposed he must have spoken to the men sometimes. He could remember a fight – someone hitting him over the head to break his grip on a hard stringy throat, a voice saying: 'It's your own fault, Jim. I warned you. The little bugger's mad as a gelded bull. Just keep out of his way like I told you, can't yer?'

He supposed the man had chiacked him about his size; he couldn't recall. Queer!

Grief, remorse, self-pity – he had experienced them all. Then one night he realised that what had been distilled from all these painful sorrows was purest rage.

It was rage at life, fate, whatever it was that had distorted him in the womb and made all his life dependent upon that fact, no matter what hopeful lies his parents had told him.

For weeks the rage trembled within him, and then it, too, came to terms with its causes.

'All right,' he thought. 'What else have you got in store for me? What else can you take away or do me for? Nothing.'

And he didn't know who or what he was thinking at: life, or time, or the stars stabbing down at a land as indifferent to those things as it was to human existence. It struck him then that all he had or ever would have was himself, and a moment to be himself in; and the knowledge was complete and exhausting.

'I'm me,' he said. 'And no one can take that away unless I let them.'

And as dog-weary as if he had won a fight, or come to the end of a long road, he rolled in his blankets near the banked fire, and fell asleep.

During this time he occasionally met someone who'd read a newspaper, or had heard the rumours that had flown round Ghinni Junction at the time of the inquest. One of these men had come from as far away as South Australia, so Jackie had no doubt that the story had been spread all over the country. Three or four wanted to talk to him about it, for crude curiosity's sake. The sympathetic ones said nothing, but their eyes waited for him to speak.

Others used the tragedy of the bushfire to have a go at him, and in the early days he seemed always in fights. Once or twice he was thrashed; another time he was cautioned by a country sergeant.

'What do you want me to do then?' asked Jackie, snuffling blood. 'Stand there like a pint of milk and let them say I burnt my wife and kid to death?'

The sergeant was elderly. 'It'll die down, son. And in the meantime just try to turn these remarks aside. You can't fight the world.'

'Can't I?' said Jack. 'Watch me.'

But the gossip did die down, and Jackie ceased to be wary each time a newcomer arrived at camp.

In the end, the old poisoner had gone on a bender that had sent him out of his mind. Trussed in the back of a wagon, dribbling and goggling, he had been taken to the railway and a train flagged down so that he could be carried to hospital. Jackie had automatically inherited his job.

It had been good for him. It kept him busy all day, for he rose in starlight and did not cease working until he had set his bread and soaked the porridge oats and parboiled a heap of potatoes for the following day's breakfast.

Those first months were something to forget, and he had almost forgotten. The challenging sparkle that had enlivened his glance had gone; he had become much soberer. The mouth-organ remained in his back pocket unplayed. At night, now and then, he turned to embrace Maida. Other times he dreamed so vividly that the firm, rubbery body of his son was dancing in his clasp that when he awakened he found his arms crooked as though to hold a little child. There was a strange feeling about his arms – in truth, perhaps left over from the healed burns – that they were always holding something. But it was nothingness.

Astonishing to think they were gone, his wife and son. Carlie, nephew of Blind Hof, great-grandson of old Martin, stature and weight and strength in his genetic keeping, Maida's Germanic hair

274

on his head, yet with his father's vitality and inquisitiveness – of this Jackie was certain – sparkling and jumping inside that head. All that potential, for strong manhood, for imposing height – over six feet tall, the doctor had said, six feet! – all gone in a flash. While Jackie Hanna, the oddity, the little turd as Piper Nicolson had said long ago, was still running around alive and well.

And Maida – how brief had been the time of her happiness! And she had died without hope that the day would come when her husband would understand and accept her love and care for her weakling brother, would understand her desperate duplicity, her debilitating fear that she would be found out.

He remembered the night she had persuaded him to come to her room. Looking back, he could see now that it was a simple plan to have him caught in the act by the old mother. Yet Maida had not been able to carry it through: she had let him escape.

It all seemed so far away and meaningless now that she was dead. His heart ached for her. It ached for himself. What was living all about?

Now his mother was dead, too, and Jerry was alone in Kingsland, battling along, not knowing whether the news of Peggy MacNunn's death had reached her son or not.

He turned out the loaves, steaming wheels with a black blush of burn down one side where the camp oven was wearing thin. He tried the brownie with a length of fence wire, observed the latter's brightness, and turned out the primitive cake to cool.

Almost without his own knowledge or volition, he had learnt to bear his sorrows like a man. Grief was intermittent now. When it returned, as it often did, it was almost as sharp as ever. But at least now he had the consolatory knowledge that he just had to bear it for a few hours, a day perhaps, and it would recede once more.

In twos and threes the men rode in, ate quickly, drank their scalding tea, smoked a cigarette in the meagre shade of the trees, and hastened away again. They were lean as bones, several of them black. The dust lay like fine fur on their hat-brims and across the wet stains where their shirts stuck to their backs. They had brought a stray with them, a youngish man who had tried to cut across the dry country to jump the train at Chipp Creek, where the engine slowed on the long hard grade.

He was not the first hobo the men had found, some of those in the past beyond saving, or already stiffs, mummified and black as Pharaohs. One man who had been fat, Jackie recalled, was nothing but a bag of basil and bones, the ground beneath and around sodden with grease sucked by the sun from his corpse. Beside him was a gladstone bag, with a clean shirt and underwear, a fountain pen, and the man's credentials as an accountant.

'Poor town buggers, silly as cut snakes. Think thirty miles of scrub and gibber as safe to cross as Collins Street. Don't let this one eat too much for a start, Jack, and if he wants to hang around till Thursday he can go in with you to Chipp Creek.'

The man was very sunburned, his lips blistered like sausages. Late in the afternoon he recovered, and came over to Jackie.

'Anything I can do, mate?'

Jackie jerked his head at the bucketful of potatoes. 'Peel 'em if you feel up to it.'

The man sat under a tree, handling the knife awkwardly, glad to find himself alive and still going.

'Thought I was going to do a perish back there.'

Jack told the man about the lift available on the store wagon. The man's eyes lit up, but only momentarily.

'Heard there was work going up the line a bit. But I dessay it'd all be gone by the time I got there. Story of me life since I got the boot from me real job.'

He brought the potatoes over to the fire. He had wan sandblighted eyes and a gamey smell.

'You one of them drorfs?' he inquired.

'Yeah,' said Jackie. He offered the man his tobacco pouch. It was grabbed eagerly.

He had the gaunt jaws, the decaying teeth common to the un-employed. Other things marked them. There was the change of expression in the eyes, a sort of dumb defiant self-consciousness, and then a wildness – a hostility ready for hostility even before it appeared. The older men quickly got a hangdog, beseeching expression; the young ones developed a snarl; the kids looked bewildered.

So did Jackie judge the huge calamity that had come upon his

276

country by the human detritus that washed up upon this distant sand.

'Like a mug of tea? Cut yourself a hunk of brownie, too.'

The hobo, starving again after his earlier meal, ate savagely. With mouth full, he told Jackie a rambling tale of being laid off from his boot factory in Balmain, Sydney. Two year ago now; nothing but casual work, and bloody little of that.

'A good clicker I was.' His tone, like that of most of the hoboes to whom Jackie had spoken, was aggrieved. 'Done me time, come out of it a first-class tradesman, and what happens? Laid off. Wife had to go back to her parents; I hardly ever seen my kid. Got a weak chest he has – no wonder, the rotten start he got. Not my fault. Laid off, just like that, a first-class tradesman.'

He looked with feeble rage at his hands, still faintly marked in whorl and pore with black cobbler's grease.

'It hurt at all, being a drorf, I mean?'

'No,' said Jackie.

'Just thought I'd ask like.'

Later that night, the hobo went to the camp boss and said he would do Jackie's job just for his tucker.

'You'll get a toe in the backside, that's what you'll get,' said the boss good-naturedly. 'Don't get up young Jack's nose, I warn you; he's as strong as an ox. Break your neck with one hand.'

The man looked sick, and avoided Jackie thereafter. He spent his time the next day fetching in cast branches for firewood, breaking up the thorny, fossilised-looking wood clumsily, wearing a hopeless, sulky expression.

'Think you'll come back, Lofty?' asked the camp boss, as he said good-bye to Jackie. Jack shook his head.

The boss nodded. 'You're doing the right thing. The cattle industry's dying on its feet. Sure will miss them doughboys of yours, though.'

Jack saw the grateful relief on Dad Wright's gnarled face.

When he and the hobo reached the siding, the man scuttled away with a grunt, not looking at him. All around the lines vagrants were lolling in the long hay-like grass; there were twenty or twenty-five of them. Jackie knew that wherever a train slowed down, men of this description jumped on like fleas, to be mercilessly harried by train guards and railway cops, thrown off in desert places, or perhaps left alone by a good sport who risked his own job to turn a blind eye to poor devils legally forced to wander. To be eligible for unemployment benefits they could not stay in one place for more than a specified time – in one State a week, in another for only a day. It was the responsibility of the police to keep this army of homeless travellers on the move. They were an itinerant labour force, dirty, flea-ridden, riding bikes and old sulkies, bashed-up lorries and cars; they included families, couples, solitary wanderers whose only hope of a roof on a winter's night was to commit some petty crime and get collared for it.

Looking at them, Jackie wondered what it all meant, why a land overflowing with productivity should thus be forced to a standstill, whirring helplessly, while her people starved. Jack had better ideas than most about the realpolitik of the Depression. The reasons why it had happened seemed clear to him. What was baffling was why it had been allowed to happen.

An elderly man with a collapsed face, a burred chin, approached him, bummed a cigarette, sat near by. He was so thin his clothes looked empty.

The old man blamed everything, the War, the Depression, on *them*, faceless pullers of strings – politicians, churchmen, bankers – who had manipulated the country into ruin for their own benefit.

'Well,' said Jackie, idly, 'we've got a Commonwealth Labour Government now, anyway.'

The old man became furious. Thin pink ran down his hairy cheeks.

'Sure we have, at bloody long last. But how do you expect them poor sods to clean up years of mismanagement? Put the whole country into the hands of the Jews them last jokers did, and now Scullin and his mob are supposed to fix everything up in a year or so. While They sit back and smoke their cigars and laugh at us. Them! A marvel a man don't run berserk.'

He was ferociously alone, his wife dead, his daughter in hospital with 'chube trouble'. He had broken his bottom denture and there was no hope of repair.

'Who'd give an old ragbag like me a job? I keep me good navy

278

in me swag for interviews, like, but how can you friggenwell look like a decent workman when your front tats are gone?' He gave Jackie a half-embarrassed look: 'Your monicker Hanna by any chance?'

Jackie nodded.

'Thought so. My married daughter, she lives in Ghinni Junction where the inquest was held.'

With relief Jackie heard the snoring of the train far away. He climbed up the embankment fence, saw the black serpent switching its tail through the blond grassland. The sun ran up and down the rails like quicksilver.

'I'd better get down there and flag her down,' said Jackie. The old man sighed briefly, came to the point. 'Couldn't spare a few bob, could you, mate?'

Jackie gave him three shillings, which was almost all he had in his pocket besides the train fare which the camp boss had advanced on his cheque, and the old man scuttled away, not looking at him, triumphant and hating himself.

Before the train was due, the men vanished like rats in the long grass. Jackie boarded it, and all through the long dreary night he awakened at intervals to think of the hoboes, frozen stiff on the splintery floors of open trucks, bumping and hammering over the lightless land, their eyes bunged with coal-dust, bellies growling. On the way from nowhere to nowhere, and for what?

'Being out of luck is like being sick,' thought Jackie. 'No meaning, no use.'

He found comfort that he would soon be seeing the Nun: it was like looking forward to a sunny day.

In a starry pre-dawn he changed to a slow freight train, fruitvans and tarpaulined trucks, and three dog-box carriages dredged up from before the Boer War. The passengers had been travelling most of the night. They slept wearily, all their heads nodding in unison like seaweed in a current. The only seat left was in front of the WC; every so often Jackie had to get up and turn the seat up so that people could get to the lavatory.

At first light, people awakened, dirty-eyed and stiff, yawning, grinning – a kind of simple comradeship amongst them. There was small talk about the slump, unemployment, how many miles to the next halt for refreshments.

When he left the train to wait for the passenger train which would take him to Kingsland, he saw three hoboes being dragged from under a tarpaulin. One looked drunk or unconscious.

'Bloody cockroaches!' said the porter, secure in his uniform.

The passenger train was crowded. Jackie rode on the platform, leaning against the washroom door, watching half-dazed the trees whipping away beside the line, and in the distance other trees changed by mirage into fuming islands, trunkless, afloat in heat.

Shortly after seven the next morning the seamed green hills of his native town rose before him. Stiff as an old man, he left the train, washed his face in the familiar waiting-room, shaved in cold water.

He thought he would have a drink at the early-opener before going home.

He walked into the Princess May, and in the time it took him to move from the door to the bar the talk stopped and the silence gathered about him. He knew the two kinds of silence, the silence that is, and the silence that's made; one is dumb and the other has meaning.

He knew which one this was.

'Well,' he thought, 'the story's been here before me.'

He lowered a shoulder and let the swag drop, slapped the dust out of his trousers, meantime glancing casually around the saloon. Strangers mostly, some looking familiar as though they were older copies of boys he had gone to school with. But all silent. A museum of dummies.

'Middy,' he said.

The barman didn't move. Jackie looked at him coolly.

A year ago he might have felt outraged, bewildered. But that was a year ago. He stared at the barman.

'Did you hear me, mate?'

The barman swivelled an eye at his boss in the little office off the lounge. The publican came behind the bar, stood in front of Jackie, his hands flattened on the counter, his smooth woman's arms showing to the folds of the rolled-up silk sleeves. His name was James Tidey.

Someone yelled from behind Jackie, 'You ain't wanted here, Hanna.'

'Get your swag,' said James Tidey, 'and get going.'

Jackie glanced around at the men. Some looked away, some grinned, others stared him out with a virtuous challenge.

'That's how it is?' said Jackie.

'That's how it is,' said the publican.

Jackie picked up his swag. 'Shove it then,' he said, and turned for the door.

As he went he heard a voice say self-righteously: 'Good on yer, Tidey. A man has to draw the line somewhere. I mean, his own wife and kid . . .'

He walked down the main street. Kingsland didn't look different, except for the garage where the Chinese General Store used to be on the corner. But the town had a scaly, run-down look, not paintless, but with everything years overdue for repainting. Jackie halted here and there, looking for familiar names on signboards, trying not to look at the people who peered out of windows, drew each other's attention, hurried past. His heart pained him. He was no longer a boy but a man; yet he was wounded that this, his own town, should believe such evil of him.

His step quickened as he saw the Nun come out of Hanna's and sprinkle the sunny pavement with a bottle of water, preparatory to sweeping it. Jackie withdrew a little to one side to watch him. The Nun's face had changed; temples and jaws were prominent; the skin of his throat was loose.

'How are things, Dad?' he asked softly.

The Nun jumped. Joy lit him.

'Ghost!' he said. 'You little son of a gun!'

They embraced each other out in the street, punched each other wordlessly, then drew apart with foolish smiles. The Nun blew his nose, wiped his eyes.

'Better cut this out. People'll think we're a couple of poons.'

He walked Jackie through the shop, which seemed dusty, desolate in some way. It was only when Jackie was in the familiar kitchen behind that he realised the shelves had been half empty, tinned food arranged in a single line to cover the hollowness, apples and potatoes laid out on paper instead of being heaped in baskets and sacks.

'And you been travelling all that time! Days! Bet you're empty as a boot. I'll have a feed ready for you in two shakes.'

'But the shop?'

The Nun shrugged wryly. 'Ain't going to be a rush. Never mind that. Sit down, me old Jack. How's things been for you?'

'About as bad as they've been for you, I guess.'

'Yeah. Musta been a knock, coming on your other trouble, I mean.'

Jackie nodded. He suddenly felt depleted, exhausted. He sat down in his mother's chair.

'Couldn't believe it when I got your letter. I thought she was built to go for ever. I wish I could have been here when it happened, to help out.'

'That's all right.'

The Nun slapped fried eggs and bacon on a hot plate, began to make toast on a long fork thrust up against the fire bars. He laughed. 'Remember how your mum always burned the toast, every bloody time? I bought her one of them electric toasters before she really got crook, but she was scared to use it, thought it might blow up. She went on charring the toast and swearing about it. Gawd, Jack, she was a woman in a million, she was.'

His voice shook. With dread Jackie averted his eyes from the Nun's crumpling face. He knew that if his stepfather broke down he himself would be good for nothing. Fortunately at that moment heavy boots sounded in the shop, and a voice shouted:

'Hey, Nun, where you keeping yourself? Got that chook food bagged for me?'

The Nun blew his nose shamefacedly, wiped his eyes. 'It gets me now and then. Sorry, Jack. You bog in now.'

He limped into the shop, and gratefully Jack began to eat.

That night he climbed along the bough and into the treehouse. The door had swollen with rain; he had to shove it to get in, and it squalled off its hinges. The treehouse itself had become very small. The floor was a foot deep in leaves, there were damp patches on the ceiling and the walls, and birds had nested in the roof, leaving behind them on the rafters archipelagoes of white dung.

He stood there as though in a dream, feeling unreal, seeing Cushie and himself lying there on a blanket, Cushie giving a cry of pain and saying, 'Don't mind. It doesn't matter if you love me, Jackie.'

But he had never had Cushie in the treehouse. It was just that as a boy he had so many times dreamed of having her there. What she had said had been said in her own bed, in Moys' house, that long-ago late spring.

Sharp as a knife were memories of other times with Cushie, the sweetness and the confidence of them, no thought of pain and bereavement. Ah, more than that, no knowledge of them!

What had happened to Cushie in the years between? He had gone so long without thinking of her, so that his love for Maida should grow unimpeded. Did she ever think of him, his golden-haired princess? The games they had played: silly as owls they'd been, as though life were a fairytale and everything came out all right in the end by Divine Law. He tried to imagine Cushie there, in the treehouse, grown-up. She'd be tall, like her mother prob-ably. But he was still the same size. Perhaps she'd despise him, be horrified at what they'd been to each other for all those years.

He climbed back through his window, began to take off his clothes. The grief for Maida and Carlie, as it often did, took him by surprise, freezing up his throat, darkening his eyes with its sheer physical onslaught. He knew it was all mixed up with the death of his mother.

He heard the Nun moving up the stairs, dragging his leg a little. The older man looked in the open door to say good night.

'How long you going to stay, do you think, Jack?' he asked, before he saw the young man's face.

'For good, if that's all right,' said Jackie.

The Nun sighed. 'It's all right, boy. It's grand.'

He shook his head. 'You don't really know, do you,' he said, 'until it happens? You can't really guess how awful it is.'

Jackie nodded.

'Christ, we're a pair of poor broken-up bastards, aren't we?' said the Nun, and he turned away to his own room.

Jerry was more cheerful the next day.

'With you here it'll make all the difference. I guess I was getting to be one of them lonely old roosters, losing interest in everything.

We'll go to the football, sink one or two at the old Princess now and then, eh?'

He saw the expression on Jackie's face and added hastily, 'Oh, you needn't think I'll lean on you like. I've got a bit put away, and your mother's insurance, though the doctor got most of it, which was to be expected, and there's the shop.'

Jackie told him baldly of the occurrence at the pub the day before. The Nun flushed.

'Them beer-sodden hooers! And Tidey, always on the side of the cash register, that one! Scared to serve you in case they took their boozing elsewhere.'

He fumed on. Jackie said, 'I suppose the rumours were bad here in Kingsland? I mean, just after it happened.'

The Nun nodded uncomfortably. 'Flying around, they were, after the inquest. That bloody little nancy of a boy of my poor sister Eva is still going around Ghinni Junction talking about it, so I've heard. Him and one of the brothers is working down there now. Country people – you know how they like a commotion to yarn about.'

'Mum never felt there was anything in it?'

'Never entered her head. I put a flea in a few ear-holes, I can tell you. Thought it was all dead and forgotten. But just fancy them mugs at the pub still at it after more than a year! A man can't win.'

Jackie smiled. 'Well, my shoulders are broad. They'll soon get used to the sight of me round the place again.' He walked over to the window.

'Moys' still a boarding-house? No mistake, it looks a wreck.'

Jerry surveyed it. 'Not a lick of paint since the Moys left it. Ah, poor old Mrs Driscoll can't make a go of it. Who can afford to live in a boarding-house these days? She had five single men only eighteen months ago, good wages coming in, glad to pay for their laundry done and a nice hot supper of an evening. And what happens? All five put off within six weeks. God knows where they are now?'

'On the roads,' said Jackie.

Jerry looked at him anxiously, 'Can you fathom it, Jack, why we got this slump?'

Jackie tried to explain, but Jerry wasn't listening. He was just talking, asking questions, to keep his mind off loneliness and sorrow. So Jackie stopped explaining economic theory, and said gently, 'I've got a snapshot of Carlie, my little boy. Would you like to see it, Dad?'

Jerry took the snapshot, already browning a little, and looked for a long time at the baby, sitting up laughing in his cot on the veranda.

'What colour eyes, Jack?'

'Blue, but they might have gone brown like Mum's. Maida always thought they might.'

Jerry handed back the picture. 'Funny, ain't it? The world full of rotten parasites living on their neighbours' blood, politicians sitting pretty while a thousand men fight like devils for one job, murderers, wife-beaters, and yet they live on and on while a beaut little bloke like that has to go. Bloody unfair, that's what it is.'

The two of them stood there, not knowing what to say to each other. Then the Nun limped into the shop and rattled tins around. Jackie washed the dishes, standing on the three-legged stool his mother had bought him many years before. He tidied up, shaved, tried to pull himself together.

Later on he said, 'I thought I might go up to the cemetery to see the grave.'

The Nun confessed he had not gone for several weeks.

'It's a bloody woeful place,' he said. 'Gives me the willies. And your mum's no more there than you are.' He drew on his cigarette. 'Ah, what's the use of codding meself? A man's a cur. I can't bring meself to go there; that's the strength of it.'

'I'll just take the weeding fork and the clippers,' said Jackie with pity, 'and see that all's right.'

The Nun nodded. He trailed into the shop, opened the door wider, let the damp wind blow into the mouldy staleness. The shelves were half bare, but what did it matter? No one had money to buy food any more, let alone grass seeds and hardware.

'It's worse than it was after the Boer War,' he thought, taking the broom and beginning to sweep. But it was worn down to a stub, with a long silly tuft of whiskers on one side. The broom was banjaxed like everything else.

'I don't know whether to laugh or cry, and that's a fact,' he thought.

The graveyard was on a hillside, all the graves looking uphill, as though the departed had turned their backs on Kingsland. Perhaps there'd once been the idea of building a church on the crest, but there'd been no money.

The place communicated its silence, as a desert does, or endless grasslands. Jackie found himself listening for the swish of his feet in the untended grass, the roll of a pebble. Where were the birds, the insects? Only the melancholy drip of water from the sodden trees disturbed the air.

Here and there the worn and dimpled grave-stones had fallen into the grass. Some had sunk up to their shoulders in bowers of briar, or leant forward as though in a reverie, the tall fennel and Queen Anne's Lace reaching up to meet them. On the cracked and tilted slab before a tall cross a pool of rainwater had formed, and two little birds, sky-coloured, were bathing there. This pleased Jackie, and after the two little creatures had flown straight up and away he was further pleased to see that the grave was that of his grandmother, the old woman Hough, who had died before his birth, and whom his mother had nursed for years. Her husband was there too, Native of King's County, Ireland, Plumber of this town, Much respected, Deeply regretted, Died of sunstroke, 4 January 1881.

He knew his mother would be near by, and at last he found the grave, still new-looking after three months, with a counterpane of gravel and a glass bowler hat covering artificial flowers. Jackie crouched beside it, began to clip the matted grass, trying not to look at the inscription. He felt destitute of either grief or comprehension. It was as useless trying to think of his mother, quenched, changed, under that stone as it had been to realise that the body of Maida had turned into a charred log. But he looked at last, and read: 'Margaret Euphemia MacNunn, beloved wife of Gerard MacNunn and loved mother of John Luke Hanna. 1875–1930. The Lord giveth and the Lord taketh away. R.I.P.'

Where had she gone, with her hearty laughter, her indestructible courage, her gusto for ordinariness which had turned life into

286

richness? It was not like her to leave those she loved bereft. Dying was out of character for Peggy MacNunn.

And yet Jerry had said, 'Don't be sorry, me old Jack. You didn't see her at her worst. She hated being not able to breathe properly. Everything. Don't be sorry.'

If she were able to speak to him she would. If he could be quiet enough he would hear. And kneeling there he tried to quieten his whole being and listen.

'Oh, my dear boy, don't grieve. There'll be others to love you,' said a voice. Jackie, with flopping heart, leapt to his feet, to see a young woman in a black hat and carrying a bunch of flowers, staring at him aghast. She stammered, 'Forgive me, I thought you were a child, kneeling there. I didn't mean to startle you.'

Jackie made a gesture towards the tombstone. 'In a way, you were right. I'm her son.'

He wished she would stay, speak to him. But he had frightened her with his oddity, his lack of stature. She disappeared amongst the dripping trees, half running. Jackie turned towards the gate, and once, when he saw her at the end of a long aisle of tombstones, he waited until she had passed, so that she would not be further disturbed.

On the way home, passing the rows of cottages that stood where there had been paddocks, a market garden where once Sallycamp Creek had spread out to form a bog where the children of Kingsland speared mud eels with bits of fence-wire, he saw the same old willows growing along the big creek. And he remembered that he and Cushie Moy had, as one of their secrets, often buried bottles containing newspaper headlines, marbles, treasured fragments of this and that. In some magical way they had become hostages to the future, bribes to time. They had stopped burying bottles when they were eight or nine, but Jackie could remember where most of them were – under the shop in the dry cementy earth, beside the back fence-post, and here, near the highest willow.

Now that he had the weeding fork, he thought he would dig it up, if it was still there.

The soft-drink factory that had opened after he left Kingsland had closed last month, hit by the Depression. The company was going into liquidation, the Nun said, and a lot of people had lost what was left of their savings. But the creek was still polluted from the factory sludge. Near the willows sluggish bubbles came to the top of the water as though from half-flat ginger beer. There was a dirty smell.

He found the buried bottle without trouble, pulled out the rotting cork, and shook the contents onto the ground. A torn-off headline: 'Terrible Losses at the Marne, Fought to Last Man, French Heroism.' The hand that had fallen off Cushie's doll. Some blue beads. His first communion medal. A blackened halfpenny.

He sat there looking at the hoard, wondering where the hopes had gone, all the frail faiths of childhood. He put all the things back into the bottle and threw it into the creek.

As he came down into the town he met a knot of schoolboys, kicking stones, yelling, pushing one another, on their way home for midday dinner. They stopped dead when they saw him, mouths fallen open in theatrical shock. Jackie had met this comedy routine before, and passed by without a look. But the tallest jumped in his way.

'What is it?' he shouted. 'Who sawed him off?'

Jackie waited, looking up at the boy steadily.

'He don't as much come up to my belly-button,' marvelled the boy.

'Get out of my way,' said Jackie. 'Joke's over, buster.'

For a moment Jackie thought that his sharp, schoolmasterly tone had carried the day, as it so often did, but the boy recovered from his momentary surprise and jeered, 'Make me move, go on, you freak, make me.'

The other boys came up behind Jackie, half-thrilled, half-abashed. One shrilled, 'You really a freak, mister?'

'No,' said Jackie peaceably, 'I'm a dwarf. Now cut along, will you? I've got work to do.'

'What kind of work?' asked the first boy. 'Setting fire to more women and kids?'

Jackie fixed his tormenter with a stare that made him burst into artificial mirth.

'You half-witted creep,' he said. 'You don't know what you're talking about. Now, move!'

He stepped forward abruptly, and the boys scattered briefly, so that he walked between them and out along the footpath. He had no wish to force a physical confrontation; it would ruin his chances in the town if he had a scrap with school kids. He walked on, keeping his pace normal.

'Yah, you oughta be hung, yer murderer!'

A stone hit him in the middle of the back. Others went wide. He walked on.

'Got no guts. Won't fight! Come on back here and Shorty'll clean you up. He's just about your size!'

They followed him, pelting him with clods of earth, horse manure, pebbles, until at last they tired of the game and galloped away to their homes. Jackie, tense with fury, tried to calm himself. He entered the back gate of the MacNunn home, and removed his soiled clothes and washed himself before Jerry came in from the shop. He was cheerful.

'Had a really good day, couple of decent orders,' he said. 'You've brought me luck, me old Jack.'

Jackie smiled, knowing that the customers had come in to get a look at him.

At the weekend the Nun did the washing, laboriously scrubbing his shirts and white aprons on a washing-board, hanging them up every which-way on the line.

The neighbour next door put her head up above the fence. 'He's that independent.' She smiled. 'I'd do his things with my wash, quick as a wink, but he won't have it. How are you, Jackie? It's been too long since we seen you, dear.'

She had always been a pleasant, sensible woman, a woman who'd had her own troubles.

'You heard about my poor Jim dying? Ah, he was never the same after the War, with his lungs, you know. That cruel gas.' She sighed. 'And now your dear mother. We were neighbours for – how old would you be, Jack? – well, that makes it just on twenty-six years. And never a cross word did we have.'

Jerry said kindly, 'You come in for a cup of tea this arvo, Mrs Early. Jackie and me will be real happy to see you.'

'I will,' she said with pleasure, 'and I'll bring some hot scones. Remember how I used to make little tiny fairy scones for you and Cushie Moy to have feasts with, Jackie?'

He didn't want Mrs Early to come in and reminisce about his childhood, but he knew she would.

There she sat, soft big country face, brindled hair chopped off as all the women's hair seemed to be chopped off nowadays, drinking her tea, placidly enjoying the scones.

'I fancy that Mrs Moy and the girls went off to England. She had a sister a Lady or something. Never liked that woman, somehow. Even took her husband's body to Sydney to get him buried. Kingsland cemetery not good enough for her. Jesus, Mary!'

A deafening crash of glass from the shop made all three jump to their feet. The teapot tipped over and drenched Mrs Early down her front. She jumped up and down, holding her dress away from her body, screeching, 'I'm scalded, I'm scalded.'

Jackie raced into the shop, the Nun limping after him. Almost the entire front window was gone. As they gaped, a huge glittering sliver detached itself from a corner and speared into the floor.

'Oh, God, oh, God!' groaned Jerry. 'Them bastards!'

He pointed to a dozen large stones on the floor.

'They musta thrown them from a car. But bloody why, Jack? How can I ever pay for another window? Forty, fifty quid it might be, and I can't even meet my gas bill.'

Jackie had clambered over the window frame and looked up and down the street. No truck or car was to be seen, not a person except an elderly man and woman staring from across the street. Jackie called, 'Did you see who it was? What happened?'

But as one person they put down their heads and hastened away.

To his stepfather Jackie said, 'It's because I'm here. I'm sorry, Dad.'

The Nun raved: 'What have you done? Nothing, except lost your wife and son. That coroner never cast no suspicion on you. Nobody did except that crazy boy. God, I would never have thought it of Kingsland, my own town, thirty years nearly I been here, and your mother born here . . .'

They could hear Mrs Early snivelling in the other room.

'Lord, she got burned, didn't she?'

But Mrs Early, soaked and stained, was weeping about something else.

'Just look out the window, Jackie. Oh, it's too bad. So mean and paltry. The pigs. That's what they are, pigs.'

Jackie looked at the wet manure that had been pelted at the Nun's washing.

'Mine, too,' said Mrs Early. 'Oh, I'm that ashamed, Jackie. So soon after your mum going and all. All her lovely sheets, ruined. And look at my white marcella quilt! Oh, I feel quite sick.'

That night the Nun was still shaken, red patches on his cheeks, eyes restless, voice sometimes trembling in a way Jackie had never heard before. He could not eat his supper, throwing down his fork, swearing.

'It musta been kids! Musta!'

'Maybe the cowshit,' said Jackie. 'But don't kid yourself about the shop window. There's an element here that wants me out of the town, and they won't be satisfied until I go. That's why Mrs Early copped it too. Any friend of mine is marked.'

'But why? Why should they want to go on believing something that ain't true?'

'Chance for a bit of fun, bit of devilry, maybe,' replied Jackie. 'And my being different from them, that alters things more than you think.'

'You mean you sometimes got picked on for this when you was out west?'

The Nun saw Jackie's hand steal up unconsciously and finger the scar on his cheek.

'Now and then,' said Jackie.

'They must be bloody mental,' said the Nun.

Jackie shrugged. What was the use of trying to explain the meagreness of some minds.

'Dad,' he said, 'we'll leave things for a bit to see if there's any more funny stuff. Maybe they've got the dirt off their livers with breaking the window, who knows? But if it keeps on, I'd better be on my way. I can't have you copping it rough because of me.'

The Nun's face twitched. He turned away, stumped out of the

room. Jackie heard him pacing up and down in the darkened shop, swearing at the boarded-up windows, getting lamer and lamer. At last when Jerry's limp had become a drag, Jackie went down to him.

'You're as bad as a restless bullock,' he said. 'What about a bit of shut-eye?'

The Nun groaned. 'Honest, Jack, I'm flummoxed. I just don't know what to do.' He gestured around him. 'Everything's falling to pieces.'

'I've got some money saved,' said Jackie. 'I'll buy a new window. But you know I'll have to get out of Kingsland before it's put in, or they'll smash that as well.'

The Nun was aghast. 'Ah, Ghost, I thought you'd be home awhile. God, boy, I dunno what I'll do when . . .'

Jackie heard him heavily ascending the stairs.

They did not speak of Jackie's departure again. It was understood that he would stay. Intermittently stones were thrown on the roof, obscene words regarding Jackie were chalked on the boarded-up window. The small remaining flow of custom to the shop dwindled to a trickle. Debtors began to press Jerry and he returned from an interview with the bank manager looking like a man who had been dealt a mortal blow.

'They're going to have to sell me up to pay the mortgage.'

'Here,' said Jack, 'they can't do that. What about the Moratorium Act that was brought in last December? That means you can postpone payments for a couple of years, if the slump doesn't end before that.'

The Nun shook his head drearily. 'The bank manager explained that this isn't a real mortgage: more like a loan made to your father, your real father. And it don't come under the Moratorium. He called it a lien, not a loan. Imagine! Your mum's shop, supposed to come to you. Ghost, she'd clobber me if she knew.'

'I'll go along and see the Bank,' said Jackie.

The Nun's face filled with hope. 'Yeah, you got education, you know about figures. Tell them I'll work like stink, anything, long as I can keep the shop for you like your mum wanted.'

The town seemed full of men standing in knots on corners, in the shadow of doorways, around the bandstand in the park.

Disgruntled, shabby men they were, mazed by what had happened to them, bewildered by the mysterious forces that had robbed them of their livelihood, separated them from wife and children, abraded their self-respect as breadwinners and independent people.

Most of these men were of an age to have been to the War. They had fought for their country, but their country, at least as represented by the Government, would not fight for them: gutlessly it had kowtowed to overseas financiers, promised faithfully to be good, to keep up interest payments, and prune wages, pensions, and public works regardless of human suffering.

'*Them!*' thought Jackie.

Looking at the burned-black raggle-taggle of itinerants, Jackie was filled with bitter rage. He thought of the Nun, a man who had worked like a dog all his life and now was about to have the fruit of his labours taken away. The Nun hadn't even taken out the lien on the shop and dwelling; Walter Hanna had done that before Jack's birth, when the council forced him to demolish the old wooden veranda that had projected over the footpath from goldrush days, and build a proper frontage with a display window. All these years payments had been made on the loan, covering two or three times the original sum; but now the Bank wanted its capital, and so that was that.

It struck Jackie that this faceless Them really looked like a pound note. What was going on at this disastrous period in history was a contest between men and money, and money was winning hands down.

A sparkling anger filled all his veins with energy.

'Up you!' he said. 'You won't get him, not while I'm around.'

All the vitality and formidable protective instinct of his nature that had once been diffused around his mother, Cushie Moy, Maida and the little son, suddenly focused upon his stepfather. That decent man wasn't going to do it hard if Jack Hanna could help it.

Three or four weeks later Jerry MacNunn went up to the convent where, so many years before, he had found work and good friends.

A mountainous young postulant showed him into the parlour. It smelled of lavender floor polish and a faint indefinable mustiness that Jerry attributed vaguely to holy water.

Sister Bonaventure of twenty-five years before had been tall and handsome. Mother Bonaventure was small and stout, with a knobbly white face like a cauliflower.

'Ah, Mr MacNunn.'

She seated herself with composure, indicated a chair, upon which the Nun gingerly got half of his behind.

'Sister Mary Justin tells me you have been good enough to bring us the gift of some useful items from the shop.'

'Yeah,' said Jerry huskily. 'Nothing much. Chook food, and seeds and things, and some tinned stuff. Thought you could do with it here.'

'It's terrible, Mr MacNunn,' said the old woman. 'So much hardship everywhere. So many businesses closing. And this to happen to you, above all people, after all your sorrows and heartbreaks. It must be hard for you not to give way to despair.'

'Mighta done that,' admitted Jerry; 'but young Jack said he'd stick to me. Him and me are going on the track together.'

The old woman shook her head dolefully. 'That clever young man! So much promise! But is there no way to live except to become a vagrant?'

'Guess not,' replied Jerry. 'We got to keep on the move now we're unemployed otherwise we won't get sustenance, you see, Sister, Mother. But it ain't as bad as it sounds. Young Jack talked the Bank into letting us keep the little lorry I used for deliveries when Mrs MacNunn was still with us, and we've covered it in and made a little turn-out of it, where we can live while we're looking for work. Snug as two bugs we'll be. Jack's that cheerful, he's a godsend.' He broke off, grinned. 'There. I didn't come here to jaw, just to give you these few things and say hooroo for the present.'

'The Sisters and I shall pray for you and Jack,' she said. 'And you must not lose faith. You must believe that there is good fortune just around the corner.'

'Betcha,' agreed Jerry.

She smiled. 'Remember when I caught you at the steamed pudding?'

'Did I bog in! I can taste that pudden still.'

They talked a little about old times.

'You've never thought about joining the Church, Mr Mac-Nunn?'

'Never,' admitted Jerry.

'Fair enough,' she said. As they shook hands, Jerry saw a tear in the corner of her hazy old eye. He gave her a hug, the stiffening of her veil sounding like gunfire in his ears.

'You little beauty,' he said.

The mountainous young postulant who waited at the parlour door nearly fainted with shock and horror. But Mother Bonaventure merely straightened her veil and returned to her chair. When the postulant came back to see if Mother required anything, the old lady said, 'There goes the finest Christian I have ever known.'

'But he's not even a Catholic,' gasped the girl.

'And what makes you think that God is a bigot?' inquired the old woman haughtily. She made a slight pooping sound and glared accusingly at Sister Mary Justin, who turned crimson, muttered, 'I beg your pardon, I'm sure, Mother', and hurriedly retired.

The Nun had many qualms about leaving Kingsland and setting out on the track with Jack. Often before they left he woke up in a cold sweat, thinking, 'Leaving everything me and Peggy worked for!' Then he would recall that in effect all these things had left him already; the very bed he tossed in belonged to the Bank.

He had no one but young Jack. Everyone belonging to him was dead except that set of ratbags at the orchard in High Valley, and he wouldn't touch them with a tarry stick. His old friends were either all dead or driven away from the town to live on sufferance with married sons or daughters. The Nun himself was only forty-eight, though when his leg was bad he felt more like sixty-eight. He wouldn't be due for a pension for many years, even if he could live on such a pittance when it came his way.

Sometimes he sat up in bed and groaned with despair. There seemed no way to turn at all. No wonder old Piper Nicolson had drunk himself to death; it must have looked like the only way out for the piper.

Yet he wanted to keep on living with young Jack, to have a mate to rely on and do things for, and crack a joke with.

'And Jack can't stay in Kingsland, that's for sure. The sods. Ghost, I been ashamed!'

Sometimes in the early morning hours he felt like dropping his bundle, except that he could think of no place to drop it. His leg, as though in malice, went through one of its painful spells; he felt as if he had a blunt peg forcing its way through his flesh. He was agitated by the possibility of his becoming seriously disabled while he was away west with Jack, being a burden on the young fella. Jack maybe beginning to resent his presence.

He put all this to Jack, in a stumbling manner, and Jack laughed.

'I'm not broke. You've got a few quid. And we have the truck. We're rich compared with most.'

So, when it was time for them to leave Kingsland, Jerry put a good face on it, did a bit of boasting in the pub, saying it was high time he had a coast around the countryside, and that there were probably whips of casual work for two jokers with their own transport who could turn their hands to anything. He was greatly encouraged by the looks of envy on the faces of other customers who would have given anything to get away from anxious, whinging wives and half-fed kids.

'If the worst comes to the worst,' bragged Jerry, 'we're going on to the Big Smoke to get a start on the Bridge. I've always wanted to see that Bridge. You know they got the big arch finished now, but there's plenty to do yet, maybe three years' work in that old Bridge.'

Only Mrs Early came out to wave them off, wiping her eyes with her apron, looking old.

'Don't look back,' she said. 'Start a new life.'

But Jack did sneak a look back.

There was a big tree in Moys' old garden, its leaves Oriental yellow. Beautiful, it was, standing there richly clad and confident of many more autumns in which to live and turn gold. But Jackie knew that Mrs Driscoll, who now owned the house, was going to knock it down this winter for firewood. She had had all the other trees cut, and the wooden gingerbread pulled off the veranda, for the same reason. The tree was a bit like Maida, standing there, not knowing what was in store for it.

He pulled his thoughts away from Maida quickly, and from his back pocket took his mouth-organ.

'That's the ticket,' said Jerry gratefully. 'Give us a tootle to cheer us on our way.'

On the fringe of Kingsland, where the old gold town had once stood, and the stone buildings had crumbled until in 1930 the first relief workers had pulled them down, an unemployed camp had gradually grown up. Its residents called it Happy Valley. Jerry had never seen it, so as they drew level he stopped the truck to have a rubberneck.

'God,' he said, 'I never dreamed! I never dreamed it was as big as that!'

The camp was scattered over half a mile. People had tried to find privacy by building their bag humpies in the lee of sandy hummocks, mullock dumps, piles of shattered masonry from the old buildings. The bags had been cut open, nailed to crudely shaped frames, and weatherproofed with a coating of lime and fat. The roofs were of bark, of kerosene tins opened out flat with a tin-opener, or bits of corrugated iron salvaged from the Kingsland tip.

Women were cooking breakfast on open fires; blowflies spiralled in hosts above rubbish holes; children hurtled here and there.

Jerry was aghast. 'I never thought to come and have a look. When I heard of it, I always thought, ah, ten or fifteen shacks, maybe. But there must be three hundred tents and humpies here. Think of winter time! Ghost, it must be hell.'

The kids had pointed and laughed at the lorry. It had never been a beauty, and looked worse now that bows had been fixed across the tray and covered with a canvas tarpaulin that could be eyeletted down against the weather.

'Looks like a flamin' circus rig-out,' Jerry thought.

Inside they had ticks filled with clean hay, cooking gear, a drum for water, hurricane lamps, a box for clean clothes. But Jackie fretted.

'We need a dog, that's what we need, to keep an eye on things when we're away. Something with teeth like a crosscut saw.'

They carried very little money. Jack knew all the tricks about safeguarding money in the bush, and he had persuaded the Nun to send his small savings in the shape of money orders in registered letters addressed to himself at post offices here and there along their prospective route.

They intended to drift slowly south, but by unspoken consent they first turned west, so as to detour around Ghinni and the Dovey. They had applied for track cards before they left, and it was the most demeaning thing the Nun had ever done, standing there like a big sook in the line of men, till he had to front up to a police constable he'd known since he had to cuff him for snitching handfuls of dried apples from the barrel in Hanna's.

'Good luck, Mr MacNunn,' he said kindly. 'Next year you'll have a good old laugh about all this.'

The Nun couldn't help it; he was too ashamed to meet the young chap's eyes. He mumbled something, pulled down his hat-brim, and cleared out of there like a scalded cat. He looked on his track card as a certificate that he was a failure, a man who had lost his livelihood, his stepson's inheritance, his wife's home.

Jack felt as though he were facing into a cold wind with which he was well acquainted. It was no colder than it had been for a long time now, but now it seemed that it blew more strongly.

So they jolted south-west, hoping they could pick up harvesting or digging or other agricultural labour. There were occasional rumours of operations recommencing on the panicky public works that the previous Government had started and often abandoned, repairing rabbit and dingo fences, driving railway tunnels half-way into intractable hills, draining swamps that no one wanted to culti-vate anyway.

'They tried, I suppose, poor cows,' commented Jerry.

But Jackie, more cynical, suspected that the demoralised quar-relling State Government had been less concerned with the life-support of the workless than with their threatened coherence under the banner of this new thing, communism, now running like a fire in bracken amongst the unemployed, flaring up in unions that had suffered in recent years. Who could blame the thousands of miners, their families reduced to starvation and homelessness during the protracted coalfields lock-out, fired on and beaten up during the Battle of Rothbury, when pickets endeavoured to prevent a mine being worked by scab labour – who could blame them for snatching at any straw, any ideology that promised a better pie in the sky?

'This new joker Lang,' said Jerry. 'He'll sort things out. Hotter than a tomcat full of curry, he is. You just wait, boy.'

The new State Premier was a courageous and undiplomatic radical whose unorthodox statements had already shaken the Commonwealth Government. Jackie knew little about him, and he had not yet been so conditioned by severe hardship that his mind was stimulated by the sound of any new name, any new proposition.

Their first week was not a good one. The road was potholed, rutted, coral red, an Etruscan road; bushes beside it were enamelled with dust, the truck itself red all over. And everywhere travellers, some on rusty bikes, but most trudging with swags up. Dirty faces swinging towards them when the lorry ground up behind them. Suspicious faces, disordered with the pouches and puckers of long-standing fatigue.

Jackie was adamant that none of these swagmen be allowed in the back of the truck.

'If they can fit in the cab, all right,' he said. 'I'll go round to the back. Anything we've got in the back we need, and we're not losing it, so that's flat.'

'Cripes, you're getting stony-hearted, son,' said the Nun.

'Better stony-hearted than stony,' replied Jack.

The Nun sulked a little. After the Boer War he had been on the track, and his experience was that when times were hard people drew closer together, looked after each other, and did in fact share their last crust.

Jack agreed. 'These travellers have a code all right. Ratting the swag of a fellow stiff is out. But compared with the hoboes you and I are millionaires. So we're fair game.'

'Something's gone out of him,' Jerry pondered, 'or come into him. I dunno whether I altogether like it, bloody little firecracker.'

Jerry did not realise that Jackie's hard-line attitude was because his stepfather needed protection. Within three days Jack saw that Jerry was not physically fit enough for a vagrant's life. His limp, though he tried to conceal it, seemed worse; he slept little; but he tried to make the best of it.

'I'm just green. End of a week I'll run rings round you, me old Jack. Compared to the veldt, this is a picnic.'

'You're jake,' said the younger man carelessly. He shepherded Jerry all he could without the latter's noticing, was up early to light the campfire and cook the breakfast, changed tyres on the truck, fetched firewood, walked around the towns hunting work for them both. Once or twice when there was work for only one, he let Jerry have it, figuring that it would buck him up, make him feel useful.

They had luck at first, near Glen Ida, stooking and general labour with a wheat cocky – thirty bob a week and food in the kitchen with his shy wife and nudging, snickering kids.

'I know the pay's not up to rates,' he said, 'but the tucker's good. Not like last year, when we lived mostly on boiled wheat.'

The children's teeth were chalky and the last baby had rickets.

Jackie played his mouth-organ for the children while the wife and the big daughter washed up. The daughter was a colourless lump, with straight red hair and tiny wombat eyes, glowering about something, flouncing and banging pots and plates until the mother in an undertone told her to stop performing.

Jerry and the wheat cocky sat on the veranda and talked Depression, the farmer saying that if the prices didn't come up this year they'd have to walk off. He and two others were the only survivors in the district. The wheatgrowers' Depression had started years before, with a sequence of big droughts and small yields.

'I've got a bonzer harvest this year,' he said. 'Never seen anything like it. But they say the price will collapse. I suppose the farm will end up in the claws of the Bank like so many others. That's what they're doing, you know, grabbing bankrupt properties to sell later on, the bludgers.'

'But there's that Moratorium,' said Jerry.

The cocky pulled a long face. 'Don't affect me, mate. They got a lien on me crop, you see, and that don't come under the Act. I'd cut me throat, honest, if it weren't for the missus and the kids.'

He was a phlegmatic man, but Jerry could hear the terror in his voice.

He took Jerry down to the homestead fence to show him the crop. Most of the harvesting would be done by people round about, to be paid in wheat.

'Pretty, ain't it?' said the farmer, watching the wheat turn silver in the fading light. 'Makes you wonder.'

Jack sat on the veranda in the twilight, and after a while the daughter came out and sat on the steps. She had in the meantime drawn on a Joan Crawford mouth with the lipstick her auntie had left behind, and she kept touching it with a finger so that he would be sure to notice. She was bursting to talk to someone younger than her parents.

She told him morosely that her father had sent away her sweetheart, the farm handyman – that was why Jackie and his father were getting work on the wheat. The boy and her were real stuck on each other, but her dad thought she'd get into bother, if Jack knew what she meant, if the boy stayed.

'He's that good looking, real romantic,' she said. 'Big brown eyes.' She brooded. 'Someone else will get him now that he's in town.'

'Well, if he's keen on you . . .' began Jackie awkwardly.

'Oh, you!' she snapped. 'What could you know about love?'

'Lorraine!' called the mother from inside. 'What are you doing out there? Come in here at once.'

The girl muttered something, scrambled up like a cow, and barged inside. He heard her snarl, 'Course I wasn't. Flirt – with him? You must be barmy.'

Jackie walked away into the vegetable garden. The girl had seemed to him to be calamitously ugly and dull; she had nothing, not even the grace of youth. But she thought she was fit for love, and Jackie completely on the outside of it. It wasn't the first time the assumption had been made, and the girl was a moron; but he felt as sore as a boil.

'Up you, you mudhopper,' he thought.

It was an autumn of hard yellowness. The stock ponds grew shallow and slimy, the sun shone from a steely sky as though it would never go away. The wheat cocky gained hope with every day; when thunder sounded as if someone were rolling stones around in the sky, Jerry could almost see him tremble. 'God, I hope it's heat and not rain!' he said. Neighbours and all worked as though the devil were after them.

Towards the end of the harvest, the wheat cocky's wife, still awkward and shy, said to Jackie, 'There'll be a dance on in town, Saturday, at the Masonic Hall. You might like to go.'

For a moment Jack thought she was suggesting he should take the big daughter, but instantly realised that the girl would never be allowed into town in case she met the ex-handyman.

He said, 'Better not, I guess.'

'They're real nice people,' she offered. Jackie shook his head.

The Nun was vexed with him.

'You seem to forget you're a young fella,' he said. 'The way you go on, you might be forty.'

'I feel bloody forty,' said Jack, grinning.

'A lot of crook things have happened to you for a young chap,' said Jerry; 'but they're over now. You need a bit of fun, chat up a girl. Tell you what, I'll drive you in, and maybe get a drink somewhere myself. Hear the news in this godforsaken hole. What about it?'

Jackie thought about it. 'I used to like dancing.' He laughed. 'Scared of a knock-back, I suppose.' After a moment he said, 'Sod 'em! Let's go.'

Just before Jerry got the truck moving, the daughter, her eyes now invisible with crying, ran to Jackie and pushed a note into his hand.

'He might be there,' she hissed. 'Vic Tollery – you ask for him.'

The wheat cocky appeared from the veranda as if by magic, snatched the note from Jackie's hand, grabbed hold of the girl and shook her.

'You bloody mug! You won't be satisfied till he's got you up the duff, will you?'

His voice was so hoarse it was scarcely recognisable. The girl began to roar, 'I love Vic, I do, I do.' In her woe her face was positively grotesque. It was impossible to believe that anyone loved her in return.

The agitated Nun put the truck into first with a sound as if the gear-box was full of bottle-tops. The lorry kangaroo'ed forward and nearly destroyed a home-going fowl.

'I love him,' they heard the girl howling hysterically.

The Nun safely got the truck into second and coasted away into the twilight. 'Gawd!' he said. 'I wouldn't have daughters for quids.'

Glen Ida lay comatose in the long iron shadows of a majestic tor. Apart from the railway and the wheat stores, it had nothing. The only two-storey building on the main street was the corner hotel, a William IV fire-trap with rusty iron crochet on long verandas over which the louts leant on Saturday afternoons, languidly spitting at the passers-by.

Atrocious music, almost drowned by the rhythmic thunder of feet, came from the Masonic Hall. The doorway was constantly filled with silhouetted figures that shoved each other in or out. Jerry's heart sank. It looked like just the sort of place where, out of sheer witless skittishness, the boys would get onto one like Jackie, and then there'd be a brawl.

'Come and have a beer with me instead,' he said impulsively.

Jackie gave him a grin. 'Sod you, too, son,' he said. He climbed down out of the truck. 'Pick you up at the boozer later,' he called back.

The Nun sighed, and drove down the road to the pub.

But Jack, too, had misgivings. He wished to hell he hadn't been so stupid as to come. But he couldn't let himself down now. He danced well. He had learnt properly at school, and in Kingsland he had managed to get plenty of partners even amongst the tall girls. Maida could not dance, of course, but he had taught her, and they had often skipped around the cottage floor to the strains of Lufa's fiddle. Long ago that seemed! The memory seemed to bring back the Dovey, its blurred glass at sunset, the bog cotton flying white flags in the swamps. Wonder what old Lufe is doing now?

So almost in a dream he dropped his two shillings in the box at the door and walked past the boys clinging to the area around the entrance as if something would savage them if they moved out of it. They fell silent, gaped, made dumb-show gestures at each other as he passed; but he did not see. He moved to the edge of this masculine enclave and watched the dancers.

Girls! They were everywhere, far more of them than there were youths, hovering around their dowdy mothers seated at the edge of the floor, fluttering about the refreshments table, dancing with young men, with each other, even standing in clusters against the walls, looking eagerly towards the boys. The smell of them was in the air – freshly washed hair, perspiration, powder. Jackie marvelled that he had forgotten so soon. He looked at their dresses, the long flared skirts of that year flapping around their art-silk stockings. Cape sleeves, long diagonal frills, little peplums fluttering over their hips. How beautiful they were, hypnotised by their own movements, floating, dreamy, eyes half-closed, even when clutched by red-faced rustic Frankenstein monsters in stone boots.

A hand touched him. One of the boys, an artless expression clamped on his face, said, 'You dance, mate?'

Jackie nodded, waiting for the sting.

'None of us are game to go and ask a sheila for a hop. What about you?'

Jackie looked along the rows of girls, picked out one in a coin-spotted green silk dress, and went straight towards her. She was talking and giggling to her fat mother, and did not look up until he was beside her.

'May I have the pleasure of the next dance?'

The girl looked up, down. Her face suffused. She whispered, 'I don't think I will, thank you.'

'Go on, June! Do you good,' said the fat mother. She smiled at Jackie, open and friendly. The violinist tapped his bow on his music stand and announced the next dance. Jackie took the girl's hand. She did not pull it away; so, speaking a little awkwardly about the music, the floor, the crowd, he led her onto the floor. Just before the music started, he looked up, saw her red face, her lip caught under her top teeth like a little child's. She was embarrassed out of her wits.

He said gently, 'It's no good, is it?' and released her hand. She almost jumped away from him, fleeing along the wall to the other girls. Jackie, feeling that something should be said to the mother, returned to the fat lady, pulling a regretful face.

'Never mind, dear. Sit down and talk to me a minute.'

Jackie did so. She said something about silly girls without the sense they were born with. But Jack was remembering the soft cool feel of the girl's hand, her thin fingers lying in his.

'Like to dance, do you? I'll bet you're light on your feet. I'm that keen on it meself, you wouldn't believe. But nobody ever asks me to dance; I'm too stout. Wouldn't care to, would you?'

He thought she was joking, and smiled.

She chuckled. 'Think we'd make an exhibition of ourselves, love?'

She had a pretty, satiny face, a wreath of chins, and lively dark eyes. He said, 'Maybe better not. But thanks.'

He walked away a step or two, then he thought, 'Blast them all, why not?' and turned around and went back to the fat woman.

'If you're game, I am,' he said, and took her dimpled hand.

She was a real little butterball, less than five feet high, as rotund as a tank. She floated as lightly as a girl, on tiny feet that bulged over the sides of her shoes. Keeping her eyes shut, she swayed from side to side, saying 'M'mmmm, m'mmmm' as if he were kissing her.

The pair of them seemed to be down amongst other people's hips. After a while Jackie was aware that, perhaps in amazement, other dancers gave them them right of way; he could hear stifled giggles. His partner said, without opening her eyes, 'Pay no attention. Let's knock their eyes out.'

Jackie caught a glimpse of his late partner, standing there with some big ginger yob, scarlet-faced, paralysed. He gave her a wink as he glided past. And so, spinning, reversing, fancy-stepping, they whirled right up to the rostrum, stopping under the very bow of the violinist. He nodded approvingly, and repeated the last dozen bars, so that Jackie and the fat woman were able to whirl right back down the hall again, and he landed her, breathless, in her own chair.

There was an outburst of laughter and clapping.

'Gorgeous,' gasped the fat woman, flapping at her face with a handkerchief. 'Haven't enjoyed myself so much for years.'

He fetched her a raspberryade from the buffet. The dancers were again circulating, and as he walked around the edge of the floor several people nodded or smiled shyly at him. When he returned to the fat woman he found her daughter standing beside her, on the point of tears, her lip stuck out, muttering, 'Never live it down . . . I could have died . . . making such an Aunt Sally of yourself.'

'You'll survive, June,' said her mother in a voice both cold and sad.

Jack stood around watching another dance, and then unobtrusively left the hall. He found the truck standing near the pub, and climbed into the cab. He undid the neck of his best blue shirt the wheat cocky's wife had so kindly ironed, took out the studs, and pulled off the collar, folding it carefully. He felt neutral. His emotions were indolent. Had he expected anything else? Not really. Did he care about the girl's reaction? At heart he was indifferent to it. What was the matter then?

'I'm lonely. But lots of people are lonely. Most people. That fat lady. People like me, though – are we lonelier than others?'

He could feel the melancholy standing there like a grey fog, ready to wash over him. He turned his eyes to the street. Pandemonium was still going on in the Masonic Hall. An old man drove down the middle of the road in a sulky. He was asleep; the reins were looped over his clasped hands.

From a half-lighted side street came a curious trio, a pregnant coursing dog of silvery colour, a portly man in carpet-slippers, and a young woman in a flowered cotton dress. As they came closer, Jackie saw that she was being led by the hand, as if she were a child. She was terribly scarred down one side of her face and neck, and there the hair had grown back in an unnatural, brush-like manner. She chewed serenely.

The man was looking into parked cars. He was delighted to see that the truck was occupied, smiling at Jack in a guileless, merry way. He came to the point at once.

'Want a girl, mate? Five bob. Say hullo to the gent, Milly.'

The girl said, 'Hullo, good-looking.' She took the sweet out of her mouth and looked at it with pleasure, saying, 'It's orange now. It was green before. I like changing balls, but lickerish's me favourite. I go nap on lickerish.'

The man smoothed back her hair. 'Well, what do you say, mate? She ain't no Rhodes Scholar, but what she ain't got up top she makes up for down below.'

'Not tonight, thanks,' said Jack. 'My father'll be coming in a moment.'

'Think he might . . .?'

'Not him,' said Jackie. 'He's religious.'

The portly man sighed, resigned. 'Ain't done too well today, and that's a fact. All these flighty sheilas in town for the dance. Undercutting poor Mill. Eh, Mill?'

The girl gave him a smile both half-witted and of striking sweetness.

'Like a smoke?' The man passed a packet of cigarettes to Jack, settled down for a yarn. The bitch, her silken skin twitching nervously, pressed up for warmth against the girl. The man admitted without pressure that he had been the cause of his daughter's misfortune.

'Poor Milly, she was cleaning the kitchen stove with polish watered down with spirits, and I came in and flicked a fag end into the tin not knowing. Whoosh, you never saw nudden like it. It was the shock that turned her head, too. She never spoke for four years, just sat there with her tongue poked out. But you're right as rain now, aren't you, Milly love?'

She looked at him with adoration. He took from his pocket a brandyball, picked the fluff and hairs from it, and gave it to her.

'Yeah,' she said. 'I take my brain tonic and I'm real good.'

'And who makes up your brain tonic, Milly pet?'

'You do, Dad.'

There was on her face a seraphic happiness. She put her scarred cheek against her father's shoulder, snuggling it like a child.

'Take you home to bed soon, Mill. Good girl.'

To Jack he said, 'We're leaving town tomorrow. Stinking new

307

sergeant, standover man, not an ounce of reason in him. Said he'd do me for immoral earnings. Said Milly had to be put in care. Did you ever! Milly's staying with her Dad, aren't you, pet? Look, asleep, just like a bubba. Never think she was thirty, would you? Well, come along, Jess.'

He toed the bitch, who leapt up with a yawn of joy. He nodded to Jack, and the three of them vanished into the dark beyond the lamp-post. Jerry appeared, full but good-tempered.

'You been waiting long, me old Jack.'

'Just come a few minutes ago,' lied his stepson. The Nun got behind the wheel. 'Can't feel me leg, so I must be sloshed.'

The drive back to the wheat farm seemed to be interminable. Jackie remembered the look on the mad girl's face, and envied her savagely. Imagine envying that poor mutilated ninny! He tried to feel disgusted, but his own honesty defeated him. Ah, but she was *cherished,* and she knew it.

This intense longing to be cherished came back to Jackie again and again. The light grace, the kindness of the fat lady, vanished from his memory. She was old, a mother, *old.* He remembered only the thin girl's fingers of her daughter. The girl's spotted green dress fluttered interminably through his dreams. He wanted a young woman in his arms, thin quick fingers to caress him, tickle him, tug his hair. Like Cushie, like Maida. He tried to recall Maida's face, but it had become wan and indefinite. And Cushie's face was that of a child.

It wasn't just sex he wanted. There was plenty of that around, even for one not like other men, what with all the girls getting a crust on the streets with the slump. He faced it, he wanted to be loved and treasured, not by Jerry, not by kind fat ladies, but by a soft warm girl of his own age. In bed that night he frantically searched for Maida's face.

'I can't have forgotten.'

All he could remember were words that described her, eyes a dark grey-blue, long straight hair, a brown mole like a moth between her armpit and left breast, a crooked little toe where the wheelbarrow had run over it. But he couldn't see her any more. It seemed the final deprivation. He fell asleep into a desperate dream of searching, and awoke sobbing: 'I'm sorry, Maida. Don't go away', and was terrified in case Jerry was awake and had heard.

At the end of the job, Jerry was pleased that he had stood up so well to the work. To have a few quid in his pocket made him feel secure. He spent most of it on repairs to the lorry – a new carburettor, a second-hand spare tyre that was better than his own. Jackie was against this.

'She's going all right. Better to hang on to the cash till we see how things turn out. We've got no prospects at the moment.'

But Jerry laughed. 'Ah, don't be a wet blanket. Come on, give us a blow on the mouth-organ.'

To the strains of 'Pretty Redwing' and 'Juanita' they ground away south through a greenish-blond landscape, shrunken creeks showing islands of sand, abrupt wooded hills with weathered outcrops like castles. There was an airy dry feeling in the atmosphere. Lightning sometimes flashlighted the west, but there was not a drop of rain to lay the dust. Gradually Jackie began to feel cheerful again.

There was a big unemployed camp at Til Til Flat. They thought they'd put up there for a day, to hear the work rumours. In the dry weather it had a curious carnival air, quite tidy and clean, with tents and tarpaulin lean-tos rigged up amongst the pepper-trees, campfires wagging under billies and frying-pans. There must have been forty people there, most on foot. Jerry parked the truck a polite distance from the rest. Children were splashing in the creek downstream, women were rinsing clothes farther downstream still. Jerry found it delightful to hear human voices, smell food cooking.

'Makes a man feel sorta homesick, though,' he confided to Jack as they rumped around their fire after they'd eaten.

The woman of the family near by, having washed her dishes, came over to them with a lump of brownie wrapped in a clean tea-towel, and introduced herself as Mrs Bead. Having found out their names, where they'd come from, and where they were going and why, and after looking around to see if any of the youngsters were in earshot, she said, 'You see that little old green van there, with the curtains across the back? Well, there's a villain got a girl in there. His own daughter! She's a bit dippy, poor thing, and all scarred. You never seen such a mess. But him! He's been going around to all the men in the camp taking orders.'

Jerry looked at her, baffled.

Jackie said, 'Well, what do you know? Milly!'

The woman gave him a suspicious look. But she was embarrassed by him, so directed her conversation to Jerry, talking furiously: 'Don't you see? He's selling her. Oh, it's dead positive lousy. This is a respectable camp. Me and my hub are going in to town tomorrow to get our dole, and I'm going to tell the constable what's going on, my very word I am!'

'Don't,' said Jack impulsively. At Mrs Bead's outraged look he said, 'The girl's happy and well cared for. If the authorities knew they'd put her in a lunatic asylum.'

'But what about the you know what?' she screamed righteously.

'Gosh, I don't know,' said Jack. 'All I know is that she'd just fret herself to death away from him. Why don't you just let things be, lady?'

'Let things be! With prostitution going on? There, I've said it, and I don't care. That poor girl! It's my duty as a mother to do something about it. And as for you, you ought to be ashamed. I suppose you've been at her yourself, you horrible little monster.'

Jerry rose. He had become thinner in later years, but he was still immense. He towered over Mrs Bead.

'I don't take words like that about young Jack here. You just trot back to your own camp and take your disaster with you.' He shoved the brownie into the woman's arms. Uttering huffing cries, she almost ran back to the old car that was her family's mobile home.

Jack explained to Jerry his brief meeting with Milly and her Dad in Glen Ida. Jerry was shocked by the whole thing. But Jackie said, 'Don't knock the situation until you see her, Dad.'

Jerry shook his head. 'I can't fathom you sometimes, and that's a fact.'

But later he went with Jackie to the green van, standing back and looking furtively at Milly while Jack told the father of Mrs Bead's intention. Jerry saw that Milly's bare arms were plump, her hair was clean, and the bits of her face that were not purple were soft and relaxed, almost motherly. She sat with her arm around the serpentine neck of the coursing bitch.

The father, peevish and disappointed at the idea of moving on again, agreed that it was the best thing, and said he'd hop it straight after breakfast. Meanwhile Milly had gone up to Jerry, smiled and said, 'You got anything nice in your pocket for a little girl?'

Jerry gave her some chewing-gum.

'Ghost, it's awful,' he said later. 'That poor kid. Only a child really, ain't she?'

Before they blew out the lamp that night, Jerry said, 'Well, maybe you see things clearer than me, me old Jack.'

He awakened late that night with the feeling that someone was in the back of the lorry with them. Jerry lay motionless, listening, his hand closing noiselessly over his heavy torch. He heard a stealthy sound beside him, and switched on the torch, simultaneously saying, 'Stand where you are!'

He saw the greyhound bitch almost on top of him. She was picking up his false teeth from the saucer where he had deposited them. At the same moment Jackie sat up with eyes squinched against the light, saying, 'What's up, who's that, what's the matter?'

Jerry threatened the animal with the torch, shouting, 'The bludger's got me teeth!'

The dog laid back her ears and showed him eyes like pips of smoked glass. Jerry was in agony.

'Holy hell! Drop them, you cow!'

The dog backed warily away, holding the denture between her own teeth as though she were a freak with three sets. Jackie fell on the floor and rolled around, shouting with mirth.

'Do something, you little bastard!' yelled Jerry; but his stepson was incapable. Jerry seized a fry-pan and crashed it down on the dog's head. There was a crunch, and the denture, now in pieces, vanished into the dog's mouth. She chewed hurriedly, seemingly unharmed by the blow, jumped lightly from the tailboard, and disappeared into the dark.

Jerry sat down, his head in his hands.

'You wouldn't believe it,' he said. 'Me choppers eaten by a dog. You – ' he snarled at Jack. 'Fat lot of use you were!'

Jackie sat there weeping with laughter. Jerry lifted the lamp and looked at himself in the shaving-mirror.

'Hell, I look ninety. Who's going to give me a job? They'll think I'm on the old-age pension anyway. A man's a bloody guy. And how am I going to gnaw me way through me tucker? Eh? Stop cackling, damn you!'

'We'll just have to find a dentist and get some more made,' said Jackie, controlling himself. But Jerry would not be comforted. They couldn't afford it; new teeth hurt like blazes. They'd have to hang around while the dentist made them; he'd bloody well starve to death; twenty quid they might cost.

Jack said they'd have a go at Milly's dad tomorrow. They might get a few quid out of him towards the price of the new denture.

'You bet I will,' said Jerry, raging. 'He must be rolling in dough, all the money that poor silly bint makes for him.'

At daybreak he was still simmering. He got up, dragged on his pants, combed his hair with his fingers, and went over to the van. Milly's dad was lighting a fire for breakfast, Milly, with crusts at the corners of her vague eyes, was sitting on a box near by, taking pipe-cleaner curlers out of her hair. She gave Jerry a benign smile.

Milly's dad listened to Jerry's complaint, clucking sympathetically.

'Sure they ain't around somewhere? I mean, she wouldn'a swallered 'em – not good for her. Milly, you go and look in her nest.'

'Think I want 'em now,' shouted Jerry, 'after they been in a bloody dog's gob?'

They found a tooth or two, a fragment of bright pink. Milly's dad was penitent, but unhelpful. He said he was stony.

'Tell you what – when the bitch pups, you can have a young 'un.'

'I don't want a flaming coursing dog,' yelled Jerry.

'Serious mistake, mate. It might make your fortune. Tell you what then, mate, you can have a free go at Milly.'

The girl nodded amiably, putting a chocolate in her mouth, the corners of which quickly became brown.

'Spare me days,' muttered Jerry. He became aware that he was shirtless, still in his grey-flannel undershirt. He backed away, mumbling, 'Beg pardon, miss.' Automatically his hand lifted to raise his hat but he realised that he had forgotten to put that on, too.

'Going bloody senile,' he muttered, as he returned to the lorry. 'Forget my fly buttons next.'

The incident affected Jerry profoundly. He did not think it a joke, and managed only a false grin when other members of the camp chiacked him about the loss of his pearlies.

Money would be short until they got to Pyramid, where their next registered letter waited. They had to line up several times in dole queues at country police stations and get their issue. Jerry dreaded and loathed this – answering questions, how long since you last drew rations, where did you work last, how much did you earn, right-oh, no hanging about, only one day allowed here, move on for the next issue. It hurt Jerry so much that he felt a little scornful of Jackie, who didn't seem to care, but bowled up to beery, crusty sergeants playing his mouth-organ or whistling, cracking jokes with the other doley-ohs and generally behaving as though he didn't know what it was to be ashamed.

'You bet I'm not ashamed,' Jack said. 'These big fat john hops big-noting themselves because they're in the position to hand out ration tickets to people with more brains and less luck than themselves! I'm not without a job because of my own fault. I've worked when I could get a job and I'm willing to work now. And as for you, you fought for this damned country once, and if it hadn't been for your crook leg you would have been in the last War too, I bet. You fought for it, so let it keep you now. Five and bloody sixpence worth of tucker a week! How lousy can you get?'

But not all the country police were rough and ready. Those who were were often afraid of huge idle crowds of unemployed settling around threadbare towns. To move on the stranger, and move him on quickly, was not only the law; it also seemed the easiest way to prevent crime and annoyance.

The winter set in before the Nun and Jackie reached Pryamid. They had gone two weeks without a day's work. The Nun's stomach was out of sorts, his leg ached with the cold, and Jackie had subsided once more into gloom. He was so morose that when the Nun saw a couple of bike swagmen boring head-down through the rain ahead of them, he said abruptly to Jack, 'I'm going to give them poor wet cows a lift.'

Jack said grimly, 'They're not getting in the back.'

The Nun exploded. 'Blast you, boy, do you think everyone's a bloody bushranger? One of them can sit up front with me and you can get back with the other one and the bikes. Maybe that will shut you up.'

Jackie sulkily pulled up his coat collar and went around to the back. He helped lift the bikes up onto the deck, and said to the younger man, 'You can ride with me. Your mate in the cab.'

He saw the man give him a curious glance, and then a half smile, and knew that the cyclist had understood why. Jackie felt ashamed, and tried to ease his conscience by being especially friendly to the man.

These swagmen were very much alike, brothers perhaps. Both were pink, soapy men, their small bones cushioned, their eyes friendly and blue. Jackie thought immediately of the Gumnut Babies, diminutive naked beings that populated a children's comic strip in one of the newspapers. His companion mentioned his and his mate's names – Mutt and Jeff, Bluey and Curley, or something – but to Jackie they remained Bib and Bub.

The elder one, now in the cab with Jerry, wore gold-rimmed spectacles. The younger, Bub, spoke well in a mild, modest tone. Jack was not surprised to hear that he had been a schoolmaster.

'When the Department cut salaries,' he said with a rueful grin, 'I got up on my high horse and resigned. A mug – half a loaf being better than no bread.'

Jack enjoyed his company. They discoursed over a wide range of topics. Bub was not long away from Sydney; he spoke of the new militancy amongst the workless, the formation of the Single Men's Association, which battled to prevent evictions, barricading houses and fighting off police and specials with stones and cudgels.

The lorry pulled up. Jerry climbed painfully out and walked round kicking tyres, cursing. There was a slow puncture in a back tyre.

The rain had receded into a ruddy western nimbus, the air had taken on the chill of evening.

Bib said, 'If you could run her onto the grass, we could camp here and change the tyre in the morning. There's a decent bit of shelter by the lake. Unless you're in a hurry to get in to Pyramid.'

Jerry looked at his son, who nodded. The she-oaks were already gathering dusk into their gauzy recesses. Pelicans came down out of sombre pink light into shadow, skating in to land on water slick as a polished floor.

Bib and Bub were well-equipped. They had a hurricane-lamp and a square of waterproofed canvas they cast over a pegged-down sapling for shelter.

'You bog in with us though,' called Jerry jovially. They demurred, saying they had little to contribute to a meal except bread and tea. Jackie cooked eggs and fried up some tinned meat, opened a can of condensed milk for their tea.

After the meal Bub took the dishes down to the lake to wash them, and Bib, lying back smoking, noticed the mouth-organ in Jack's pocket.

'Play, do you?' He remarked diffidently, 'I used to sing a bit, smoke-ohs and so on.'

'Give us a few choruses then!' demanded Jerry eagerly. ' "Reedy Lagoon" 's a good one. And "Red River Valley".'

The moon rose, the lake became steel, the islands of debris were clots of black wool that stirred now and then with an uplifted wing or bill. Jerry was entranced; he had never had enough music in his life. He lay back and smoked, fell into half a dream. Bib had a sweet tenor. He knew the words of many songs, 'The Hawaiian Farewell', 'My Old Kentucky Home', 'Thora'. The last made Jerry blow his nose surreptitiously. It had been Peggy's favourite, always made her blub. 'It's that sad, it gets me fair in the gizzard,' she used to say.

'Give you a hand with the tyre in the morning,' said Bib, kicking out the fire. He said to Jack, 'I've a few newspapers in my swag, if you'd like to have a read before you go to sleep.'

Jack was delighted. He and the Nun never thought to buy a paper; their itinerant life isolated them from the stationary world.

All they wanted to know – news of jobs starting, seasonal agricultural work – they picked up from other wanderers.

Jerry turned in at once. He said drowsily, 'Real good wasn't it! The singing. Glad we ran into them two. Decent fellas.'

Jackie sat on his mattress reading the newspaper by candlelight. It was a Sydney paper, old James Jackaman's newspaper. Cushie came momentarily into Jack's head: queer it was, holding the paper started by her grandfather, a kind of remote link. He put her out of his mind hastily.

He saw that there were enormous tram losses, because of 'the new habit of walking', that five thousand women had applied for relief; a dole inspector had been attacked with a pickle bottle; and in his sermon on the previous Sunday a clergyman had said that the Depression had come upon the people of Australia for their sins.

'My God!' murmured Jack, shaking his head.

The Nun raised a face fractious with sleep and said, 'Here, what about putting the light out and getting some shut-eye?'

'In a minute, in a minute,' said Jack. 'I'm just finding out why you have no teeth and neither of us has a job.'

A new soup kitchen had been opened, and there was a frightening photograph of downcast, shabby men in a queue half a mile long. In an attempted eviction at Bankstown the house had been barricaded with sandbags and barbed-wire. Amidst showers of bluemetal, the police had made repeated charges with wire-cutters. One constable had sustained critical skull fractures. Sixteen men arrested.

He turned to the leading article. The new Premier, Lang, had evidently announced that his Government would default on the payment of interest on London loans.

'Hey, look at this, Dad!' said Jack. 'This Lang, what a pepper-pot, eh? What a nerve! Dad?'

Jerry snored on. Jackie returned to the leader, which was written in an awesome tone of outraged majesty. The Premier had committed the sin against the Holy Ghost, *he had repudiated*. The leader writer himself, it was evident, had suffered some gross offence to his finest principles. His moral sense had been violated. Jackie burst into chuckles. He read on, grunting and rocking around with delight. The tender concern for money that was shown here! Wrap it in a blanket, careful of its little head! Yes, yes, over the page is a picture of a thousand starving men looking for a pannikin full of watered-down sheep's-head soup; but never mind that. Here is our darling, our precious guarded one, the all-holy quid. No sacrifice of yours is too great to keep it safe.

The young man put the paper aside. He pondered over this whole world of power and ownership he'd scarcely ever thought about.

'Christ,' he thought. 'I'd like to know more about all this.'

The Nun grizzled. 'Gaw'sake, put the light out.'

Jackie said, 'Oh, go to sleep, you old coot. I'm just cottoning on to something.'

He blew out the candle and lay down. He meant to think about it. A few snickers escaped him. But he was too sleepy to think.

They awakened in the morning to the noise of the pelicans going off fishing, a dazzle of black and white, the sun shining fuzzy pink through their throat-pouches. It was a beautiful day, winter standing on tiptoe somewhere but not here, earth like a big warm placid beast stretching itself in the sun. It was a countryside of lombardies, ash, and chestnut, and its colours were bronze, sepia, and malachite. Far away on greenish slopes of downland stood the town of Pyramid, red-roofed, all in a huddle like a village in an Italian picture.

Jackie cooked breakfast and the Nun and Bib and Bub got to work at once on the lorry. They ate, killed the fire, and prepared to leave. Jerry cranked interminably, Bib had a go, so did Jackie. But they couldn't as much as get a wheeze out of the engine. Scarlet with exertion and wrath, they stood around the truck, cursing.

Bib said in his diffident way, 'Used to know a bit about engines. D'you mind if I have a go? You have tools with you?'

He looked carefully over the engine, nodded: 'Think I can get her fit enough to limp into Pyramid to a garage, anyway. But it might take me all day.'

It was agreed that Jack should take one of the bikes and cycle into town, pick up his ration issue, and bring back some food.

The Nun gave him the last of the change in his pocket. He winked.

'Get a couple bottles of beer, too. We'll have another sing-oh tonight, eh? Cheered me up real good.'

It was only four miles to Pyramid. Jack bowled along, touching the pedals with the toe of his shoe every time they came around, wishing he had longer legs but managing satisfactorily.

He whistled as he went, looking around him at the lovely flatland, which seemed to have been settled long before. Everywhere were falling fences lost under wild roses and black-berry canes, ruined stone houses picked bare as bones, a derelict coaching inn with a slate roof slipped down over its eyes like a decrepit hat.

He jolted over railway lines, past a criss-cross signal, and straight into the main street of Pyramid, a paintless, barbarously run-down town. He got his rations, and wandered around looking in the shop windows, enjoying his independent solitude.

The pub was not open for him to buy the Nun's beer, so he looked around for a park, and found one already dotted with loafers. It was sunny and green, around a pocket-sized stone church with an immensely tall thin tower that stared through the brightness with a Cyclopean eye.

'How you goin', mate?' said a voice.

Jack rolled lazily over to see the speaker. He was an obvious hobo, his swag beside him. He was the merest scaffold of a man. The skull poked through the facial skin; his hands were like bundles of sticks.

'Ah, giving me the once-over, I see, mate.' Lifting his lids he gave Jack a brief glimpse of a knowing goanna eye. 'It's a blessing, I tell you, looking so crook. The women can't bring themselves to tell me to frig off. I tell you, dig, there was one sheila, housemaid in a temperance hotel, that kept me for a whole week in an airing cupboard. Warm! I coulda lived there for ever. It's looking crook that does it. I can cough like a consummo, too.'

He coughed like a consummo for Jackie. Jackie drowsed, while the professional gabbled on. He always wore sandshoes, he said. He looked at them complacently, large, stiffened with mud.

'I'll give them a nice white up with Bon Ami when I get to

Rungil Ponds,' he said. 'Clean shoes help a man's self-respect. They go down with the sheilas, too. Got a sister at Rungil Ponds; jumping the rattler there this evening. Might winter at the Ponds, now I come to think of it.'

'I've never jumped a train yet,' said Jackie. 'Bit tricky, is it?'

'Naw!' The thin man spied a little woman trotting up to the church, coughed like a consummo at her. She broke into a canter, clutching her handbag.

'Well, mate, you might say I'm a regular compendium on the old King of Spain. I've travelled on the free all over Australia. Riding on the buffers, now, that's dangerous; cold and dirty and bloody hard on the legs. Wouldn't do you, mate, you ain't got enough leg, anyway. And these mugs that lay flat on top of a van. Gawd, you wouldn't credit such nongs, would you? First low tunnel, and they're ten pounds of raspberry jam. No, I'll give you the drum.'

'Any work at Rungil Ponds?' asked Jackie.

'Only the tunnel, far as I know,' said the professional. 'Stinking, cold, wet work – wouldn't have it on meself. They're always losing men that can't stick it like. Might be worth trying, if you're stiff for a few bob.'

Jackie picked up the beer and a couple of ounces of ready-rubbed tobacco for Jerry, and pedalled out of town again. It was dinner-time, and he hoped that Bib and Bob would have rustled up some kind of a meal from the bits and pieces in the tucker-bag.

As he rode around the reedy shores of the lake he was surprised not to see the truck. For a moment he thought he must have mistaken the location of their camp, then he noticed the Nun down by the water. Jackie shouted, 'Hey, what's going on? Where's the lorry?'

The Nun jumped up. He had a wet rag held to the side of his head. It had dribbled pink all down his shirt.

'Ghost, boy, I'm glad you're back.'

Jack jumped off the bike. He saw the Nun was alone. There were tears in his eyes as he stammered something, and turned away. Jack said, 'Here, sit down on this log. Let me look at your head.'

There was a long contusion, and a lot of blood in Jerry's thick hair. Down his left cheek there was another welt, already blue and purple. He winced as Jack fingered the head wound.

The Nun groaned with rage and mortification. 'Them pair of dingoes! Who'da thought it, Jack, who'da thought it, so nice and friendly and all? Singing "Thora"! Christ, what a mug I was, walked up with my mouth open. Well, you always said some people weren't to be trusted, and if I'd listened this wouldn't have happened. Gawd, a man's a bloody nit. Ought to be put away.'

Jackie threw some wood on the fire, refilled the billy, and put it on to boil. He looked around to see what Bib and Bub had left them. Not much. When the water was warm he bathed all the blood out of Jerry's wound and had a good look at it.

'Not too bad,' he remarked. 'Might need a stitch or two though. Now, shut up and have a smoke while I throw a bit of food together, then you can tell me about it.'

It became obvious now that one of the two bike swaggies had interfered with the lorry's engine during the night.

'I thought we might as well have a swig of tea while they were working on it, pretending to work, I ought to say,' he said bitterly. 'So I started the fire and I was down at the lake getting water when I heard the motor start up. You coulda knocked me down with a feather. Here was the older one, that four-eyed goanna, in the cab, backing her up, and the other one chucking everything, the bike, everything, in the back.'

It had taken Jerry a moment or two to 'realise that Bib and Bub were going to drive off without him. He ran towards them. The truck stalled momentarily, and he grabbed the handle of the cab door.

'Then that other snake came round from the back with a branch or something, and gave me such a whang over the head – Strewth, did I see stars! I fell on the ground, and he gave me another one. I didn't as much as get a punch in, not one lousy little punch. And all the time four-eyes was screeching, 'Put the toe in, Vinny!' But he didn't wait, just jumped in the cab, and the lorry druv off that way, the way we come yesterday. God, Jack, I feel such a mug. Need me head read.'

Jack put into the pan the mutton chops he had just bought,

sliced up some onions and tomatoes and added them. The catastrophe of the truck's loss had numbed him. They had nothing,
not even blankets.

He thought of the many times his stepfather's calm good sense
had brought him out of confusion. What had he said that time
when the old piper had shouted something hurtful at him during
the War? That there were patterns in life and living, and just
as you thought you were to be swept out to sea a current would
bring you back to shore again, and someone waiting.

Well, he thought, turning over the chops with a green twig,
now it's my turn. I've got to keep Dad going, see things don't
get too hard for him. And if ever I meet that pink pansy with
the tenor voice again, I'll kill him.

Aloud he said, 'Quit blaming yourself, Dad. That pair were
smoothies. Come on now, sit up and have a bite.'

'Bite!' said the Nun dolefully.

'Gum, then. Just get something inside you and you'll feel better.
You're going on as if the truck is gone for good. Later on, when
you feel yourself, we'll walk into Pyramid and report the theft
to the police.'

Jerry brightened. 'I didn't think. Course, there's the number
plate and everything. Stolen vehicle. We might get it back quite
soon. Thank God I had my wallet on me, with me dole card and
your mum's picture and me glasses. And we've got that bastard's
bike, too.'

'And money waiting for us at the Pyramid post office. So things
aren't so bad.'

Gradually Jerry regained his calm. 'Sorry, Jack. Nearly did me
block for a bit there. Makes a man feel useless not even to get
a punch in. Wouldn't have been like that once, you know.'

'Won't be again, either.' Jack grinned. 'What about a beer? One
less to carry.'

On the long hot tramp back into Pyramid, Jackie went over
the situation in his mind. He did not discount the gravity of their
position. Alone, he could have managed as other single swagmen
did. It flashed across his mind that having his father along was
as burdensome as having a woman with him. He pushed the
thought away, then admitted to himself, 'No, I have to be honest:

that's just how it is. Willing, good company, but not physically up to it. Poor old joker, cracking hardy!' Aloud he said, 'How you going, Dad?'

'Good-oh,' said Jerry. 'Howsabout a squeal on the face organ? Not "Thora" though.'

So, with Jerry wheeling the bike with their few possessions in the carrier, Jackie playing 'The Drover's Dream' and 'Wallaby Stew', they entered Pyramid, going first to the post office to collect their money, and then to the surgery, where Jackie left Jerry to get his scalp stitched, while he went on to the police station. The sergeant gave him little hope of getting the truck back. Once the vehicle got over the border they had Buckley's.

'Worth our hanging around in Pyramid for a few days?' asked Jack. 'I've got the Dad with me, and he's got a crook leg as well as the crack on the head from that lousy bastard.'

'Makes you sick, don't it, people acting like that to each other in times like these?' He was a decent man. 'If you're absolutely stony I could vag the both of you for forty-eight hours. The wife's a good cook. Chance to have a lay-up and some regular washing and feeding.'

Jackie laughed. 'The Dad would never come at it. He's old-fashioned.' He added, 'What'll I do with the bike?'

'Take the bloody thing away and sell it,' said the sergeant. 'I never seen it, never heard of it.'

Jackie checked with him about the railway tunnel at Rungil Ponds.

'Yeah, you might land a bit of navvying there. There's a swine of a foreman – men coming and going all the time. Bit on the short side for a shovel though, ain't you, mate?'

Jackie shrugged. 'I'm strong as a horse. Always something I can do.'

The sergeant said awkwardly, reddening, 'Hope you don't mind my asking, being small like – born that way, were you?'

'Yep,' said Jack.

'The wife's having a kid, you see,' said the sergeant. 'Just curious like.'

'Don't worry, sarge; not much chance of its being like me. I'm

322

one in a million. Well, tooraloo!' and he swanked out of the police station.

Outside he found his hands tightly clenched. He thought, 'Right-oh, right-oh. You'd feel the same way.'

During a meal at the Greek's, Jack put it to his stepfather that he should return to Kingsland.

'I've been thinking. Maybe you could board with Mrs Early. If I went outback again I reckon I could get a cook's job at a shearing-shed or with a road gang. I'm a good cook. Better than Socrates here.' He gestured at the greasy eggs. 'I could send money home.'

The Nun looked as if Jackie had hit him. The young man hastened to say, 'Look how long you stood by me when I couldn't get a job. Give me a chance to get my own back, Dad.'

The Nun was deeply affronted. 'Tell me straight, Jack, am I holding back?'

'Not a bit of it,' said Jack. 'It's just that if we don't get the truck back – and there's not much hope of that – it's going to be a hard winter.'

'I've known hard times,' said the Nun angrily. 'Wasn't no picnic in Africa.'

The young man longed to yell, 'You witless old goat! You were seventeen then, with two whole legs!'

But he was not able to do it. Love for his stepfather enfeebled him. He said appeasingly, 'We'll leave it for now, then. See how we manage.'

Secretly Jerry was alarmed, almost panicky. He felt he couldn't face returning to Kingsland. 'Ghost, I got no one but Jack, really. I gotta hang on to him until I feel more meself.'

Yet at the same time he was sorrowful, humiliated, that this should be so. He had spent twenty years being a father to young Jack, being around to tell him things, chiack him out of bawling when he fell over or things went wrong, carry him home from the football when it was late and the kid was tired. Ghost! Looking back, Jerry realised that he'd not known how happy he was in them days. Little Jack, his little tiger, never giving in to anything.

'I can't lean on the boy, Ghost, no. Not yet,' he thought, in real torment. The fact that Jack was a dwarf seemed to make it all the worse. 'The size of him and all! I got to hold me end up somehow, and maybe things will work out.'

So he stood up straighter, never mentioned the pain in his leg, spoke as if he didn't have a care in the world. When the sergeant, after three days, could give them no news of the truck, he said cheerfully, 'Well, me old Jack, I vote we hop the train to Rungil Ponds, and see what's offering.'

As the train left the station, and the livid light of the green signal dipped into the truck and out again, Jackie exhaled with relief. Though he had followed the thin professional's advice, Jerry and he had had a tense, anxious hour, dodging around the dark good-sheds, seeing the train approach from the north, the engine throwing a red glow over the long black snake behind. As she stood snorting on the loop, they scurried across the rails on the offside, threw their swags into an empty louvre, and jumped up after them.

'Are you sure it's the right one?' whispered Jerry.

'Yeah. All freight except for the one carriage. She's picking up two or three passengers now. I saw them on the platform with their luggage.'

When they were well away, they unrolled their swags and wrapped blankets around themselves. The bike had been sold for four pounds; they had, at the same auction room, obtained second-hand flannel shirts, a torch and batteries, blankets and a metal water-bottle, a few odds and ends such as a cut-throat razor and a towel. They had a tucker-bag, and just before the shops shut Jerry had bought a bag of terrible comestibles called 'faggots' to keep them going through the night.

The stars streamed overhead, sometimes obscured by smoke. The wind whimpered with a shrill human voice. Jackie pulled the doors shut, but the truck was still full of wind and coal-dust, stinging their eyes, chokingly cold. There had been four trucks covered with tarpaulins, but the professional had specifically warned against riding in them.

'I'll tell you for why,' he had said. 'A truck with a tarp over it is like a locked house. Get in there and it's breaking and entering. If they collar you, you'll do a stretch. Also, it's a favourite dodge of railway guards and cops to crawl over a tarp belting it with a wooden waddy. If you're lying underneath on top of the load you could get a fractured scone.'

The train tore through the night. They expected to go through Rungil Ponds at first light. Jackie dreaded the time when they would have to alight, dropping off the train as she slowed at the first halt signal approaching the station.

'Still,' he comforted himself, 'older men than Dad have done it without breaking a leg.'

They ate their faggots, now cool and greasy, little flowerpots of sawdust, ground up fag-ends of corned beef and stale sausage, pepper, fat.

'Ugh!' said Jack, and disgustedly fired the peaty remnant into the darkness. 'I'd rather do a starve.'

He rolled himself in his blanket and fell asleep as if into a pool of oil. Jerry, too, his back against the wall of the truck, his head on his chest, slept intermittently. When he awoke he felt as if every bone in his body had been dislocated. The pain of straightening his neck as he raised his head was unbelievable. My bloody napper must weigh a stone, he thought. He became aware that the train was slowing, the wheels clicking and bumping into a slow glide.

He gripped Jackie's wrist. The young man awoke instantly.

The train jerked to a halt. Reverberant noises in the chill silence, lights touching the tops of trees, vanishing. Jackie cautiously peered out.

'She must be watering. No sign of any town.'

A boot crunched on gravel. The door was slid open, and a lantern shone.

'Cold night, ain't she?' An amiable rat face looked up at them. They were speechless.

'You can ride free far as you like, for all of mine. I just came along to tip you off that we got Owen up front.'

Jerry said, 'How'd you know we was here?'

The guard was amused. 'Saw you get on at Pyramid, course. Green, ain't yer? But Big Owen's a thorough-going bastard and I wouldn't like to see the kid stop a clout. Take the hint, mate, and slip off right now. Strike due west, two-three miles, and you'll come to the main south road.'

He lifted the lantern to see them better.

'Christ, you ain't no kid! Well, spare me days!' He looked closer at Jackie. 'Ain't you that dwarf fella that was mixed up in that funny case over Ghinni way?'

'It was a bushfire,' said Jack. 'An accident.'

'Oh, yeah,' said the guard. His face changed, hardened. The whistle blew. He stepped back. 'Well, a man can make up his own mind about things like that.'

Without another word he strode off. Jerry said uneasily, 'Who's this bloke, Big Owen?'

'Don't know. But I think we ought to get off.'

Jackie began swiftly to roll up his swag, urging Jerry to do the same. But it was too late. The train started, gathered speed. Jack swore. He stuck his head cautiously out of the truck. The night plunged past, faster and faster; there was a smell of swamps and wet coal. Water glistened in spectral patches.

'Missed our chance,' said Jack. 'Bugger it. We'll have to wait for a grade.'

'But we'd be in the middle of nowhere,' protested the Nun. He couldn't see Jack's face, but he said, 'You know who this Big Owen is, then?'

'Never heard of him; but from the way the guard spoke he can't be anything but a railway cop, and a well-known one. He won't be well-known for his cheerful disposition.'

Jerry was inclined to argue. 'Ah, the guard was a decent fella, he wouldn't pot us.'

'Not you, maybe. But he'd gladly see me hanged. Now look, quit the arguments, Dad. The next time she slows, we'll scarper.'

'We could take him,' growled the Nun. Jackie let him talk on, knowing that it would calm him. He himself waited, alertly, listening to the sound of the wheels. The moon came up, but the countryside only hung suspended, faintly high-lighted. No feature could be discerned except black fins of hills against the sky.

Jack carried a map in his pocket. He spread it out on the splintered floor, held the light of the torch close to it. He figured that they were still sixty or more miles from Rungil Ponds.

Suddenly there was another man in the truck. A great shadow

leapt across the circle of torchlight, the map skidded away under a heel, Jack saw the Nun, who was on his feet, whip up his left arm to block a descending blow, and drive his own right fist into the centre of a block of semi-darkness. A waddy clattered out of the man's hand, and he doubled up, making sounds like a roaring horse. Jackie seized the waddy, stood ready. He shouted to his father:

'Get the swags to the door.'

The man's hand shot out, grabbed Jackie by the hair. Instead of jerking backwards, the young man leapt forward, bringing his head up under the other's chin with a sodden smash. At the same time he seized the man by the throat, and wound his legs about his body. They crashed into the corner, floundering in the noisy darkness, the torch rolling back and forth and casting a weird, fluctuant light upon the louvres, a hulking shoulder, Jerry lurching around shouting.

Jack yelled, 'Keep back, keep back! I can take him. Get to the door!'

It was like a small monkey fighting a big monkey. In spite of Jack's exertion of his great strength, his opponent managed to roll sufficiently to get some of his weight on the younger man. Slowly he forced Jack's shoulders back against the floor. Jack dug his thumbs in at the corners of the jaw. The slewing torchlight showed a congested face.

Out of the corner of his eye Jack saw his father hesitating beside the sliding, clanking door, the darkness running beside the train, prickly pears coming at them like grey giants for an instant and then vanishing. He heard the hammer of the wheels change as the engine took the weight of the train on the grade. He choked out, 'Not yet, Dad!'

Under his head he heard the metal grip and gride; the whole orchestra of groans and clacks and rattles changed its tempo, the buffers clamoured. He shouted, 'Now! Jump!'

He sensed, rather than saw the doorway become empty.

The face goggling into his own was dark with blood. With a fearful effort he thrust back the chin. The veined eyes rolled up and the body went flabby. Jackie squirmed out from underneath it. Every muscle in his body was shaking, but he could not afford to wait. He stuck the torch inside his shirt, dropped out into the darkness, and rolled like a ball down the embankment. He crashed against the base of a prickly pear, and a thousand steel hairs pierced him. As he tottered to his feet he saw the tail of the train swing around the curve ahead.

He rested a while, feeling nauseated, exerted to the last ounce of his strength. He heard a faint coo-ee, picked up the torch, and stumbled through the faintly moonlit scrub to look for Jerry. It was freezing. The wind fingering his many abrasions was as sharp as metal. He found the Nun at last, propped against a tree.

'You all right, Dad?'

The older man said anxiously, 'Christ, boy, I didn't want to leave you back there.'

'Something the matter?'

'Just landed a bit heavy, that's all,' said the Nun. 'But I dunno where the swags are.'

'I'll find them. Don't move from there.'

It took Jackie twenty minutes of searching along the embankment: the Nun had thrown the swags too wide. Jack shouldered them and trudged back to his stepfather. In the dim, lemon light of the torch the older man's face was cadaverous. Jack took fright.

'You've broken something!'

'My leg,' gasped the Nun. 'Something's bust.'

A large blue protrusion on his upper thigh had split open like a thin-skinned pear. Pus and blood gushed out. Jackie looked at it aghast. Jerry, half fainting, leant against the tree.

'It's been coming up this last week, that bit of shrapnel, I suppose, but when I landed, I bust it . . . Oh, God, Jack . . .'

Tears of agony ran down his face.

Jack turned the torch on the wound, which was like a huge burst abscess. Protruding from the depths was a discoloured piece of metal, shaped like a corroded knot of cord.

'Christ, Dad, why didn't you say something? You silly bastard, why didn't you?'

But Jerry could not reply. He leant against the tree, his teeth chattering with cold, uttering now and then, 'Ahhh! Ahhh!' in a low anxious tone.

Jack unrolled his swag, found their towel, which was filthy. He got out his clean shirt.

'Oh, God, boy, not your shirt,' babbled the Nun. 'And don't let the muck get on my strides – I'll have nothing to cover me bank account.'

'I won't,' said Jack. He made the shirt into a pad, mopped the gullied flesh gently. 'Try and stick it, Dad. The bleeding's not too bad. And I can see the shrapnel.'

'Where?' cried Jerry, brightening. 'Let me see the bastard.' But even as he leant forward he grunted and slumped against the tree once more, half-conscious.

Quickly with the cloth Jackie dragged long strings of clotted pus and mucus from the hole, pressed gently, forcing the blood to flow once more. He took hold of the metal, tried to withdraw it. It shifted soggily. The Nun shouted hoarsely, and Jackie desisted.

'A doctor could get it out. We've got to get you to a doctor,' said Jack. He looked at the sky. 'A couple of hours to dawn. I'll light a fire and make you comfortable.'

He bound up the wound and covered the Nun with a blanket, then gathered together dusty twigs and bark and lit the fire. Jackie boiled the billy, made tea, and put steaming hot cloths on the Nun's leg.

When, at last, the Nun fell asleep Jack hunkered beside the fire, smoking, gazing into the flames, wondering how he could get him to a doctor. The map had been left in the louvre truck; he had no idea if there were any towns between here and Rungil Ponds. Absently he sucked the skinned places on his hand, rubbed his painful knuckles. He became aware that he hurt all over and his back was on fire with the cactus spines. He slept little.

At dawn he was as stiff as a board. The Nun was still asleep, his mouth sagging, his face wan. Jackie was relieved, for he had feared blood poisoning and fever from that open wound. Pulling up his coat collar against the needling cold, Jack scrambled up onto the embankment, looked all around for smoke from chimney, any sign of human life at all.

It was wilted country into which they had jumped, cur country, licked by nature. To the south were long meandering hills, worn by ancient ice or water, hairy with low grey vegetation. Crows kaa'ed lonesomely. To the north was a wide plateau. A listless wind picked over ragged scrub. Here and there were sandy patches already hopping with rabbits, small grey dots like fleas or lice. Jackie wondered it there were a rabbiter's camp where he could get help, or where Jerry could lie up until a doctor was fetched. He sniffed, trying to pick up the dankness of mud, or foul sedge, for almost all the water they had carried was gone.

He looked up and down the permanent way. It was so quiet he could hear the sand whispering along the rails.

Hearing movement, he glanced down to see his stepfather, trailing his blanket, lurching out of the scrub. Jerry was pale, but he looked better than he had done the night before. He was vexed with himself; ashamed to meet Jack's eyes.

'Bit of an old woman, I guess. Sort of a shock it was, that was all.'

Jackie lit the fire again, put the remains of their water in the billy.

'If your leg needs fomenting I'll use it for that; otherwise you can have a cup of tea.'

He removed the blood-stained pad. The wound had collapsed on itself like a toothless, oozing mouth. Raw tissue surrounded the metal slug, angry-looking. The Nun stared at it.

'That bugger has given me hell for over thirty years, d'you realise that, Jack? And now here we are, face to face. Gawd, I'd like to get the bastard out. Have a go, Jack, go on, and if I yell, don't pay attention.'

Jack hesitated. 'I don't like to, Dad. It's a doctor's job.'

They had bread and a bit of cheese in the tucker-bag. Jack made tea in the billy, stirred it with a green twig, poured it into the enamel pints. Colour came back into the Nun's face.

'I never even said anything about that fella in the train,' he said apologetically.

'Forget him,' said Jack, slapping cheese on the bread.

'But how'd he get in there with us? Ghost, I nearly jumped outa me skin. But I fended off that right of his, didn't I, eh? Just reflex, it was.'

'Fast as lightning,' said Jack, passing the food to Jerry, who champed, saying, 'He musta come over the top of the truck. You reckon? What scum, eh? Woulda thrown us off, you know.'

Jack wondered how many of the hoboes found dead and mutilated beside the line had been thrown off by such as Big Owen, murderous hulks who'd had a whale of a time during the War and now found their métier in the Depression, bashing up tramps.

'Think he might lay a complaint for assault, though.' Jerry was worried.

'Not him,' said Jack. 'Can you see him spreading around the good news that a dwarf stretched him out? Just the same, that guard picked me, and I'd be easy to find. Still, I've got to chance it, so stop worrying.'

Far away he heard a dog barking. He bounded up on the permanent way, stared around. The sun was rising and mist, steaming in feeble wisps, marked the course of a creek. Then, as the sun rose higher, Jack saw a twinkle amidst distant trees. It was the reflection of an unpainted corrugated-iron roof.

But that homestead was perhaps four or five miles away.

He said to the Nun, 'I'll go there, and get help. We could get you on a horse.'

'I can walk,' said the Nun firmly. 'I'll make it there on foot.'

Jackie could not dissuade him. He re-bandaged the wound, got the trousers back on him, rolled up their swags, and they set off.

It took them the best part of the day. The young man cursed and abused the older one for his stupidity and obstinacy, but the Nun wouldn't give in. Every time they stopped for a rest, the Nun dug a few more cactus spines out of Jackie's back. They were already inflamed and festering.

By the time they came in sight of the dwelling a morose silence hung between them. They were closer to disagreement than they had ever been. Jackie went a few steps ahead, carrying the swags, his stomach growling. The Nun tottered along behind, pain plucking at his leg at each step. The muck from the abscess had oozed through the bandage and hugely stained the leg of his pants. Jerry could think of no way he could clean his trousers; he felt so feeble and light-headed that tears came into his eyes at the thought of this fresh calamity.

The dwelling in the wilderness was a shack, built of a mixture of unpainted timber and packing-case sides. It was a rabbiter's hut. Skins hung drying on wires, and on the veranda traps were piled. But it was in its way neat and weatherproof, the grass was cut, and a rose bush bloomed meagrely near the steps. Fifty yards away a comatose creek sulked in a chain of shallow pools.

Three heelers, excited and hostile, met Jackie. He thought it prudent to coo-ee to the householder. Immediately a woman ran forth, booted the dogs away, turned welcomingly.

Weary and depressed as he was, Jackie could not help grinning at her expression as she looked at him.

'Yes,' he said, 'I'm a dwarf. Jack Hanna is my name.'

'Well,' she said swiftly, 'whatever your shape, you've a grand pair of eyes on you.'

She helped him to get Jerry into the house, her strong shoulder of far more value than his. She was the rabbiter's wife, a gaunt, rusty Scotswoman from whose craggy face looked small eyes blue as butterflies. They laid the exhausted man on the sofa, where he instantly fell asleep.

As the housewife slapped saucepans and pans around on the grid over the open fire, Jackie told her what had happened. She said decisively, 'Well, my man can drive him into town as soon as he comes in from the traps at sundown. And in the meantime I'll take a peek at that leg in case it's gathering.'

'He'll fight you,' said Jackie. 'He'll give you a battle for the pants.'

'We'll see,' she said, smiling. 'Sit down and eat, boy. You must be famished. On the track, are you?'

Her name was Het. She had a dappled neck and big pale hands, well used to skinning rabbits. Jackie tried to be jaunty and saucy; it was an attitude that always softened and amused women, but once he had eaten his head almost nodded into the remnants of the treacle pudding that lay on his plate.

Het never saw a soul from one month's end to the other. She was famished for conversation, for her man was a silent one. Even though she saw the young man was almost asleep, she went on talking, looking at his dusty black hair, home-cut, so that it curled in harsh tufts, his long eyelashes on his cheeks.

'Times I walk over to the railway line,' she said, 'just to see the trains go past and wave to the passengers. It's a long toddle in the heat, but there, a person needs company. Sometimes they throw me the day's newspapers!'

She touched Jackie's cheek with her hard finger. 'It's a lonesome life here,' she said, almost inaudibly. 'Gey lonesome.'

Then she shook him gently. 'Up with you, lad. Undo your dad's braces and lift him at the middle, and we'll have breeks off him before he can bellow.'

The Nun awakened with a horrified start, and tucked his shirt down between the legs. Het laughed. 'Here's a towel to cover yourself with. Now then, let's have a look at this mess. Ugh!'

'It was a Boer done it,' said Jerry.

'Aye, I see,' she said, and she seized hold of the discoloured metal, gave it a twist and a yank and, to the accompaniment of a mortal yell from Jerry, had it in her fingers.

'What are you squealing for, man?' she asked in amazement. 'It was just sitting there. Now, I'll just slap a bread poultice on that, and swaddle you up, and you'll be fit enough to sit up and eat a meal like a gentleman.'

'God, woman,' said Jerry, holding his leg, his lips drawn back from his teeth like a dying dog's, 'you're bloody murder!'

She laughed with delight, jeering at him: 'Look at him there, the little old cold lad, bare as a trout, sitting on his bum bones glaring at me!'

Brisk and matter of fact, she put a hot poultice on the abscess, bound it up, oblivious of Jerry's ruffled mortification, gave him a safety-pin to hold the blanket around his middle, and bade him hobble to the table. Jackie grinned; Jerry gave him a wry shrug.

The hot food put heart into him, and he was relieved to see that Het had his trousers stretched out on an ironing-board, sponging them briskly before ironing them dry.

Her husband, Donaldson the rabbiter, enjoyed the company of strangers. He had the odd, smiling timidity of those who rarely see other human beings, keeping his eyes cast down as he ate. His wife told their story, and he listened as absorbedly as if it were new to him, nodding at intervals with a curious complacency. He and Het had been amongst the British immigrants who flooded into Australia after the War.

'It took us three years to make up our minds,' she said. 'Then

333

we packed up and went, assisted. Wild black men in the streets we expected, kangaroos – och, were we green! But soon we were doing well. Heck had a bicycle shop, fittings and services: it was a goldmine. The whole world was in bicycle breeks, it seemed.'

'Aye,' said Heck.

'You mightn't think it,' she said, 'but Heck has a grand business head on him. He saw the slump coming eighteen months before it arrived. Saw it clear as a vision. "Het," he said, "we're selling." So we did.'

Heck, pleased but modest, gave Jerry a gratified wink and nodded.

They had travelled round the country in the old car, picked at last on this piece of Crown wasteland out of Wilga – and without permission built the shack and set up rabbiting. They had between them a mutual enjoyment of their shrewdness, in 'seeing it coming', unlike other people who hung on hoping for the best and lost everything. They beamed at each other now in innocent smugness. Yet Jackie, now restored to his ordinary wits, read on each face separate terrors and longings never as much as hinted at.

The old car was like a hearse, a tourer with its back seat removed. Heck used it to take his pelts to the dealer, and it smelt of animal and saltpetre. For five miles there was only a bush track, he said, leant on by scrub and impassable in the wet. Sometimes he and the wife lived on rabbit and damper for weeks at a time.

'But, losh! We're better off than most.'

When they left the shack, Het gave Jackie a kiss and a hug.

'I'll bet you've a sweetheart, with those bonny eyes of yours!'

'If you weren't married, I would have, for sure,' said Jackie.

She hooted with laughter, but Jackie saw tears in her eyes.

When Donaldson left Jack and the Nun in Wilga, he tried to push five shillings into Jerry's hand.

'For the doctor,' he said. 'He'll no' work for nothing, that one.'

'No,' said Jerry firmly. 'We're right for money. And we thank you and your wife. Great. We won't forget it.'

334

'Did you believe all that?' asked Jackie, as they sat in the waiting-room.

'Na,' said the Nun. 'Poor as abo. fleas, them two. If they ever had any money, it's all gone long ago. But they got pride. And you can't lick people like that.'

Jack grinned. 'Never in a million years,' he said.

The doctor looked at the slug with interest.

'I'll have that for my curiosity cabinet,' he said. 'I'll have it for my fee.'

The Nun was cranky at having to let it go, though he realised it was the sensible thing to do. As he explained to Jack, it wasn't so much that he'd miss it after thirty-two years, but that he didn't like the idea of it in that cabinet, along with the jar of kidney stones – enough to sink a rowboat, the Nun said – and the woeful things pickled in jars, and the baby's skull with three eye-holes.

The doctor wasn't a bad fellow. For a bit of firewood-chopping from Jackie, he allowed them to bed down on clean sacks in his garage that night. His little daughter, eyes rounded with excitement at the sight of Jack, ran out with a tray of hot food for them, roast beef and beans and potatoes, and rice custard to follow. The Nun nearly cried, it was so good after the dog's dinners they'd been having.

'Ghost,' he kept saying. 'Ghost! It's enough to make a man say grace.'

Before they went to sleep, he said, 'That quack says my leg'll mend up like new, and my health'll improve, too. It'll be real queer not to have a crook leg all the time.'

Later Jackie heard him say, to himself, 'I used to be a very enjoying sort of a fella.'

In spite of his reassurances to his stepfather, Jackie was uneasy during the three days they remained in Wilga. He knew that the railway cop might well have laid a complaint against him. The guard, prejudiced by his false ideas, might well bear lying witness. So when the doctor said that Jerry could safely move on again they hitched a ride on a produce lorry going south, for the rumour was that the Government was about to start tree-planting on the desolate plains.

Jerry was tired. He felt much older than a man not yet fifty, as though the stuffing had been knocked out of him somewhere. And he worried at the thought that he and Jack might just have to wander around the country like two winds blowing side by side, getting dirtier and more bedraggled, more depressed and hopeless, until at last they were just two odd-looking derelicts – down-and-outers, just like all the others. He thought, almost with resentment, 'I just wish Jack would take it into his head to alight somewhere.'

Immediately he reproached himself. 'God, a man's a bastard. The little fella can't enjoy it any more than I do. But who's going to give a steady job to one like him, when there's full-sized men ready to work their guts out for their grub and a roof?'

Jerry realised he was just homesick: 'All I want is to be back home with Peggy.' It occurred to him then that a man was not homesick for places as much as for people and time. He was homesick for eight, twelve years before. And such an ache seized him that he had to pretend to be asleep in case his face gave him away.

They hit the bottom of the pile at a pig farm a few miles west of Edith, a hamlet straggling about a railhead and a bacon factory. The word had gone around that Council was beginning new roadworks outside the town.

'If we don't get a start there,' said Jack, 'that'll be it, eh, Dad? Sydney or bust.'

The last of their money was at the Edith post office in a registered envelope, waiting to be picked up. It would cover fares to the city, with a couple of quid over.

They had begun that day in good fettle at Crimea, twenty-five miles from Edith, where they had had a few days' work bagging potatoes. They had landed a reasonable kip in an empty louvre truck in the freight yards; but when daylight came and the iron argument of the yards began they slipped out and drifted down the main street.

Every third shop was boarded up, its doorway filled with dirt and blown papers, and occasionally a blanket-wrapped body. Jackie combed his hair, looking into a mirror in a shop window.

Dreary garments hung on huge cardboard blow-ups or pho-tographs of girls' faces and shoulders.

Jerry blew on his fingers. A dybbuk wind rushed up the street, hating everything it touched. At the end of the road shone a soli-tary square. The smell of new bread came to the travellers. A real pain seized Jerry's belly at this odour.

'Could you do a bit of fresh bread?'

'I could eat the bloody baker.'

They had no need to check their money. They knew to a half-penny what they had. Enough to spend a night at a boarding-house in Edith, have a bath and proper shave, wash their shirts, a few bob to get them out to the job, supposing they were lucky enough to get a start.

'Two bob over,' said Jack. 'Come on, mate!'

The baker was a lively monkey with light blue eyes in a brown face of antique beauty. His name was Vince Panebianco.

'Funny, eh? White bread! Here, you come and sit down in the warm near the oven.'

He was so glad to have company in the melancholy dawn he almost danced from the door to the bread trough he was cleaning. Thankfully Jackie and Jerry entered that small crammed haven of heat and light. They tried to buy something, but he would have none of it, pressing a rubbery new loaf upon them, scraping around in a canvas bag, finding a red pear of cheese and cutting off two thick slices.

'I know, I know! I was on the road. Two years! No track rations then either. Terrible! Living like a stray dog! I lay out in the rain in a paddock, hoping to catch some sickness and die. You believe me? What your name, little one? Jack! Giacomo! You have room in the stomach for a hot pie, Giacomo? And you, mister?'

'Oh, you're a gent, you are,' groaned Jerry.

The pie was so boiling hot he couldn't eat it. He wobbled a mouthful from side to side of his mouth, his eyes rolling.

'But how did you come to be a baker, Vince? What hap-pened?'

'All the time I was on the road, starving, begging, hoping to die, there was this letter following me around, this post office, that one, where is this Vince Panebianco? Is he dead, is he in prison?

But at last it came to me. In this town. Crimea. It said my uncle was dead. In Naples. He had left me a little money. What will I do with it, I said? I was standing out there on the footpath, there! I saw the bakery. The old man was sick, he wanted to retire. I went to him and said: for a year I will work for nothing, do all your work. You be the padrone, sit there in the easy-chair, tell me what to do, teach me! Then I shall buy the bakery. So it has happened. I am most fortunate man. But I do not forget what it is like on the road.'

All the time he had been talking, the baker had been loading loaves into huge trays. Jackie and Jerry helped him carry them out and slide them into the back of his little van.

'Where you going, then, which way? I go as far as the Four Mile, on the Edith road. Good!'

He filled their tucker-bags with buns and bread. They set off, the earth wheeling down into the sun's steady light, the paddocks starched with frost. The frigid air seemed to scintillate; the steely sky softened, became a sweet blue.

'Listen!'

As Jerry and his son got down at the four-mile peg, the baker leant forward, held up a finger. A bird in a tree cried out a long incomprehensible message like a muezzin.

'When you think all is spoiled, all is over, then comes God with a hand to help. You remember!'

He smiled, waved, turned the van down a pinkish mud road that wavered between the chocolate fields. The two travellers shouldered their swags and continued along the road to Edith. Mile after mile there was no sign of life. Yet this had been a populous region; grey, derelict wooden farmhouses, crazy toppling barns stood here and there amid lime-yellow groves of winter wattle.

Farther on, perhaps six or seven miles from Crimea, the warming air had the fresh odour of frost-bitten soil, and sometimes, hidden by wind-breaks of macrocarpa or tall holly, they saw homesteads amidst potato and turnip paddocks. But they had food; there was no need to go asking for a hand-out.

On these long tramps the Nun liked to talk about his early life with Jack's mother, how she had looked when he first saw her: 'Pouring hair oil outa that little green cask on the shelf, you re-

338

member it, Jack? And spilling it all over her feet. Buttoned boots she had, brown ones.'

The younger man listened with pleasure. Still, it always amazed him how his stepfather could speak so freely, and with such enjoyment, of his dead wife. He, Jack, could scarcely bear to think of Maida or Carlie; but Jerry was comforted by his memories.

They ate and rested at midday, hoping some vehicle would pass. Two hoboes, an oldish man and a stripling, passed, going at a steady, mile-eating rate.

'You for the roadworks out of Edith?' called Jack, and the elder one replied in a refined voice, 'If we're not too late!'

After they had begun walking again, three bike swaggies in a loose group, as though they travelled together but were not friends, overtook them. They passed half a dozen large trucks carrying pigs, gravel, green produce, belting along at forty miles an hour and not even slowing when Jack held out a hand.

At half past four Jerry was ready to drop; it was all he could do to get one foot in front of the other. The sun had set, and the air was biting.

'Well, mate, we aren't going to make the metropolis before nightfall,' said Jack. 'Better look for a place to camp before the dark comes down.'

'Right,' said Jerry, forcing good cheer into his voice. Jackie saw how fatigued he looked. He thought, 'I'll have to find a homestead and put the nips in for a doss in a toolshed – anything out of the frost.'

In half an hour they had come to a small flat beside a creek. It was sheltered only by the ashen ghosts of ring-barked trees. A campfire waved despairingly in the wind, one of the bike swaggies trying to shelter it with his army surplus overcoat. As Jerry and Jack approached the fire died.

They saw a woman, bundled in a drooping coat, skulking around picking up fallen branches.

'Good day, all,' said Jerry cordially. 'You ain't got any Grand Hotel here, eh? Isn't there a better place than this?'

'You find one, let us know,' snarled one of the cyclists. 'We been scouring around for an hour. No bridges, no trees, nothing, and a ten degrees frost coming on.'

The woman, meekly holding her bundle of sticks near by, said shyly, 'But those two other men went up to the farm to see if they'd let us take shelter somewhere; so it might be all right.'

She put down the wood like an offering beside the bike swaggie and crept away to sit on a suitcase beside an elderly man with scooped-out cheeks and no overcoat. She put her arm around his shoulders as though to keep him warm.

Jackie saw that quite a small crowd had collected in this place that would be a pleasant camp in summer. Now it offered nothing but wretchedness.

'Don't worry, Bert,' the woman said to her companion. 'The farmer is sure to help. He wouldn't be so inhumane.'

'Well, what do you think?' murmured the Nun to Jackie. 'Better move on, or what? Hang on, here comes someone.'

Jack saw that it was the good walker with the refined voice. He had a badly sunburned face, a clue to his greenness as a vagrant. He was accompanied by a nervous, silky boy.

'Sorry,' said the older man to the group. 'I saw the farmer but he absolutely refused to let us shelter in any of the farm buildings. Said he'd had too much thieving. Slammed the door in my face.'

'He was awful,' said the boy.

Jerry could sense the sullen resentment amongst his companions. He remembered the same thing in the army, an electric undercurrent of surliness, dangerous as rage. He lit a cigarette, drew on it luxuriously, said, 'Have a draw, mate?' and passed his tobacco pouch to the most hostile of the solitaries.

'Well,' he said, 'the way I see it, we can't freeze to death for want of trying. I reckon we ought to all go, in a deputation like, and put the hard word on him. When he sees we have a lady with us – Ghost, he'd have to be a bit of a stinker not to change his mind.'

'Two ladies, if you please.' The carefree toot came out of bleak dusk, followed by another woman, clad as if for the city in a red wool coat with a standing possum collar. She was a short girl with a big ginger head and a battered green suitcase. She hammered up to them on thin hard legs ending in small patent-leather hoofs.

340

'And where did you come from, baby dear?' asked a bike swag-man jeeringly.

'Out of the blue and into here,' she answered blithely; 'and you watch it, big boy, because I've got a kick like a mule.'

'That's a chromo for sure,' whispered Jerry to Jack. 'I can tell one a mile off.'

They all trailed up the track towards the homestead. Jack was interested in the chromo, who looked as if she had recently been wet and rough-dried, and whose face was anaemic and pinched under the gamin grin.

She whispered to him, 'Crumbs, I'm perished! Let me hold your hand, darl', and gave him a marble paw.

He said, 'We've got some tucker. Buns, and fresh bread.'

He saw the glisten on her brown eyes as she rolled them.

The homestead was lit for evening. Dogs ran out barking hysterically.

'You speak for us, cock,' said a loner to the Nun. 'You've got the words like.'

There was a murmur of assent. Jackie saw a scuffle at the window, and a child's voice shrilled, 'They're back again, Dad ... lots of them.' The door was flung open, and light slanted across Jerry. He could see only a thick-set shape, its hair sticking up.

'Evening, boss,' said Jerry civilly.

'Never mind the flamin' chat. Come to the point.'

'Well, it's like this,' said Jerry, 'it's no night for camping out, mister, and we got two women with us ...'

'None of my business!'

'Aw, have a heart,' pleaded Jerry. 'We only want a roof to doss under. We're not asking for a hand-out, just something to keep the frost off.'

The farmer burst into an impassioned, rambling diatribe about the damage that had been done in the past to his plough-shed, gravel in the engine of his tractor, tools stolen. He'd made up his mind and that was that.

'The moon'll be up soon. You can walk into Edith and get your-selves vagged. Forty-eight hours free lodging and scoff. No, I made up me mind and yous aren't going to move me.'

He turned his head and barked a rebuttal at someone behind him, probably his wife. The chromo, sharp as a tack, cried loudly, 'You there, missus, there's an old lady with us, how'd you like to be her, eh? Out of doors on a night like this?'

There was no answer. The door slammed. The young boy began to whimper, and the older man put his arm about him. 'Maybe we can walk into town, Gordon. It'll be all right.'

Jerry said, 'Well, I'm not walking anywhere. I'm done to a turn and I don't care who knows it.'

'We'll just go and bunk in one of his sheds and be damned to him –' began Jackie. The door flew open again, and the farmer shouted, 'And don't think yous can go sneaking into me out-buildings, because they're all padlocked.'

'That won't stop us setting fire to them, you dingo,' yelled back one of the men with bikes. The door slammed once more.

'Got by Moonlight out of Murphy's Paddock, that one,' said a solitary, hoarse with rage. He raised his voice: 'You bludger, you hear me? I hope you rot!'

'Stuff him, I'm off,' said the second solitary. He picked up his bike and wheeled it away down the dark track.

Jerry said, 'Hang on now, folks. There's bound to be some place the bastard couldn't lock up. Excuse my French, girls. We'll have a look for it.'

'There's a hurricane lantern in our swag,' said the educated man.

Followed by the excited, sidling dogs, the little cavalcade trailed about, following the lantern, until they came to a low structure. The stink at once identified it.

'Here we are,' announced Jerry. 'Your five-star pub for the night, ladies and gents.'

The chromo snickered. 'Oooh, you're a wag, Pa.'

The educated man lifted his lantern and looked inside. 'No pigs in it now, anyway. Floor's pretty dry.'

'Gawdelpus,' chirped the chromo. 'They'll never believe it in Bourke Street. Well, if it's either this or freeze to death, I'm for it.' She led the way, gave a yelp. 'Got a tenant already, comrades.'

The light showed a figure rolled in a blanket in the recess behind the heavy gate-post.

342

He seemed to be in a stupor; the smell that hovered about him like a fog declared him to be a methylated spirits drinker.

The pig-pen was in poor condition. The sheets of iron on the roof were rusted and gapped; some were missing. It was in the process of being cleaned out; a shovel and rake stood against the wall. The refugees crowded in. The man with the lantern hung it on a nail.

While Jackie and another man tried to start a fire in the lee of a stone trough outside, the three dogs hung about, their lean bodies vibrating with cold, then they slunk away. The wind doused the fire. The travellers could not even boil a billy.

'And that scrooging bastard's up there, with his gut full, and his feet to a lovely blaze, you can bet.'

The enormity of it gave them a simple unanimity. They looked at each other with solemn, meaning grimaces. Jackie, dulled with cold and fatigue, realised that any of them could have murdered the man without a second thought. But the final catastrophe of the campfire had rendered them all impotent. Jack opened the tucker-bag, brought out Vince Panebianco's charity, said, 'Might warm us up. Come on, lady, have something. What about you, mister?'

The elderly man, palsied in the wind that knifed through the cracks, took a bun. He said gently, 'It's very good of you, young man.'

The meal finished, they talked desultorily, huddled in bits of old tent, blankets, canvas ground-sheets about the lantern, as though it gave off warmth as well as light. There were now nine of them, counting the metho. drinker who was muttering in a half-delirium. The two remaining bike swaggies and the man and boy were going through to Edith. The older woman, her head sinking on her chest with weariness, and her husband, were heading for Werris Creek.

There was a commotion outside the pig-pen, dogs barking, a lantern swinging, and the farmer came in.

'Gawdelpus, it's Attila the Hun again,' remarked a wiry, aggressive young man.

The farmer began to rave. 'The bloody nerve of yous lot. Louse-ridden no-hopers. Get off my property. I'll put the dogs on you.'

'You set any dog on me and I'll gum it to death,' began Jerry in an effort to lighten the atmosphere. But the farmer roared on: 'I don't want none of yous here. I'll have the lot of you for trespass!'

Jackie saw now that the man was scared of them; he had been forced by fear to make a stand.

'Right,' he said. 'You do that, mister. And we'll just have a kip until you come back with the coppers. We're not leaving, and that's it!'

'What kind of a man are you?' said the older woman faintly. 'You ought to be ashamed.'

'All right,' blustered the farmer. 'But I want you out right smart at sun-up, you hear? I got pigs coming in before nine o'clock and I want to get this pen put in order.' He glared threateningly around at them, still keeping his rage on the boil in spite of defeat.

As he withdrew, the chromo stuck her tongue out at him. 'I got a ticket in this new lottery. If I win it I'm gonna come back here and set a match to that stinker's house.' She sighed. 'Oh, what's the use of talking?'

They all felt the same way. One by one they rolled in their blankets, tried to go to sleep. Jerry had his hat rolled up for a pillow, Jackie his boots.

It was fearfully cold. Both of them were trembling right through to their centres. The cottony blankets were no protection from the knifing wind. After a while Jerry groaned, 'Chris'sake, boy, come closer and keep the cold off me back.'

Jackie lay down behind Jerry, pressing close. A feeble current of warmth circulated between them.

'Can I put my hands on your stomach, Dad?'

'No, you flaming well can't. Gawd, it's unbearable. I can feel my blood setting like a jelly.'

Jackie murmured, 'Don't never be bitter, Dad.'

'Don't you mock me, you devil,' growled Jerry. But in the darkness he grinned.

It was a long time before anyone got to sleep. The metho. drinker near the door grumbled and uttered thin cries. One of the two loners coughed intermittently, a hideous smoker's cough, as though he had a chestful of custard.

The chromo yapped, 'Can't you shut it up, you coughin' 'orror? How the devil can you afford smokes these days? That's what I'd like to know, eh?'

Through the rents in the iron roof big stars glared down, like little mirrors, doing their huge slow dance in a delirious nothingness. Jerry remembered being cold under the same stars in Africa, frozen, he was, so that the blood from his wound congealed in a stalactite of black glue. Who'd believe you could be cold in Africa?

Half-way through the night, with Jackie snoring, Jerry, in a half-doze, became aware of an insistent noise. The woman in the far corner was crying.

'Ghost, lady, can't you be quiet? It's just as crook for all of us.'

'I think my husband's dead,' she said.

Jerry was aware of nothing but fury. Bloody inconsiderate old cow, just as a man got half-way thawed. He heaved Jackie away. No wonder he was feeling warm. The boy was broadcasting heat like a little oven.

'You got a candle or anything, missus?'

He heard her gulp, try to control herself, scratch a match. A faint light bloomed and wagged in the far corner. Jerry got to his feet, all bent over like a damaged cockroach. He felt as if he had been mangled. Jackie fell back, still dead to the world, his arms outspread in the slimy mud. Jerry could have kicked him.

He went over to the corner. The old man was as dead as mutton: fatigue, hunger, and cold had got him. He wore a good suit, now threadbare and stiff with dirt. He had one eye open, and the candlelight put a curious opalescent glaze on it. His knotty hands, still clasping the blanket, had thickened blue nails.

'He's gone, isn't he?' said his wife tremulously.

''Fraid so,' said Jerry, closing the eye. He felt a swine for being so annoyed when she had awakened him. He looked at the poor woman. She was crouched against the wall, her head wrapped against the cold in a dirty white tam-o'-shanter, so that she looked like a half-barmy Welsh bard. Jerry took the blanket off the corpse.

345

'Here,' he said. 'You wrap this round you, missus; no sense you getting crook, too.'

By now everyone was awake. The educated man relit the lantern. There were mutters and low conversation. The chromo sat by the widow, taking off her own coat and putting it over the woman's thin shoulders, patting her arm and saying how terrible it was, poor thing. Jackie and the swaggie with the cough went out into the white world and got a fire going near the swill trough. They boiled the billy.

'Christ, what's the country coming to – old man conking out in a pigsty, dying like a bloody dog? Only two or three hours to daybreak. Better get the police – best thing, eh?'

At the mention of the police the metho. drinker, tocsin apparently sounding through his daze, leapt out of the pigsty with his swag in his arms and hurdled away into the darkness.

'And good riddance to you, too, Douglas Fairbanks!' remarked someone.

The chromo came over and murmured to Jerry, 'She wants his jaw tied up – it's dropped, love. I can't come at it somehow.'

There was nothing to do it with but one of the widow's stockings. The foot was full of holes, and cardboardy with dirt. Jerry tied up the jaw, straightened the man's arms and legs.

Jerry said to the widow, who was being comforted once more by the younger woman, 'We'll wait for the farmer. He'll have a ute. To get into town with, I mean.'

As though he had pressed the lever of a siphon, she began to weep and talk. The old man was not her husband, so now she would not get even a pension. He was only sixty, though he looked seventy. He just wasn't fit for the hardship.

My Bert, she called him. We've been living together all these years, his wife being a very hard, unforgiving woman. Bert owned two cottages, you see? That was all the income we had. But the tenants haven't been able to pay rent for two years, so we had nothing, you see? Bert wouldn't put them out, poor souls. What's the use? So when we came to the end of our savings, I asked my sister in Werris Creek if we could stay with her awhile. But we only had train fare for one, and I wouldn't leave him; so we both went as far as Gunnedah, and then we thought we might get a lift. But it was all too much for him . . .

346

The chromo pressed the poor creature's head against her bosom, rocked to and fro, said, 'He just went to sleep with the cold. Didn't know a thing about it. Half his luck, eh?' she added, looking around at the others and giving orders with her eyebrows. They hurriedly grunted assent. But not one of them wanted to be the stiff stretched out in the pig-pen.

A cold rage fermented in Jack. He sqatted silently by the fire, feeding it with bark, and replenished the billy as it emptied; but inside he was so angry it made him feel light-headed. To him the dead man called for defence, revenge. The cruelty, the humiliation of it – a respectable old man ending his life in a pig-pen, and one where he had been allowed to shelter only on sufferance. Jack couldn't wait for the farmer to make his appearance.

In the grey gelatinous dawn the farmer came down, stamping in his gumboots, nose red and damp.

'Come on, yous,' he said. 'Sun-up I want you mob outa here. Them Tamworths will be here in a few hours, and I wanta get the pen cleaned up.'

'Shut your face,' exploded Jackie. 'A man died in there last night. Talking about pigs when a poor decent man has snuffed it! You just bloody well go back to your nice clean dry house and get out your truck and go fetch the police.'

'And not another yap outa you!' shrilled the chromo.

The farmer turned pale. He looked at the group confronting him, grainy eyes, home-cut hair, faces full of enmity, the men in army overcoats, dyed blue, flapping around their shins. He had been working himself up all night, determined to clear them out at the first streak of dawn. Rabble, he called them to his wife. He hated and despised them because they represented something he was afraid of becoming. They were a phantom threat.

Now he said, 'This true?'

'My oath,' said one of the solitaries. 'Satisfied now, Kaiser Bill?'

'You got no right – ' shouted the farmer. But he was drowned with boos and cat-calls.

The Nun said, 'Here, mates, put a sock in that. The boss here didn't knock the old chap off. He would have died a bloody sight sooner if he'd had to camp outside. I'm sorry, love,' he added to the widow, who hid her face and sobbed again.

'Here!' cried the chromo, putting on a comical face of surprise. 'You on his side, eh? Throwing in with the trumps, mister?'

'I'm no trump,' said the farmer, dark red now with distress and resentment. 'I'm just a working man like yous. Jesus, do you think us on the land has had it easy these past years?'

But he was lost under the cries directed at Jerry: 'Crawler! Can't stand a man who doesn't stick with his own.'

Jerry said to the farmer, 'Be obliged if you'd get the johns, mister. Soon as you can, eh?'

Jerry's urgent nod sent him off. The Nun turned to the group.

'Ghost, you can be a lot of boneheads when you like,' he observed. 'That poor sod has no more control over the times than we have. No use abusing him. Waste of breath.'

He sat on his heels, taking an occasional slurp from his tin pannikin, leisurely and undisturbed as ever. Jackie watched him, amazed at the way he took control of this crowd of hungry, angry, unreasonable people. And as the Nun talked, Jackie himself began to feel that he had been an idiot.

'No wonder They can push us around,' he thought. 'Most of us haven't any brains.'

'If the old man had been allowed to doss down in a garage or toolshed he mightn't have died,' argued the educated man.

'True,' agreed Jerry. 'But if the farmer's had the bad luck he told us about, tools pinched, vandalism, maybe worse, his daughter done over or his wife terrorised – eh? Can you blame him for locking things up? I mean, we ain't all angels just because we're outa work.'

'Just the same, the bastard is better off than us,' said the younger solitary angrily. 'He could afford to take a risk.'

'Well, take this fella's pigs,' Jerry said. 'How did he buy them? Overdraft from the Bank, you can bet your boots. So he don't really own them. Still, he has to feed and house them, and maybe they're pretty well all he depends on to feed his kids in a few months' time, after he pays back the Bank, that is. But if they die, because there ain't no shelter for them, seeing that there's a mob of unemployed camping in their pen, then the Bank gets paid just the same, but the kids don't eat. He's banking on them porkers.'

'Human bein's come first,' growled someone.

'Yeah, granted; but the human bein's the cocky's thinking about are his wife and kids,' said the chromo. She slapped Jerry on the shoulder. 'Regular bush lawyer, aren't you, Pa?'

When a young boy and girl came down with a basket from the homestead a little later, the hoboes meekly accepted the food that was offered. Only the widow, exhausted with grief, slept under the chromo's red woolly coat with the wet-dog collar.

Jackie's mind was buzzing. Whereas the Nun had spoken out of his simple wisdom and knowledge of humanity, Jackie had absorbed the idea in an intellectual flash. Of course you couldn't blame property owners: they were just part of the enormously complex human scene. Property hadn't done the old dead man any good because it wasn't *producing* any more. The times had made it barren.

The policeman, a fatherly old buffer, said to Jerry, 'Ought to get up some kind of a fund for the lady, to get her to her sister's, cope with the funeral. Now, my cousin's manager of the local rag. How about a couple of you going in to see him? I'll come along. Lend a bit of weight like.'

'Leave it to me,' said Jackie.

On the way into Edith his thoughts were still busy. Property, now. It was a commodity, and its value varied from year to year, month to month. And money, what was that?

It was a commodity too.

Jackie felt as if lightning had struck him. Why hadn't he realised it before? It was something that Banks hired out, as loans and mortgages and overdrafts, cheap when nobody needed it much and dear when they did. They were money shops.

What, then, did the unemployed have to offer?

Labour. Another commodity. The work of their hands. All they had to offer. All their eggs were in one basket, so that if nobody wanted what they had to sell they were stonkered.

Jack thought, 'Funny how a man doesn't catch on, eh? But I could learn about all this, learn how to protect myself. Strength!

That's what would come out of knowing such things. By heck, I will learn about it, too.'

He was all on fire with it, but they were coming into the town, so he resolutely turned his mind to his companions. He said to the young woman, 'Have you a job to go to, miss?'

'Oh, I'll manage. I turn me hand to anything, you know. I'm a barmaid by trade, but I can cook, clean. Willing to work for me keep if it comes to that. Oh, I get a bag of laughs out of life.'

'You were really good with that poor old chook,' said Jerry sincerely. 'Dunno what we'da done without you.'

She shrugged. 'We're all human, Pa. Eh? Can't say truer than that.'

A moment later she was making their companions smile with a recountal of how she'd landed at the pig farm.

'Got a lift with an egg man. Well, we're not past the first bend before he's putting my knee into gear. Fair enough, I think. Well, I mean to say, nothing for nothing in this great world. Then up goes the hand under my skirt like a starved rat. I got a toehold on his ear and pretty near took it off its hinges. Truck goes into ditch, omelettes everywhere.' She roared with laughter. 'I beat it over the paddock and the next thing I knew I was in a pig-pen. It's the luck of the draw, boys.'

'I don't think she's a chromo after all,' whispered Jerry to Jack, in mortification.

The story of the old man who expired with cold and exhaustion in a pig-pen was the subject of that day's editorial. It was picked up by the wire services and reprinted all over the Commonwealth, for in its squalid way it seemed to symbolise the apparently unsolvable plight of the unemployed, now totalling thirty per cent of the population, working women not counted. Those in work struggled with radically reduced wages.

In her grandmother's old home in Sydney, Dorothy Moy read the story, and saw that John Luke Hanna had been spokesman for those travellers who had been with the dead man during his last hours. She was alone, and lonely, and for some time after she had put down the paper walked up and down the drawing-room, seeing her tall slender figure move like a ghost or shadow in the greenish Victorian mirrors, whispering to herself, 'He's getting nearer.'

The little town of Edith was generous, and the fund opened for the de facto widow of the dead man quickly climbed to £400, a large sum for a district getting along on the smell of an oil rag.

On his way down the main street after leaving the newspaper office, Jackie Hanna saw a fourpenny bin outside a second-hand shop. It was full of dirty old books. There he found two textbooks on economics, so tattered that he bargained the shopkeeper into letting him have the pair for fivepence.

6

Jackie Hanna, Cushie Moy

1931-1932

6

Although it was spring, the evenings still belonged to winter. From the Harbour blew a pinching wind, smelling of cast-up seaweed and dying mussels, and turpentine logs tethered in rafts in Black-wattle Bay. Dorothy was glad the fire had been lit early in the drawing-room. Granny's brown plush chair was still drawn up beside it, her knitting bag pinned to the half-bald arm.

'Shall I have it put away, Miss Dorothy?' the housekeeper had asked months before, after Clara Jackaman had died. Dorothy shook her head.

The woman hesitated, saying at last, 'Excuse me, Miss Dorothy . . . forgive me, Miss dear. It's not my place, but I know Madam would wish . . . you should go out more. It's not good for a young person. You have to get over it. Mrs Jackaman would want that.' And she began to cry herself, her wholesome pink face putting on a grimace of shame and distress.

Dorothy put her arms about her, let her cry. Mrs Marion had come as housemaid to Jackaman Court more than thirty years before, when old Joseph Jackaman had died and left the ornate Victorian house to his estranged son, James. She had married James's first butler, dead a long time now. For the past twenty years she had been Clara's faithful servant and perhaps only true friend.

After a while Mrs Marion said, 'We shouldn't grieve for her. She missed Mr James so much, and then there was the other – her little weakness.'

For Clara, old lady Jackaman, that genial, succulently kind old

355

woman, passed over with impatience and a faint disdain by her snobbish daughters, had been a drunk. She had always been fond of a little tiddle, a tiny drop, a spot, phrases which she had accompanied by a roguish or deprecatory twinkle. But after the death of James she had flown to the bottle for everything – sleep, surcease from grief, loneliness, even her own shame and distress at her drunkenness. When her daughters had discovered her disgraceful secret she had been so humiliated she had drunk more than ever. There had been no one but Mrs Marion to protect her until her grandchild, Dorothy Moy, had come.

Sitting solitary beside the fire, Dorothy thought of that afternoon, so long ago, more than six years ago, when she had left Claudie and Iris and taken a taxi to Jackaman Court to ask her grandmother if she could stay with her. The taxi-driver had been plaintive. 'Why didn't you say you wanted to go to Rag Castle, love? All this time looking for Whatsname Court!'

The house was of a style often seen in the older-settled Sydney areas, a fanciful Gothic castle with flat roof and corners enriched with turrets prickled like lobsters and encased in verdigrised copper. The small-paned windows were set in deep embayed arches, and here and there on the sandstone walls were niches as though to hold statues instead of the wind-sown ivy that tumbled or stirred like green banners.

She was ushered in by a flustered maid, and stood bewildered amongst her luggage on the black and white tiles of the cavernous hall. Then suddenly, down the staircase, came lurching and tripping her grandmother, with her hair fallen in thin plaits down her back, her face puffy and blotched. After her hastened a short, wiry, uniformed woman.

'Granny, what's the matter?' cried Dorothy, hastening forward to catch hold of her grandmother as she reached the foot of the stairs. Clara wept. 'Is that you, Dorothy? Is it really you?' She seized the girl frantically. 'Don't let her get me, lovie. I'm frightened of her nose.'

As Dorothy looked, the short woman put a firm hand on Clara's arm and said authoritatively, 'Now, Madam, stop playing up. Come along with me at once.' Dorothy saw that she did indeed

356

have a huge lilac beak. Over her head the girl saw Mrs Marion, looking agitated.

Dorothy said, 'You don't remember me, Mrs Marion? I'm Miss Isobel's daughter.'

'Oh, Miss,' said Mrs Marion in a curious embarrassment, 'we didn't know you were expected. Madam isn't herself. Now, Madam, let Nurse take you to bed, you're not well.'

The old woman turned upon Dorothy such a disordered face that the girl said, 'I'll take her. Just show me the way.'

She had realised at once that Clara was drunk, and was dumbfounded. Did grandmothers get drunk? Her own grandmother? Such compassion and love swept over her that her eyes blazed, and the nurse fell back angrily, her nose turning a darker shade.

As they passed her, the old woman slurred triumphantly, 'See? My little granddaughter is going to look after me. And you can get out of my home, and take your boko with you.'

Thinking of that evening, Dorothy could only recall herself and Mrs Marion half-carrying the heavy old lady up the stairs, and a scene of extraordinary unlikelihood going on in the hall: her Aunt Australia suddenly entering the front door, in a grey fur jacket, pulling off her hat as she came; the nurse losing her head altogether and shouting, 'That's the end. I give notice. Boko indeed! Just the kind of word I'd expect from a common old boozer.'

'Bring the car around for Nurse Riding, Robert,' Dorothy heard Australia's voice order some hitherto unseen manservant. 'As for you, Nurse – get your things together immediately.'

When Clara was in bed, singing and muttering, Mrs Marion hovering beside her, Australia came into the room.

'Disgusting cow, I'm glad to see the back of her. Never happy with her. Well, Dorothy, what brought you here this afternoon?'

Dorothy said, 'I want to stay with Granny for a while, if she'll have me. I've had some upsets.'

Australia glanced at her sharply. 'And do you still want to stay, now that you've participated in our domestic dramas? I must warn you, they occur frequently.'

The girl nodded.

'Right,' said Australia. 'Mrs Marion, you could put her in the green bedroom?' Suddenly she gave a harsh chirp of laughter. 'Boko! That did it. Touch her boko and you've touched a tiger. Good for Mother.' She turned abruptly, saying over her shoulder. 'No one but Miss Dorothy and myself for dinner tonight, Mrs Marion. We'll have it on the table in the bay window. Seven thirty, Dorothy.'

The bay window was full of flowering plants. Through the silken leaves of begonias Dorothy saw a lighted ship, towering over the house, only two hundred yards from the window.

'Yes, we're just above wharves, docks, fitting yards,' said Australia. 'The place is bedlam sometimes, with maritime noises. Then there's dust, dirt . . . oh, the whole district is running down like a clock. It's absurd that Mother should stay here by herself in a grimy industrialised dump.'

'You don't live here, Aunt?' ventured Dorothy.

'I've an apartment on the roof of the Emporium,' said Australia. 'But since Mother really took to sozzling, I'm nearly always here. Mrs Marion is devoted, but I can't leave all the burden to her. Mother must have someone with her most of the time.'

'There's me,' said Cushie. Australia shot her a look.

'You've cleared out from the Duchess of York Annexe then, have you?' she asked.

Dorothy shook her head. She said, 'I'd better tell you the whole story. You mightn't want to have me here.'

She told the tale baldly, as if she'd read it in a police report. Australia smoked, stubbing out her cigarette and lighting another immediately. At last Dorothy stopped. She said almost inaudibly, 'I suppose you're shocked.'

'No,' said Australia. 'I'm too old.'

Dorothy giggled nervously. 'You're a funny aunt.'

'Compared with my sisters,' said Australia, 'I certainly am. We won't let them know anything of this. It's your personal affair. So tell me what you want to do now.'

Dorothy said, 'I don't want to go to England with Mama and Daddy. I feel I can't go back to being . . . being a daughter.'

Australia widened her eyes. They were of a peculiarly attractive smoky blue. Her lashes were dark and curly, though her shingled

358

hair was greying. She said, 'You're astute, my dear. My sister Isobel is not going to take kindly to being defied, however.'

Dorothy said in a low voice, 'I didn't mean to hurt Mama and Daddy, you know. And I get on very well with Granny.'

She began to cry silently.

Australia sat smoking, not saying anything. The window filled with fireflies – masthead lights, fuzzed portholes. She could hear the ferries grunting across the Harbour. She remained silent while the girl wept, recognising the monstrous simplicity of this young creature, victim of the terrible fevers of youth.

Recalling her own girlhood, she saw her niece as a similarly shapeless character, directed by nonsensical yearnings and ideals, hedged in by merciless prejudices and great barren despairs.

'All,' thought Australia wryly, 'to be pruned and deflated by life.'

'You'll despise me,' muttered the girl at last, 'for being so silly.'

'No,' said her aunt. 'I don't think you're silly at all. It's just that you've been expected to know things intuitively when it's quite impossible for you to do so. It's a mistake most mothers make with girls, I think. A nice girl ought to know without being told. But if she doesn't, it's her fault.'

Dorothy looked taken aback. Australia could see that she was thinking, 'How does this old woman know?'

'Come on. Off to bed,' she said briskly. She had a pleasantly fogged voice, doubtless from the cigarettes.

So began Dorothy's years with her grandmother. Old Clara was in raptures. She was a sweet-natured woman, a little frightened of her fashionable, patronising daughters. She enjoyed simple pleasures, cups of tea, a game of cards, lots of chat. She was adept at hiding bottles, in her wash-jug, amongst her hats, in the toy cupboard in the old nursery. But Dorothy kept her busy, so that she had little time for solitary drinking. Besides, she was happier. She did not need liquor so much.

Australia said, 'I was at my wits' end. Thank God you came along.'

In effect, Clara became Dorothy's baby, a good-tempered, boozy old baby, docile and kind. Granny could be very gritty though, where her principles were involved. She wrote a hard reproachful letter to her daughter Belle about the abortion, and Isobel wrote a frigidly angry one to Dorothy, accusing her of treachery and lack of honour.

So when Bede Moy died with another heart attack it was Olwyn who broke the news to Cushie. It was fortunate that Clara was in the middle of a long drinking-spell; the girl had so many cares that her sorrow at her father's death could not be indulged. Clara, drunk, was a compulsive talker. She babbled most of the night about old times and forgotten people, old Joey Jackaman and the devil he was, how frightened of him all the girls in the workroom were; young James with his red hair and his trace-horse, which he would hitch onto gentlemen's carriages at the bottom of steep Druitt Street to help pull them up to the top, sixpence a time; and how one day he hitched onto the vehicle of a young gentleman with a pug face and hair even redder than the urchin James's, and how he turned out to be Henry Parkes, who was to be Premier, and, long afterwards, the Father of Federation. That was James Jackaman's start in life, said Clara.

She spoke, too, of old Joey's wife Beck, whose name had been given to Dorothy as her second. She was a black-eyed Cornish-woman, some said a gipsy, who could read and write, and had a certain refinement. She died in 1868.

Sometimes early in the morning Mrs Marion would come and whisper, 'You go to bed, Miss dear. I'll watch her now.'

But Dorothy could not sleep. She roamed the vast empty house, twelve bedrooms, mostly shut up now, smelling wanly of lavender and naphthalene, bedrooms once occupied by Clara's large family. She imagined the girls dancing, running up and down the stairs, in those days of bustles, ostrich feathers, magnificent baroque hats. Australia hanging the black flag out the window on Mafeking Night. No, that would not have been here, but in the house Clara and James occupied before old Mr Jackaman died. But to this house, Jackaman Court, wicked Australia had run away to live with her wickeder grandfather, because her father would not let her be independent, would not allow her a position on his news-paper, and she had shouted at him that she would rather kill her-self than just be a lady. So old Joey had let her learn the ropes at the Emporium, at first merely to spite James. And when he died, as the bells were ringing for Federation in 1901, old Mr Jackaman had left Australia full control of the great store.

Dorothy wondered if her own father had ever been in this house. But it was unlikely, for he had been only an accounts clerk on Grandfather's newspaper, the *Nation*. She stood in the dark room, her head downcast, leaving herself open to the pure grief she had for her father. How well she understood now the pathos of his life, his struggle to rise above that dock-side family into which he had been born! His had been a slender character, she could see that now; his small ambitions had seemed great to him – respect at the Bank, a secure job, childlike vanities. They seemed like buttons and brass farthings to his daughter; but he had worked for them; they had been his right. Yet she had, in all innocence, helped to take them away. She knew her mother would tell her, one day, that she had contributed to Daddy's death, and perhaps she had.

Yet, standing in the dusty, junk-choked room that looked out over the long green garden, and the locked go-downs above the mouldering Jackaman jetties, she did not feel guilt. She had accepted that no one could come into another's life without consequences. Jackie had taught her that. She would not want him to feel guilt for anything in her life.

'Dear Daddy,' she whispered. 'Dear Daddy. I always loved you, no matter what you were like really. I just loved you, Daddy.'

There was something sweet and archaic about this room, isolated on a kind of quarter-fourth floor above the servants' attics. It opened on the roof to the south-east, but on the other three sides was lit by rose windows as though it had once been a chapel. It was papered with a silk-stripe paper, powder-blue and cream; there were shreds of a Chinese rug upon the once-polished floor. It was called the French room by the servants, and Australia had told Dorothy that her grandfather Joseph had built it as a boudoir for his mistress, Ottilie, whose romantic taste it had been to dwell, as it were, in some remote eyrie. Where had she gone, that Frenchwoman? What had happened to her, was there a picture of her anywhere? There was scarcely anything left of Ottilie but the little room, where the sunrise now filtered in, incandescent through the Rossetti-like clovers of the windows.

Dorothy knew that she should tell Claudie of her brother's

death: she was sure that Bede's widow would not inform her. In all this time she had scarcely thought of Iris and Claudie; she had been too occupied with Granny. But now the two of them, their disparate faces, came before her, and the girl was ashamed to think that she had intended to break the news to Claudie by letter. Iris would never write: she would go and see someone who had tried, however hamhandedly, to be kind to her.

She was nervous as she walked once more up the grubby, askew top-end of Elizabeth Street, full of sunshine and rumbling traffic. She went to the salon, where Claudie and Iris would be at this time of day, and was bewildered to find that it had vanished. In its place was a Chinese grocery shop.

She went across to the house. It seemed different. The minuscule garden was full of dead grass, garbage, and paper blown in from the street.

She knocked, the door cracked open, and she saw a pitiless dark eye, a downy yellow ear.

'Is Mrs List still here?' she asked. 'Or Mrs Pauley?'

'Gone away, gone away!' shouted a furious voice and the door whacked shut abruptly. She stood a moment, thinking, both puzzled and at a loss, and a voice said, 'Ay!'

She had never seen the man next door at close quarters, but he had recognised her at once. He was an elderly shiftworker, peevish and bleached.

''Ere,' he said, 'wasn't you next door there for a bit some munce back?'

'Yes,' she admitted. 'I haven't been in touch. I . . . didn't know Mrs List didn't live here any more.'

His eyes glistened. 'Then you don't know what happened? Come in 'ere and sit on the gas-box and I'll tell yer.'

Shrinking, Dorothy listened. He told the story of Virgie's visiting three or four times, punctuating it with righteous cries of 'Serve 'em right! Keep low company and you end up in the gutter – good place for'um, specially that vicious little madam. Nearly dragged me out the winder on me bonce, she did one night.'

It seemed that Claudie had become hysterical, Virgie had forced her way into the house; when Iris had tried to keep her out, Virgie had smashed a bottle on the step and attacked Iris with it.

'Blood! Gawd! All over the veranda it was – turn a man up. And that big drunken hooer carrying on like a mad wrestler: Jack Dempsey wasn't in it. Took four cops to get her in the wagon, and one of them took a jab in the shoulder. I tell yer I was glad I wasn't on the night shift, I wouldn'ta missed it for ten quid.'

'Was . . . was Mrs Pauley badly hurt?' asked Dorothy.

'I dunno. They took her to St Vincent's. And the dumpy one, Mrs List, she come back a week later and took away her furniture and everything. Not a word to any of us, oh, no! Them in there now, they're Assyrians, bloody cannibal lot. Killed a sheep in the backyard last Sunday. Ah, ugly!'

Dorothy excused herself and went away. She caught a tram down to the *Nation* office and looked the case up in the newspaper files. It was much as the neighbour had said. Virgie had been tried and sentenced to two years for assault with a deadly weapon. Iris's injuries had been facial.

Dorothy was aghast. She felt that she was a catalyst, bringing changes and disaster. Wherever she went. But in time her good sense reasserted itself. Claudie's reaction to her older sister was none of her fault, neither was Iris's protective instinct towards Claudie. Yet Dorothy was bitterly aware of the deficiencies of her conduct while she was with the two women.

Some years later she was waiting for a tram at Circular Quay when she noticed Iris amongst the crowds pouring off the Manly ferry wharf.

Iris's face was scarred and puckered across one cheek and down her neck. She wore an upturned hat, and seemed to make no effort to hide her face. She looked calm and pleasant, a little more matronly and heavy than when Dorothy had seen her last.

By the hand she held a plump fair-haired girl of three or four, dressed up like a doll. Dorothy was thunderstruck by the little one's resemblance to herself. There was no doubt, this must be a child of Claudie's. As she gazed, Iris lifted the little girl and, holding her most tenderly, hurried across to the tram stop.

Dorothy was at first shaken by this unexpected occurrence, but gradually pleasure filled her mind. She thought again and again of Iris's protective gesture, the absorbed look on her marred face, the air of happiness that surrounded her.

She told Clara, and the old woman nodded sweetly, saying, 'Perhaps they needed you to happen in their lives.' But she was tipsy that day, and Dorothy smiled and paid no attention to her remark.

The self-disgust that Dorothy felt after she had visited Strawberry Hills did much to stiffen her resistance to her mother, who brought Olwyn to Sydney not long after Bede Moy's death.

Clara fell to pieces as soon as she had Isobel's telegram saying that she would spend a week with her mother on her way to London, where she was going to live with her brother Titus.

Australia said downrightly, 'You can stay sober for a week. You must, Mother. That child Olwyn looks a stickybeak. Sharp as a tack, as well. Do you want Laetitia and Titus to know – about this?' Clara had snivelled and wailed.

'It's not my fault, dear,' she said tremulously to Australia. 'I just can't help it. It was different when your father was alive.'

'We aren't blaming you,' said Australia; 'but the London mob would be horrified.' She commanded inexorably, 'On the wagon while Isobel is here! I mean it, Mother.'

'I'll help you, Granny,' said Dorothy. Clara leant on the girl's breast and sobbed and wheezed. 'I can feel my asthma coming on already,' she whispered.

The truth was that Clara was frightened of Belle, frightened of raised voices, hurt feelings, emotional disturbance. And things turned out as badly as she had feared. The first night, for instance, the shrill voice of the monkey-faced Olwyn; barks, splutters; Mrs Marion up all night with the child's inhalation tent; breakfast late in the morning; and then Isobel calmly announcing that she was going to take Dorothy to London.

Clara lit an asthma cigarette, holding it self-consciously with tiny golden tongs.

She said, 'She's happy here, dear. Why don't you leave her? Her nerves . . .'

'Oh, nonsense!' said Isobel irritably. 'Nerves indeed! She hasn't a sensitive bone in her body. Don't tell me she cared even about her poor father's death.'

'Did you?' asked Clara sulkily, and then was so terrified at what she had said that she began to cough spasmodically. Isobel walked restlessly about the room, offended by the sight of her mother, stout, shuddering old wreck, with a doughy face that looked as if it had once belonged to someone with a larger skull. Clara's vulgar bog origins were there to be read on that subsided face, and Isobel felt that in some way this was an impertinence.

Clara, in her turn, looked furtively at her youngest daughter, so striking in her mourning, courageous and iron-willed as ever. And her heart began to wallop sickeningly.

Isobel said, 'Mama, I must take Dorothy with me. You must see that there are so many advantages for her in London.'

But Clara could not see anything except a future without Dorothy to lean on and laugh with. Her lips wobbled; she longed for brandy, sleep, oblivion. She felt uncontrollable panic. 'I want her to stay, she's all I've got now.'

Isobel, overcoming her impatience, stroked the thin flat coils of her mother's granite-coloured hair. 'Dearest, don't you want to see Dorothy well and happily married?'

'Not every girl wants to be married,' muttered old Clara hopelessly. 'Look at Australia. She's very content as she is.' And she burst out crying, for she had never thought that Australia was content at all.

'Oh, dear Lord,' she sobbed, 'I'm selfish, that's what I am. Just thinking of myself. You'll have to leave it to Dorothy.'

Leave it to Dorothy? Isobel could have laughed at the old lady's simplicity.

'I've got myself all upset, dear,' Clara said pathetically. 'Would you ring for Mrs Marion?'

The housekeeper tenderly assisted the old woman from the room. 'You need a rest, Madam dear,' Isobel heard her say.

'Oh, Mrs Marion,' said Isobel, 'please ask Miss Dorothy to come to the drawing-room, will you?'

As she went out the door, Clara turned and cried with infantile spleen: 'And when her father died she cried for a week!'

Isobel waited. She thought how little she and her elder daughter had said to each other the previous evening, when Australia and Dorothy and a manservant had met the travellers at Central Station, fatigued and travel-stained in spite of their sleeping compartment. Olwyn had looked like a plucked sparrow, hideous in her black, Isobel had to admit. Her tall sister, on the other hand, had in six months changed from a gawky heron to a woman. The girl's hair had ripened in colour; she moved with a touching grace.

On the way to Jackaman Court, sitting side by side as they were, Dorothy had scarcely uttered a word; but Isobel had caught the girl looking at her shyly, as though she were a stranger.

Now it was morning and time to get things straight. Dorothy entered the room, kissed her mother. Her head was not bent as it might have been a year before. She sat still, looking at her mother warily. Isobel smiled charmingly.

'Oh, Cushie,' she said, 'we've had our troubles, you and I. We've been estranged perhaps. I've said harsh things, I know, but you'll never understand a mother's distress when such things happen. But there – the bad times are behind us now. Let us be friends, darling.'

'Of course we are friends, Mama.'

Isobel patted her hand lovingly. She began to speak of London's pleasures and sights, balls at Aunt Laetitia's gorgeous house, trips to the Continent, the Alps, down the Rhine.

'Isn't it exciting? You will be such a success, Cushie, for I must admit you have turned into what poor dear Daddy would have called a peach.' She sighed mournfully, and in that second of near-silence Dorothy said, 'I'm staying here, Mama.'

'No, darling. We're sailing on the twenty-second.'

'I hope you and Olwyn do go Home, Mama. It will be lovely for you. But I'm not going.'

'Don't be absurd, dear. You belong with me and your sister.'

Dorothy shook her head.

A bright rose stained Isobel's cheeks. 'My dear, may I point out that you are only nineteen. I still have authority over you – and your income.'

'I don't care, Mother . . .'

Isobel flew into an imperious rage. 'How dare you defy me? Haven't I suffered enough because of you? And now you want to bury yourself here with an old woman. Grandmother will become feeble, will be bedridden, you'll have no social life, you'll be an old maid!'

'Oh, Mother, I don't mind any of those things. I love Granny. I feel that this is my home.'

Isobel straightened her back. 'You are coming to London, Dorothy.'

'How will you make me, Mother?'

For some time Iosbel felt profoundly diminished by her defeat. She did not let her feelings show on her face. She carried it off well, smiling, saying, 'She's such a sentimental little ninny, you know, Adela. Adores her Grandmamma. You should have seen her face when I suggested she stay, just till Olwyn and I get settled in London! Silly little thing! So happy. I felt that it might be for the best . . . she's highly strung, you know.'

'She looks as strong as an ox to me,' observed Adela, in her magisterial tone. She still thought she was speaking to natives, though she and her husband were now home in Sydney for good.

Not Adela, nor Anna, that venomous mosquito of an elder sister, guessed Isobel's real feelings. Her face remained serene, her voice sweet, but she bled. She knew that Cushie understood that she was fighting for her life, the life she would have had if she had not married Bede Moy and borne his unsatisfactory children. That was the secret affront, that this daughter of Bede's understood and pitied her because she had wasted her life.

Cushie had gone beyond her reach. An inexplicable pang went through her. For a moment she thought she must be ill, she was so cold. But looking about her she saw that it was a bright warm day. It was just that the years before her appeared like the frigid slopes of an unknown mountain, its peak cloud-hidden.

For Dorothy her love for her mother had changed. It was no longer demanding. Once she had felt that she would wither, die, because her love was not reciprocated as she needed it to be. She knew now that to love was the significant thing.

When the Moys sailed on the twenty-second, it was Olwyn whom Dorothy regretted, the tart little creature whose affection she had never done anything to deserve.

'You're doing the right thing, Cushie,' she had said. 'I must say I have my doubts about Uncle Titus. Something rather disagreeable there. However, I shall outgrow him. But London's for me, I think.'

Already, by the time they left Sydney, Isobel was referring to the sophisticated child as *une belle laide*, born to be chic, one of those girls who set the style, become the rage. But Dorothy could see that Olwyn had thought of this long before her mother did.

That had been in 1925. And now it was 1931, and Dorothy was sitting beside the fire in what had become her own drawing-room, opposite her grandmother's unoccupied chair. Mrs Marion came in quietly, said, 'Time you went to bed, Miss Dorothy. You'll be going out early in the morning again?'

'Why, yes, Mrs Marion. There've never been so many people waiting as there are now.'

Her bedroom was now the French room. It was piercingly chill up there on the roof; the cold struck through the windows like lances. There was a hot-water bottle in her bed, but she could not sleep.

She had put delicate French furniture into the room, buying it cheaply at an auction room full of treasures from bankrupt estates. She wondered who had owned it, or if Ottilie had had similar furnishings. Ottilie, too, had lived here during a great Slump which almost destroyed the young colonies. Joey Jackaman would have ruthlessly cut staff, turned his older domestic servants into the street, told the others that the same fate awaited them if they didn't work longer and harder. Joey was an opportunist; he would have turned the eighties slump to his own advantage. Probably he had made Ottilie do without her carriage, chopped her dress allowance in half.

Dorothy was twenty-five and in the family was already regarded as an old maid. Only that day at luncheon Aunt Adela's ridiculous pot of a husband, retired from the Indian civil service, had bumbled at her, 'Don't expect you to remain long in maiden blessedness, m'dear! The news will soon get around about the Mater's will.'

Aunt Adela had stabbed him with a look like a needle, and Dorothy replied neutrally, 'Nothing can be done about Granny's will until Uncle Titus arrives from England.'

'Oh, quite, quite,' muttered Aunt Adela's husband, and went on to talk portentously about the new firebrand in Germany, the leader of the National Socialists who, in the Reichstag elections of September 1930, had emerged as a major party, with 107 seats as against their previous dozen.

'That Austrian blackguard will topple Hindenburg yet,' he pronounced. 'At least the old man is an aristocrat; he has the right to the Von, you know.'

'Say what you will about Herr Hitler,' cried Aunt Anna in her uncommonly bitter tone. 'But what about this beast in our own State, this Lang, this Bolshevik, who has had the gall to *repudiate!*'

'Interest on *British bonds!*' buzzed Anna.

Anna's military husband, who could turn his face red at will, turned it red: 'And announces that he is going to do it *again*, the scoundrel!'

There was a hush at the blasphemy, broken only by the agitated tinkle of a Waterford wine-glass against Aunt Adela's gold tooth.

Dorothy, who had been abstracted and bored through the meal, looked at them closely. People of straw. She could almost see it sticking out through the nostrils of Aunt Adela's husband, as if he'd been a mummy.

She could just imagine Jackie Hanna taking him off, his bogus English accent, carefully acquired in some inferior Calcutta club, the lip, the nostrils constantly on the move as if the straw itched.

She asked, 'Why not?'

'Why *not*? Why not *repudiate bondholders' interest?*'

Aunt Anna's husband outdid himself, turning ruby. The air was full of agitated talk, to each other, themselves, scarcely to the girl at all. Dishonour. Mother Country. All we owe. Hardly hold my head up. Bounder. Foundation of whole monetary system. Only young woman. Can't expect. We'll all be ruined. If this goes on. The newspaper. The Shop. Australia so foolish. So obstinate. Bonds. Shares. Terrible times.

'Yes,' said Dorothy. 'But Mr Lang is not repudiating interest payment. He is postponing it because of the slump.'

'You know nothing about it!' snapped Aunt Adela.

'Yes, I do,' replied her niece. 'I read. I go to meetings. I listen.'

369

'Dishonourable behaviour – shocking,' said Aunt Anna's husband. 'The nation's name will be mud.'

'But, Uncle Austen,' protested his niece, 'England's name wasn't mud when she accepted Mr Hoover's moratorium on war debts. And it wasn't mud when the American government gave her reduced interest rates on her own war debts. Surely in bad times like these everyone requires negotiation? And that's what Mr Lang has asked for.'

The clatter broke out again, drowning her. Only young woman. Can't expect. Mother Country. Bounder. All be ruined. The newspaper. The Shop. Bonds. Shares. Terrible.

Aunt Anna's husband, now pale, shouted, 'The fellow's a communist.'

'But he isn't,' cried Dorothy. 'The communists hate him. They say so.'

'He's a National Socialist then, like that blighter Hitler!'

The man looked as if he were about to have a seizure, so Dorothy subsided into silence.

Aunt Adela's husband commented disparagingly on the cricket season, and gradually Uncle Austen came back on the rails. But once, in the middle of the other man's anecdote about Cartwright's rotten show in Bombay, actually when the Viceroy was present, Uncle Austen said to his wife in a hoarse whisper, 'It's the principle of the thing, the principle!'

After that he regained his normal colour, leaning back and gazing around the table complacently. He had defended the god.

They departed immediately after luncheon, Aunt Adela skewering Dorothy with a stare hitherto reserved for sweepers.

'Live and learn, my dear,' she uttered. 'Dear Titus will straighten out some of *your* modern ideas.'

The manservant escorted them to their cars. When the man returned to the all, Dorothy inquired, 'Am I mistaken, Robert, in believing you were listening?'

'At first purely by accident, Miss Dorothy.' His lips twitched. 'But it was so enlightening that I ... ah ... lingered.'

She turned away to hide a smile. He coughed formally.

'Excuse me, Miss Dorothy, may I ask if you have ever attended one of the Premier's public meetings?'

'No,' said Dorothy. 'But I'd like to. Very much. But I don't care to go alone, and so . . .' She shrugged.

'There's one in Prince Alfred Park next month, Miss,' he said eagerly. 'If it would be in order, I could escort – attend you. But we could not take the car close to the crowd. They tend to be unruly.'

'So I imagine,' said Dorothy. 'I'd enjoy that, Robert. Thank you for suggesting it.'

She and Robert attended several meetings. The grim disaster of the Depression became more intelligible to her, and her understanding of her grandmother's pity for its victims more complete.

Now she thought of those gaunt crowds, faces uplifted, mesmerised, as indeed she often was herself when the Premier spoke. She thought of the luncheon, her Jackaman relatives, her mother's face. As sleep eluded her, she became more and more depressed. She should not have spent so many hours that evening scratching over old memories. She dreaded having to see Titus again; that was why she was so deeply distrait.

The wind shuffled along the roof like an old man, throwing handfuls of leaves and little twigs at the windows, a lonely, lonely sound. Stars sat like apples on boughs not yet fully leafed. Just as old Joey Jackaman had modelled the exterior of his house on one he used to pass in London with his rag and bone cart, so he had had his garden planted solely with deciduous trees, like a London park. Only the go-downs, which Joey had used to warehouse his imports as they came off the jetties, retained their Malayan profile, a dense black zigzag against the dodging lights of the Harbour.

'Those go-downs!' lamented Dorothy. 'Oh, Granny, why did you choose me? I'm not the right person, I'm afraid.'

But she knew why. Clara had trusted her to carry out what she wanted her to do.

She got up at last and huddled in a blanket before the heater. If she was so cold, what was the state of the people in the terrace houses on the steep hillsides of Balmain? Most of the tenants were on sustenance, she had heard; electricity and gas had been disconnected. Landlords had given up trying to get rent. If they evicted these wretched people, what other tenants could they get? It was better to have the houses occupied than open to vandals and squatters, or burned down by the vigilantes now banded together to prevent evictions.

So often she had seen the scruffy children foraging for slack around the ships' coaling dumps. They even shovelled up the dust, moulding it with clay into chunks of fuel. Clara had watched them, tears in her eyes. Supplying coal to the poorer parishioners of her parish church, St Mary's, had been one of the old lady's many charities. That pig-pen, where Jackie had been – how arctic that must have been, for an old man to die!

She had thought of Jackie many times that week. It was partly because she was troubled about the will, and Uncle Titus; for when she was troubled she always longed for Jackie. But mostly it was because, from a Pitt Street tram, she had seen a dwarf in the lunchtime crowd, and had thought he was Jackie. She had jumped off the tram at the next stop, hurried back towards King Street; then knew she had lost him, and felt faint. As the crowd parted like a current, she saw him again, crossing over by Farmer's, and instantly obscured by the hips and thighs of passers-by.

Breathless, she caught up with him, touched him on the shoulder, knowing the moment she did that he was not Jackie, however changed. He turned a face stiff with displeasure. The family resemblance between dwarfs made the girl's heart thud. In consternation she stared, seeing only vaguely the aged features, large melancholy eyes. In a cultivated voice he hissed, 'How dare you, young lady?' and she realised that he believed she had touched him for luck, as so many people had once touched Jack Hanna.

She said, 'I beg your pardon. I thought you were a friend of mine.' But her voice was so low, his outrage so great, that he did not hear her, and moved away, rigid with dignity.

'I'm so sorry,' she murmured again.

She longed for Jackie. He'd know what to do about Titus Jackaman, what was the best thing to do. He still seemed to her to be the most resolute and steadfast person she had ever known. She had been a witness to his early life. No one had been as well acquainted with it, not even Mr and Mrs MacNunn, for he had always put on a good face for them. But she knew. She knew how he had learnt to endure people's curiosity and silliness, their irrational antipathy, and turn the tables with a joke. She remembered his panic when he could not get work. But he had never broken, never given way, not even with those half-crazy people at the orchard above Ghinni.

She did not know why he had married; she only knew that it must have seemed to him to be the right thing to do. But even that had gone awry for Jackie. In 1929 she had read of the inquest on Maida and Carl John Hanna, and the pain she felt made her realise that the mysterious ties that trembled like electric filaments between her and Jackie were still there. For it was a pure pain, unsullied by jealousy. She felt hurt for him because she loved him, and his suffering was hers.

She had thought then, 'I'm being sentimental, romantic. How people would laugh, even Granny maybe! First love. Never forgotten. It sounds silly, childish.'

Still, it was true. And so she turned away from old Clara's loving attempts to bring eligible young men across her path; she ignored Australia's brusque, sisterly demand: 'Do you want to turn out a dried-up old spinster like me? It has its drawbacks, you know.'

In 1929, when firms first began to reduce staff, and the first crepitations of the world-wide Depression were heard, Clara Jackaman had organised amongst her more charitable friends a free breakfast in the Domain for the increasing numbers of workless men. Until her death, in the autumn of 1930, Clara had always managed to be sober enough to go to the Domain on her Sunday, and Dorothy accompanied her. Now it was Dorothy and Mrs Marion. They joined the small team of men and women who handed out the soup, bread, and hot coffee to those who had slept in 'the Dom' the night before.

The previous Sunday they had had food for two hundred, and there had been nearly four hundred in the queue, frowsy, rubbing their cold arms in the first rays through the trees, yawning and shivering; some inert and defenceless, their heads drooping like those of old carthorses; some cracking jokes or being fierce and contemptuous towards the 'do-gooders'.

'Don't let that bother you,' Clara had said. 'They feel like that because we've got something to give away and they've nothing. We'd be the same.'

Clara herself had once been like that. Her parents had both died in the cholera that followed the Great Famine in Ireland. She had been brought up in a Kilkenny workhouse and at fourteen sent out to Australia and indentured in Joseph Jackaman's sweatshop in George Street. There she had led the life of a slave until young James had run off with her.

When Jackie and Jerry MacNunn arrived in Sydney it was spring, curdy green leaves on the crippled plane-trees, and the evergreens glistening with sugary coal-dust. The Nun rubbed a little between thumb and finger, saying, 'It's sharp, too. Can't do a man's lungs all that much good.'

All the way down in the train his spirits had been sinking. As he stood amidst the demented sounds of Central Station, he felt vulnerable.

'I'm like a shelled snail,' he thought. But young Jack looked around with an awed, exhilarated glance, saying, 'By gum, every-thing's so big!'

'Wait there, Dad,' he told the Nun, and bowled up to a bobby standing statue-like near the winking Arrival Indicator to ask him where they could spend the night cheaply.

'Cheapest is the City Refuge, son,' said the policeman. 'You can walk there, too.' He pointed out the direction, calling after Jackie, 'Better have a bite here first. You'll get sweet damn all there at this time o'night.'

So they bought hot pasties and ate them walking along to the refuge. It was a hard-featured building with the date 1887 incised over the door, and a streak of vomit beside the steps. Jackie went in, came out quick smart. 'All full up. Good thing, too. Stinks. The bloke said there are seamen's boarding-houses down by the docks. Come on, Dad. Down the hill.'

The Nun followed him submissively, stupefied with weariness and with the noise. The offensive odour in the air reminded him of heated dirty metal, or acid chewing through wood. They found a boarding-house, paid their money in advance, and were shown to a cubby with a spavined double bed.

'Maggoty dump,' muttered Jerry.

'Never mind,' said Jack. 'Just for tonight, eh?'

Jerry didn't like to remove his clothes, for the blankets were mildewed and the sheets smelled of phenyl and were unidentifiably smudged. At last he pulled off his boots and lay down on top of the bed with his own track blanket over him.

'I'm stonkered,' he said.

Jack took a pack of cards from his pocket and slipped a couple over the holes in his boot soles. 'Think I might go out for a wander,' he said. 'It's only a bit after eight.'

'Don't lose yourself,' grunted Jerry. 'Put the light out as you go, will you, mate?'

With the boy gone, he felt as if he had dropped into a sea of pumice. Everything abraded feebly, yielded, fell away beneath him. His sense of hopeless dismay was so profound it was near panic. He wanted to get up, run like blazes out of this place, jump any train anywhere. The city noises clacked in his ears, his head. He couldn't think. Everything was wrong. There was not even any true darkness outside the window, only a church spire scummed over with green reflected from some illuminated sign. After a while he saw a blister pearl appear from behind the spire. He lay there, scratching, looking at it dully for several minutes before he recognised it as the moon. His scratching became frantic, and he lit a match to see what was biting him. The whole wall was hung with tiny black berries. As he gaped, they broke their ranks and vanished.

'Ghost!' groaned Jerry. But he was too bushed even to get up to put on the light. He sank into sleep, and the bed-bugs came out in their thousands and nearly ate him alive.

Jackie's reaction to the big city was altogether different. In a daze of delight, he walked around the streets, down to the Darling Harbour wharves, lined with ships like moored churches and palaces. Behind high tin fences men laboured; he could hear steam panting, winches squealing, clangs and rumbles, distant shouted orders. He thought, 'People working everywhere, there must be jobs for us somewhere.'

The lights fascinated him, the topaz and diamonds, the red glare and the foggy pearl. There were lights high up in the air as if they were on poles or mountains, and lights deep down in valleys – dazzling clots and strings and nebulae. The city seemed to sprawl everywhere. As far as he could see there was no darkness ungemmed by windows, street lamps, the little searchlights of moving cars.

He thought, 'Oh, God, this is for me. If only I had come years ago!'

He turned and almost ran up the hill to the big street along which they had come from the station. George Street. It shone at the top of the hill like a luminous vapour, pierced by the glittering squares of display windows. It was a late shopping night. The shops had not long shut, and the street was crammed with people. Trams moaned and crashed past with what seemed perilous speed.

Scarcely anyone stared at Jackie, not even children. Nor did they look at each other. They were shabby people, but the shabbiness was not humble but brazen, devil-may-care. He saw a man with the seat half out of his strides, showing dirty underpants, and no one even glanced at him. And an old woman in bedraggled skirts, wearing a man's felt hat and carrying a birdcage containing an outraged cat, and again no one looked.

The multiplicity of goods in the show windows astonished Jack. He gazed at them like a savage, uncomprehending. Yet it was the Depression! What could this city not produce in better times?

A tiny newsboy ran past him, squalling incomprehensibly, thrusting papers under people's arms, grabbing their money, not interrupting his chant as he did so. 'Paper, mister? *Sun* Final, Sports?'

Astonished, Jackie saw that the paper-boy was an old dwarf, even smaller than himself, with a face creased like a dry passionfruit. Jackie smiled at him, wanting to say something, but the dwarf did not even see that Jack was the same as himself. He ran on, hoarsely shouting. On his back was pinned a yellow *Sun* poster which said BRITAIN GOES OFF GOLD STANDARD.

The occurrence delighted Jack. He felt that he had in effect become invisible. He was just part of a Sydney crowd.

He found his way back to the boarding-house unerringly, as

though his very skin told him which way was Central Railway, which the Bridge.

When he lay sleepless beside the snoring Nun, he could still feel the fierceness and swagger of the city. It was in the air, like a half-mad glitter, unlike anything he had ever known, and yet uncannily familiar.

'This place is like me. Like what I used to be when I was a kid, before High Valley and all the rest.'

It was extraordinary. The furious chemistry of the city had half-poisoned or half-intoxicated him. He could not sleep. All he felt was a wild longing for morning to come, so that he could go out into those streets again. Some time in the night he heard thunder like bronze gongs, and rain falling as if from a bucket. Water overflowed the gutters with the sound of rivers, plunged down the broken spoutings like waterfalls. And this excess, this violence, seemed so right for Sydney that he fell asleep again like a trusting dog.

In the morning both he and Jerry were marked all over with swollen welts; their shirts were speckled with blood exuded by the glutted bugs. The musky smell of the insects was in the air.

They had a cup of tea and a slice of currant cake at a corner shop, glad to get away from the lodging-house. They saw now that they were in a congested, ugly part of the city. Factory chimneys blew out low streamers of pungent smoke, stridulous groans sounded from the docks below. Yet the sky glistened like a child's eye.

'Bridge first, eh?' asked Jack.

They had scarcely rounded the corner before they saw it, a monstrous hump jamming the end of the road, hanging the sky obliquely with a net of scaffolding. It was like the cadaver of a dinosaur being dissected by ants. No photograph Jerry had ever studied had come within a mile of showing the Bridge's soaring massiveness, the grace, the power.

'Gawd,' Jerry kept saying reverently. 'To think that they can get that great bugger to stay up there! Would I think myself lucky to work on that! I'd be like a dog with a tin tail.'

All the way to the Bridge they saw men standing in knots on

corners, in doorways. Some were dejected and gaunt, others challenging or cynical. The Nun looked at them, perturbed. Jackie scarcely noticed them. The sunny city shone around him; he knew his previous night's reaction was heightened, as though he'd had half a dozen beers. He felt skittish, and winked at a sluttish woman banging a doormat against iron rails.

'You dinky little bantie,' she croaked in delight. 'Come in and have a cuppatee, come on.'

The prodigious structure of the Bridge was crawling with men.

Notices were nailed everywhere: No jobs. No Work for Casuals. Keep Out. No Vacancies.

Still, Jerry approached a foreman with a pencil behind his ear. The man was civil. 'You're about eight years late, Dig. She's just coming up the straight now. Expect to have her opened next March.'

'You'll be clearing up for years,' protested Jerry. 'Look at the place around here. You'd think the Huns had been shelling it. Labourers . . . you'll want labourers. Me and the young fella are real good on the shovel.'

Jackie could see his father was disappointed. He said cheerfully, 'Well, we didn't expect to hit it first time up. Tell you what, we'll find a decent doss somewhere and count up our dough, and work out a plan of attack. What about around here somewhere? Handy for the Bridge. We'll go and ask every morning till they're sick of our dials around the place.'

'What's this place called, then?' wondered the Nun.

Jackie found out that it was Dawes Point, commonly called The Rocks. It was a dilapidated district, a stony backbone of a peninsula full of jump-ups and fall-downs, dog-leg flights of perilous steps, crumbling rows of stone tenements leaning against each other for support, bald waste sections where starveling women hung their washing and scurfy kids ran and squealed. These youngsters had legs blotched with festers or impetigo.

Jerry spoke to one of them, holding up a penny so that the child grinned ferociously.

'Where's a place to get a good clean room, Snow?'

The child considered. 'The Buggerin' Barn is full up. But there's Towser's two and a zac for the room, and get your own tucker.

And if you're down and out he'll let you have a pozzy in the basement for nudden.' He gaped frankly at Jack. 'What made you like that, mister?'

'Smoking,' said Jack.

The boy snatched the penny and flew away, stopping momentarily to point a thumb at a tall house on the upper level of the cobbled lane. On the way they passed a tottering cottage surrounded by a crowd.

'What's going on, missus?' Jerry asked an aproned woman. She said tearfully, 'Rotten shame! How they can! The Atkinsons are being sold up.'

Later Jerry was to get used to these pitiless slump auctions; but this, his first, filled him with a raging contempt. During Atkinson's long unemployment the family little by little had become bereft of all comforts.

'All the bedding they got is sugar-sacks and newspapers,' Jackie heard someone say. 'Aw, they tried but. Poor woman, she tried to keep the children looking decent.'

Even their funeral insurance, dearest possession of the respectable poor, had lapsed. Now they were being sold up on the spot to reimburse the landlord for portion of the rent arrears. No notification had been given.

'They put it in the newspaper; that's the law,' explained an old man. 'But fancy spending penny'appeny on a sausage wrapper! You can get coupla stale bread rolls for that.'

The husband was out looking for work, the wife alone and half-silly with terror. She sat on the floor in the small front room, her head pressed into the stomach of a fat neighbour, refusing to look as the linoleum was torn up and sold for five shillings, the kitchen table carted away on someone's back, the very cups and saucers of that morning's breakfast taken off the sink. For, in spite of the sympathy of the crowd, the frequent vicious heckling of the impervious auctioneer, there were plenty of bidders. Jackie himself bid for and obtained for three shillings the absent Atkinson's toolbox.

The Nun was flabbergasted. 'I'd never have thought it of you, Jack! God damn it, you're a rat. How in hell will that poor devil ever get a job without his tools?'"

As he spoke, an overalled man came out of the crowd, tapped

Jack on the shoulder and said, 'Give you six bob for the lot, Shorty. There you are, a hundred per cent profit.'

'No, thanks,' said Jack. He turned to his stepfather. 'See?' he said.

But the Nun didn't see, and strode along for a hundred yards, ranting, until at last Jack got sick of it and said brusquely, 'You've got a big mouth, Dad. I bought these tools to give back to Atkinson. I could see that big cow back there was just itching for them.'

The Nun grunted, then exploded into laughter.

'Stuck me neck out, didn't I?'

'Get it chopped clean through one of these days, y'long streak,' replied his son.

When Jack took the tool-box back to the distraught wife she insisted that he take something from the box for his trouble. As he shook his head, backing away, a neighbour growled, 'Don't want her to feel under an obligation, do you? Ain't she got enough to put up with?'

They opened the tool-box, showing a meagre accumulation, a claw hammer with only one claw, a set of chisels and screw-drivers, a blunt saw, a workman's few odds and ends. Amongst the worn but well-looked-after collection, Jack noticed a pair of hair clippers.

'I'd be much obliged for those, lady, if you can spare them.'

She nodded, suffocating with tears.

Jackie said, 'What will happen to these people? Where will they go?'

'Liverpool, La Perouse, one of them unemployed camps. Poor cows. Four kids, you know, and she's got shocking legs.'

The Nun expressed the opinion that Towser's house stood up only because it was too silly to fall down. It was a blighted yellow, its iron lacework torn off years before, its verandas death-traps of rotten boards. When they knocked, Towser himself appeared. He was a strong middle-aged man with sharp hazel eyes and a lumpy contentious nose. Towser had an educated accent, and a voice both challenging and mocking. His real name was George Vee, and Jerry disliked him the minute he saw him.

Both he and Jack instantly realised the origin of his nickname when he laughed – an eruptive bark as if he were about to have a seizure.

'Bit of luck you caught me,' he said. 'I was just about to go off with the old truck, woodbusting. Jock will show you the room. Four bob for the pair of you. Jock!' He yelled down the stairwell to a black hole at the bottom. He added, 'Jock's an old Wobbly – IWW. Camps in the basement.'

A stout man with white hair growing straight up from a gibbous skull took them upstairs.

It was a terrible house, full of old dry disconsolations. The floor was covered with a mosaic of broken lino, compacted dirt squeezing up through the cracks like tufts of felt. Even Jackie felt uneasy on the stairs, as though there were spooks all around, wheezing, coughing, feeling crook. The air smelt of damp wallpaper, clothes dried while still dirty, and the sad saps of man.

'Archie wack,' said the old man, taking them into a pitch-black room.

'Reckon he's half sawney?' said Jerry out of the darkness.

'Got a case of galloping tongue-tie,' said Jack. Chuckling, he struck a match and held it high. In the gloom there showed two stretchers, a table with a gas ring and a basin.

Jerry saw a gas bracket on the wall. He lit the gas, and a blue fishtail sprang up, bubbling.

'Ah, hang this, Jack,' he said. 'There's no window at all. It's a flaming wombat hole. Think what it'll be like when the real hot weather comes.'

'You looking for a belt on the ear?' demanded Jack. 'Sure, this is a hell of a place, but it's a roof. Better than a drain-pipe or a pig-pen. I've never heard so much moaning.'

The Nun tried to pull himself together. His naturally sanguine temperament struggled with his abhorrence of the city. His face was set against it, and he was powerless to change.

While he was shaving he talked to himself, and once Jackie was troubled to hear him say, 'I feel as if me arms was tied down.' His hair became greyer, his face fell into folds like an old flag. Jack, seeking for some remedy, said, 'Would you feel more like yourself if we could get you some teeth?'

The Nun said absent-mindedly, 'Oh, yes, me tats. I can do without them a bit longer, me old Jack.'

What he felt, without putting it into words, was that his life was receding into a small cave. Hope had seeped away. In the country things were cruelly bad, but you weren't able to see it all in a birds'-eye-view as you could in Sydney. Men waiting all day to get food coupons checked or changed; going home empty-handed to starving wife and kids; going back the next day; standing in the sun till some officious pannikin boss let you through the turnstiles.

The immense, apathetically orderly crowds of the unemployed affected Jerry like a slow suffocation. He knew that every third breadwinner in the country was out of work, that the end of each year cast upon the streets hordes of youngsters whose chance of getting a job was nil. But he had the impression that he was seeing them all at once. They were an army, down at heel, inglorious, despondent. They raked in garbage-tins, stirring around in the muck; they prowled the streets, trying to sell things, packets of flower seeds, sugar scoops made of tin, jars of homemade jam and pickled onions. Sometimes they had sulky, reluctant children with them as though to emphasise their need. While Jerry was still decently dressed he was often stopped and asked for the price of a pie. He thought he would remember those hangdog faces, sockless ankles, and collarless necks until the day he died.

'Ghost,' he sometimes said to Jack. 'What's it all about?'

He came very quickly to the place where most of the unemployed were already, a critical point where he felt convinced that there was an enormous enemy out there – faceless, ravening, pitiless. Jerry didn't know what to call this enemy, but Towser called it capitalism.

Jackie saw very clearly that Jerry was bewildered to the point of paralysis. There was nothing solid for him to fight. He could not play a man's part because he couldn't see where a man's part lay. He had always thought of himself as having his head screwed on the right way, but intellectually he was now like a cast sheep. So many of the older men were like this, like blind dogs, apprehensive, listening hard for a clue, jumping and snapping at any threat-

ening sound. Others were cowed and docile. Often they killed
themselves, and the papers gave gruesome details of their deaths,
employing a righteous approach as if the bankrupt grocer
who sliced his own throat had in some manner let the country
down.

Jack and Jerry were often themselves part of the speechless,
dawn-lit rush, walking three or four miles to some factory which
had advertised a vacancy only to find that there were sixty or
eighty men camped there before them.

'They read the newspaper, of course,' explained Towser, 'when
the job pages are tacked up outside the office. Some of them wait
there from two or three in the morning.'

Jackie began to get up in the moonlight, to run through echoing
streets to the *Nation* office, where the presses rumbled in a subterranean beat, and the lighted galley-board was surrounded by
hordes of dark, shivering figures. He was too small to read the
Wanted ads, but there was never any need. Someone was always
reading them aloud, and the crowd dwindled in accordance with
a constant, agitated movement, as men in groups hastened away
to the industrial suburbs. Some already wore overalls and carried
tools and packets of food, as though to impress a prospective boss
with their desperation.

If there was no vacancy that seemed a possibility for his father
or himself, he went back through the chill streets, passing an
occasional waterproofed policeman propped in a dark cranny like
an image. It was his game to pretend that Cushie Moy was walking
with him, laughing, hand in hand, up alleys where dew-fall had
glazed the tiles of mouldering, airless houses, and there was a smell
of garbage and rat-holes.

In this game they went down to the sea, and sat on the massive
wall that was all that was left of the long-demolished Battery
of Sydney's first garrison years. They looked at the mountain of
the Bridge, blotting out the spangled northern shore, and he said,
'Why didn't you tell me that Sydney was such a . . . was so . . .?'

But even in the dream he could not think of the right word.
The city had spoken to him, and he did not know how or why.
There was nothing seductive about it. Its haggard Victorian

dilapidation was not picturesque. With a native hardihood, it sprang from its cruel past with an unquenchable joy. This was its charm for him.

Maida would have been frightened of it. It would have rolled over her like a steamroller, as it had over Jack's stepfather.

He tried, in love and tenderness, to bring his wife's young face before him. But it seemed wan and out of focus. He thought, 'I was true to you, Maida, really true. You and Carlie, you couldn't have been more cherished.'

Carlie! When Jack thought of him his heart melted. Sometimes he still had sore pangs of grief for Maida and Carlie, but more and more when he thought of the little boy he thought of him alive, jumping up and down in his cot, his hair so fine it floated. The gaiety of that baby! He was so pleased to be alive he spent his seven months beaming about it.

Astonishing to think that there was no more Carlie except in his memory, and maybe Lufa Morgan's. Jack thought of good old Lufe in the cream boat, glissading over the red-dawn river, the water birds rising, banking away, long legs dangling down like those of mosquitoes, Lufa turning his shy crooked grin upon some other offsider. But perhaps he was no longer on the Dovey. Maybe the Depression had got him too.

But it was never Maida who was with him on these solitary mornings when the sea slapped half-asleep at the foot of the old wall and lights looked up out of it like drowned faces.

What was Cushie doing, wherever she was? Was she content, did she know love? Or did she feel as he did, that they had always been two sides of one coin: she, in her physical perfection and defencelessness, like a beautiful gentle bird, he so small and grotesque, and yet hardy, full of purpose?

Sometime during these weeks he understood that he was a whole man again. Workless, always half-hungry, the seat of his pants so darned it was like sitting on a cushion, with not a thing in the world to give him hope, he laughed aloud, knowing that his spiritual centre of gravity had righted itself. The whole world was trying to climb a greasy pole, but he wasn't.

'I've climbed mine,' he realised.

Walking home, he remembered his stepfather saying that he

could feel his muscles deteriorating. 'Gives me the pip. I'll turn into a flaming slug. Ghost, if I could only dig some spuds, load a truck, any bloody thing. I'd do it for damn all, just to have something to do.'

Jack thought of his own mental muscles sagging, turning into perished elastic. He fetched out his books again, and bought more from the Paddy's Market opened the year before in a cavernous tin shed at the Haymarket. Books could be bought there for a penny, even less. Jerry looked at them sometimes, jaw-breaking stuff.

'What you ought to do, me old Jack,' he suggested, 'is go to one of them night schools.'

Everywhere charitable organisations, churches, Government committees, provided free and almost free education. Towser was cynical.

'It's to keep the workless off the streets,' he said. 'Keep 'em busy so they won't dream revolution. Like those wool-masters in the old country that made their apprentices do an hour's compulsory education after a fourteen-hour day feeding the loom.'

'Bloody hell,' said the Nun. 'Do you want it both ways? The old country got thousands of people who could read and write out of it, anyway. And I notice you don't have any more fourteen-hour days.'

Towser grinned. He lived to argue. He belonged to the Unemployed Workers' Movement, organised to prevent evictions and the brutal stand-over tactics of some dole inspectors.

Jerry's antipathy towards Towser had not decreased. He said, 'He's a ratbag. Don't know why you don't tumble to it.'

'Takes all sorts,' said Jack. 'At least he tries to help people.'

It was true that Towser was a lenient lodging-house keeper. There wasn't one of his tenants who'd be an acquisition to anyone. The richest were the pensioner couple who were scarcely ever seen, so timid and reclusive were they. Others came and went, ratty-looking drifters, who probably did Towser out of even his two and sixpence a week, and stole everything that wasn't nailed down into the bargain. Then there were the derelicts in the twilit basement, kept in order by Jock.

The thing which was secretly shameful to both Jerry and Jack was that the dreadful house had become precious to them. It was a bolt-hole. Each found a certain relief in the knowledge that when they came to the end of their resources Towser would let them doss down with the cockroaches.

The Nun groaned with self-disgust when he thought of it. A roof was a roof when winter came: he had to use his common. But it made him feel he was under an obligation to Towser, that they all were: tame people the man liked to keep around the place for some purpose of his own.

Since he had started at night school Jack spent all his spare time studying. He could smile now at the education his parents had thought so remarkable. It was better than that of his Kingsland schoolmates, and that was all. It was not a powerful enough weapon to overcome the drawback of his dwarfism, but it was a start, and it could be improved.

'But why all this economy?' asked Jerry. 'What do you see in this witch-doctor stuff?'

'It just fascinates me somehow,' said Jack.

'I can't fathom what good it'll do you.'

'There'll be something.'

Jack felt an increasing power and energy; he longed to get his teeth into something. Sometimes he felt that it could well be the world; he wanted to shake it like a rat. But playfully. He could not hate the world now that he knew it better.

His specially made clothes were now all worn out.

'I'll never get a job in these togs. I look like a chopped-off Charlie Chaplin.' So he went to the Clothing Relief Depot, to be knocked back with, 'I dunno, dear, we never seem to get any second-hands from midgets.'

So he went to the principal of a nearby boys' school, a Christian Brother whose own long black habit looked done for, and asked if there were any old school uniforms about the place.

The principal was saturnine and pragmatic. He had no romantic ideals about Lady Poverty, knowing that the old girl was rarely dignified and austere, and tended in real life to have her front teeth missing and a grimy smell. Compassionate as well as wry, he was pleased to be able to find in a cupboard a navy serge uniform from the days when the boys wore uniforms and not just any clothes their parents could fossick out of charity depots and second-hand shops.

'God, Brother!' said Jack, dismayed at the little bum-freezer coat with the badge on the pocket, the trousers with legs twice as long as his own.

'Don't knock it till you've tried it,' replied the Brother tartly.

In the empty schoolroom Jackie stripped off unselfconsciously, and the man looked with pity at the large, muscular calves and thighs, the pot belly, and the backside that curved out as if to balance it. The angular deformity above and below the knee-joint was now very pronounced. While the Brother was thinking about this, he noticed that the young man was giving him a genial glance.

'Picture, aren't I?' said Jackie with a teasing wink.

'You've a ton of cheek, I'll give you that,' said the principal.

By this time the boyish charm of Jack's face had gone, vanished into a gauntness that made his unusual features all the more noticeable. His eyes were as fine as ever; and he used them like swords or lances, fixing people with them until they almost forgot the oddities of his anatomy. The principal felt it almost as a blow that these splendid grey eyes, with their thick eyelashes, should belong to one so devilishly treated by fate.

Jack took away the uniform to a tailor who no longer had a shop, but still did some mending and alterations in his tenement front room. He looked at it doubtfully.

'I'm only a coat-hand,' he said. 'Do you want to risk the strides?'

He made a good job of both, and Jack felt a new man. His shoes were still calamitous, and at interviews he had to be very careful never to turn up his soles.

A few times Jerry got as far as an interview, and once he had a start on a building job. He said he was a carpenter, though he was only a useful handyman. He might have weathered it, except that the work was three floors up, and the height nearly destroyed him. He had to creep along the joists on his hands and knees. The other carpenters carried him, in the way they had, so that he'd collect at least a week's wages when he got the bullet.

The Nun mentioned this loyalty when he went to console him-

self with a beer at the Hero of Waterloo. And someone said that
he had heard of ten or twelve fellas at a time, workmates, who
were stood down rather than have one of them sign the wages
book for the award wage when he was forced to accept only half
of it.

'You mean employers come at that, the mongrels?'

There was a general laugh. 'Come down in the last shower,
mate?'

As for Jackie, he had never been within whistling distance of
a job. They took one look at him, the faces that were twin brothers
to those who had looked at him with embarrassment or outrage
in his youth. But to that was often added a careless brutality and
impatience: 'Your own brains ought to tell you you're unsuitable.
I'm a busy man.'

From the desk to the door, Jackie bristled, longing to turn
around and spring at the barbarian, squeezing his chicken neck
till his tongue came out. But underneath this brief tumult was
an uncritical and impersonal understanding of the man's position.

Once indeed he turned about and said, 'I'm a good book-keeper,
sir, and you don't need height for that.'

The man stared, his pulpy face swelling with blood pressure
or affront. Jack thought, 'He's in a funk for his own job. If he
takes on a dwarf there'll be someone after his hide and he can't
risk it. He'd rather play safe with a full-sized man with half my
qualifications.'

The man's face deflated, and a cryptic expression passed over
it. He brought out five shillings. 'They're rotten bloody times, old
man. Will you take this and get yourself a decent feed?'

Jack instantly saw that the man needed him to accept the
money, either to prove himself humane or to prove that the unemployed had no pride. So he took it, with grave thanks, and observed the manager's relief.

He's like that pig-cocky who tried to turn us out of the pen
that cold night, Jack reflected. Every time he sees a man without
a job he sees himself. Poor bastard, he's haunted. They're all
haunted.

When he got home, he found the Nun, with a butter-box set
up in Towser's backyard, giving passers-by haircuts for threepence

a shot with the departed Atkinson's clippers. He sometimes made a shilling or two this way. Jackie stood near by, seeing how Jerry's neck had become stringy, and his big corded workman's hands soft and pinkish from lack of manual labour.

The Nun had convinced himself that he hid his depression successfully. Carrying it off, he called it, cracking hardy. But to Jackie he was like a pane of glass. He began to feel much older and tougher than Jerry, profoundly defensive of him.

But communication between them had slowed like a stream of glue. Jerry mostly wanted to yarn about Kingsland – what had happened to this person and that – stories about Peggy; but he didn't like to. Once he said unexpectedly, 'D'you remember, me old Jack, the way tomato plants smell with the sun on 'em?' and then was silent, fearing that Jack would tumble to his homesickness and think him an old granny. So there seemed little to talk about as they trudged from factory to foundry, shop to market garden, soup kitchen to ration-ticket depot. The fatigue of the constant walking wore down any desire to converse. Getting one foot in front of the other, that was the day's problem.

Sometimes Jerry thought he'd try somehow to get back to Kingsland. It'd be no harder there to make out on the five and sixpenny ration ticket. A bob to the baker, two bob to the butcher, a bit of tea and sugar, a small tin of condensed milk. Make sure the shopman gives you a receipt, and no tobacco, you hear! Those in work aren't paying a shilling in the quid unemployment tax so that you stiffs can have a smoke.

But in Kingsland he'd be alone. Loneliness was the worst, the wicked thing. Towser's house was full of Alone people, like Jock. Even Jock's past had vanished. The violent anarchy, the prison, the floggings of his young days, were like a set sun; there was a diminished glow of it in his eyes sometimes, but not often. He had no comrades left any more. Not even the communists seemed to have heard of the IWW – the Wobblies. It was all Lenin and Trotsky with them – and Joe Hill hanged and forgotten, martyred Joe.

Jock's name was William Isbister, but there was no one to call him Will any more. Not even Jerry could bring himself to it, somehow.

'I sometimes think it was all a dream,' said Jock. He had become more intelligible as Jerry got used to his accent. As well, he always put in his teeth when he went upstairs to play draughts by candle-light, for the Nun always contrived to have a bit of food ready for him.

Jock thought Towser a champion. The only point on which they disagreed was over the Premier of New South Wales, J.T. Lang. Towser maintained that this strange, powerful man was fascist, like Mussolini in Italy, or the rising trump in Germany, Herr Hitler. But old Jock thought that Lang was true Labor, putting the working man first, not like them gutless bowsies in Canberra.

Whenever Mr Lang spoke in public, Jerry and Jack would walk miles to listen. He was a spell-binder, delivering short barking sentences, straight-forward and non-ambiguous. Immense gatherings of unemployed hung on each word, hope sparkling once again in their bloodstreams. They stood in domains and dusty parks, most of them unmoving while thunderstorms in summer rage burst out of the scalding skies, and Lang talked on under a big black umbrella. There was savage heckling and cat-calling; often fights started amongst the audience. The mounted police were always there, their glossy horses unmoving at the edge of the crowd.

Once Jack and his father, because they had waited most of the afternoon, were just below the bandstand from which the Premier spoke. Jack looked up at the enormous height of Lang, observed the dark suit, the dark hat set with clerical demureness above a long smooth face, hollows for eyes, with nothing to prove that they were there but a flinty gleam reflected from a nearby gas-lamp.

It was a critical time for the Labor Premier. The oldest, most heavily industrialised State, New South Wales had always had a reputation for intransigence. Now people spoke openly of secession, even civil war. For more than six months the State had defied the Commonwealth Government, a Labor Government that had come to office two days before the Wall Street crash in 1929: to inherit the consequences of the witless extravagances, the lack of foresight, of its predecessors.

Its leader, the dedicated and honest James Scullin, had when in Opposition consistently condemned the rash borrowing of the then Government. He was a prophet destroyed by the authenticity of his prophecies.

The terrible task confronting the Prime Minister was complicated by a powerful and obdurate Opposition Senate, which defeated and delayed all attempts to ameliorate the desperate condition of the Australian people. As well, Scullin had to suffer this Old Man of the Sea, the demagogue Lang, a lone mutineer, formidable, impossible to intimidate, who uttered blasphemous strictures against the Mother Country of a kind hitherto heard only from bolshies.

At the Premiers' conference earlier that year, Lang's motion to postpone the payment of interest to bondholders had been received with consternation. One member of the Opposition, whose destiny it was to become Prime Minister and an elder statesman, announced that he would rather see every man, woman, and child in Australia starve to death than have a single British bondholder wait for his money.

Jack could feel the electric thrill amongst the crowd as Lang spoke. It was sunset, and the red light was hard and bright on the stems of dusty palms that looked like upright serpents, unnatural, not like plants.

'My friends,' said Lang. 'The bondholder has a mortgage on your sweat.'

He repeated it softly, in a penetrating near-whisper, and there was a hideous roar, as of bears caged. The mounted policemen sidled their horses closer.

A man near Jerry shot up a black-woolled fist and shouted in a ringing Welsh voice, 'Fair go, mister! D'you think they're better off than us in England? They're starving in their thousands and I've seen them, mister.'

Many English voices spoke. The swarming immigrants of the twenties boom shrieked out their defence of their country, their disillusionment with the new land to which they had been driven by the tottering economy of Great Britain. A brawl or two broke out, a horse was ridden into the crowd.

Dorothy Moy saw the sunlight red as blood on an upraised baton, someone dragged a bundle of old rags out of the crowd.

Robert said cautiously, 'I think I'd better get you out of here, Miss Dorothy.'

She said, 'I'd like to hear more. That man ... he's tremendous.'

He said firmly, 'Begging your pardon, Miss ... You haven't seen a crowd lose its head yet, Miss. I'd appreciate ... There could be rough stuff ...'

She saw he was excited and tense. 'Would you like to stay, Robert? I'll walk down to Parramatta Road and get a taxi.'

But he disapproved of the idea, and took her away to where the big black Packard waited, a safe distance from the meeting.

So she missed seeing Jackie Hanna.

Lang waited till the noise had died down. He spoke directly to the Welshman. 'You speak in defence of our brothers in England, my friend.'

The Welshman was hoisted up by his mates. 'Unemployment is worse there than here ... starvation ... miners ... mines shut down ... bloody misery ... my dad ... brothers.'

Lang said, 'You are right. Britain has a greater rate of unemployment than ours. It began earlier, it may go on longer. But those of whom you speak, the miners, your family ... *are they bondholders?* Were they able to invest millions in overseas loans? Man, I am not saying that it is the ordinary British working man but the bondholder who has a mortgage on your sweat.'

He waited until the roar had died away, and added, 'It will do that prosperous gentleman no harm to wait for his interest.'

Jack Hanna yelled, 'Tell us what the loans were for, Mr Lang.'

He saw the gleam of the man's eyes as he turned towards him. 'You ask what the loans were for. Much of this enormous sum went towards ordinary national development ... railways ... secondary industry ... port improvement. But ...'

Jack admired the long significant pause. He thought, 'That's good. That's where I'd put it if I were up there.'

'But ... a good proportion of British loans at high interest were made to equip and support the AIF so that Australian soldiers should be able to fight Britain's war in far-away countries ... in France and Palestine. Shall I repeat that, ladies and gentlemen?'

During the outcry that followed, Mr Lang stooped towards Jackie.

'Will you come up on the platform, sir?' he asked.

Jerry thought, 'Gawd, don't go, boy, he's only asking you because you're a dwarf. You'll make a guy of yourself, Jack!'

But already Jack had swung himself up on the platform, was shaking hands with Mr Lang, who looked all the taller because of the young man's lack of stature. There was a murmur of surprise from the crowd, a ripple of laughter. Jack turned to face them immediately.

'That's right,' he shouted, 'I'm a dwarf. Does that mean I don't eat? Does that mean I don't need a job? Does that mean I haven't a right to self-respect?'

The crowd responded, laughing and whistling. Though it was approbatory, it was a frightening sound, like the breathy howl of an organ pipe.

Jackie shook his clasped hands over his head like a boxer, and turned back to the Premier, who said, 'May I know your name, sir?'

Jackie told him. He was amused that the Premier should call him 'sir', and not 'boy', or some half-jocular nickname, which had been his lot since he was a child. But Mr Lang addressed him as Mr Hanna, and asked him if he had any more questions.

Jerry was both awed and baffled when he talked it over with Jack afterwards.

'Don't you tumble?' asked Jack, grinning. 'He knew I'd ask the right questions. So that he could give the right answers. Like when I asked him to explain why the Commonwealth Government was suing New South Wales. So he could tell the crowd that as soon as he refused to pay bond interest last April the Federal Government went creeping off and paid it, and are now dunning New South Wales for reimbursement. Everyone knows the facts but he wanted to put it his own way, so as to get the reaction he wanted. Like a comedian and his straight man.'

The Nun couldn't fathom it. But Jackie remembered the faces, thousands of them, looking for a saviour, waiting, needing to be reassured, to be told they'd survive, that things would come good again, that they'd make it in the end.

He thought, 'I could do what Lang does. I could do it better.'

As Christmas neared, various religious and civil charity depots dispensed Christmas cheer to the needy. There were haunting scenes of crowds queueing in the sun for five or six hours waiting for a depot to open. Jerry had stood in a few of them. He was embarrassed to do so, but his wistful longing for a shirt with an unfrayed collar was too much for him. Sometimes he thought he might even land a pair of boots.

He sincerely enjoyed the deplorable hassle when a mob, driven wild by heat and impatience, rushed a depot and caused a ton of potatoes, four hundred cabbages, and nine hundred pumpkins to vanish in seven minutes flat.

'I timed them,' said Jerry to Jack. 'There was not a bloody thing left but the do-gooders, and they woulda snitched *them* if they coulda eaten them. But they was all wire and gristle.' He added, 'I could do with a toothful of Christmas duff, couldn't you, me old Jack? Crikey, your mum used to make a corker pudden.'

So they walked all the way out to Glebe Town Hall, where a Christian Ladies' Guild was giving out Christmas puddings to genuine cases.

They arrived good and early, and Jack thought it was a bit unnatural that there were no more than twenty or thirty people around the door.

A curdled-looking fellow looked over Jerry and Jack's susso cards penetratingly, hoping to find that they were out of date or fraudulent. At last he said reluctantly, 'I can only give you single men's puddens, you know.'

'Go on, show us the married men's puddings,' urged Jack, who was beginning to feel a bit of a devil. 'We want to see what we're missing.'

The clerk sneered, and thrust two muslin-wrapped black grapefruit across the counter. They were as hard a boulders.

The clerk chopped out a few words. 'You boil 'em up,' he said.

'Merry Christmas,' said Jack, but the man made no answer.

'Ah well,' said the Nun forgivingly, 'maybe he's a Jew.'

They walked down towards Broadway, through the old wide streets bordered with crumbling houses, shops squeezed between them, run-down working-class hotels. The Nun felt wambly. They had had no breakfast but a cup of tea.

'Might have a gnaw at me pudding,' he said. 'Just a taste, like.'

'Has to be boiled up,' said Jack. 'Smiley said so.'

The Nun peeled off the muslin. 'Smells good,' he said. 'Spice or something.' He took a sacramental mouthful.

'Single men's puddings!' scoffed Jack. 'Did you ever hear such damned rubbish?' He turned around. 'How's the Christmas cheer, Dad?'

'Like a gobful of black kack,' said the Nun. He spat it out, and bowled the remains of the pudding over a wall. 'Flaming sod!' he barked with irrational rage. 'They think anything is good enough for us, even if it would drop a pig in its tracks.'

'Ah, knock it off, Dad,' said Jack. 'It's only a bloody old spotted dick. Don't do your block.'

'It's not only the bloody old spotted dick,' cried the Nun, looking wild. 'It's everything. I'm fed up, boy!'

'On the wing!' said Jackie swiftly, and he showily passed his single man's pudding to his father, who caught it automatically and drop-kicked it down the street.

So they toed it down the footpath, Jack fancily dribbling it, the Nun occasionally getting in a neat one with his better foot, both of them letting out yips and cheers which made a passer-by say reproachfully, 'Yous unemployed don't appreciate nothing.'

The pudding survived for a couple of hundred yards, and then Jack skilfully punted it through the door of a fish-and-chips shop. There were brays of panic from within, as though the wrecked and wobbling comestible were horse dung. Jackie and his father discreetly vanished up an alley.

Jack made no more reference to Jerry's outburst. He knew Jerry would be abashed because of it; but his heart ached for the older man. As they passed the brewery stables, he said, 'Why don't you give them a go for a job? You've had a lot to do with horses in your time, and you were a mounted man in the Boer War, weren't you?'

Jerry demurred, saying there'd be a sign out if they wanted anyone; so Jack put on a madman's face and growled, 'Get in there before I flatten yer.'

He sat on the kerb outside to wait. There was a little tree near by, a poplar putting up a fight for life, all its frail threads of roots under the concrete. This rachitic tree was the only green thing as far as Jack could see. He looked at it, drowsing in the sunshine.

After twenty minutes, the Nun came out, wiping his mouth.

'The yard boss give me a cup of gunfire,' he explained. He stood awkwardly, scratching his neck.

'Well?' demanded Jackie.

The Nun said, 'I dunno why you sent me in there, me old Jack, but I got a start.'

They punched each other back and forth all the way to the corner, laughing aloud. Jackie detected a note of hysteria in his father's voice. He said, 'We'll take a tram back to the Point. We can afford that now you're a working man. Have a feed and talk it over, eh?'

From the time the first adventurous excitement of going on the track had seeped away, Jerry had felt wryly that the words of a popular song described him to a T.

> *Show me the way to go home,*
> *I'm tired and I want to go to bed.*

And all at once, as though God had had a gutful of his secret, constant grizzling, there was this job: lowly, dirty, but one where a man could feel at ease with himself. The yard foreman, who had been at the Boer War himself, and had got Jerry the job on the strength of Jerry's own service, was as rough as a bear's behind. But he was a just boss.

'Name of Heenan,' said Jerry. 'Tough. Ghost! He could wear a taipan for a necktie.'

The stables had been there for ever. They were built of Pyrmont stone and pit-sawn kauri thick as ships' timbers. The yards were paved with stone setts pocked by the hooves of generations of dray horses. The brewery had been there for ever, too. Governor Macquarie had drunk the first ale drawn, back in Waterloo year, 1815. He had toasted the Duke of Wellington in it, and the brewer of the time had put the Dook's tin-opener profile on his labels. The stables had been there when the Surry Hills were green, and through the Haymarket ran a tidal creek visited by whimbrels and swans and wild duck, with a little causey across it.

Jerry was one of twenty or more yardmen. There were other men and boys about the place, old codgers in the harness room, young whipper-snappers, sons of the other men mostly, who took the teams out to Centennial Park for their green feed over the weekend.

There was something wholesome and old-fashioned about the place: the pump splashing on the cobbles, the gaslights in the stalls, the smell of saddle soap and metal polish, manure and liniment, the huge placid beasts being shoved around and shouldered over by the sack-aproned men.

There was accommodation for single men above the stables. Room there for Jerry, if he wanted it. But he was doubtful about leaving the young fella.

'You off your loaf?' demanded Jack. 'You move right in there. Save fares. You can get up later in the morning. I'll ask Towser if he's got a smaller room I can have cheaper. Go on, do you good to be on your pat without me hanging around.'

So Jerry moved into the loft, into a chaff-sprinkled cubicle that was full of sunlight all day, and caught the westering sun over Darling Habour and the droughty plains beyond, so that Jerry could lie on his stretcher and sunbake if he wanted, after he'd knocked off work.

'I feel like all me Christmases have come at once,' he thought.

At the same time it half killed him to leave Jack in that dump in The Rocks, in that room where a man had to light a match before he could find his nose to scratch it. And there was Towser. Jerry was sure that as soon as he was out of the way Towser would move in, ear-bashing the boy, feeding him all this bloody bolshie stuff.

'You just watch out for that flaming Rin-Tin-Tin,' he cautioned Jackie. 'Yes, I know, you got more brains than me, but I know men. And my nose tells me that fella's a bit off.'

'Ah, go on,' Jackie chiacked him. 'What's the matter with Towser, poor coot?'

The Nun brooded. 'I just feel it in me bones. Maybe it's the way he's always letting on he knows more than everyone else, about what's behind what Scullin is doing, what Lang's after, what's gonna happen in Germany next year. You'd think he had the Holy Ghost sitting on his shoulder like a pet budgie.'

'I've got exams coming up. Just forget him, Dad. I can look after myself.'

Cleaning up a tired horse, Jerry thought remorsefully that he'd had a bit of a neck to talk to Jack like that. The boy was twenty-five, had more brains than you could shake a stick at. He could handle bloody Towser.

The horse was rain-soaked, ears down, its hocks caked with mud. It leant its head against Jerry docilely, blowing down his neck.

'Oh, turn it up!' grunted the man in mock irritation, giving the animal a heave. The creature arched its thick neck and nibbled softly at his ear. It gave Jerry an almost sexual pleasure; he felt a vagrant longing for the sturdy joys of human love.

All up and down the line of stalls he could hear the rough voices of men pretending anger, the clonk of buckets, hands slapping broad withers, the ring of hoofs on the cobbles as the incoming teams arrived home and the boys removed the harness.

He gave the horse a little hay while he washed the muddy hocks, looked for bruises or stones, carefully dried and brushed out the long white feathers. The Connellys, who owned the brewery, were finicky about their transport stock; at least once a week some member of the family inspected the animals minutely. They were show-pieces, not only of the brewery, but of the city.

Brushing the horse with firm, reassuring strokes, Jerry marvelled at how quickly he had got into the way of things. Heenan no longer inspected his work daily, though he still made his random raids on the stalls. But Jerry had always been at home with horses; it was cows that got on his hammer.

He put his face against the animal's side for the comfort of warmth and an animal smell. Its coat was full of gritty city dust and he sneezed, then brushed more vigorously, finishing off with a leather, following the lie of the coat. He washed the nostrils and the dock, put a blanket over the back, measured out the dry food. He slapped the horse on the rump as he passed.

'Lucky old devil!' he said; and, taking up his bucket and brushes and cloths, he went on into the next stall.

Every evening the men were given a bottle of beer each. They sat in the harness room, yarning over it, secure in the knowledge that at Connelly's, anyway, the Depression was outside. Then Jerry used to clean up a bit and go down the road for sausages and eggs at a little eatery where there was a decent woman who always gave him an extra fling of mashed potato. He had one day off a week, and he usually spent part of it with Jack, slipping him ten bob for some tobacco or whatever he needed. Jack demurred, but he could see it was a great joy for his father to be able to sling him a few bob to help out.

'It's only a loan, you know, Dad.'

'Too right. One of these days I'll put the nips into you for it.'

Jerry bought himself some teeth for thirty shillings. A nasty blue-white colour they were, like cheap cups. But they didn't hurt too badly, and the difference they made to his face was amazing. The woman in the hash-house said he looked fifteen years younger. He felt she was right. The next week he thought he might buy himself a two-and-sixpenny white shirt at Murdoch's; but instead he took young Jack to the pictures, and they had a great old roar at Laurel and Hardy. He began to enjoy wandering down George Street of a Friday night . . . the lights, the liveliness and noise of it all.

It had been many years since he'd really looked at girls. There seemed to be millions of them, flappers, Jerry called them, swishing around in long flared dresses with fluttering sleeves. He liked that. During the twenties all the girls had looked like pillow-cases. These ones wore tight little hats aslant over their thin eyebrows, and almost all of them had round red lipsticked mouths, like gold-fish, Jerry thought.

Once or twice a young woman of a different sort gave him the eye, and Jerry was tickled pink. He wondered if poor old Jack was getting any, and sighed. He'd never liked to ask.

Although Jack missed his father, he was relieved to be by him-self. The presence of the older man for so long, and through such hard times, had been a strain. He was fatigued with being cheer-ful. There was a peculiar freedom about being able to look despon-dent if he felt that way. He moved into a room at the top of the house, separated from the slates by discoloured wallboard with holes chewed or punched in it. Towser said he could have it for nothing if he gave him a hand twice a week on the wood run. As Jackie's savings were almost down to nothing, he accepted this offer gladly and without any sense of obligation; for it was no joke running in and out of houses, up stairs most of the time in that locality, with sacks of firewood. Towser picked it up for free out on the Liverpool plains, and sold it for a shilling a bag. On the other days old Jock helped Towser, and Towser gave him a few bob pocket-money for the job.

Jack's new room was the size of a bath-tub, and the bed was a shocker. He was banjaxed when he tried to work out what shape of a human had created the big sag in the middle and the wee sag in the bottom right corner. He stretched a piece of plank from the windowsill to a fruit box and made himself a table to work on. But it was simmering hot up there under the roof, and what with the rubbishy food, lack of sleep, and solitariness, he began to feel a disagreeable debility. He felt he was getting as flimsy and spent as the old house languishing about him.

Having to sustain Jerry's optimism had kept him going. Now there seemed little to bother himself about. He finished his examinations at night school, and did well, he thought. He read the newspapers at the library and followed with a languid interest all the fights in the Federal Labor Party. He voted for good old Scullin in the elections, but wasn't surprised when the ragged hopeless remnant of the party was kicked out of office, to be replaced by a kind of bastard coalition which included several Lang-Labor types who had seceded from Scullin.

'So the Big Fella's brought Scullin down at last,' commented Towser. 'He'll bring himself down yet, you'll see. He's over-reached himself.'

Jock, his strong old face flaring red, gobbled something at him. It was the first time Jackie had ever seen Towser's faithful follower overtly enraged with the master. Towser grinned. 'Sorry, Jock,' he said. 'I know Lang's your hero. But that's how I feel.'

Christmas came and went. In January the New South Wales Government announced that it would pay no more overseas interest until more stable times returned. The new Prime Minister,

Lyons, attached New South Wales revenues, and Lang retaliated by suspending the collection of Commonwealth income tax. The harassed community saw the State as a runaway horse heading for some frightful precipice. The New Guard, a quasi-military citizens' organisation devoted to the defence of monarchy, law and order, and property, drilled publicly and played war games in Sydney's parks. The communists issued fiery statements, and the *Workers' Weekly* announced that once in power they intended to expel all Governors and other representatives of British finance, withdraw from the Empire, and set up a workers' and farmers' republic.

The Jackaman sisters and their husbands felt cold winds blowing all about. Under the circumstances the terms of old Clara's will, particularly in that area relating to the establishment of a shelter for destitute men in the old waterfront go-downs, seemed catastrophically improvident. All that money being dribbled away, *going out of the family,* in an absurd cause!

They made no bones about letting Dorothy know what they thought about it.

'Mother was merely buying her way into heaven,' commented Aunt Anna, but she at once saw her mistake when an expression of mulish affront settled over the young woman's face, reminding Anna disturbingly of Clara herself.

Jack Hanna still walked miles every day looking for work. He made some fleeting social contacts, and attended some of the many free lectures in church and Masonic halls. He heard about Douglas Credit, Keynesian economics, socialism, radicalism, evolution, the truth of the Bible. It was during a lecture on the Holy Land, with lantern slides, that he realised he was really attending these free shows because of the cocoa usually passed round afterwards. The Church of England often provided biscuits and rock cakes as well. Girls handed round the cocoa, and he thought he might get friendly with one. But he never did. He got smiles, sometimes a shy word or two about the lecture or the weather or even the rock cakes. He wasn't backward. He asked two or three of them if they'd care to come out for a cup of tea; he tried hard to get up a conversation, even about the stupid lolly-tinted slides; but he had no luck.

He was not hopeless. He was just lonely. One Sunday morning, looking from his high window across the sunny, deserted streets, across the steely glass of Darling Harbour to the smoking chimney-pots of Balmain, he found himself crying. He didn't know whether it was the smoke, which spoke of Sunday dinners being put on, and people who at least could sit down with other people to eat, even if the dinner was no great shakes. Or perhaps it was the church bells ringing across the water from the spires that spiked up from Balmain's cobby hills, reminding him of bells jangling through Kingsland and other towns like it, snoozing Sunday towns, like cudding cows, and the huge lovely sky over all.

Cushie's people had lived over there, in Balmain or Birchgrove, above the great dock, on some lean road carved into the hillsides, amidst Moreton Bay fig-trees, or even apple-trees.

He hadn't cried since Maida and Carlie died, except in the night, dreaming, that first year.

'This won't do,' he thought. 'This bloody well won't do. A man could go off his scone this way.'

So he walked out to Surry Hills to see Jerry, who was camped on his bed in his groom's cubby-hole, his teeth in a glass on the floor beside him. Jack didn't like to wake him up, but Jerry was thoroughly pleased to be wakened. He went out and bought some pies, and a slice each of khaki boiled pudding with a blob of sweet sauce on it. It was supposed to be hot, but was little more than feverish.

'Wire in, me old Jack,' invited Jerry. The two men ate grate-fully, Jerry talking enthusiastically: how he enjoyed the work, the other blokes, real decent. They called him Mac. He supposed he might never be called Nun any more. Seemed queer! His cubby-hole would be bonzer in winter, warm as toast, and not a flea. He did not see his humble service to animals as being humble. It was just wonderful luck, you wouldn't believe it. And Heenan had given him a pretty broad hint that he might be put on per-manent. He'd have to have a word with them up top first.

Here Jerry lowered his voice. One of the blokes, silly mug, had been caught smoking in the loft. It was his job that Jerry might inherit.

'You've got to think of the horses, you see,' he explained.

Jack realised then that his father had stopped smoking. He was profoundly impressed. It made him realise as other things had not how important this job was to Jerry. He felt that perhaps older people needed satisfactory jobs even more than young ones; they had narrower worlds. They needed hard edges, secure boundaries to their lives. Somehow this made Jerry seem remote: Jack had never felt this before.

He listened, grinned, joked, and all the time there was this unassuageable pain of loneliness in his heart. It wasn't a boy's loneliness any longer, but a man's. He felt he might go through life with this longing, this sensation that there was a pit inside him, never to be filled. He faced up to it, looked at it carefully: it was like a kind of haunting, as irrational and inherently terrifying. Now he knew he had seen its traces on many faces. It was what made old people withdraw into themselves, peering out suspiciously through tiny windows at the world, as the reclusive pensioners of Towser's house peered at him. It was not that they were defensive in their loneliness: it had changed them to a different kind of person, that was all.

'Well,' he said, not to himself but to the loneliness, 'see how you get on with me, sod you.'

For some time now George Vee had been nudging him in his gentle, off-hand way, to join the Unemployed Workers' Movement, to help in their fight against evictions particularly.

'Just join,' said Towser. 'Be there. Lend weight.'

'On the principle that every little helps?' cracked Jack.

Towser said seriously, 'It's just a kind of demonstration, you know, drawing attention to the uselessness of evictions. Some landlords can be easily intimidated. You'd be surprised.'

'To tell you the truth,' said Jack, 'I've no fancy for being arrested and thrown into pokey.'

Towser laughed. 'If it came to that, there'd only be a fine, and we've got together a small fund to cover that. But mostly we can get out of the way before the police can grab us. They don't really want to get us, you know, they just want to evict families without opposition.'

Jock said belligerently, 'A man has to do what he can. It's to do with self-respect, you understand?'

Towser laughed. 'Watch out, Jack, or he'll mow you down with solidarity and the immortal band of brothers.'

Jack thought it over. Maybe it'd be a bit of a lark, if nothing else, and give him something to talk to Jerry about. Even though the Nun disapproved of Towser, he was strong on solidarity and sticking to your mates. So he told Jock and Towser that next time there was a picketing he'd go along with them.

In the meantime he thought he'd try a new tack to cure his loneliness. He began to hunt up girls.

The district was full of prostitutes. If you turned over a stone they'd dart in all directions like slaters. But he did not have enough money for the professionals, even at Depression prices. He went around the streets looking for amateurs, usually in couples, self-conscious and giggly. The first one he approached said, 'No, I couldn't reelly, I reelly couldn't, I mean reelly', and hurried off hoop-backed, swinging her patent-leather handbag in agitated arcs. 'Come *on*, Dulcie,' she called from a distance. Dulcie, tittering, shot after her. Jackie heard the first one say, 'No, it ain't a kid, Dulcie. Use yer skull. I tell you it ain't. It's one of them freaks.'

At last he cornered a jumpy girl with a murky skin and a cast in her eye. When he spoke to her she scrambled off a few feet like a spider, looked over her shoulder apprehensively, and let out her breath. 'Crumbs,' she said, 'you gave me a start speaking to me so sudden. Ain't you little! My cousin Kev was one of youse. Gee he was cute. He died young but. Me name's Valda.'

She was willing, even for the five shillings he had, and talkatively led him to 'a good place', along alleys that sunshine had not warmed for more than a century, the pavement sticky, the interstices of the clammy walls clogged with slime, and into a cleared space under the dark approaches to the Bridge. The monstrous structure reared over them like an anaconda, fuzzed here and there with clusters of spotlights where men were still working, for the Bridge was to be opened to traffic in a couple of weeks.

Valda led the way to a patch of grass she knew. She wore green woollen gloves, which she would not remove.

'Can't, dear. I got this dermo, see? That's why I got the bullet from this sandwich place where I was working. Oh, it was a lovely place, as much as you could eat really, with crusts of loaves, and fag-ends of devon and fritz, and ham that had turned funny. Well, come on, love, I'm a bit pregnant and I don't exactly feel a box of birds.'

Whether it was the dermatitis, or the gloves, or the pregnancy, Jack found himself useless. Embracing that body was like embracing a plank with a faint firm bulge in the middle. She became bored and cross, though she tried to hide it. Her cozening servility, plus the gloves, put Jack off more than ever, and his annoyance at himself at last boiled over into a shameful contempt for her. He jumped up, put himself to rights, listening with one ear to her gabbled reassurances. It wasn't his fault ... often happened ... he'd be good in a minute or two ... the tales she could tell.

'Oh, shut your mouth, you silly cow,' he said roughly.

To his amazement she flew into a temper. No need to ... just because ... calling names ... people have feelings ...

He had thought a girl like her would be hardened to obscenity and abuse. And after all, 'silly cow', what did it mean? Nothing. Then it struck him she thought she wouldn't be paid, he'd wasted her working time. As she flounced off, he ran after her and thrust the Nun's five shillings into her hand.

'Here.'

She whirled and threw it at him. 'Call me silly cow!' she snarled at him. He could see she was searching for some wounding epithet. He waited, knowing that it would be some reference to his dwarfism, for it always was. At last she bawled, 'Silly cow yourself, with knobs on!'

The schoolgirl insult, her independence in throwing the money at him when she needed it so badly, seemed to him to be admirable. Skinny little solitary, with all the trouble in the world, no brains to speak of – she still valued her self-respect, and if anyone had a go at it she was ready with a kick in the shins.

Even if he could have found the coins again in the semi-darkness, he scorned to search for them. They were a monument to Valda.

Going home, he felt as cheerful as if the encounter had been as physically satisfying for him as he had intended it to be.

Somehow the incident had put him to rights. He even found himself whistling.

'You've got to laugh, eh – me old Jack? – you've got to laugh,' his father often said, and he was right. Jack wanted badly to tell him about the woolly gloves, but he thought Jerry might be shocked.

A week or so later Towser told him that a family was being evicted from a house in Newtown. The landlord was a notoriously hard nut; they had been up against him before.

'This time we'll stay put as long as we can, really give the bastard a good go. Are you game, Jack?'

'That damned, mildewed lot!' commented Australia. She paced around the room puffing like a chimney, bent over with a paroxysm of coughing, and angrily flicked her cigarette into the fireplace. Dorothy noticed how thin she was. Her sharp pink face was worn, her narrow sophisticated nose had a touch of the town rat about it. 'Hell, I'll have to stop it. I'll kill myself with these blasted fags.'

'She's very nearly an old woman,' Dorothy thought.

The following day Australia was to sail to San Francisco with her business manager. She tried, from genuine kindness, to conceal her irritation with her niece.

'Talk, girl,' she shouted silently. 'Say what's on your mind, and go away and let me get on with things.'

But Dorothy did not know where to start. How could she explain her fears? 'Don't go away, Aunt Australia. Stay and help me ... help me do what? Be firm with Uncle Titus. More than that. Help me not to say Yes when I want to say No. But I can't say that to her, I'm too ashamed.'

She gazed at her aunt, desiring only to see a vigorous ally who would guess what she needed and supply it.

But Australia was too tired, too impatient. She found herself speaking, more to take her attention away from the girl's anxious face than to distract Dorothy.

'. . . we are extended dangerously, so I called the family together. Thank God I've retained 52 per cent, but the family has the rest. I asked them to forgo dividends for a couple of years, plough in some more capital until things looked more stable. And with one outraged, foaming voice they said they couldn't afford it. Victoria, the old humbug, fell back in her chair and limply whispered something about indigence. Reduce staff, they said, cut costs. I told them I had cut costs to the bone for more than two years, but reduce staff I would not.'

Dorothy suggested, 'Wouldn't it help if you did?'

'I won't do it,' said Australia shortly, looking around for her cigarette-case. 'They're already rostered, by their own agreement. Only four days a week for the last year. Most of them have been with me for twenty or more years. There are several who worked for Grandfather Jackaman. No, I shan't reduce staff.'

'It's good that you feel like that,' said Dorothy.

Australia smiled briefly. 'Well, the radical newspapers have fitted all of us employers out with horns and tails, but there are plenty of firms in Sydney that have retained full staff, believe me. Austen says it's my baronial complex; that I enjoy having a thousand people dependent upon me for a stable existence. God, how I detest that man. How could Anna –?'

'And you think you can raise finance in Philadelphia?' asked Dorothy, without interest.

Australia nodded. 'Without risk to Jackaman's, I trust. But . . . well, never mind.'

She felt an objective tenderness for the girl. Poor little devil! She'd have to say something, and quickly, or the child would be here all the afternoon. 'Now then, it's Titus worrying you, isn't it? He wants to set aside dear old Ma's dream of turning the go-downs into shelters, grab his share of the maintenance fund? Of course he does. Why on earth did silly Mother bring him in on the project?'

'She said I would require a man's assistance and intelligence,' Dorothy said. 'All women need a man to lean on, she said.'

'Hell!' said Australia, laughing. 'My brother Titus isn't a man, he's a bandit. That mother of mine! She never ceased seeing Titus as the pitiful little twelve-year-old that Papa sent off to England to be educated to be the century's most accomplished editor. Poor Papa, that was *his* dream.'

'He says I owe it to him because he's given a home to Mother and Olwyn all these years,' said Dorothy, pursuing her own train of thought.

'What a hide he has!' exploded Australia. 'I don't doubt that your mother has kept the seductive devil in comfort from her own purse, not to mention the trust my father established for Olwyn.'

'And mine,' thought Dorothy, who upon gaining control of her capital at twenty-four had found it greatly diminished.

'Look,' said Australia, 'you're not in any way bound by Mother's will. You don't have to feel guilty if you consider you aren't equal to the responsibility. The whole thing's at your own desire and discretion, if I remember the wording of the will. Titus can't force you into one decision or the other; but it's to be expected that he'd try to pressure you into the one which brings him money.'

'But I want to do as Granny asked,' said the girl. 'She trusted me. That's why she asked me, and not someone else.'

'Oh, my dear,' said Australia, 'and that's why the old puss sidled off to that shabby little solicitor to make her will. She knew very well that Jackaman and Jackaman would argue her out of something so quixotic and sentimental.'

'But why shouldn't Granny have what she wanted?' asked Dorothy. 'Even if no one thinks it sensible?'

'If that's how you feel about it, then tell Titus to go to blazes.'

'The family think he's right,' admitted Dorothy. 'My mother writes letters . . . and Uncle Titus is very persuasive. I get – upset.' She added despairingly, 'I'm not like you, Aunt Australia. You're so firm about everything. You aren't tempted to give in just so all the fuss and argument will stop.'

'Damned nonsense!' said Australia. 'Take a stand and stick to it. What does it matter what any of them say? Sod them!'

It occurred to her then that there was something soft and humid about this niece of hers; something old-fashioned and last-century. Maybe her shrewd old mother had been right – here was one girl who needed a man to lean on. But not, for God's sake, Titus.

Dorothy, thinking she read disapproval, even contempt, on Australia's face, jumped up and said nervously, 'I shouldn't have taken up your time, Aunt. I do know how busy you are. I was inconsiderate. Of course I'll work it out some way, I have to, I do see that. But I seem so – stupid.'

She was a pretty creature, Australia thought, melting as she gave the girl a hug. The fragility of youth's form and appearance gave the woman a pang. Still, the girl would have to shoulder her own temperamental disability; she was no longer a child.

Australia's head felt empty, and at the same time achingly crammed. There were so many things to think about, critical aspects of her trip to the United States. Beside them a charitable old woman's romantic bequest seemed both ludicrous and trivial.

She realised she was sitting there remembering the day she had left her father's home. Why had she left? To flee from the domination that was driving her mad, from an opposition that afflicted her so much it would have been easier by far to concede. The vehemence and despairs of the young girl she had been! Her terror of her mother's tears and loving pleas, lest they disarm her! Who could have thought that such violence of emotion could ever be extinguished, almost forgotten?

It seemed to her now that she had been extraordinarily like Dorothy, conditioned to terror of disapproval, feet and hands chopped off so that she'd fit into some Procrustean bed designed for her by loving and well-intentioned parents.

'Poor little beast,' she said mournfully, referring not to Dorothy but to the girl she herself had once been.

When Dorothy returned home, she heard Uncle Titus's voice in the drawing-room, talking to Aunt Adela. There was another letter from her mother on the tray in the hall. She could not make herself even pick it up. It would be another demand, couched in playful, affectionate words, that she be sensible, co-operative with Uncle Titus, whose judgment was so good, relinquish dearest Grandmama's idealistic scheme. Olwyn would be presented soon ... long to see you ... darling Dorothy ...

The young woman could almost hear her mother's endearments following her as she went to the door of the drawing-room. Uncle Titus must be getting desperate, she thought: calling up reinforcements. He sat there smoking, smiling his enigmatic smile while Adela talked at her. She found that by tensing her shoulders, compressing her knees, squeezing herself into a rigid defensive bundle, she could bear it. At last she looked at Uncle Titus and muttered, 'Next week, say Thursday or Friday. I'll have made up my mind by then.'

'Dearest child,' he protested, 'you're such a tease. It isn't fair to me, is it, Adela? You know how important it is for me to get back to London. Can't you decide before Thursday or Friday?'

He came forward to take her hands, put his arm about her shoulders in the careless manner he had. She rose quickly and moved towards the door. He made her flesh cold. When as a young girl she had shied away from him she had been wiser than she knew. Who and what was he? She had no idea. He had no observable qualities except his formidable zeal for getting his own way. Amusing, bland, sweet-tempered, he applied relentless pressure, overwhelming all in his path like a ton of ice cream.

She escaped through the door, hearing Aunt Adela fizz: 'I might as well talk to the air. She's nothing but a flapper. Flighty. As much brains as . . .'

Dorothy reached her bedroom as though it were a rabbit-hole, gasping with anger and fright. She had seen the fleeting expression on Uncle Titus's face. She knew what she was doing. She was withholding safety from him, and he hated her for it.

She felt sullen anger at their insolent assumption that she could be coaxed and bullied at their will. Not one of them, not even Australia Jackaman, had inquired what Clara had really wanted to achieve. Without honest investigation, they had inferred that their mother had been virtuous but a little feeble-minded, sentimental, and ignorant of the world. Not one of them remembered that Clara knew the hardest aspects of the world better than any of them. She had wanted to rescue the helpless and manipulated from their fate, as James had rescued her. And as her knowledge of humankind had grown, Clara had wished also to assist incompetents, drunkards – those who had built their own wretched fate.

Dorothy knew, because Clara had told her, that the old woman had loved her children just because they had been her children. She didn't care at all for the people they were now, but forgave them for the phantom child's face she could still see in each one of theirs. She said that Britannia and Adela had been such impetuous, loving little rogues.

Dorothy understood her grief. It was terrible to think that two loving little rogues had turned into a pair of she-bigwigs with grey wire wool coiffures, blancoed noses and discreetly red geisha mouths.

Only Titus had not changed for Clara. Australia had been right. Even though the old mother had seen her adult son from time to time throughout the years, she had always continued to regard him as the delicate-featured child, standing at the ship's rail in the cold wind, trying not to cry. Clara had been guilty. She knew she should have put up a fight to keep him at home till he was older.

Dorothy went down the back stairs and took the key of the go-downs from the board in the back porch. Mrs Marion appeared, wiping her hands, saying, 'Everything all right, Miss Dorothy?'

The woman was afraid for her job, as Robert and the others were. Rag Castle had been their home so long. The weight of responsibility for these familiar people, and for all the strangers that would pass through the Jackaman Shelters if they ever came to reality, pressed upon the girl crushingly. Her face must have shown something of this, for Mrs Marion took a step forward: 'Miss Dorothy . . . has something happened?'

Dorothy shook her head and continued on her way through the chestnuts and beeches.

The go-downs were immense forsaken caverns; the hardwood beams that bridged their derelict vacancy were like fire-blackened trees. They were full of anomalous shadows, like men hanging. Amongst the many odours of mice and decay, there was an Oriental smell – musty tea, sandalwood, stiffly dressed madras and calico.

It was a place for lizards and cockroaches, and tree roots insinuating themselves through wall cracks like slim white serpents.

Clara had taken years to work out her plan to convert the old storehouses into a refuge for destitute men. She said: 'There's always someone to look after little babies, but people think there's something low and disgusting about homeless men . . .

'It seems to me, dotie,' she explained to Cushie, 'that to love the unlovable is very hard; but it's what the Lord requires of us.

'Dormitories here,' she pointed out, 'and there cubicles for washing and shaving. Kitchens here, and a place where they can wash their clothes and hang them out to dry. Clean clothes are very important, especially for a man who has been used to them. It's a scalding shame for a decent man to have to go and look for work when his collar is black with dirt and grease.

'What a blessing it is, pet,' she had said to her granddaughter, 'that Balmain and Birchgrove are running down so fast. There'll be more and more workless and pensioners coming here. They automatically go to the bottom, you know.'

All Clara's plans, sketches, and notes were with the solicitor with whom she had made her final will. Undoubtedly the whole scheme would eventually be taken over by a competent committee; but the entire mechanism had to be set in motion by Dorothy Moy.

Dorothy had never guessed that Clara had intended to designate her. She had thought the plan for the Jackaman Shelters was just an old lady's benign fancy, something to keep herself busy. It was obvious that Clara intended her granddaughter to be the superior partner. Titus had been brought into it as adviser and protector for a young woman who looked as if she would never marry.

The terms of the bequest were simple. If Dorothy did not choose to proceed with the project, Jackaman Court and its estate was to be hers unconditionally. The fund Clara had provided to maintain the shelters was to be divided at once, three-quarters to go to Titus Jackaman, and the remaining quarter to Dorothy Moy.

When the girl had first learnt the contents of the will, she thought that Clara had conceived this plan as a gift to her, Dorothy Moy, as a means of filling absorbingly what Clara foresaw as a barren future for an unmarried woman. Probably she had believed the Emporium occupied such a place in Australia's life. Her nineteenth-century thinking followed such simple paths.

Now that she had had so much opposition from Titus and the Jackaman aunts, Dorothy thought she understood Clara better. Clara, like Jackie, had never asked her to be anything but what she was. The bequest was not for her benefit, but for the benefit of the unlovable and destitute, as Clara had plainly said. She had involved Dorothy only because she took it for granted that trusting love would be met by trusting love.

'But I'm not strong enough. I can't trust myself,' Dorothy thought. The emptiness of her heart was like the emptiness in the go-downs: full of old ghosts, with faint signs of past activities and prosperities, a hollow place where riches once had been. She thought, 'I don't want to be alone. I want to be with someone to love. But there isn't anyone now.'

She had tried for more than six years to become stable, serene, and mature. She had learnt from them all, Clara, Mrs Marion, the durable, brusque Australia. She had thought that the distraught, foolish Cushie of eighteen had vanished for all time.

Yet, even before Titus arrived, Dorothy had intimations, like the faint queasy tremors of distant earthquakes, that Cushie still lived, baffled, easily intimidated, a person trained from infancy to be an appeaser, one who would abjectly agree to something against her own will, solely to get away from the aggressiveness of others. She wondered whether all infants were as malleable as she had been. Her only defence had been to be submissive. Perhaps Olwyn's had been to develop bronchitis.

She could see now that she had never stood on her own feet. Twice she had made the gesture, when she had left Claudie List's house, and when she had refused to go to London. But she had not done that alone. Each time she had known her grandmother was there, loved her, would stand by her. Perhaps she never would be able to do anything alone. The years with her mother and the conditioning by her mother were too strong.

In her dealings with Uncle Titus she had followed the diagram her childhood training had laid out for her. She explained, listened, placated; she felt that he must be right; it was natural that he should know more than she. She wavered; saw with fright the phantasm of her mother's face looking from those handsome features; heard in Titus's authoritative masculine voice the tones of her father's. He would keep on at her until she was swamped, until at last in sheer fatigue and hopeless detestation of the situation she would concede – and betray old Clara.

Returning slowly to the house, her head bent, she thought, 'Why do I even think of fighting them? What's the use of it all?'

As she hung the go-down key on its nail, she was submerged in despair. A life without love, what was it?

Mrs Marion came to meet her, saying, 'Mr Titus and the ladies have gone, Miss Dorothy. They said they couldn't wait any longer. Miss Dorothy, you look tired. Shall I send a tray up to your room, perhaps?'

Dorothy nodded. She recalled that the following morning she was on early duty in the Domain. The idea wearied her. The whole thing seemed witless. The poor were always there, always.

'Not these poor,' Clara would have said.

Jack was taken along by Towser and ceremonially introduced to the Newtown tenants, the Murrays, but they were too agitated even to look at him. The wife had the bossed jawbones and frog eyes characteristic of those who had spent a long period on an inadequate diet. The man was in a sweat at the prospect of eviction, but even more disturbed by the strangers who had occupied his home since the previous evening. He had put on a spunky, even pugnacious expression, but his adam's apple fidgeted. Three young boys snoozed on a mattress on the kitchen floor, and an aged father incessantly complained of the radishes and late beans trampled in the backyard.

The woman whined a litany: 'They're going to get us into terrible strife, Roy. What will me and the kids do if you're put in the cells, Roy?'

The cramped Edwardian villa was set askew to the street in a long row of identical brick dwellings. By the time Towser, Jock, and Jack Hanna had reached it, at four in the morning, the members of the Movement had barricaded the bottom floor with sandbags and snarled about the entire building with barbed wire.

Jack had been taken aback. 'This what you call picketing?' he demanded. Towser replied absently, 'We're putting up a bold front. Intimidation. Come on, better get inside.'

Sparse groups of people stood around in the lamplight; others gaped sleepily from windows. Men still worked on the glittering fuzz of wire. Jack knew then, as well as later, that that was the moment when he should have walked away. But he didn't. There were too many staring. So, half-undecided, half-intimidated by the resolution of his companions, he crawled through an aperture in the wire, which was then secured behind them.

Jack felt he was what Jerry would call a hairy goat. Certainly Towser and the old Scotsman had not misled him; but they had not said anything to correct his misconceptions either. But then, did they know he had had altogether a different idea of what the Unemployed Workers' Movement did?

Thus castigating himself, he emerged into a stuffy little front room, piled haphazardly with half-packed domestic goods and congested with men.

The house was lit with candles, and the quivering light gave a curious dolls'-house effect to the place. The electricity had been cut off months before, when Murray had been sacked and things began to slide. Around the bay window stood eight or nine men, peering dourly through the entangled wire into the windswept, dimly lit street. Jack was irresistibly reminded of pictures of beleaguered patriots during the Irish Revolution. Weapons lay to hand – pieces of iron railing, metal pipes, batons loaded with melted lead.

A couple of the men chaffed Towser about the under-sized members he was forced to recruit nowadays, looking meanwhile at Jack with a friendly grin.

'That one's been pruned too hard, Towser. You'll never get a crop.'

Jock growled, 'Shut your gob, you, or I'll shut it for you.'

The man was painfully taken aback. He said to Jack, 'Only a joke, son, didn't mean anything, like.'

But Jock glanced furiously about, challenging anyone else to have a go at Jack.

Since their departure from Dawes Point, Jock's personality had altered more and more. His flat cheeks were carnation; his white hair seemed electrified. He had the elated expression of the old campaigner back on the familiar terrain.

Jack said to Towser, 'I'm not struck on all this. What's going on?'

Towser said in his indifferent tone, 'Publicity mostly. Landlords get scared when there's a demonstration. Public opinion makes them think twice about evicting a family. It's all a matter of strategy.'

Jack jerked his head towards the window. 'That your public opinion out there in the street then?'

'That's it,' said Towser. 'They fight our battles for us. We give them a focal point.'

'Then why the hardware?' inquired Jack, picking up and hefting one of the waddies.

One of the men at the window said contemptuously, 'If you left your guts at home, stub, you better scarper off and find 'em before the johns arrive.'

Jack shot back: 'My name's Hanna, and you bloody well call me that if you've anything to say to me, mate. And get this straight, anywhere I go my guts go too.'

The man grunted, turning to the window. The street lamps had been turned out; a wan pearly light filled the room. Towser said, 'Take it easy for a while, Jack. We don't expect the police to arrive till seven or so.'

The men were tired. Some gave great yelping yawns; one or two slept. A woman with a worn, aggrieved face, the skin marked in square ruckles like the side of a crocodile handbag, came around with a big teapot and enamel mugs. She said the Murrays had dropped their bundles: they weren't worth fighting for – squibs, timid as bandicoots.

Jack was interested to see the men's deferential attitude towards Towser. He was obviously the boss man. Yet he had an aloof demeanour, as of an officer towards his men. He dropped a suggestion here; a word of commendation there. The orders were given by a couple of subordinate urgers, peremptory and tyrannous, enjoying almost voluptuously this brief opportunity to wear the iron heel.

The men in the house were a strangely assorted crowd. Amongst them were grey-haired ex-tradesmen, frayed, but with the signs of old respectability upon them, particularly about their boots. There was a fellow with dented scars and an ear that was a cartilaginous frill. His mate, an immigrant with no teeth, had a moustache that had retreated almost into his nostrils; he had lost hope, was beaten. 'What can ye du?' he repeated. Most of them were stringy working men, long enough out of employment to be sore, if not bitter. Yet there was about them a grim hilarity that Jack immediately recognised: their nameless, formless enemy had, even for a brief time, taken on flesh.

After the wretched flounderings of months or years, they were offered something solid in the shape of an intractable landlord and a mob of cops who were being paid to harry them. They gratefully accepted the chance to come to grips with these symbolic foes. They were showing-off, too, chiacking the crowd outside, the tenants, and each other.

Towser was speaking earnestly to the Murray family. He had ruffled the hair of a little toad-eyed boy who had awakened, and drawn from the anxious woman a ritualistic smile. The old father had fallen asleep with his face squashed on the table like a half-empty leather sack. Jack watched Towser covertly.

The Nun's animosity towards Towser had previously awakened in Jackie an idly defensive attitude towards the man. He watched him now and realised that he did not know him at all. He supposed he was a communist, working to turn this ill-assorted gang of malcontents into a cell, or whatever it was that the Russians called their workers' groups.

The newspapers called the Unemployed Workers' Movement 'communist'. Whether they meant Marxian or Tolstoyan was anyone's guess: so little was known about Russian Communism since the Revolution. Anything politically unorthodox or socialist in tendency was described as communist or subversive.

Towser was, in fact, a type of man of which Jack had had no experience. He was a quasi-intellectual of a kind later to become both recognised and exploited by radical political movements. He was a loner.

He had experimented with Marxism, but had no real feeling for it. The rigidities of its structure seemed to him to resemble the endless rules with which little boys hedged their games about. Excellently educated, of good family, he had had a shifting, unsatisfactory life until he discovered that by some peculiarity of personality he was able to put a bee in another person's bonnet, give him something to think about.

He came gradually to regard himself as a primary cause, a light-bearer, not corrupting, but awakening.

He took delight in his nickname. It was a *nom-de-guerre*, an adjunct to his private underhandedness, which loved conspiracy, mysterious comings and goings, secret hidey-holes, *not leaving tracks.* He lived poor, but he had kept all the money his mother had left him. It tickled him tremendously that he should gather and sell clothes-props and firewood while he had eight thousand pounds in the Bank. Not that he cared deeply for money; it was just another funk-hole. If he chose he could vanish from The Rocks, without a word, leaving all his belongings. He could imagine how this would add to his legend.

He had found his perfect place amongst the discontented unemployed of that district. Far from having any true notion of democracy, such men were ever on the watch for a strong, articulate leader. But there was not sufficient challenge for him there, so he had expanded into the more disorderly and subversive area of the Movement. Something in him craved the exhilaration inherent in the uncertain nature of these brushes with authority. The risk fed the witch-doctor in him.

At first he had just left ideas lying around, which the current organisers could pick up or not. But they always did. Then, almost imperceptibly, he found himself a leader. To him it was half a lark, half a gamble with his own power. There was little danger. As he had told Jack, the landlords tended to concede quickly. On the few occasions when certain of the Movement's members had been arrested for disturbing the peace, Towser had paid their fines 'out of funds'.

But lately he had had an intuition that it might be a good idea for him to go to prison for a short time, just as a gesture. Jock, the old revolutionary, over-simplifying in the romantic manner of his type, often said, 'The martyr's blood is the seed of anarchy.'

Towser hankered to see how far he could go without getting into overt trouble. There were reckless men in the Movement who had long advocated a real siege, just to test the police. Towser had planned carefully that this Newtown eviction, should it come to violence, would reap maximum publicity.

Jack Hanna knew none of this. He only knew that George Vee was not an easy man to interpret. There was one thing he did know. The Newtown house was prepared for a long defence. He had prowled about, noticing the supplies of food, the washing tubs and bath filled with water, in case the police cut that off. Most ominous of all, the bedrooms upstairs were piled with bluemetal, like heaps of mullock.

'Ammo,' thought Jack. His original alarm had subsided and he felt a fatalistic calm, as though he had been brought to this place deliberately. For some time now, in spite of his consuming loneliness, he had felt that he could cope with anything. But he didn't know how he could handle a Donnybrook with the police, if such eventuated. He didn't want to go to prison, even for twenty-eight days. But here he was, and here the situation was; a test perhaps, some part of the growth he had felt with such sensitive acuteness at different times of his life. He waited, saying no more. The sun came up, dark red in a bank of rain-cloud. Some time later from the crowd outside there arose a greedy groan. Two vehicles full of police had arrived. Jack saw the men in the room exchange glances half-cocky, half-apprehensive.

Towser said, 'You go upstairs to Jock, will you, Jack?'

At the same moment there was a crash of glass from above, and Mrs Murray yipped shrilly. Jack ran upstairs. Jock had bashed out a window. He stood there statuesquely, a piece of stone in each hand. Jack could see that he would not care if he were picked off with a pistol or rabbit rifle. He had been martyred before, and he could take it again. It was one thing he was good at. His deliberate exposure of himself to police identification fitted some dramatic picture he had, as did the unnecessary smashing of the window.

His voice was tremulous with excitement. He chuckled meaninglessly. 'Will we show them, eh, Jackie? Heck, it's grand!'

The sultry sun poured yellow smoke over the street, where the excited crowd had been swelled by women with milk billies, men on their way to work or unemployment depot, people hoping to see fun or violence. The police were mostly young constables, with three or four pot-gutted upper ranks to give orders. They were greeted with cat-calls, thrown potatoes, obscene noises; but the crowd parted meekly enough to let them through.

Briskly the constables advanced with wire-cutters to gain access to the house, but they were repulsed with showers of bluemetal from the upper windows. Some marked with dirt and blood, they withdrew for a conference. One of the constables hastened away, probably to phone for reinforcements, a tail of foul-mouthed urchins mocking his every movement. Jock chortled hysterically. He raved out something at the retreating officer but no one understood a word.

Jack thought, 'This is crazy. We haven't a hope in hell.' Yet he continued undecided, thinking still that Towser must surely know more than he.

He was increasingly uneasy. He didn't like the looks on the faces of the other men, their discomfort and false humour. He wondered if they felt the same hope – that Towser had something up his sleeve.

'Seems like we're going to be on the flickers,' he heard someone say.

On the roof of a shop near the corner a man hauled a movie camera through the window, and set it in position. Jack looked around for Towser. The expression that dodged across the man's face was absorbed and personal. He looked to Jack as if he were shaking hands with himself.

'He arranged that somehow,' Jack thought.

By now the mob was immense, restless and shifting like a football crowd. A car like a cigarette lighter purled up and brayed impatiently. A policeman, looking nettled, ran over to speak to the driver.

Towser pointed. 'There's the worthy landlord, Jack.'

'He's got guts to come here today, give him that,' commented someone.

'He's an arrogant idiot, that's what he is,' snapped Towser.

In a moment the car was invisible, the focus of a shrieking, tussling mob. Batons flashed, fell; the crowd coalesced; someone with a bloody head lurched out of it; a woman holding a child with one hand hammered at backs and shoulders with the other. From above, the police seemed both disorganised and panicky, shoving here and there, lashing out with batons, re-grouping in parties and charging back into the skirmish. From their opponents arose a boisterous yell that made Jack's hair bristle.

The car reversed erratically, bumping packed bodies, people fighting to get out of its way. It shot up onto the footpath, turned round a lamp-post and was gone.

The sergeant in charge shouted, 'Mr Murray, the landlord has offered to provide you with alternative accommodation if you let us remove your furniture with no further trouble.'

There were whoops and yells from the tenant's wife, who seemingly had made a break for the front door. These were cut off abruptly, as though by a hand, and Murray himself replied in a gruff quaver, 'He can go to hell!'

The mob cheered warmly, and Jack hoped that their acclaim reassured Mr Murray, so plainly coerced into this affair.

Towser, however, shrugged away Jack's misgivings. 'Just a lot of fireworks,' he said. 'The landlord always gives in before things get too bad. Besides, they know now that if they do get the tenant out someone will set a match to the property.'

The man keeping cockatoo on the street corner bellowed up to the windows: 'You in there! Three more cop cars just turned in by the shops.'

The two urgers conferred briefly with Towser, and the older one turned to the uneasy defenders: 'Well, what about it?'

Jack felt spontaneous admiration for the men, grinning at each other, pulling comic faces of alarm or belligerence, even the old gentlemanly tradesmen, but unanimously deciding to go on with it.

Towser gave a few calm orders, this man to defend that window, the others to hand up bluemetal, this pair to go down and see that all was ready to withstand a rush at the front and back doors. He said to Jack, 'Go out on the balcony, Jack, and tell 'em that we intend to stay here until they winkle us out.'

In involuntary co-operation Jack turned towards the little bird-cage of iron that opened off the bedroom window. Jock's hand came down on his shoulder.

'No,' he said, 'not Jack. You keep well back, lad.' He turned to Towser. 'The rest of us have a chance of not being identified,' he said. He bit out the words with such choler that Jack heard every one of them. Even so, it wasn't as much the words as the voice that riveted Jack; there was some unidentifiable iron in it. Towser said authoritatively, 'Do it, Jack.'

'I'll do it myself, George,' snapped out Jock.

Before Towser or Jack could speak, pandemonium broke loose outside. Hitherto the noise of the crowd had been loud enough, as they harassed and abused the police, getting in a trip or a king-hit whenever there was an opportunity. This was different, a strange snoring howl, as though those who emitted it were out of breath. Jack ran to the window. He saw many more police; they seemed to be everywhere. Four or five of the younger men were levering sheets of corrugated iron from a nearby fence. He saw at once that the police would use the iron as shelter while they hacked through the barbed-wire defences.

The moment they made a concerted rush at the house the crowd turned berserk, rocking the police cars, clouting the windows with lengths of iron railing. They got one over on its side and a high-ranking officer spilled out of it like a blue shellfish. The crowd had now swarmed into the next street; trams were held up, bells clanged, whistles blew. A newspaper photographer standing on top of his car was shaken off and vanished under running feet.

Meanwhile the battle of Murray's house continued, with the police making repeated sallies under their primitive shields whilst barrow-loads of bluemetal descended upon them. One young constable with a head of curly dark hair became caught in the barbed wire like a cast sheep.

'Look at Janet Gaynor!' yelled the whooping, triumphant defenders.

Jack could see Janet Gaynor, scarlet with mortification and rage, struggling there like a fly in treacle and yelling to his mates to get him unhooked. Someone took deliberate aim at him, clipped him along the jaw with a stone that took off the skin like a razor. Bright blood dribbled all down the boy's neck and shirt. Two of his comrades jerked him free from the wire and dragged him away. He fought them wildly, mad to get back for revenge.

After that there was a short lull. The defenders were panting. They wore excited, dazzled expressions, like young boys at a football match.

Jack said, 'Look, mates, we can't win! There'll be real bloodshed. We can't get any more men inside to help, but they can bring reinforcements from all over the city. The game's over, why not face it?'

They looked at him with soured contempt.

'What the hell are you, you sawn-off squib?' A surly red-faced man spoke.

'I'm someone who can see a dim outlook when it's in front of my nose,' barked back Jack. 'Come to that, I don't want to do three months chokey just because of someone else's comic-strip ideas. There must be a better way to fight evictions than this.'

They turned away from him. One or two looked at Towser in dismay. One said, 'If you were a foot higher, I'd belt your ears off.'

But he was too small for them to clout. He had offended against the first law, that of solidarity. There was nothing to do but ignore him. This they did with dignity. But they were rattled.

He said with rage, 'Don't you see? The Murrays will be chucked out just the same, and we'll be jugged, and not just for disturbing the peace, either. What's the point of that?'

At that moment Jock emitted a growling roar, and barged out onto the balcony. His body was so large, the space so minute, the men inside the room could not see what was happening. A terrible sound, as of worrying hounds, came up from the crowd. Jack saw that the youthful constable, Janet Gaynor, determined to regain face before his comrades, had been legged up to the balcony. He seized Jock around the neck. The old man was as thick as a log, strong as an ox for all his age. It seemed that he grabbed the young man by the hair, and back-handed him across the temple with a closed fist. Jack could not really see. All he saw was Janet Gaynor flying backwards over the balcony. He landed in the nested wire, and hung there as limply as if he'd been crucified. Blood poured from his head.

'Jesus, you've killed the bastard!'

There was a concerted rush for the stairs. Jack heard the defenders jamming, cursing, fighting on that narrow descent. Almost simultaneously he heard something heavy, an axe or crowbar, bashing down the back door. It struck him: 'We're done. They've got us.'

Someone was shoving him, gabbling. It was Jock.

He gobbled something about, 'Your father. Bathroom. Will ye hurry!'

Jack was shoved into the small cubby-hole smelling of gas. Jock was savage, half wild, face convulsed into knots of muscle. He pointed to a tiny manhole in the high ceiling.

'No need for you to get took. You've had nothing to do with us. Quick, boy, up on my shoulders.'

Almost dazed, Jack leapt up on the man's heavy shoulders. He could not do more than push aside the manhole cover with his fingertips.

'Jump, sod ye! Are you paralysed? They'll be upon us in a moment!'

As Jack leapt for the manhole, Jock gave him a toss like a wrestler. The young man seized the edge of the hole, dragged himself up, was in a mousy darkness.

'Pull the cover across, blast ye!'

As Jack did this, careful not to disturb the dust that furred the edges, he saw the old man lurch away from the bathroom. There was a noise outside on the stairs as of fighting dogs, yells, the crack of batons, then a diminishing commotion. Heavy footsteps sounded through the bedrooms, into the bathroom. Someone said, 'Got a full bag, Kev. Right. Now we'd better clear the tenants out.'

The other man said, 'Fair go! It's starting to rain.'

A retreating voice rumbled, 'That's their look-out. Ought to have accepted the landlord's offer before it was out of his mouth. Lot of nongs.'

The rain made gloved tappings on the slate roof. After a while Jack crawled cautiously along a beam pocked with dry rot and blanketed with dust. There was a ventilator under the gable. He scraped away a little of the dirt and peered out. He could see very little, but people were walking and running away from the scene. The autumnal rain came down in a violent intermittent swish. He heard thunder. There were angry noises in the street. No doubt the members of the Movement were being thrust into paddy-wagons. He heard vehicles starting up, but could see nothing.

424

After that followed rough thumps as the Murrays' furniture was moved out. Mrs Murray's voice was raised in a long ululation. Car and perhaps truck doors slammed; horns blew continuously.

Jack lay in a daze until the street at last fell into a city silence: motor horns, the constant low hum of traffic, the brattle of the trams beyond the corner. He lay flat on the beam, his toes hooked over neighbouring beams. 'God,' he said to himself. 'God!'

It could scarcely be more than nine or half past now, but he was trembling with fatigue. He lay in the twilight of dust and unfamiliarity; he heard something whisper across the rafters, mouse or cockroach. He thought that perhaps he was reacting from shock. The blood from the young cop's head, redder than poppies. The look on Jock's face. He cautiously shifted his legs onto the beam, relaxed along it like a hibernating snake. Now there was no sound except that of rain mumbling on the roof, glugging down the pipes.

He supposed that Jock, Towser, everyone in the house would be arrested, Jock certainly on a serious charge. How they must be feeling, those men with families! In his strange state, suspended between real awareness of his predicament and a kind of dream, Jack experienced an emotional empathy with those basically defenceless, easily manipulated men. He knew their inborn longing for a master. There was always something to take advantage of this vulnerability – Marxism, Fascism. Soon the nations would blow the bugles and involve them all in war for some trumped-up ideal, kill off the surplus, whip up the money-making industries, fill the coffers. He felt a glum wonder at humanity. Did anyone at all ever do anything for anyone else for disinterested reasons?

Yes, Jerry MacNunn did. The Nun had been an ideal of fatherliness always before Jackie. It had been his part in life, though he had been unselfconscious about it. Thinking of him, Jack smiled appreciatively and almost immediately fell asleep. Some time in the afternoon he awoke, heart thumping, to hear prowling footsteps in the silent house, a voice calling cautiously, 'You there, Shorty? Shorty, it ain't the johns, it's me from next door.'

Jack remained silent. He heard the man come into the bathroom. There must have been flaked Kalsomine from the ceiling fallen in the bath; dust perhaps from the manhole. The voice said, 'You up there, Shorty? It's Snowy Jackson from next door. I seen you go in this morning but I didn't see you come out. Knew you must be still here holed up. Come on down, mate, I can get you out the back and into my place.'

There was nothing to do but to trust the man. Jack moved aside the manhole a crack, saw an oldish face, a drab spike of hair. The man wasn't a copper, anyway. He said, 'Thought you might be up there. Come on, mate. Shake a leg. I got this feeling that someone will set a torch to this house.'

He led Jackie through the rain, the disorder of spiralled wire, torn-down fences, trampled vegetables, into his own house next door. A woman lent Jack a dry shirt that came down to his ankles, and fed him, gabbling all the while. 'You can't stay here, no matter what Dad says. You gotta get out soon as yer can. We got enough trouble, up to our ears in it. God, things are terrible. But the Murrays will be all right now. Never wanted any of this hullabaloo, Mrs Murray told me. They gone to Redfern, I heard, sharing with another family. But that poor young policeman, I mean, a dirty copper and all that, but young. Poor boy.'

'Is he dead then?' asked Jack, as she paused for breath.

She pulled an ominous face. 'Fractured skull, I heard. I mean, sounds bad, don't it? Not good at all, fractured skull.'

When his clothes were cleaned and ready to put on, Jack thanked the neighbours and slipped over the back fence into the alley and made his way by other streets to a tram-stop in Parramatta Road. He scarcely knew what to do.

He was sure that the police would have searched the house in Dawes Point for subversive printed material, weapons, names of Movement members. They were already convinced that it was a Bolshevik group, and old Jock's long record of violent disaffection would not disillusion them. Where then did he, Jack Hanna, stand? He was not a member; his name would be nowhere on the Movement's lists. Still, any of the other tenants, the cowed old-age pensioners, one of the half-dotty metho. drinkers in the basement, had only to say they had seen him going off on the truck with Towser and Jock and his goose would be cooked.

He got off the tram some distance from his own street, and

swung himself up on the stone wall where he had sat so often in imagination with the soft, listening ghost of Cushie Moy. The rain had gone. Little vessels came out of Darling Harbour, passing under the arch of the Bridge as though through a demi-lune gate. In the rich sky sunlit turrets of cloud stood in a row. The men in the house were still in his mind. He saw clearly that their major strength, their solidarity and their terror of betraying it, was also their weakness. Mindless attachment to solidarity had trapped them into staying in that house when their own common sense told them the battle was fruitless. He thought, 'The only solidarity they believed in was what Towser decided. But there was never any proof that his decision would be the right one.'

Then he thought, 'I won't go back to the house. I'll break off connections with Towser right here.'

The moment this thought entered his head he had a powerful sensation of inevitability, as though destiny had pushed him into a corner where he must sever his association with the house. At the same time he was afraid. He knew then that the decaying old dump had indeed been a bolt-hole. He was crestfallen to think that he, Jack Hanna, should be so abject as to be daunted by the thought of losing a roof – and such a roof.

'I'll go to Dad. He'll sneak me into the stables for tonight, anyway, and I'll decide what to do.'

But he was reluctant to lose his books and few belongings. How could he replace them?

He resolved to march boldly up to the house, wearing the mask of an innocent man, pretending he'd just been out to look for work, resolved to brazen it out if any rozzers were lurking in the hall-way.

Half-way up the stairs he saw the male pensioner peering around a timidly-held door.

'The demons been here! Took away a whole sack of Mr Vee's papers and things. Asking about you, they was.'

'What did you say, Pop?' asked Jack, a cold lump of trepidation forming in his stomach.

'I said I didn't know nothing, supposed you was out looking for work as usual. Dunno if they believed me though.'

The old man's eyes were red as blood with some inflammation.

He kept dabbing the run-off with a grey rag.

'That was mighty of you,' said Jack sincerely.

The old man grabbed his arm. 'What will become of us all if Mr Vee gets put in clink, boy? The dees said maybe the house would be shut up. Me and the wife, we don't know where else we'd go for half a crown a week.'

He was servile with fright and self-pity, looking pathetically at Jack. 'What's Mr Vee done, son? And them demons said Jock was in serious trouble.' He added absent-mindedly: 'There's a joker in the basement in the rats, terrible noises, like a steam whistle. I asked the dees to take him away but they said it wasn't their business.'

Jack went on up to his room. There were so few things in it he couldn't be sure whether it had been searched or not, but he felt it had. He thought he could smell cigarette smoke in the air. He found a little food, and rolled it and his clothes and some personal belongings in a blanket swag. He slipped a few books into his pockets. Taking what was left, cups and saucers, a frying-pan, the rest of the books, he went down to the pensioners' room. It was some time before he could cajole the old man into opening the door.

He said, 'I'm going to stay with friends for a few days. Would you take the rest of my stuff and keep it in your room till I come back? Especially the books.'

'What if the dees come back and ask me?' faltered the old man.

'You don't have to admit to anything, Pop,' explained Jackie. 'Tell you what: If I'm not back in a fortnight, sell it all, do anything you like.'

The old man was not grateful. He knew Jack's belongings would only fetch a few pence from the second-hand shop, and he'd have all the trouble of carrying them there.

Jack walked away without looking backwards, feeling strongly that he had finished with the place. More than that. Something had finished him with it, pushed him out, because other happenings were waiting for him elsewhere. He fancied perhaps they were connected with the Nun. His steps quickened as he thought of talking it all over with that tranquil man amid the smell of straw and manure and feed, and the gentle sound of horses moving in the stalls below.

He was ravenous. It was late afternoon. He had had nothing to eat since he left the Murrays' neighbours, and God knew that had been lousy enough, a cup of tea and a scone as flat as a boot-sole.

He heaved his swag into a toast-rack tram, and swung himself up easily. A couple of people looked at him in their indifferent city way. It struck him then that it was a long time now since he had remembered he was a dwarf. When he had, it was about as important as remembering that he had black hair.

In this bone-shaker tram, built like a wooden ship or railway-carriage of the previous century, he realised at last that what his mother had planned for him had come to pass.

It seemed a funny time for it to happen, when he was stripped of all the world held valuable, job, roof, wife, son, human love – perhaps even his freedom if he were to be involved in the catastrophe of Jock and Towser.

Windows facing the westering sun were incandescent. A reflected fire filled the tram. The man opposite him had dazzling squares of red moving in his glasses. He said, 'Well, Lang's opening the old Coathanger next week. Going to be there, mate?'

There were hurdles and hoardings for half a mile along the approaches to the Bridge. Men spidered around the pylons and below the arch, stringing light bulbs on loops of cable.

'There'll be millions there, millions,' said the man, as pleased as if he had built the Bridge himself.

Before they had reached Park Street, Jack realised that he could not, after all, ask for Jerry's hospitality. There was Heenan, the righteous foreman. It was impossible, unthinkable, to put Jerry's job in jeopardy. Jerry's happiness had to be protected. Jack couldn't help grinning. It seemed to him that he was carrying on as if he were his old man's father. Somehow they had swapped roles.

'No sweat, me old Dad,' he thought; and he left the tram at the corner and walked up towards the Domain.

A southerly was rising, a chill rampaging wind. It punched the big traffic lamps over the intersection, tossed the thick mops of the trees that were already losing leaves. He looked up towards Oxford Street, wondering if he should spend his last remaining money on a decent meal. But the hunger seemed to have died out of his belly. He had, anyway, some edible odds and ends in his swag. So he cut across through the trees and went on into the Domain.

There were already crowds of hoboes there. The police had almost given up patrolling it and moving them on; for where were they to move to? It was wasted effort. Jack had heard that the cracks and shallow caves in the sandstone on the other side of the Dom, facing Woolloomooloo Bay, were permanent homes for down and outers, an *al fresco* lodging-house all along that historic shore.

Jack merged with the hundreds of wandering men. The thought came that he should try for a bed at the City Shelter, or at one of the religious organisations' refuges, but it did not linger. He had had enough of that. He had camped out before and would again. He went looking for a tree, a rock, to keep the southerly's teeth away.

The curiously indifferent peace that had come to him in the tram persisted. He had taken some sort of involuntary step forward or outward in life: just as, on that long-ago early morning, he had accepted that he was Maida's husband, and had turned away with unselfconscious resolution from his boy's dreams of Cushie Moy; just as, out in the wilderness, under those unappeasable stars, he had known that he could survive grief, rage, anything.

The regular dossers knew just where the feral wind from the Harbour pounced, getting between ribs and into hollow teeth, making life close to the ground unbearable with whipped-up grit. Thus, already, with the afterglow still steady in the west, and only a few street lights showing on the overturned keel of the Darlinghurst ridge, all the good positions seemed taken.

'All right, all right, mate!' Jack said a dozen times as a feature-less bundle snarled at him.

He threw his swag at last behind the robust legs of some marble statesman who stood, head bent, hand caressing fleecy chin, think-ing about Free Trade, or Federation, or Repulicanism, or some other issue of the eighties of the previous century. He wore a frock-coat, this statesman, for which Jack was heartily grateful, since its spread kept the wind from him. He sat there watching the lights across the Harbour appear like a fine dust of mica, hearing big ships farting out near the Heads, and seeing little ones shuffling rapidly towards Circular Quay.

Jack chewed slowly at the bread and meat he had brought from Towser's house. The cold, the long hunger, the fatigue and excitement of the day, had put him into a passive state. He didn't know whether to keel over with weariness or just wait for the thoughts to come into his mind where he could look at them.

He threw the gristle to the ruby eyes that flitted amongst the bushes.

Something abided. Perhaps it was God, as the song said. Or mankind. Or both, waiting, enduring for each other. His own life had been short, and he had, he supposed, little real knowledge of mankind. Sometimes he thought of it as running on rails, like trams, towards an unknown and unidentifiable terminus. But people like Lufa Morgan, his mother, the Nun, Het and her rabbiter, even Milly and her Dad, they were there to teach him something. He knew now that he had learnt not only to look but to see.

Like that knowledge in the toast-rack tram that he wasn't a dwarf. Some fellows, six feet high, burly as bulls, were midgets inside. Kewpies. Soft little mice. But he wasn't. He was a full-sized man, and nothing could alter that any more.

He remembered Maida calling him her little tiger. The Nun had sometimes called him that, too.

'Well,' Jack thought, 'I'm not little. But I can be a tiger any time I want to.'

And he let out a snarling roar, so that something in the bushes, creeping up to rat his swag, emitted a sputter of fright, and rose to its feet and blundered away.

Jack laughed. He rose and stretched, looking around at the town's stars and suns and coloured comets, the hard shapes of buildings suspended in halated metropolitan light. His sense of identification with the city's sturdy vulgarity, its rough beauty, resolved itself into words: 'You game old bastard!' The words rose out of love.

431

The southerly had spent itself, but the air was like an ice-box. It smelt pungently of ships and petrol, the ashes of a bonfire where the Domain keepers had burned swept-up leaves that day. Jack rolled in a blanket, lay along the plinth behind the statue, his head on his swag, his face protected by a newspaper, and his feet propped against the statesman's marble box of a right boot. He wondered about Jock, furiously trying to deliver his story to some policeman who couldn't understand a word of it. Towser, too – the many inexplicable things about him. Brains, though. Beside him the other men in the Murray house had seemed as straight-forward as horses or dogs. But there were oily patches in Towser that Jerry had sensed; something false, a corrupt smell of self-indulgence – something that Jerry had sniffed and recoiled from.

Yet Jack was grateful to Towser. The man had recognised some-thing in him; that was why he wanted him in the Movement, why he'd tried to get him out on the balcony where the photogra-phers could catch him. Towser had spotted that, as part of a public *persona*, dwarfism was irresistible; people couldn't help looking, lis-tening, half-amused, half-admiring that big ideas could come out of so small a body.

Jack remembered then how that crowd had listened and watched when Mr Lang was speaking to him, even though he had been consciously only a stooge for the Big Fellow. The feeling of incipient power had knocked at him then, even a sense of inevi-tability, when he had thought: 'I could do this better.' His interest in the world of politics and power, half-glimpsed as yet, was like a seductive landscape hidden in mist.

An intuitive excitement made him tremble. It seemed as though everything had been leading up to this moment when he was dis-armed of everything but knowledge of himself.

To dismiss dwarfism as a burden was one thing; but to make an asset of it was a challenge, tomorrow's challenge. He felt a salty joy in his own toughness.

After he had been asleep for an hour or two, the stray cats crawled out of the bushes and ate the crumbs he had left on the steps. One, further from death than the others, able to hoist itself up the steps, slept against him for the sake of warmth. After the sun rose, it tottered away.

Before seven Mrs Marion and Dorothy Moy finished dispensing hot coffee and soup to the long line of gaunt men and a few dishevelled women who had been waiting at the usual place in the Domain since dawn. Some at the end of the queue missed out; there was no more to give them. They dawdled away, swearing or doleful. Robert heaved the big milk-cans that had held the food into the back of the van and waited for the women.

Dorothy said, 'You go on home, Mrs Marion. I'll walk across the grass and get a taxi. It's such a peaceful morning.'

It was her frequent custom, but Mrs Marion said, 'You look a little peaked, Miss Dorothy. And it's Sunday. Wouldn't you like to rest today?'

But the girl shook her head, smiling good-bye as she walked away across the wide sunny downland, the sea its fence on one side, the city on the others. There was scarcely anyone about now. Only a few bodies, too sick or drunk or numbed with sleep to go looking even for free food, lay on seats and under trees, covered with newspapers, blankets, flattened cartons. So great was their disorder and decrepitude that they looked as if their owners had thrown them away. Dorothy looked at them in despair, feeling Clara Jackaman leaning over her, leaning on her.

Her despondency was so great that she looked at the day as one might look at a flight of steps, the minutes occurring one after the other, each to be surmounted. Yet she was acutely aware of her surroundings: the church bells already quarrelling plaintively across the water, the long leaves of the Judas thorn turning towards the sun like hair blown all one way, the dark paths the feet of cats and men had left across dewed grass, the lovely light.

It occurred to her that a state of cowardice, courageously acknowledged, might be the start of something else; but she could not think what it could be. She felt then with certainty that no one would ever love her, that she would turn into another Australia Jackaman, that life would not round into anything. And

433

while she suffered this affliction, another part of her mind pronounced decisively that such melancholy was what all young people felt, that it vanished with youth.

She turned aside, as she usually did, towards the statue of Sir Henry Parkes, the Father of Federation, the man who had first dreamed of pulling together the cluster of remote, squabbling colonies into one commonwealth, the man who had set her grandfather James on the road to prosperity, and been his faithful friend. But in the statue's face, both leonine and senile, she could never find any sign of the red-haired, pug-nosed firebrand her grandmother had often described to her.

Behind the statue she saw a child sleeping, rolled in a dark blanket fuzzed with dew, a newspaper over its face.

Her heart jumped in compassion, then in painful shock. The figure was too substantial for a child's. As though in a dream, she lifted the newspaper from his face.

It had changed so. For a second she thought she had made a mistake. Then her memory of the boy's face was merged in the reality of this sleeping one, a man's face, faintly lined, a bare spot in one eyebrow, a puckered scar on his cheek. The face was no longer handsome; it had set in the lineaments of the dwarf family, formidably strong.

She did not wonder what that face had to tell her; she accepted it.

Jack opened his eyes to see the young woman, golden hair bobbed, green leaves behind her, an anxious sweetness on her face: Cushie Moy magically transformed from girl to woman.

He sat up, his first thought a confused consciousness of his disarray, his unshaven face. He had dreamt so often of finding Cushie again; he had wanted their meeting to be in some way ceremonial.

'Oh, Cush!' He threw aside the blanket, made a gesture of helplessness.

Her eyes said, 'I've found you.'

It was so clear a voice that he asked, 'Have you been looking?'

She nodded, sat down beside him, and put her arm round him.

He said, 'I thought you were in England, years ago.'

After a while she said, 'Do you remember when we went up into Paddy's Range looking for the other dwarfs?'

'Yes.'

'Dwarfs make swords and crowns and rings,' she said.

'Do they, Cushie? Still?'

'Yes.'

He leant his head against her. He felt her heart beating. It seemed that he had always felt it beating, ever since he was born.